CW01647106

Kane Unmanned

Wolfwere Series Book 5

Dick Wybrow

Dee Dub Publishing

Chapter One

I felt strange.

And for once, it had nothing to do with a six-foot-seven French Canadian with the most extreme multiple personality syndrome the world had ever seen.

"Where do we go from here?" Kane asked me as I stared into the warm embers of the setting sun. Not in panic or dread or overcome with fear that I had to get my boy covered or "woof!" Just enjoying a smoldering ribbon along the horizon.

Shuffling down the dusty steps of the St. Louis warehouse, a little hop from the last stair, I realized something odd.

I wasn't terrified.

Of course, my anxiety train still chugged along like a cross-continental express with busted brakes.

We had to find Marata and Doc Hammer, who were now working together. The message they'd carved into the brick hadn't been just monster graffiti.

"Animals first."

That had been a declaration. An invocation.

And I'd have bet money—not mine, but Kane's, of course—that the message had been for us.

Hammer would have overheard us talking about taking out the NextGen, back before we'd even known what they'd been called. When Marata had hoofed it from the Covenant HQ near Atlanta all the way to St. Louis, she'd have been craving a major top-up of her "go juice."

I bet when she first saw her old boss, she'd been ready to slice the woman to giblets. But Hammer was a schemer and knew the only thing Marata had any love left for were animals. To the extreme. If Marata had shown up to a PETA rally, even those folks would have gone, "Yo, dial it down, 'k?"

"Marata used to be a Covenant lab scientist," I said to Kane as I ambled back to our rental car. "She'd worked on the virus that eventually made the Enhanced. And the NextGen."

"NextGen came from me," Kane said solemnly.

"Sure, but it all started with Marata's team. And she'd worked under Hammer, so those two have a relationship."

Kane grinned. "One where Ilsa Hammer tried to kill her, yes? I think this is not a good relationship."

I thumbed the key fob to open the doors on the Honda hatchback. Kane groaned when he looked at it.

"Car is so small."

"It's not the size that matters, Kane," I said, opening my door.

He scowled at it. "Is very small. Size does matter."

I felt like I'd scored a small win. I got one guy to admit it. Even if he was really a wolf.

When I hopped in, I heard my phone chiming and snatched it off the faded dashboard. Twenty-seven minutes until sundown. For three minutes, it had been bleating out panicky warnings to an empty car.

Kane squeezed in butt first, looking like toothpaste trying to climb back into its tube. He tugged his legs up and had to shift his knees toward me just to get the door closed.

"Comfy?" I said as he twisted to get his seatbelt on. "Since we didn't see Doc Hammer's entrails draped around that place, she'd have made a deal to save her life. The only deal that Marata would have been interested in."

Kane nodded. "Foot rubs and back scratches."

"No, man," I said and laughed. A month with the guy, and I still couldn't tell when he was just screwing with me. "When I was at the zoo with Gregor, I was going to be torn to pieces and she didn't give a damn. Just watched the show."

"She helped me in Atlanta, I think," Kane said, fumbling with the lever on the side of his seat. "Gave me a shot of her go juice."

"But that's my point. She knows you ain't a human," I said. I started the car and carefully wove around the busted crates and jagged metal strewn around the lot. A flat tire was the last thing we needed. "In her eyes, you're a wolf. When she said to me 'he is we,' that was not just about being an Enhanced. She meant animal."

"She is not."

"Marata sees herself that way now. And hitting you with the go juice was just to help you kill the Enhanced people. 'People' being the operative word."

I jumped at a horrific ratcheting sound as Kane disappeared from view. When I looked over, he was lying against the rear seat, staring at the ceiling.

"Unintended," he said with a small smile on his big bearded face. "But more comfortable. No need for motel."

"Upgrade time, baby. We're getting a *hotel*," I said, heading down the gravel path toward the main road. When it turned to grass and we bumped along, he jolted and bounced. Stubborn as any dude I'd met, he just crossed his arms and pretended to enjoy the ride.

"Room with tub," he said.

"Can do. Wolf needs his bubble bath," I said. When my tires hit blacktop, I punched the gas.

Kane closed his eyes. "Marata thinks she is animal. How does this matter to us?"

"She's still brilliant. Batshit insane, sure, but wicked smart."

"Hammer is also bat crazy."

"Right. And not stupid either. Their Enhanced bodies are a wreck but not their minds. A bit jumbled, though. Marata remembered the code for her lab, but it took her a while. With the two of them together, they can fill in the gaps the other can't recall."

"Mère and Père did this."

"Your human parents planned the destruction of all humans on the planet?"

"I do not think so, but it is good to have hobbies when old. Keeps the mind sharp," he said, and I could hear the smile in his voice. A very human kind of cheek. "But one would often remember what the other had forgotten."

"So you're saying Hammer and Marata are like an old married couple? Aww, how sweet!"

I felt his tender hand on my arm. "You will have this one day, too, Emelda. Not the people-killing part. But a partner to share your life. As I have."

The light ahead turned from green to amber, so I gunned it. By the time I got to the intersection, it was solid red, which earned me an angry horn blast from the driver of an eighteen-wheeler who'd had to jam on the air brakes.

"It is better lying down here," Kane said. "This way, death will be a surprise."

Chapter Two

We'd spent a comfortable night in a hotel and, indeed, wolf got his bubble bath. By the time he'd finally extricated himself from his bubbly bliss, I'd been fast asleep.

At first light, we got back into our cramped rental, and I'd pointed our car southeast. We needed to find where Hammer and Marata had gone to launch their "animals first" plan. I could only think of one place to find those answers: a bland office complex that served as the secret headquarters of Covenant back in Atlanta.

And where my friend had nearly been tortured to death. If he had any anxiety about returning, he was hiding it well.

"I think one day, I would like to see California," Kane said, lying very comfortably in the busted car seat. "It would be very nice to look around for a while. And, for a change, not to be shot at."

"Or bitten."

"Or swiped with spiky claws," he said, his warm laugh rolling up my arm and gently squeezing my shoulder. "Your mother, she lives in California, yes?"

I nodded, fiddling with the radio. When I realized he was actually waiting for an answer, I clicked the radio off. "Yeah, I'm pretty sure," I said. "Working at a flower shop, from what I remember. Or a bookstore."

Kane shifted his weight to turn toward me. I sighed inwardly.

"You do not know this?"

Waving my hand at the windshield and the world outside, I said, "I've been, you know, busy."

"Family is important."

"Yeah, so I'm told."

He grunted and settled himself back into his seat, closing his eyes. "But not all family. Some are not so good. I remember one wolf, what humans might call an uncle, and he caused much trouble. Always would encroach on the territory of other packs, get chased, and run back to us."

"Bringing trouble back with him, yeah? I know people like that."

"We took care of this."

I tilted my chin toward him, waiting for clarification.

"We ate him," Kane said. He crossed his arms and nestled his shoulders deeper into the seat.

"Damn, really? Don't forget a birthday in your family."

"No, no! With this, I am joking." He leaned forward, very pleased with himself. A little boy in the back seat of a passing Chevy waved when his head popped up. Kane waved back. Then his playfulness melted away. "He was banished. Forbidden from returning."

"Harsh. Might have been better if you'd eaten him."

Kane cleared his throat. "Did you also endure such a thing? Banishment?"

"What?" The question shocked me, and I drifted into the next lane. The Chevy's horn warbled at me, and I slid back with an apologetic wave. I did *not* get a wave in return. "Why would you think that?"

"Ta mère, yes? Your mother and you do not speak."

"Ha, no. That was self-imposed. We had a rough couple of years before I moved out," I said. "It might be another couple of years until I'm ready to revisit the idea of a visit."

That got a grunt out of him.

"I understand," he said then added, "Okay, I do not understand. But I understand that you understand, so this is acceptable."

"Glad I've got your stamp of approval," I said. "We'll patch it up one day."

"You have time, so this is good," he said. "Unless she is eaten by a pack of wolves."

"Nah. You guys wouldn't like the taste of her. Sour. Bitter."

Kane laid back in his seat again. "Put gravy on top and not so bad, I think."

Steering down the same Atlanta streets as we had a week earlier twisted my stomach into knots. I'd watched Tech Sergeant Gregor die at the

Covenant HQ. Kane had nearly died there *twice.* Had he not transformed into the wolfwere, he would have.

And so would I.

Kane sighed when he saw the building come into view. "It feels like farewell tour, yes?"

"What?"

He pointed to the massive, black-windowed office complex ahead. "Like rock band on one last concert tour. Going to cities we played music in. Except these are places we fought monsters."

"Strange analogy."

"Derelict factory where you ran from Marata. Here, now, where I was hung from a wall for days." He nodded slowly. "Coming to the end, yes? Maybe we have to make a Minnesota small-town stop."

"Hell no," I said, chuckling. "Not if I can help it."

After the battle that had taken place in this building, it hadn't been a surprise to find the Covenant building closed. Not satisfied with just dropping the gate arm, they'd installed concrete bollards to keep anyone out. Six of them in pairs, blocking the short entryway. Leaning up in my seat, I could see two cars in the parking lot.

So the place wasn't entirely empty.

"I bet Hammer and Marata went to one of Covenant's old lab sites, and the only way we'll find it is by getting in there and poking around."

"Why an old site?"

"Animals first, right?" I said, slowing at the gate. "They'll need a lab to extract the virus to create their Enhanced army."

"They could just bite, yes?"

"I think it's more than just infecting someone. Cal Davis had been one of their soldiers and had undergone months of medical treatments to handle the transformation." I shook my head slowly. "You remember Bridget Mills, right?"

"Yes, the Minnesota woman bitten by my brother."

"Right." I'd forgotten Cal had been the son of Kane's human parents. My friend considered him family. "She'd been feral. Enhanced but, you know, wrong because she'd changed without the benefit of those therapies."

"Marata and Hammer were both bitten," Kane said. "No treatments."

"Exactly. And they're kind of..." I crossed my eyes and stuck my tongue out, which got a grin out of him. "But like Cal, Gregor *had* gone through the program. Those two had all the enhancements and none of the weirdness. Strong, agile, and most importantly, they could carry out instructions given to them. Perfect little soldiers."

"Which is what Doc Hammer will want for the animal army." Kane rubbed his chin, nodding. "Yes, I think you are right."

I pointed at the gate and cement barrier. "Man, they really don't want anyone going in there," I said, driving past. "No one's in the guard shack."

Kane dropped back into his permanently reclined seat. "Maybe building is abandoned, and they have left doors open for us. This would be nice."

"Ah, no," I said. "There are two cars parked out front. Somebody's home."

Making a U-turn, I returned to the main road and headed toward where I'd seen a subdivision of houses being built. When we reached a cul-de-sac, encircled by empty homes, I parked the Honda so I could think.

"What about the spooky zoo where you were almost eaten?" Kane asked me. "That also may be good option to find the information we need, yes?"

"My gut tells me no."

"Can your gut tell me why?" he said and giggled. "I would very much like to see this. The belly button moving like lips. 'Hello, I am the tummy of Emelda, and I have very smart things to say!'"

I tented my fingers, tilted my head back, and looked down my nose at him. "Your answer is in your question, Grasshopper."

He frowned at me. "Is this word a slur? Have you slurred me? Have I been slurred?"

"Stop saying slur," I said and shivered. I'd never realized how nasty the word sounded. Of course, I'd never been hit with a slur word salad before. "The zoo has bitey, chomp-chomp monster animals, wolfman. But, yeah, if we don't find answers there, it's an option."

Before getting out of the car, I scanned the nearby homes to see if anyone was watching. No cars in driveways. No curtains in windows. Some of the houses were half finished, and all of them looked empty. Like the developer had started, um, developing then went broke.

Or, more likely, someone bought them out, so they didn't bring any people in. How much money did Covenant have at its disposal?

Steve Janus had said billions. Must be nice.

"Doc Hammer was pretty high up the food chain," I said, running my fingertips through my hair. "She'll have been privy to the locations of their secret labs, and that knowledge was likely the reason Marata didn't tear her arms off." I nodded to the tree line next to the cul-de-sac. "The back of Covenant's HQ is just through those woods. Inside, we should be able to find a list of those sites."

Kane grunted. "You are so clever to work these things out," he said.

When I looked at him, expecting a mocking smile, I didn't see it.

He caught my expression and shook his head. "I mean this very much, Emelda. You are a brilliant woman."

I stammered for a moment, unsure what to say.

"Beauty and brains," he said, and a big smile split the beard on his face.

"Wow," I said. "No one's ever—"

"You are the brains," he said. He popped open his door and rolled out. Flipping a mane of long dark hair out of his face, he added, "And I am the beauty."

Chapter Three

I checked the moon app on my phone. Three hours until dusk.

The first word that came to mind when considering how much time until we got mooned was "plenty." But I didn't dare say that out loud because I'd gotten that *so* big-time wrong before.

I'd never been a superstitious person, but here, I was worried that if I even *thought*, "Oh, we've got tons of time," the Dark God of Irony would smite me with his bad karma stick.

Stick? Did gods have sticks? That didn't seem right.

"You have become quiet," Kane said, staring over my shoulder at the rear of the Covenant HQ building. We'd tromped through the woods and hidden in the shade of a line of cedar trees. He leaned down to my ear, whispering. "Are you assessing threat and devising smart plan to get inside? What are you thinking?"

"Hmm," I said, rubbing a spot of dirt off my cheek. "I think menacing gods would wield staffs. Not sticks."

Without missing a beat, he said, "Also, I have heard them to carry a stave, which can double as a weapon."

"Right." I squinted at a pair of massive gray doors next to a cement ramp. Trying to pry those open would make too much noise. "Stave. Where'd you hear that?"

"In stories read to me as a boy," Kane said. "If twirling is involved, they may also utilize a rod."

"No," I said, my eyes drifting over the rows of dark windows to another door on the corner. It looked like an employee entrance for evil scientists, bloodthirsty henchmen, and corporate accountants. "And I think some angry god twirling his rod isn't the image I'm going for."

"Yes, ma mère told me this can make you go blind."

"What?" I half turned to him.

He blinked. "What?"

From our vantage point, we could see the far edge of the front lot. I motioned to the two vehicles I'd seen earlier. "They must be the security guys."

Kane leaned forward. "How can you know this?"

"Because it says Concord Security on the side," I said. "I think that's Covenant's way of thinking it's clever since those words kinda mean the same thing."

He grunted once.

"You've got better vision than me. Can you tell from here if that door with the steps is locked?" I said, looking up at Kane. All I saw was a Brillo-pad beard and a big lantern jaw. Not that I really knew what a lantern jaw looked like, but the dude's head was enormous. "Sofa cushion jaw" didn't really have the right ring to it.

"No, it is too tiny to see this. But all the building windows have a candy coating upon them. Cherry flavor, I think."

"Wut?"

Instead of answering, he rolled back on his heels and tugged me deeper into the shade of the trees. "A large bald man with a formidable belly has passed by a candy window."

"Where?"

"Should I point?" he asked me. "I feel pointing would be something I should not do."

"Yeah, don't point. Good instincts."

"Of course. I am wolf."

"Yeah," I said, leaning forward to the balls of my feet. "What do you mean candy coating? Tinted?"

He grumbled. "Tinting is like the windows of the death car we had in Mexico, yes?"

"Right. Like the hearse."

"No, not like this." He leaned in, almost resting his chin on the top of my head. "Red shine."

"Red sh—" I nodded. I'd seen that plenty back in my breaking-and-entering days. "Shatter detection. That's laser light. You can see that?"

"Lasers? Like space fights?"

"Yes and no, but heavy on the no," I said. "It just means busting a window is not an option. Damn. I'd hoped that when they shut this place—"

Kane growled, and I hugged the ground. Totally still and quiet, I waited for him to tell me what he'd seen. He didn't.

"What?"

"Huh?" he said then coughed softly. "What is what?"

"You growled. What did you see?"

"Just clearing throat," he said, a smile in his voice. "Apologies."

I heard a skitter in the trees to my right and stiffened, but I saw nothing there. When I looked at the building, I spotted a guard passing by the window. A stocky older guy with a salt-and-pepper crew cut. So, not bald. Two guards inside.

I looked to my left, where a huge divot had been carved from the grassy hillside. Three cement walls held the soil back, making a space for a dumpster. One of its thick rubber lids hung open.

Another scratch and shuffle to my right. This time, I could see a line of scraggly bushes swaying. Had the bald dude snuck up behind us?

Again, Kane growled. He'd spotted someone.

Spinning on my knee, I retreated deeper into the woods and searched our surroundings. I put my hand around my back. Right. I'd lost my slingdart in the floodwaters at the convent back in Mexico.

The bushes fluttered, and I raised my fists, ready to strike. Yeah, my punch doesn't do much, but I do have a wicked combo: my punch, Kane's punch.

Our stalker poked out of the underbrush and blinked two beady eyes at me, twitching its head left and right.

Kane let out another low growl.

"Cut that out," I said. "It's just a damn squirrel."

"Ha. Ha," he laughed, in a stilted and very not-laughing way. "Yes. Just a squirrel."

I frowned at him. "You couldn't tell by the smell of it?"

"Yes."

Waiting for more of an explanation but not getting it, I returned my focus to the building. Now, I couldn't see either of the guards. The squirrel skittered back into the bush, and I heard Kane shift his feet.

"Forget about the damn squirrel," I whispered and nodded to the single entrance on the far left. "It's a long shot, but I'm going to check that door. I bet that's where the workers used to come out."

"Will that not be locked?"

Ducking low, I crept toward the cement bay with the big dumpster.

"Sometimes, employees prop doors open. Smoke breaks and stuff," I said, walking in a crouch. "Maybe someone jammed a rock in the gap and forgot."

"Yes," Kane said, nodding quickly. "Good to check."

Crab walking to my left, I kept spindly bushes between me and the Covenant building. The five floors of office windows felt like demon eyes watching my every move.

I dropped flat when I heard an odd snorting sound. When I looked back, Kane was holding his hands out, pushing downward.

Dude *snorted* at me.

But he could also see much better than I could. I spread my arms and legs out and lay on the grass. I watched him as he watched the building. He twitched his head to the right, then back at the windows, then to his right again.

"Forget about the damn squirrel!" I growled at him as quietly as I could.

He raised his palms in apology, staring intently at the windows. After a moment, he nodded the all-clear.

Too exposed on the hillside, I ran to the cement wall nearest to me. Without hesitation, I dropped inside the bay and hid behind the dumpster.

From there, I peeked around the corner and got a good view of my target, a short set of steps with a chipped red handrail that led to a thick steel door. From this angle, I could also see the hoods of the two security vehicles. Would they do patrols around the complex?

The gap between where I was hiding and the rear door was about fifty feet. Crossing that distance, I'd be exposed.

Then I noticed the smell. Or rather, the lack of it. I had my cheek pressed to a huge dumpster, but no odors wafted from it. Of course, this was an office complex, not a restaurant. Maybe pencil-pusher trash didn't stink so much.

Curious, I crawled over to where the open flap hung down. Standing slowly, I shivered as five stories of windows glared down on me like a creature with a multitude of eyes watching my every move. I peeked inside the big bin. Nothing there.

Unless the trash man had come that morning, the office complex was currently closed for business.

Except, of course, for the two security guys inside.

I dropped back down and slid over to my corner perch. My nerves began sizzling like Fourth of July sparklers. When I'd been a part-time thief, that feeling had always been a bit of a rush. My body psyching itself up for a midnight break-in.

In the broad daylight, my stomach flopped around like it wanted to scramble back up to the safety of the trees without me.

Turning toward the hill, I searched for Kane to get the okay that the coast was clear. He crouched in the shadows, swaying from foot to foot as if moving to the quiet rhythm of the forest behind him.

The hunter, I thought. And it made me happy and sad at the same time. Pretty soon, the big guy was going to be out of my life. He was goofy and weird and sweet and scary, all rolled up into one package.

He held his hand out to me. Then his palm collapsed into a pointed finger, and I spun and bolted across the parking lot, pumping my arms and legs as fast as I could.

My footfalls rang off the walls, so I switched to running on the balls of my feet. That was harder but far quieter.

When I got to the red railing of the short staircase, I grabbed it and swung down, pressing my back against the wall. Up on the hill, in the shadows, Kane stalked through the trees. He nodded his big head once.

Coast was clear.

I rushed up the steps and knew my answer before I got to the top. The door was flat against the building, not propped open. And I could see the red lights of a security pad. Locked.

Reaching for the handle, I paused. Would trying the handle set off alarm bells? The better question: Would I run all the way down here and *not* try the handle?

Slowly, I pulled it down, and it moved a half inch then stopped. Nope. No going in there. And the back door didn't have a handy window to peek through.

"Shit," I whispered.

I felt something under my shoes, and when I looked, I saw four cigarette butts in various stages of squished. I bent down to smell them and winced. I'd always hated the smell of cigarettes. My grandfather smoked.

"*Mi abuelo fumaba*," I whispered to myself. "Or *fumuba*. One of those."

And they still reeked. These weren't likely from Pam the Evil Accountant who'd gone for her cancer break a week earlier. By now, those would have likely blown away in the wind.

"One guard smokes," I whispered.

I was sure I was right. Even more sure when I heard an inner door bang and clang just beyond the one I was standing right next to.

Chapter Four

People can be so gross when they think nobody is around.

Or when they don't realize there's someone just behind the corner, holding their breath and not moving a muscle so they don't get busted. Or shot.

Simultaneously, the guard farted and burped, the latter coming out with such flappy dampness I nearly hurled.

"Better the second time," he mumbled and smacked his lips.

Yep. I was totally going to puke.

With my back pressed against the wall, I could see the front parking lot to my right. Ahead, a field of dying grass. They'd built the Covenant HQ at the far edge of some developer's lot, far from prying eyes. If I tried to make a run for it, I'd be spotted by anyone looking for any reason to shoot someone.

And Burpy Dude sounded like that type.

I heard the flick of a lighter then a long pull as the guard sucked in his smoke. He blew it out with a moan. I put a fist to my lips and swallowed bile, but it was fighting me.

Thankfully, the crackle of a handheld radio distracted me.

"Mike, you near a window?"

Burpy Guard, aka Mike, groaned then keyed his own handset. "Can I get just a minute or two here? Smoke break, Izzy."

The voice said, "You've had like five."

A grunt and laugh. "Nah, bro. This is only my second."

Mike was gross *and* a liar. I'd seen the cigarette butts. If nothing else, their exchange told me his partner, Izzy, paid a lot closer attention than he did. I filed that away.

"We got some movement out there," the guy on the radio said, and once again, I stopped breathing. "Around back."

Shit!

I craned my neck up to scan for cameras. And sure enough, I was standing right underneath one. In fact, Izzy the guard could probably zoom in to see my pinprick pupils. With only a few seconds before Burpy Mike spun around the corner and started firing, I considered my choices.

Running to the field would be stupid. A better plan might be booking it down the side of the building and...what?

I'd have to cross the front parking lot then run down a long drive, weave around concrete bollards, and jump a gate. That option would also likely get me shot in the ass.

Just as I was flipping the mental coin, Mike spoke into his radio. "I'm out back," he said. "I don't see nothin'."

"Look up toward the trees."

"Trees?"

Trees?

"Yeah, there's some guy up there or something racing through the damn trees."

I heard the shuffle of hard-soled shoes and Mike muttering to himself as he stomped down the three concrete steps. His shadow poked around the corner, and I froze. Shadow Mike apparently saw nothing interesting, so it followed the guard into the rear lot.

The smoldering butt of a cigarette arced through the air and landed in the dead grass just three feet in front of me.

Mike keyed his radio. "I don't see any... hold on. Probably some kid."

They've seen Kane. What the hell is he—

I smelled something burning. Tiny flames were growing where Mike had tossed his butt. If he turned and saw that, he'd give it a big stomp of his big beefy foot, see me, and then *I'd* get a big stomp of his big beefy foot.

"Go take a look," the voice on the radio said. "That's what they pay ya for."

"For crying out loud." The guard began to walk away.

I sighed with relief and tasted smoke. Mike's ciggie fire was growing.

Dammit!

Crouching low, I peeked around the corner and saw the guy. Built like a muscular stop sign, he stomped across the empty parking lot. I took a chance and burst forward, snuffing out the tiny flames with my shoe. I was about to race back to my hiding spot when I noticed Mike the "security" guard had wedged a broken bit of brick into the back door.

Out in the open now, my own shadow tweaked left and right, unsure what to do. Obviously, following me could be a bad idea.

Screw it.

I crept up the steps, taking each on the balls of my feet, silent as a cat wearing fluffy wool mittens. Flattening myself against the wall next to the door, I waited.

This, of course, made no sense. If Mike turned, he'd see me. I pushed the gap wider with my elbow and slid inside. Dark and cold and the dull hum of electronics. I chanced a look outside and saw the security guard digging into his pocket. He came out with his pack of smokes.

When I heard his voice, I had to stifle a yelp. Echoing across the empty parking lot, it almost sounded like he was yelling in my ear.

"Aw, hell. The dude split," he said, talking to his partner over the radio. "It's hot as balls out here. I'm heading back in."

No time.

I pulled my leg in and heard a scraping sound. When I realized I'd dragged the damn brick inside, I went to jam my fingertips into the gap and got a stinging nip from the heavy door as it snicked closed.

Son-of-a...!

Jamming my throbbing digits into my mouth, I looked around the tiny room. To my right was a metallic panel filled with tiny yellow bulbs, each with markings like EV7 or MR4 and none of it meaning a damn thing to me. Opposite that, I saw long plastic tubes like fat, uncooked spaghetti of various sizes—conduit that punched through the cement ceiling to feed the room below.

The basement they'd held Kane in.

In front of me was another security door. This one bore a slender window, reinforced with crisscrossing wires in a diamond pattern. Staring through the glass, I saw *another* door on the opposite side. It also had a window, but in the meager light, I couldn't make out anything beyond it.

I tried the handle in front of me. No joy. On the wall next to the door was a black box the size of a thick slice of bread. Atop that, a red light told me that those without magic swipe cards weren't getting through. Locked.

When I looked through the window, I saw a similar panel by door number two.

Damn. Damn, damn, damn.

Through the exterior door behind me, Mike spoke into his handset. "Just some guy running through the woods. Looks like an idiot."

Then I heard his shoes hit the steps.

Chapter Five

I spun in a circle, looking for a place to hide.

Nada.

The space between the outside and inner door was as cramped as a jetliner's bathroom. No utility closets. No trap doors. No hooks laden with invisibility cloaks.

Deep breath. I had to calm down.

I prayed Mike hadn't quenched his nicotine craving and would light up another smoke. That wouldn't solve my problem, but it would give me a minute to think. Or a minute to prepare for a Mike fist to fly my way.

Hell, I'd had a fair share of fists come at me. But Mike didn't seem like the sort who'd stop after you'd belted out an insincere "Sorry, I won't do it again!"

Keys jingling.

Feet shuffling.

I heard the slap of plastic against plastic and a deep tone.

Not going for his cigarettes. Dude was coming in.

I wanted to punch the wall and stomp my feet in frustration. Anger has a doping effect against fear. A good rage can throw up a barrier, a wall, to keep all those squishy fluids from turning your brain into a damp loofah sponge.

The door beeped a few times then let out a low warning tone. I heard Mike grouse. "Damn it," he said and sighed. "Come on."

A code. He was typing in a code. The door apparently had both a key card and some numeric code.

By the time he slapped the key card onto the door a second time, I was crouched and spinning. Looking for something, anything I could use as a weapon. A broomstick. Extension cord. Hell, I woulda been overjoyed to have a spork.

The brick.

I heard the first tone of Mike's code go in and snatched the brick. Half brick, actually, because it was broken, which is likely how it ended up a doorstop. It weighed all of two pounds.

"Four," Mike said in a frustrated voice as he typed in digit two. Then he hit the next digit without voicing the number.

That was when I looked to where I'd picked the brick up. A metal L-bar lay flat against the door. Just below that, the concrete bore a dark, circular hole.

Screw it!

As the last tone chirped, I twisted the bar and dropped it into its hole. The lock clicked, and the knob turned. Then the door shook.

"Aw, hell," the guard said and repeated his entry sequence. Again. Slap, poke, poke, poke, poke. Click, pull. The door rattled again. Then the beast of a man bellowed. He yanked and shook the door handle, but the little L-bar held firm, happy in its hole.

Through the door, just inches from my head, I heard him sigh.

"Hey, Izzy?" he said and grumbled to himself. "Security bar in the back door slipped. Can't get in, so you gotta let me in through the front."

"Hold up," the voice said on the radio. "Did you see who the hell was back there?"

"Yeah, just some dumbass running through the woods like a nut."

"What the hell was he doing way out here? Those houses up the road are all empty." The other guard, Izzy, didn't sound as glib about the stranger as his partner.

"Check this out," Mike said, his words tuned up by a smile. "The guy was chasing a frigging squirrel."

The other guard keyed the mic just so he could laugh.

"Yeah. My guess," Mike continued, "is that the dumbass hid in the woods to light up and got so stoned he thought it was his long-lost dog or something."

"Where is that dude now?"

"Just kept running deeper into the woods until I couldn't see him no more," Mike said, chuckling, as I heard his shoes shuffle down the stairs. "He catches that squirrel, he's gonna regret it."

Chapter Six

"A *squirrel*?"

My voice rang off the half-built houses of the cul-de-sac. I didn't care. Lying flat in the car's passenger seat, Kane shuffled lower. I threw the door open, and he theatrically blinked at me with droopy eyes.

"Oh, there you are, Emelda," he said as if waking from a nap. "I have been here waiting for you all this time."

I kicked him in the thigh. Not hard. Or at least not as hard as I wanted to.

"So I was trying to sneak into an un-sneak-in-able building, right?" I said, bouncing my fist off the car's roof. Didn't bounce. I left a slight dent. "And my lookout is chasing squirrels?"

"No, no. Not squirrels," he said and looked past me into the woods. "Just the one."

"What... I mean, why? All you had to do was keep an eye out!"

He lowered his head and shrugged. "It called to me. But not in a 'hello, come play' sort of way. More of a 'chase me and tear my tiny limbs off' way. Which, I will admit, is a very specific call."

I wanted to be more angry. However, I knew when he reverted to human after some canine time, he always retained some traits of the dog he'd transformed into. I wondered how much human he'd carry with him once he became wolf again.

Then I shooed those thoughts away, trying to hold on to my anger. I couldn't.

"It's fine," I said and leaned against the car. "And actually, all your weirdness got me inside."

Kane shot out of his seat. "You got it? Did you get the information we seek?"

"I got through door number one," I said and dug out my phone. "But I got stopped by door number two and door number three. Your squirrel fetish only bought me about a minute."

He wrinkled his nose. "I have heard this word before. What is fetish?"

"Obsession. Compulsion," I said. "And something you can make a couple bucks off in the weirder parts of the internet."

Kane started to say something else, but I'd already found the number I needed. I held up a hand to him, waiting for my friend to answer.

"Hey, Emelda!" Denny said. "I didn't think I'd ever hear from you again."

"Why is that?"

"I dunno. You strike me as the sort of person who just disappears on people."

"Dude, harsh," I said. "I don't think we know each other well enough for that kind of..."

"Honesty?"

I laughed. I'd only hung around his mother's farm a few days, and he had me pegged.

"How is Miss Florida, by the way?"

"Mom's good. Getting geared up for canning season, so she's up to her armpits in glass jars."

"That's a visual."

I'd remembered that Denny had helped me track down my phone up in Minnesota, which had led me to the first time I'd seen one of the dead Enhanced. And when Kane had torn out the throat of one of Tech Sergeant Gregor's people. Denny knew none of that.

But he had given me a funny looks when I'd returned with a dog whose muzzle was soaked dark red.

He was a good man and didn't ask too many questions. Either he was respectful or he just didn't want to hear any answers involving blood.

"Hey, you did that thing when you tracked down my phone, remember?"

"Yeah," he said, chuckling. "Signal flare."

"Right, so since you're a bit of a tech nerd, I was wondering—"

"No, no. I am not a tech nerd."

Kane leaned in to listen. I pushed his gigantic head away and put Denny on speaker.

"Okay, fine," I said. "Tech geek. Is geek better than nerd?"

"I don't know." Denny stressed his point by crunching loudly on some kind of snack chip. "I'm not either of those things."

"You knew about the signal flare thing, though."

"Yeah. Yeah, because everybody does. Common knowledge."

I looked over at my big friend. "Kane, do *you* know about signal flares?"

"Is this where old rock-and-roll people perform during the summer? With waffle cakes and fried bananas. Yes, I know—"

"What the hell are you talking about? No." I turned my attention back to the phone. "See, Denny? We don't know about stuff like that."

"Fine," he said. Crunch. "You lose your phone again?"

I blinked. Held my phone out and stared at it. I mean, I was *calling* him on my phone.

"Listen, we're trying to sneak into a building, but there's all this high-tech security."

"What? Why?" he said and crunched faster. "No, no. Don't tell me. I don't want to know."

I smiled. "Here's our challenge: it's got electronic locks on all the doors. You need a key card and a code to get in." I paused, hoping he'd jump in. He didn't. "So, any idea?"

"Yeah. My idea is that it's private property, and they don't want you in there."

"Ah, but the problem is we really, really *want* to get in," I said. "Can't you, I dunno, log into their mainframe and see if there's a way to unlock them remotely?"

After a long, long pause, he asked, "What's the exact location?"

Excitedly, I opened my map app and read the address to him. We waited as he clicked and clacked on the other end. After a few moments, he came back on the line.

"Okay. Done. All the doors should be open now."

"What?" I looked at Kane with wide eyes. "Really?"

"No, Emelda! I have no clue how to do anything like that!" Denny said. "Hell, I got locked out of my TikTok account four months back and can't get back in. Do you know how many..."

My tech guy kept up his rant, but I'd already tuned him out. Maybe I needed someone who had access to the building already. That gave me an idea, and I opened the browser on my phone.

"Dammit," I said.

Mid-rant, Denny stopped at my interruption. "What?"

"I tried googling this cleaning company, but their page is down."

"And why are you googling a cleaning company?"

"We met these two people who, um, cleaned in the building we need to get into. They might know of a back way. Or how to get into the subbasement where they were torturing Kane."

"Torturing Kane?"

"I am okay," Kane said, leaning down to the phone and speaking far too loudly. "I killed many of them."

"*What?*" The volume of Denny's voice made the phone vibrate.

"No, no. He's joking." I made a face at my oversharing friend. "Um, is there an internet white pages anymore where you can look up numbers?"

"Ha, no. White pages. How old are you?"

"Great. So there's no way I can get ahold of them?"

A long sigh. "Well, their site might have gotten archived."

"Archived?" I said, chewing on a nail. "What does that mean?"

"On the internet archive site. What's the name of the cleaning company?" I told him, and he clicked away for a few seconds. "Yeah. I've got it here. What do you need, an email or—?"

"Phone number would be better," I said. "We're kind of low on—"

"Yep," Denny said, cutting me off. "I've got it."

"Um, Kane," I said and shifted my eyes toward my friend. "Do you know about the internet archive site?"

"Is *that* the place with the washed-up rock bands and waffle cones?"

I shook my head and narrowed my eyes. Obviously, my boy was hungry.

"See, neither of us knew about the archive site. Or the signal flare. I think that puts you in some rarefied air," I said. "Denny, the tech nerd."

He moaned. "Can I give you the number so that I can go back to what I was doing before?"

"What were you doing before?"

"Nothing," he said, "which, between *that* and this call, is my preference."

Chapter Seven

Before I could say a word, the woman on the other end of the line blurted, "Where are you?"

She sounded annoyed. Peeved. And I hadn't even said a word yet. Usually, it takes at least a minute of me talking before people get there, but she'd come in hot.

"Um, I am," I stammered, "standing in the cul-de-sac of an unfinished housing development."

"Do you see my house?"

"Listen. Is this—?"

"No, I can't imagine you do because I do not *live* in an unfinished housing development," she said. She was on a roll. "I am in an apartment building. Cozy and warm and full of furniture."

I had no idea where she was going with this.

"That sounds, you know, nice," I said.

"It is. It's got almost everything. But do you know what it doesn't have?"

Obviously, I'd already lost all control of the conversation. So, like I do when I'm in those kinds of situations, I gripped the sides of my mental sled and leaned in.

"I think you're about to tell me."

"Pizza!" she shouted into the phone. "Two of them, actually, because I don't want pineapple coming anywhere near mine." A voice babbled in the background. She shushed it. "But right now, I would swallow a Hawaiian pizza whole, because I have been waiting *an hour*!"

Ah. I got it then. "Hey, I'm not—"

"You are not *here*? Yes, I know this," she said with a full head of steam. "Because if you were, I wouldn't be able to talk to you. Do you know why I would not be able to talk to you?"

"I really don't."

"Because I would have a mouth full of pizza! If you don't—" She stopped speaking for a moment, and I heard a tinny buzz on the other end. Then a male voice, low, chattering to someone. "Pizza guy just buzzed my building."

"Great."

The woman sighed. "Now I gotta go down and get that."

"I'll grab it," the male voice said. Even over the line, I could hear the smile in the guy's voice.

"No, no. Last time, you got off on the wrong floor, said you got lost, wandered around, and ate three pieces of *my* food," she said, not even turning away from the phone, so I got an earful meant for someone else. Totally unfair.

"I am legally blind, you know," the guy said, but I could hear him trying not to laugh.

"And I am not legally buying any of that bullshit. You know this building better than I do. I don't wanna..."

Over the phone, I heard the two of them going back and forth in what had turned into a playful argument. I felt like I was intruding, but part of me just wanted to listen. Listen to two people who were just hanging out and giving each other crap.

Normal people.

Well, more normal than the life I had.

"Hey, hello!" I finally shouted into the phone. "Is this Consuela?"

The voices stopped on the other end as she shushed her friend again.

"Yes, yes. I'm going down now. Tell your pizza guy—"

"I got nothing to do with that dude, Connie," I said and then spoke quickly before she hung up. "We met you guys last week. Or the week before; it's all a blur. Remember? Me and a big guy who looks like he could have been an extra in an eighties action movie? But, you know, probably one that got blown up really early in the film."

A pause. Then: "Right. I remember you. We lost our only gig because of you two."

"I'm sorry. That wasn't... It's been a busy few weeks."

"Not for us of late. We don't have a job."

I looked at Kane, who shrugged.

Into the phone, I said, "Do you want one?"

***

When I pressed the button next to the apartment number Connie had given me, I wondered if she was purposely ignoring me. Then a voice came onto the speaker. Not hers. A guy.

"Hey, is that you, old man?"

My friend stepped up and looked at the metal box.

I said, "Just speak, and he can hear you."

"Yes, it is I. Is this the voice of Edgar?"

"Hell yeah, Kane! How are you?"

Kane smiled and looked into the apartment's lobby. "I am good, but there is a locked door where I am standing, and shaking it with vigor does not make it open."

Yeah, but it *had* gotten the attention of a very crabby woman in a very tattered pink bathrobe, who was now very pissed at us. She'd been seconds away from calling the cops until her little dog ran up to the door and panted at Kane through the glass.

He'd bent down and smiled at the tiny ball of fluff, its pink tongue lolling from its mouth. "You are very sweet," he'd said. "But I am betrothed to another."

Pink Robe Lady smiled at that and, I think, since her dog liked Kane, she'd chilled. A little. I explained we were waiting for a friend to answer. She'd hesitated until, finally, Connie's business partner answered on the third buzz.

"Con just hopped in the shower real quick," he said. "If you hurry, we got pizza up here. You could probably sneak a few slices before she gets out."

Kane frowned. "This seems like a dangerous plan."

Edgar buzzed us in.

When I pulled the heavy door open, I got hit with the sensory overload of everyday life. For a moment, I just stood there.

The comforting sounds of a baseball game flowed down the bare carpet, interspersed with some guy complaining about some player or some play he didn't like. I couldn't hear the actual words, just the grumbling through his apartment door. But to me, it sounded like happy grumbling.

Down the cement steps rolled the click and clatter of pots on a stove as the aromas of some family's evening meal dusted my skin. I heard some kid laugh then the sound of stocking feet across the bare floor. A mother's voice rang out, chasing her, maybe, in a warm, playful tone. In my mind, the little girl had sneaked a bit of the dinner and tore out of the room giggling.

To our right, the woman in the pink robe had her door cracked open as she chatted away on her phone or to a roommate. Then I realized she was talking to her dog. Sure, Doggie was probably just enduring it until she reached up for the battered tin with the treats inside, but...

Just life.

People happy. People sad and frustrated. But people living their lives, riding the ups and downs. More downs than ups, of course, but that only made the ups even more precious.

I felt Kane's hand land softly on my shoulder.

"A wolf who runs and runs can never dig a den," he said, his deep voice rattling something in my chest. "But it is only when you have a home that you no longer have to run."

My sigh rolled into a laugh, and I looked up at him.

"Did you learn that from watching crappy TV as a boy? You know, last year?"

Kane did the strangest thing. He bent down and kissed me on the top of my head.

"My wolf ancestors learn this. And this was taught to me," he said and pulled back. "I think humans knew this many generations ago. Now, they have so much noise, so many people telling them to run and do, that they have forgotten something."

I crossed my arms. "Yeah? What's that?"

"There are answers in the silence."

Clearing my throat, I cocked an eyebrow at him. "You should put that on a T-shirt, you know?" I said, fighting a tremor in my voice. "'There are answers in the silence.' Might get people to keep their traps shut."

Kane smiled and pointed up the steps.

"No way, dude. They're on the sixth floor." I walked toward down the hall and found the elevator. "Here's another one for your T-shirt shop: Don't take the stairs when a tiny room will get you there."

Once inside the rickety car, we both fell quiet. I didn't have any interest in answers that my silence might offer, so I asked Kane about Edgar.

"He seems like a good man to me," Kane said, watching the numbers above the door. "It is because of him that I escaped my imprisonment when hanging on the wall."

I remembered the image of Kane and Edgar emerging from the Covenant HQ subbasement. Lights flashing, steam rolling out from the sprinklers. And my friend looking like he'd aged fifty years in a few days.

Kane added, "Edgar did, of course, also break some bones, but that was an error. Easily forgiven."

"He did what, now?" We'd never really talked much about his time down there, but I had the sense it had rattled him more than he let on. "How did he break bones? Dude is barely bigger than me."

"When releasing the metal straps. He had a lady on his phone talking him through what to do, but it was all confusing. Button push, crunching of bones. That was wrong, so go the other way. He do this, and I was freed."

When Kane said weird shit, sometimes asking for an explanation only made things more confusing. Maybe I'd ask Edgar about it.

On the sixth floor, we got out and looked up and down the hall.

"Damn, there aren't any numbers on the apartments."

Four doors down, a man stepped out and called to us.

"Hey, guys, we're down here," he shouted. But he was facing the opposite direction, waving and calling to the other side of the hall.

When Kane and I got to the door, he dramatically flinched and spun toward us. But he had a tiny smile on his face.

"Oh, whoops," he said. "There you are."

I could see why Kane liked the guy. And they'd only known each other for all of ten minutes. Edgar had a big smile and a kind face. Good-looking face, too.

"This is your home, yes?" Kane asked as we stepped inside.

"Naw, it's Connie's place. We're just hanging out for a pizza night since we are both now unemployed." Edgar walked past the kitchen, pointing to the table where two grease-stained boxes sat.

Kane shifted his weight toward them, but I held him back. I looked at him. *Wait.*

Edgar reached out for a big sofa chair, ran his fingers across the back of it, then tumbled over its armrest. He pulled a lever on the side to recline.

"After our fun-filled night, we got a message to say the gig was 'indefinitely on hold,'" Edgar said as Kane and I entered the tiny living room. "Con couldn't get anybody on the phone, so she went to the building, but nobody was answering the door. She said the place looked abandoned."

"It wasn't like they had a doorbell," Connie said. She came in wearing shorts and a T-shirt, drying her hair with a towel.

"Hello again," I said to her, putting on my brightest smile.

She didn't smile back as she eyeballed the giant French-Canadian next to me. "Hey."

"And when Con went around back," Edgar continued, "one of those big ape guards came out and told her to take a hike."

I noticed Connie had shot Edgar a look but, of course, her friend didn't pick up on it. The room fell silent.

"She's glaring at me, isn't she?" Edgar said and gently patted his cheeks. "I can feel my face getting warm."

"There is a glare," Kane said. "She does not want you to talk so much and also does not trust us being here."

Connie pointed at my big friend and plopped down onto her couch. "You got it in one," she said then nodded at me. "I remember you with that weird-looking guy. Bad haircut and worse attitude. You dump him for this guy? At least you traded up."

"What?" Edgar said, pulling his recliner's lever, and it looked like it might launch him across the room. Cool as a river rock, he just turned his head toward his friend. "This is the guy I told you about. All hanging on the wall until I saved his butt."

"He broke my ankle," Kane agreed.

"Not on purpose." Edgar put his hands up. "And I didn't hear the clicking of crutches when you came in, so it was probably a sprain."

Kane shrugged. "Cracked bone. This is a break."

"Wait, wait, hold on. There was the military guy, but Ed, this isn't the old man I saw you come out of the basement with," Connie said, standing again and walking over to the six-foot-seven man in her living room. "Similar build. Like an oak, but that guy had to be like seventy." Up on her tiptoes, she peered into my friend's face, close enough to kiss him. "Was that your dad or granddad or something?"

To his credit, Kane kept silent.

"Same, dude," Edgar said, smiling. "I never forget a voice."

Everybody just turned to me. Well, all but Edgar. I'd kept quiet as I tried to work out what I needed to say and what I could leave out. We were there for intel on the Covenant building, and I didn't want to get sidetracked.

"It's complicated," I said, just buying time. It also bought me a scowl from Connie. "He's got a condition."

"This is not untrue," Kane offered.

"And, as you can hear, he's French Canadian," I said. "They're just different."

That got a laugh out of Edgar. "Our boy is different, all right. I'm pretty sure he took down a wall with his fist."

Before any more questions flew my way, I asked if I could sit. Connie pointed me to a cousin of the chair Edgar was lounging in. A distant cousin. One who grew up on junk food and lived in the spooky woods. It looked like it belonged in a dump, not an apartment.

Without a word about furnishings, I sat. "We just need a few answers, and we'll be out of your hair. Kane will even buy you more pizza."

"Emelda enjoys spending my money," my big friend said.

Connie picked up her slice from a paper towel on the armrest and chewed. "Now I *know* you guys are together."

"Just friends," I said, crossing my ankles, "But we really, really need to get into that building."

"Get back in?" Connie looked at all three of us. "From what Edgar told me, your big friend would have died in there without his help."

"Ah, well, I had some help too. A lovely-sounding girl talked me through some of the harder parts."

"Whatever," Connie said. "The next day, the whole place got shut down, and we're out of a sweet gig."

"We got a payout," Edgar offered. "It'll carry us the next few months."

Connie shot a look at him. "It was a pay*off*, Ed. As in, 'Here's some money, so keep your mouths shut.'"

"Who told you not to go back?" I asked.

The woman chewed her pizza and sat on the armrest of her chair. "What part of 'keep our mouths shut' don't you get?"

Edgar was more forthcoming. "Just a text. Except for the first interview, all our contact had been through email or text."

I asked, "Who sent those?"

That got a shrug from the man in the chair. "Dunno. Any time we tried emailing or texting back, we got nothing. Or error messages. Must be some service."

"Ed!" Connie growled.

"We'll give you cash for the information," I said, raising my hands. "In exchange, we'll pay your cleaning rate for another three months."

Connie chewed for a moment then said, "Six months."

"How about four?"

"Six. Months."

I looked at Kane, and he nodded.

"Fine, but only if you know anything that will help."

I explained how we needed to find some sort of hidden service entrance. We'd seen the big front doors, of course. The loading dock. And the back door where Mike the Burpy Guard had been smoking.

When I stopped talking, Connie waited for more. She looked between me and Kane. "Wait, that's it? You just want to know whether there's a secret way to get in?"

"Yeah."

She said, "And you're willing to pay for my answer?"

"Yes. As I said."

Connie folded up the rest of her pizza slice and shoved all of it into her mouth, chewing slowly. With a grin, she said, "There ain't any other way in. We had to go through a bunch of doors. Each had a key or code or a camera with a security guard to buzz us in."

"Come on," I said, flashing a glance at Kane. "There's gotta be some way."

"Ha, we were just the cleaners, chicka!"

"It's *Emelda*."

"We were the cleaning crew, Emelda. There's no super-secret way we get inside. We just went through the front doors." She sighed, and her smile dropped to a horizontal line. "But since you're paying, I mean, what about that basement ramp that opened when Edgar and this guy's dad came out?"

"Do you know how to open that?"

"Sure," she said, shrugging. "From the inside, it sounds like."

I stomped my feet. "That doesn't help us, Connie."

"Still gotta pay us."

“I said we’d pay if you helped us. Telling us ‘no, you can’t get in’ doesn’t help!”

“No, you said you’d pay for my answer, and that’s—

A high pitch whistle split the air, and we all turned. Edgar pulled his fingers out of his mouth and smiled. We waited as he pulled the lever on his chair and eased his seat back.

He said, “I know a way in.”

Chapter Eight

"No, you do not," Connie said. She crossed her arms and glared at her friend.

He took it in stride. Even if the dude had been able to see, he probably still would have. He just seemed like that kind of guy. I liked him.

"Yeah, there's a way."

I asked, "How?"

Edgar put his hands behind his head, his face turned to the ceiling. Like he was lying on the beach. "You gotta be really high to try it," he said and giggled to himself.

"Ah, come on, what does that even mean?"

"Roof," Kane said. "You are saying to go in through roof."

Edgar scowled at him, tugged on his chair lever, and sat bolt upright again. I got the feeling he did that a lot for effect. "Well, dammit, son. I was going to milk that for a few minutes, and you took all the fun out of it."

My mouth hung open for a moment. "You really meant the roof?"

He shrugged and grinned.

Swinging my head toward Kane, I asked, "You riddled that out of a bad stoner pun?"

"Stone pun? No." His eyebrows knit together, making one long one. Weird. "His face to me said 'roof.' Is roof made from stone?"

I needed answers, but the pizza aroma beckoned me. And I had to get Connie to chill, so I stood and pointed at the table.

"Yeah, get me one too," she said with a half smile. "I suppose you guys might as well dig in, since you're paying for it."

I walked over and grabbed a slice for me, non-pineapple because I'm not a monster. But for Kane, I took two of the Hawaiian slices and smashed them into a sammich because he was. And I knew he wouldn't care.

I handed Kane his pizza sandwich.

"Thank you, Emelda."

Connie made a teasing sound. "Ooo, and he's polite too? I might just steal this one from you, girl."

With both slices in his mouth, Kane said, "Alas, I am already spoken for. I await my reunion with my wolf—"

"Don't talk with your mouth full," I said, putting my palm an inch in front of his face. I shifted my hand to the side and glared at him. *Not now.* I asked Edgar, "So, the roof, huh?"

"Roof, roof," he said as if barking.

That got a snicker out of Kane, who held his hand up to the guy for a high five.

"Ed, how in the world..." Connie's voice trailed off, and her eyes turned to slits. "You mean with the windows stuff?"

Edgard nodded slowly. "The windows stuff. There's a hatch inside that leads to the roof. Flip the bar, and it opens right up."

"Right." Connie huffed. "And the only way onto the roof is to be inside."

Kane's hand hung in the air, still waiting.

I whispered, "Put your hand down," but before he could, Edgar slapped him high five.

"Ouch, so very strong," Kane said, shaking his fingers. "You may have broken another bone, this time in my hand!"

I turned to the woman. "So what does a hatch have to do with windows?"

"Part of the gig," Connie said, motioning toward the sliding glass door of her tiny balcony. "Each night wrapped up with us spending an hour cleaning the outside windows."

"Trouble is," Edgar said, thinking aloud, "the hatch is between the two wings in a tiny room. The doors on either side have codes you need to get through."

Connie laughed again, louder. Like before, it had no joy in it. "Which, as I mentioned, you can only get to from the *inside*."

"Okay, right. A hatch," I said, my voice a whisper. "There's a roof access."

Edgar nodded at me. "Smack dab in the middle of the building," he said. "The little room with the hatch is all just water pipes and air ducts, I think. Not much to clean, but I always dragged a broom through anyhow."

Kane was watching my face for a reaction to the new intel. I nodded. *Maybe.*

"Well, it's something. We just got to find a way up onto the roof," I said. "You think they changed the door codes?"

Edgar shook his head. "Naw, why would they?"

"Hold on! Why does any of that matter? You can't—" Connie began.

But her buddy was on a roll. "Nobody's in that building. Except for the two guards you saw," Edgar said, nibbling on a tiny pineapple wedge. "They might have changed the access codes front and back, but those inner doors aren't electronic. Old-school finger pads."

I knew what he was talking about. "You mean the box beneath the handle with the metal buttons like pencil erasers?"

"Exactly. Heck, those codes have probably never been changed. You'd have to pass through mega security to get to them, so why bother?"

"Okay, that's something," I said, standing and nodding at Kane. "Give us those door codes, and who knows? We might be able to pull this off."

Edgar crossed his arms and frowned. "That is a problem. There are different codes for each door, but I don't remember the exact numbers, just the finger combos to open them."

I looked between the two of them. Connie furrowed her brow.

"Well, just tell us the key pattern," I said. "Like, 'hit the second on the right or third on the left.'"

Again, Edgar shook his head. "I went through those doors so many times, I only know it by feel. I don't have any clue."

Groaning, I threw my hands up. Then I looked at my big friend. "Hell, if it's just a door, Kane can bash it down."

"Yeah, I remember he does that sort of thing." Edgar chuckled and hunched his shoulders. "But those doors aren't just regular office doors. They're heavy security doors."

Kane grunted. "Also, Emelda, the candy coating, yes?"

"What?" I said, but I realized he was right. "Yeah, smashing the door could set off the shatter detection on the windows."

Dammit, we were so close. So close!

"So," I said, "you're telling me that *if* we can get up onto the roof and *if* we can get the hatch open, we'll drop down and be trapped in a room the size of a garden shed?"

"Maybe not," Edgar said. He steepled his fingers under his chin and sat back. "You just need to bring someone with you who knows the codes by feel."

Connie wasn't having it. "Hell no! Are you crazy? We're not a part of any of this crazy shit, Ed."

"They need our help," Edgar said as if that phrase was all the justification he needed. "I know the codes to help."

"Thank you, Edgar," Kane said, kneeled down, and put a hand on his arm. "You are a good human person."

"Kind of you to say." The side of the man's lip curled up. "I think."

Obviously, the very thought of Edgar joining us for a break-in had put Connie over the edge. "This is all just stupid Scooby-Doo shit," she said. We looked at her and she blinked. "I mean, no one's going up there. This is a fantasy."

I shook my head. "If we don't get up there and find what we're looking for, it'll be more like a horror show on a global scale."

Connie blinked, swallowed, and went quiet for a few seconds. Then the anger came roaring back. "You can't even get up there! There's no ladder." She threw a hand toward Kane. "And unless your big friend can jump five stories up—"

"Can you?" I asked Kane.

"Maybe two or three," he said, shaking his head. "Not five, I do not think."

"You *can't* jump even two, man," Connie said, her laugh sounding manic. "That's twenty feet! You guys are insane. Ed, this is nuts!"

"They don't need to jump or climb ladders or slingshot their way onto the roof," Edgar said, giving my friend's hand a kind squeeze.

Kane perked up. "Slingshot? Could I do this?"

"No," I said, waving him off.

"I would like to try."

Connie covered her eyes and growled. "It's not remotely possible."

"It is, Con."

"It isn't," she said, tearing her hands from her face and rolling them into fists. "There's no way for them to get up on the roof."

"There is."

"There isn't!" she yelled, her voice so loud someone in the next apartment pounded on the wall.

I walked up next to Kane and kneeled down in front of Edgar. An urge to grab his hand washed over me, but I folded my fingers together instead.

I asked the seated man, "How?"

Edgar shrugged, and a tiny smile lit up his face. "Window stuff."

Chapter Nine

In a word, Connie was "unhappy."

Actually, she'd come up with a lot of her own words to go with that. Several of them were entirely new to Kane, and he'd looked at me to explain them. And explain how some of what she'd suggested was physically possible.

Like a nervous pitcher staring at his catcher, I wordlessly shook him off. Nope. Just let her vent.

She'd continued to be unhappy as she'd reluctantly driven to the ghost-town cul-de-sac behind the Covenant complex, partly because she'd had to drive their cleaning van, since Kane had busted the seat in our little rental and no one could sit in the back.

"I'll be fine, Con," Edgar said from the bench seat next to me. "All they need me to do is open the doors inside."

"Edgar, do you know how dangerous these people are?" she said. "No, you have no idea."

"Do you know how hard it is to find cleaning work when you can't see the broom?" he said with a wry grin. "You brought me into this outfit to work. I'm working. This will buy us six more months, yeah?"

Connie fumed as she flipped the shade down to block the late-day glare.

My moon app thrummed in my pocket. I silenced it.

The sun lay on the horizon like a discarded orange wedge after peewee soccer practice. We would have made it a half hour earlier, but I'd detoured us to the local Ye Olde Outdoorsman Shoppe to pick up a few items. By the time we'd parked at the empty housing development, we would only have a few minutes until the day became night.

Yeah.

I didn't want to have to broach *that* subject, because we were already stressing our driver to the breaking point. A conversation about Kane's nighttime sensitivity wouldn't likely calm her down. I'd have to figure out a way to keep him covered, but first, Edgar was regaling us with his plan to get inside.

No surprise, Connie was less than giddy about it.

"Kane seems like the kind of guy who can handle himself," Edgar said and playfully kicked the passenger seat. "He'll make sure I'm cool."

"He's a beast." Connie coughed out a sneering laugh. "The descender might be able to hold him, *might*, but you and him together will be pushing it."

Edgar had come up with a way to get onto the roof. However, Consuela knew the rigging better because she'd been the one who always strapped into it.

The descender let workers wash the exterior windows of multistoried buildings. As she described it, two U-shaped bars called a parapet anchor hung over the roof ledge. Once you set the anchor above the windows you wanted to clean, you spun four massive clamps to lock it in place.

From the anchor, two ropes hung down that were attached to an electronic pulley system on the cleaner's harness. Let out the rope, you go down. Hit the doohickey on the motor, and you go back up.

Each night, a section of the outside windows of the Covenant building had gotten cleaned, top to bottom. After a week of that, they'd have circumnavigated the building, and they'd start again.

On the night we'd first met them, the descender had been set up and ready to go for the night's cleaning. Then all hell had broken loose. Connie and Edgar were told the next day they were no longer needed.

The apparatus just sat there, waiting to be misused. However, it had a weight limit.

"Those ropes can handle twice his weight, Con," Edgar protested. He seemed thrilled about going over the wall. Dude was fearless. "They're not gonna snap if it's me and him."

"No, but the motorized winch can't handle Godzilla-sized people. Especially when Godzilla is carrying someone else."

It was my turn to chime in. "Actually, Kane's gonna stay in the van. They might have seen him earlier today, so he'll be here in the back. Away from the windows and covered up."

From the passenger seat, my friend shook his head. "No. You cannot do this alone."

"And," I said, imitating his voice, "you cannot go out when it is dark, yes?"

Kane spun and peered around the headrest. I almost laughed. He looked like a little kid begging to go to Disneyland.

"We will find a way," he said, flicking his eyes back toward the orange light pouring in the windshield. "I can cover up."

"That has never worked out, Kane! Not one time. A big fail every single time we tried."

"Failure is the greatest teacher."

"Not for test pilots and parachutists," I said. "And not for a... not for you."

Kane frowned. "No. Pack of two. I will help."

"How?"

"You are smart and will think of something. We do this together."

I heard a rat-a-tat click then a tapping against my leg.

Edgar said to me, "I get the feeling there's something you're not telling us."

There was no way around it. So for the next few minutes, I told them.

Chapter Ten

Edgar hopped from the van first. He had extended his retractable cane, but instead of using it to get around, he spun it like a gymnast twirling a baton, hand to hand, then caught it in his right. With his left, he smashed the top of it, retracting the stick down to a fat cylinder again. When he hung it on his belt, it looked like a jumbo-sized whiteboard marker.

"I can't wait for this," he said, chattering away excitedly. "I knew there was something weird about you, man. I knew it!"

Connie sat motionless in the driver's seat, staring at the wheel. She needed a moment.

Rubbing my palms on my pants, I asked Mr. Happyfuntime, "You *knew* the moonlight changed him?"

Edgar tilted his head. "I mean, no, not *that*. But I knew there was something just different about him."

Kane sat in the passenger seat as the last moments of the day whispered dark promises from the horizon. I watched as he reached for Connie then pulled his hand back.

"Are you okay, Consuela?"

For a moment, she said nothing. Then she shook her head and turned to him. "You guys are insane, right?" She looked through the open cargo door at me. "Right? *That* isn't possible. Why would you even say all that?"

The weirdest feeling of shame came over me. Absent was that delicious thrill that this person, who was basically calling me a liar, was about to be proved wrong.

In the past, I'd always relished moments like that. Craved them. Rolled around in their astonishment like a wet dog in the drapes.

After someone went nose-to-nose with me, insisting I'd been so wrong, their world got suddenly upended *because* of me. Because I was right!

That realization—yes, imagine that, Emelda was right!—blew the smug expression right off their face.

But as Connie looked between me and Kane, I didn't feel so right.

"Maybe this is not a great idea," I said.

Edgar was all in. "This is an *amazing* idea, Emelda!"

Inspiration for my part of the plan had come from our first run at the building. Kane had drawn one of the security guys away because he'd chased a squirrel. At night, if they saw a six-foot-seven dude outside, they'd probably shoot him.

Now, a *dog* running around, yapping and barking, isn't a threat, but if I wanted to get up to the roof unseen, we needed to distract the guards. There were cameras around the lot, and it would be best if they weren't looking at the screens when I did it.

Rather, when Edgar and I did it.

Kane put one foot out the cargo van's door then looked over at the quiet woman in the driver's seat.

"I am so sorry we brought this trouble to you, Consuela," he said. "Emelda is strong. She will keep Edgar safe."

He stepped out and slowly closed the door. We all watched as Kane walked in front of the vehicle and stared into the fading sun.

For a moment, he just stood there, in a standoff against the horizon. After a deep sigh, he began unbuttoning his jacket. The only sound in the quiet night was the tick-tick-tick of the buttons breaking free.

Edgar whispered to me, "What's happening? What's he doing?"

"He's taking his clothes off."

That got a nod out of the man. He got it.

"Why is he taking his clothes off?"

He didn't get it.

I started going over what I'd revealed in the van earlier. I'd left out the wolf part because, I mean, why make things weirder? But it was time to get into some details about his transformations.

"When he changes, he gets smaller, so the clothes won't fit. Especially tonight, because we'll have just a crescent moon up there and—"

"Right, right," Edgar said, interrupting me. "So the size of the moon, or phase, determines how big a dog be becomes?"

My jaw dropped. And not because Kane had just taken off his shirt, folded it, and laid it on the van. But, you know, that kinda would have done it too.

"Wait. That... I mean, that makes sense to you?"

"Am I right?"

"Well, yeah."

Edgar shrugged, a smile tugging at the corners of his lips. "Then I guess it does."

When I looked over at Connie, she was staring at the dashboard. I didn't know if that was because a dude was stripping in front of her or if she was just gripping the steering wheel, hoping the world would stop spinning out of control.

Her night had started with pizza. Now, a stranger stood in her headlights, preparing to turn into a dog.

The sun sputtered on the horizon as Kane tugged at his belt. I turned to Edgar.

"We're you always blind?" I said then felt sick. "I'm sorry. Is that okay to ask?"

"Totally fine. I've got retinitis pigmentosa. Some people with RP get a type of tunnel vision, but I've always been a fast learner," he said and grinned. "I can sorta see light and dark. My RP kicked up when I was a kid, and the world got fuzzier and fuzzier until it slipped away. I know it's still there. I just can't see it. Hiding on me, I'm thinkin'."

"You've got a great attitude about it," I said, feeling more and more stupid with every word I said.

"Oh, I get frustrated by it now and again. Like when somebody tells me that a big French Canadian's about to turn into a dog ten feet away, and I can only listen."

I heard Kane place his jeans on the hood of the van. His belt clinked and tinkled like wind chimes then stopped.

My eyes on Edgar, I asked, "So this all makes perfect sense to you?"

"Naw, but I know there's magic in the world," he said and tapped his head. "Maybe I'll tell you about it one day."

"We got a minute or two," I said. "Tell me now."

"Ed thinks he hears dead people," Connie said, speaking for the first time since we'd parked. "My best friend thinks he can talk to ghosts."

"Naw, I don't talk to ghosts. That's crazy," the man next to me said. "But they talk to me."

In a mock severe voice, I asked, "Are they talking to you right now, Edgar?"

He shook his head. "They're probably watching a naked dude standing in the street who's about to turn into a—"

Edgar's words were interrupted by a groan from Kane, and when I turned, he had gone down on one knee in the middle of the road.

Chapter Eleven

Kane

For a year, this curse has, um, cursed me. The transition from human to canine.

The horizon also has a transition. From yellow to orange to red then black. The day must die so that the night may come.

I can feel the prickles upon my skin. The buzzing in my skull. This time, there is an acid churning in my stomach. In my perplexed state, I do not recall whether this always happens. My mind lifts away from my body as if it does not want to be a part of this.

As Emelda would say, I can relate.

Somewhere in the sky, the predator moon has been searching for me. The night eye blinded by its sky cousin. The sun is my protector, but I am always prey. When she passes to the next world, without her grace, I am discovered.

Like now.

My limbs twitch and shake, aching as they twist into strange shapes. Not so painful to the body, but the mind, yes, the mind still cannot comprehend. *Unnatural*, a voice says. *Improper*, another replies.

My eyes close against a blinding light, but it only grows brighter. The vibrant colors of the setting sun, from birth to death, speed across the sky.

Yellow, orange, red.

The red melts and coalesces into the eyes of the beast. Staring at me. Judging me. Daring me to embrace and take it into my soul. But this is a reckless creature with a hunger for blood. Alas, it is a hunger I share, for the dark beast is within.

In bright flashes, many shapes pass before my eyes. I recognize some because they are creatures I have become.

Large head, straight back, sharp teeth.

Wrinkles where fur should be.

From thick, powerful thighs to tiny legs like chickens. I do not become chickens. However, I have become dogs that chickens could probably defeat in combat. Chickens are very angry creatures. I expect this is because they know their fate, which often involves mayo.

The beast in my mind scowls at the canine creatures that flash by. Its face twists in disgust, swiping at each, but in their ethereal form, it cannot touch them. As it cannot touch me.

At least, I hope it cannot.

The wolfwere grows more powerful within. A part of me, but apart from me. A distortion of Kane. Still me but not me. Increasingly, not me.

My legs buckle, and I stumble to the hard blacktop. I feel my shoulder hit the road just as tufts of fur split my skin. Almost as if the transition animal seeks to cushion my fall.

The air swirls around me, a torrent of sound and motion and light, as my body tenses and roils and bubbles to where it feels like my bones will crack and my blood will burst.

As quickly as the hurricane began, it stops.

I am lying on my side, blinking away blinding light. Has the moon finally left the sky to come in for the kill?

It is so bright.

But I will not die lying down!

I will face my foe. From the ground, I roll to my feet.

All four of them.

Chapter Twelve

As Kane transformed, I glanced between the bizarre scene and Connie. She had lifted her head from the steering wheel and was now watching intently, her face stony.

My friend let out a muted call, as if in pain. Had he done that before? I'd never considered it might be painful for him.

"What is happening?" Edgar whispered, shifting from foot to foot, his head twitching around like a bird.

"He's..." I started, but I didn't know how to finish.

My eyes went to Connie, who looked frozen in place. Except her eyes, which fluttered as if something in her mind said that if she just cleared her vision, whatever was happening in front of her would make sense.

Of course, it didn't make sense.

"That isn't..." she muttered, her voice drifting out the van's window. "That can't happen." She turned to me, eyes blazing. "That's some trick, isn't it? Some damn party trick!"

I shook my head.

"What are you seeing, Con?" Edgar shouted.

But she was focused on me. Eyes accusing.

"Did you guys set this up earlier today? What kind of joke is this?" she said and hesitantly turned her head back. The big man who'd been standing there had disappeared.

Where Kane had been, her headlights revealed a small black dog. It rolled to its feet, turned and snarled at the vehicle, baring its teeth at the grille.

"Holy shit," she cried out, rolling her window up. "Is that thing safe?"

"Kane," I shouted. "Don't scare the cleaning van, 'k?"

The dog blinked and flicked its head toward the sound of my voice. "Is this you, Emelda? Why cannot I see you?"

"Because you're staring into headlights, you big goof," I said and walked toward him. "Or little goof, as it were."

I cast shadows across him in zebra stripes, making him look like some mystical creature. Which, I suppose, he was.

Kane was barely bigger than a cat. A compact body with black fur and tufts of white on his legs and tiny chest. Dark hair hung from his muzzle, almost as if he'd brought his beard with him in the transition.

I felt a bump from behind.

"Sorry," Edgar said. "What... what is he?"

Bending down on one knee, I gripped Kane on either side of the head. "I'm not really a dog person. He's black and white and sort of scruffy."

Edgar hopped once—for real, the dude hopped in the air—and clapped his hands together. "What else?"

"That's it. He's a little black-and-white scruffy dog."

"Schnauzer," Connie said. I turned and saw her standing at the quarter panel, just the outline of her body visible. "Maybe a mini schnauzer, but th-that's a schnauzer."

Edgar turned toward the sound of her voice. "Is he amazing looking? I mean, this is unreal! Are you sure it's him? For real?"

"Yes, it is me, Edgar," Kane said, his tiny dog face pinching up. "Wolves do not lie. People lie."

Before anyone could ask about *that* comment, I said, "Don't get on your high horse, schnauzer dog. I think you're pretty good at spreading bullshit around."

"Of course, this I can do," he said, lifting his head in the air, a bit high and mighty for a dog so small. "I grow up on a farm. This is a simple thing to do."

"Is he talking?" Edgar said, spinning in a slow circle. "Is the dog talking? Are those words—?"

"Yes, Edgar," Connie said, her voice hollow.

Kane stepped closer to me, his head slung low. "Are they making fun of me? Have I offended them in some manner?"

"No, man. It's like they've never seen a guy turn into a dog before."

"To be clear," Edgar said. "I still haven't seen that."

I winced and closed my eyes. "I didn't... say that right. Sorry."

"I'm teasing you, Em. Can I pet him?"

Kane bared his teeth and let out a low growl.

I laughed. "He's not really a dog like that. He's still a dude. In a way." In a way that he used to be a wolf, but there was no use in confusing an already bizarre situation.

"I bet he's beautiful," Edgar said, dropping to one knee. Tentatively, he held out a hand that trembled in the night air.

At first, I thought he was shaking, afraid of getting bitten. Then I saw his face.

His lips parted to let short, fast breaths escape. His gray eyes were wide. Damp. The dark skin of his smooth forehead glowed in the headlights.

Edgar wasn't afraid. He was in awe.

Kane looked at him and slowly trotted toward the man, his claws clicking across the oil-black street. When he got to Edgar's hand, he lifted his head and pressed in.

The man next to me stifled a sob and blinked rapidly. Then he laughed. Scratching the animal's fur with both hands, gently, reverently, he laughed until tears fell from his beautiful eyes.

"You are Kane?" he said, his voice a whisper.

"I am Kane. You are Edgar." His little dog lips curled into a smile. "And you smell like pineapple pizza. Despite this, I believe we can still be friends."

I reached forward because I knew Kane better than anyone. "Yeah, you're gonna wanna chill on the heavy petting. Kane doesn't—"

Edgar didn't even hear me. I didn't exist. Just him and the supernatural dog. The man reached down and hugged Kane. *Hugged* Kane, for god's sake! Gripped him like a six-year-old with a new puppy.

"Okay," I said and scooted away, waiting for the claws to come out.

"You are magic," Edgar said, happy tears soaking into the dog's fur. "The world... I knew there was magic. I knew it! And here you are."

He gripped Kane tighter.

"You're gonna want to ease off, dude," I suggested.

Edgar pulled his head back and went nose to nose with the animal. "Thank you. Thank you for being our magic. You have brightened our dark world, my friend Kane."

I nearly fell over in the street. "Kane? Did you just *lick* Edgar's face?"

The man laughed. "I don't mind."

"Kane?"

The black-and-white dog shifted back with his hind legs, pulling from Edgar's grasp.

The man clasped his hands together, then hugged himself. "Isn't he a joy?"

Kane looked around, bobbing his head left and right, not meeting my eyes. He swung his snout in my direction, looking as sheepish as a dog can, and tilted his head.

"Strange compulsion," he said then finally looked at me. "I could not help myself with the licking. Very strange."

I was about to give him all kinds of shit, I mean loads of it, because we're friends, and that's what friends do. Good ones do, at least.

But my thoughts got interrupted by the slam of a car door.

For a second, I thought for sure the van was going to fire up and race away. Or run down the tiny dog. I went to the driver's-side window and knocked on it.

Connie stared down at the dash. The rapid blinking had stopped. All blinking had stopped. I knocked on the window again.

Finally, she rolled it down.

"You okay?"

She shook her head once then again. Then quickly, screwed her eyes up, and let out a big breath of air. "No. No, I'm not okay," she said. "But I'll deal with it later."

That sort of reasoning made me worry. Sure, I'd done my fair share of deflection. Hell, I'd done more deflection than a hockey goalie in the Stanley Cup playoffs. But we needed Connie's head in the game.

"You sure you can still do this?" I asked, nodding to the back of the van. "You know how to get that gear all set up. I don't."

She nodded once. Then her eyes cleared, and she said, "I still don't know how we're going to get those ropes down from up top."

"You said we just need to trip the two latches holding them."

"Yeah," she said. "And it's five stories up, Emelda. Unless you're telling me that thing can fly?" She threw a hand toward the dog. "It *can't* fly, can it?"

"Kane is *not* an it or a thing," I said, not hiding the anger in my voice. "And of course he can't fly. He's a dog."

"Of course?" she shouted, her anger rising. She wrenched the handle of the door, and it flew open. I had to jump back. "A human just turned into a dog right in front of me! That's not possible. That's not even in the realm of maybe. It's *im*possible. So forgive me if I ask such a *stuuupid* question as can the impossible dog fly?"

For a second, I thought she might clock me.

And her rage was fueling mine. I leaned into her and cocked a finger, ready to fire. Before I could say another word, I heard someone say, "Hup."

We both turned.

The schnauzer was standing in place, jumping. "Hup," he said. Then he crouched all the way down, his fur brushing the road, and extended his tiny legs as he lifted a few inches into the air.

"Hup!"

Connie and I both just stared at him. Kane swiveled his head toward us.

"No," he said, his claws clicking on the road as he regained his footing. "I cannot fly."

The woman next to me put her hands to her head and shook it. "I just have to get through the next hour, and then I'll have my breakdown."

"Aw, Con," Edgar said, turning toward us. "He's one of God's little miracles. Enjoy it."

She slammed the door and leaned on the window. "I will enjoy it. When this is done, we get paid, and they are gone." Connie jabbed her finger at me. "You still haven't told me how you're getting those latches free. This is all a waste of time otherwise."

I pulled the slingshot I'd gotten at the outdoorsman store out of my back pocket. I waved it in front of her. "Turns out I'm pretty good with these."

Connie laughed in that exasperated way people do when they feel they're standing still as the world spins around them. "Great," she said. "The guards will hear all the racket and be on you in ten seconds. How do you expect to pull that off?"

"Ah, well, that'll take a miracle," I said, letting out a long breath and looking over at Kane. "Just a little one."

Chapter Thirteen

A great leader once said, "I love it when a plan comes together."

Actually, I think that might have been in a movie. Or some old television show. Still, it's a pretty stellar line.

We had a plan, and it was coming together. Was it a good plan? Probably not, but a bad plan was better than no plan.

At least, that was what I was trying to convince myself.

I grunted and got shushed by Connie. "It's got to be tight. I don't want you guys getting halfway up and slipping out," she said. "Well, I don't want Edgar slipping out."

"Thanks," I said.

She tightened the last strap and took a step back to check the fit. Then she looked at me. "You really think this will work?"

Grinning, I nodded. "Of course it will."

I had no idea.

We'd crept through the trees behind the Covenant building and hidden in the darkness. Schnauzer Kane stood in the grass between my feet as we all looked at the five-story fortress. Over the next few minutes, I saw one guard and then another walking the halls on the third floor. The other levels were dark.

That was when I realized everyone around me was waiting for me to tell them what to do next. What the hell did I know?

I think a good leader, in large part, is an expert at faking it. When people ask, "Will this work?" they answer, "Of course it will!"

They don't really know more than anyone else, but if their foot soldiers think they believe it will work, it just might. The leader's bullshit fuels their confidence, and their confidence helps pull it off.

That was what I was doing.

Pretending I was supremely confident while having no idea if scaling the exterior of the building as doggy Kane distracted the two guards would work.

Especially because it relied on Kane distracting them. Although Kane seemed confident he could pull it off.

Was that fake confidence like mine? I doubted it. Kane had the unique ability to buy his *own* bullshit.

He'd trotted around to the front of the building, where the two security vehicles had been parked side by side. They were the only cars in the lot, so even he wouldn't get confused.

Was he planning on piddling on the tires? Would that be enough to draw the attention of the goons inside?

Not my problem.

I'd bought a slingshot from the sporting goods store. My slingdart was somewhere outside an old convent in Mexico, buried in a few feet of silt by then. I thought I would miss it but didn't. Still, I'd gotten pretty damn good with the slingshot.

"You sure you can trip those way up there from way down here?" Connie whispered, craning her neck toward the contraption five stories up. The descender looked like a steampunk gargoyle with its legs draped off the edge of the roof after a weekend bender.

"Don't worry about that," I said with all the BS-fueled confidence I could gin up. "I just gotta hit the two silver latches, and the cords drop down?"

Connie snorted. "Yeah. *Just* hit the plates fifty feet above our heads."

"Easy."

Connie secured the motorized winch between me and Edgar. It was about the size of a loaf of bread. Once the two ropes dropped from above, we'd loop them through the winch and ride up to the top using the controller strapped to my harness.

"Bend your knees, Edgar," I said.

When he did, I reached down and picked through the decorative white stones at the base of the building. I'd seen them earlier that day and even then thought they'd make great projectiles. Odd that my mind had immediately gone to, "Pretty! I wonder how I could make them weapons."

After a minute, I had a handful of more rounded ones because I felt they had the best chance of going in a straight line. Science. Or physics. Whatever.

I loaded the first stone into my slingshot, pulled the strap back, aimed, and let it fly.

Clank!

Connie froze. I froze. Edgar chuckled.

"That was surprisingly loud," he whispered. "Did it work?"

"No," Connie said, tugging a Velcro strap on my vest tighter. "It did not work. Unless the plan was to alert everyone for a city block that we're back here. Is that the plan, Emelda?"

I didn't bother answering. Anger simmered in my brain. I slotted another rock into the slingshot, lifted it toward the sky, pulled back, and released.

Clang!

Edgar's smile faded a little. "Did you get that one?"

"No, dude," I said and bent down to grab a slightly larger rock. I nearly fell because I'd forgotten that Edgar was strapped to me.

"Here we go," he said, giggling.

Connie had to shush him, too. She threw a hand out and steadied him so we didn't topple over.

I set up the slingshot again. "Don't worry. You know how these things go, right?" I said, aiming for my target. "It's always the third one. Adds tension."

Clang, ping!

We all stood there quiet for a moment. Edgar broke the silence. "Well, the fourth attempt will add even more tension, right?"

As I lined up, Connie put a hand over my slingshot. "It's too loud!" she hissed. "We're gonna get busted."

"I'll get it," I said, shrugging her off and lining up again. "Gimme a sec."

She shook her head. "They are going to hear that!'

Of course they would. The security cameras pointed toward the lot and around the building. We had hugged up close to the exterior wall so we couldn't be seen. But even if those cameras didn't have microphones, I was shooting rocks at the building and hitting metal. Someone inside was bound to hear that. No question.

"They won't hear a thing," I said through gritted teeth. Just as she was about to reach to stop me, I let the rock fly.

Clank, ping, whirrr.

The latch holding rope one sparked, and the coil unspooled toward the ground. Stunned, Connie took a step back so it didn't hit her. It hit Edgar instead.

"Either I got bonked on the head by a suicidal snake," he said, "or I think she got it."

My face was stoic. Flat. *Easy, I knew it would work*, my expression said. In my head, though?

Holy shit, I can't believe that worked!

"One more to go," Edgar said, turning his face up. He then thought better of it and slid to the side, pulling me along with him.

Again, I lined up the shot.

And again, Connie reached out. "That was *crazy* loud. They're going to—"

That was when we heard the barking from the other side of the building.

Chapter Fourteen

Kane

My prey stands before me.

Its eyes do not blink as it watches me stalk back and forth. I growl to show my fierceness, but it is unmoving. This is a front, for I know it fears me so.

The teeth of the creature are large but dull. Its lower lip is a rigid line, but if it were alive, it would be trembling. I am the alpha here!

I yip at it.

Hmm.

That was supposed to be a howl. A terrifying display of my dominance and power. It was not.

No matter. I will strike terror into the heart of my foe with a spectacle of my ferocious hunger for flesh and blood. Or, rather, metal and rubber. And plastic.

"Bark, bark, bark!"

Ugh.

I mask the disappointment in myself. How pitiful I must seem! If a creature such as I had appeared in the Canadian wilderness, my pack and I would have sent one of the wolf cubs to kill it. As practice. And it would have snapped this animal's curly-haired neck with a flick of its tiny baby wolf jaws.

Still, I have to find a way to defeat this foe.

This Nissan Leaf.

I believe that was what Emelda called it. A terrible name for a vehicle. A leaf is known for one thing and one thing only. Falling. I will fell this faller!

Creeping forward, my claws skittering across the blacktop, I stalk toward my target as I watch its friend in the next parking space. This other vehicle is also a Leaf. And I will not be defeated by foliage!

The wolf—even when it is a scruffy dog—finds the weakest in the pack and attacks.

I part my jaws and strike!

A black strip at the front of the bumper is my target, and I take it between my teeth. Fiercely, I bite down and tear at it without mercy. This, however, only lifts my body in the air and shakes it from side to side.

This is okay, for it is only a show that the men inside will watch. Still, I need them to come defend their pitiful cars from my wrath. I must find a way for this tiny form to threaten this hulk of a machine.

Stepping back, I leap forward and land on the hood.

"Ah ha!" I say to the frightened vehicle. "You didn't expect an attack such as—whooaa!"

I slide across the hood of the car, my claws grasping for purchase. Tumbling off the side, I clatter to the black tar of the parking lot. But I am quickly up again to my feet!

A slippery car hood cannot defeat me!

Crouching, I leap again and land but push my footpads out so I do not slide. Instead, I squeak, which sends a tremor up my tiny arms. This hurts a little bit.

I do not yield to pain. Those with wolf hearts laugh at pain!

Still, I think I may have a tiny boo-boo.

No! Fierce creatures do not get boo-boos, large or small. Even if I am not a fierce creature on the outside, I have one within. And I will not yield to my vehicular foe.

Ah ha!

I see its horn. Not the car horn, for that is inside. But a single metal horn bends from the rear of the vehicle and is pinned to the side of the car's roof. An antenna, I know this is called, but in this battle, it is this beast's horn. And a weak point in the armor of this formidable creature.

I try to walk up the windshield, but my feet only slide against the glass. They make more squeaky sad-bird sounds, and this I do not like. A reminder of how tiny this body is.

Leaping, I land on the roof and slide.

"Bark, yip, no! *Non! Arrêt!*"

I push my padded feet out and stop. I am getting better at maneuvering this dog body. Now, I am in control. Slowly, I stalk toward the tip of the bent antenna. Its weakest point. It is nestled into a black plastic casing.

I know it is just this plastic that holds it secure. Thus, I attack. First with my claws, but they are feeble, so I bend down and bite. Tiny black bits come away, and I spit them out. Very unpleasant tasting.

Once more, I bite down. This time, I use the power of the tiny body and flail back and forth.

"Grrnnn, grnnn, grnnn!"

I can feel it succumbing to my attack. The brace is moving, the plastic crumbling. I shake harder, pull with my hind legs, twist and shift.

It is working! I am breaking it free.

I hear it snap—victory!—and crunch down harder, gripping the metal rod between my tiny schnauzer dog teeth. It is mine! I have a piece—

The metal antenna begins to straighten, and strangely, I go with it. I lift off the roof of the Nissan Leaf and see the stars, a carpet of twinkling light, beneath my feet as I am launched through the air.

Chapter Fifteen

The two guards, Ezekiel and Mike, stared at the lower-left screen as the tiny dog flew out of view. Izzy thought it might have been the funniest thing he'd ever seen. Not that he wasn't a dog lover; he was. And he knew schnauzers were tough little dogs and that it would be just fine.

Pissed but fine.

"It's like a damn *dog*-a-pult," he said, wiping a tear from his lower eyelid.

Mike? He didn't find it as funny. "Friggin' mutt's chewing up my ride!"

The anger steaming off Izzy's partner only made the older man laugh harder.

"Shaddup." Mike leaned closer to the screen. "There's something wrong with the dog."

"Yep, he's about thirty feet from where he'd hoped to be," the laughing man said.

Mike smacked his coworker's chest with the back of his hand.

"Damn, I haven't laughed that hard in ages." Izzy dropped into a nearby rollaway chair and let out a satisfied sigh. "Just ain't had much to laugh about recently, is all."

Mike fiddled with the computer to zoom in the camera. It didn't zoom. The camera shifted slightly left then shook. "Damn thing. Never works right." He typed in a few more commands, and it centered itself back onto his car. "Where'd the stupid dog go?"

Izzy leaned forward, rubbing his rubbery face. "Maybe he's had enough. Ran off to lick his wounds."

"No. Look!" Mike said, thumping a nicotine-stained finger onto the screen. "The little mongrel just came around the side. What the hell is it doing?"

Scooting his chair forward, Izzy leaned in to get a better look. He wasn't sure if he could take another laugh attack. It'd probably stop his bum heart, but it might be worth it.

"I think..." the seated man said. "I think mini Cujo is coming around to face off against your car again."

Mike shook his head slowly then turned to the other man. "You think that damn dog's rabid or something?"

"No."

"Why not? It might be."

"When was the last time you heard about a rabid dog?"

The standing man leaned in closer, pulling at his lip. "A friend of a kid who I grew up with got bit by rabid skunk. Ended up with like fifty shots in his belly."

"Urban legend," Izzy said. "Nervous parents used to tell the 'fifty shots' stories to keep their kids indoors."

Mike shifted his chin to look at the other man. "Keep them inside? Mine would lock the doors to keep me out."

Izzy nodded slowly. "That tracks."

"What the hell does that mean?" Mike spun, fueled by a rage for the little dog squaring off against his security vehicle. "My parents—"

"Shh!" Izzy shot a hand up as his eyes flitted to the ceiling. "Did you hear that?"

They both quieted for a moment, just waiting in the silence.

"I didn't hear nothing," Mike said.

Izzy let out a breath. "If you're gonna talk, we ain't gonna hear anything. I think it came from the back."

"What? What came from the back?"

The older man leaned forward to grab the camera controls, but Mike smacked his hand away. "Don't touch that," he said. "Look at that little bastard! I've seen lions do that in cages. Like they're preparing."

"Ha, for what?" Izzy said, forgetting about the strange sound. Buildings did that sometimes. Especially this one. "You think that scruffy thing is going to steal your car?"

When the tiny dog on the tiny screen leaped onto the hood, Mike stumbled back, his thigh catching the knee of his seated coworker, and toppled back. He fell and landed hard on his broken pride.

"Damn it!"

"Your own fault, brother," Izzy said. With the space in front of him clear of chubby steroid monkeys, he scooted his chair forward. He rested his elbows on the table and watched the show.

From the floor, Mike asked, "What's he doing?"

"He's on your hood."

"Why is he on the hood?"

Izzy felt the giggles start to rise again from somewhere deep in his belly. He couldn't help it. "I think the little dude is lining up for another go."

Mike shot up, and Izzy braced for the shove, but it never came. Instead, the big man ran out of the third-floor video room on a tear, whipping past desks that had been empty for more than a week now.

Ezekiel would have never admitted it to his coworker, but the total stillness freaked him out a bit. Rather, that the stillness in the abandoned building didn't exactly feel still.

For his part, Mike wasn't freaked out but freakin' mad instead. Squeezing his fists together, he focused on the large office windows facing the front lot. The anger was making his head throb, and he clapped a coffee cup full of pens to the floor. The outburst made him feel better.

Mike enjoyed hitting things. Especially things that couldn't hit back.

At the largest window, he yanked on a dangling cord. The shade folded like an accordion, rising with a metallic clatter and ending with a *thunk* as it smacked the top of the window. The collapsed shade hung askew, slightly lower on one side.

The near-empty parking lot lay before him. The dead and dying grass on either side of the access road lay beyond that. Above, a clear sky of stars with a sliver of a moon.

And below, a dog was attacking his car.

Chapter Sixteen

You would have thought after I'd freed latch one, the second would be easy. I had the distance and arch down. I could just repeat what I did the first time.

"I don't remember what I did the first time," I mumbled.

Connie looked like she was going to breach birth a hay bale. Her face twisted in a painful expression as she wrung her hands hard enough to break fingers. "This isn't working," she said through gritted teeth. "This won't work."

"It'll work."

I lined up and fired off another rock with the slingshot. It pinged off the bracket with a tiny spark. Closer, though.

Connie took a half-step back, and I reached out and grabbed her shirt to hold her steady. She glared at me.

I glared back. "Stay close to the side of the building."

And she did. In fact, she leaped around Edgar and flattened herself against the wall. Her lower lip trembled, and she squeezed her eyes shut. In a raspy whisper, she said, "Emelda, I think that camera moved."

"Probably the wind," Edgar suggested.

"What wind?"

I fired another shot, and just after I did, I heard the little servos in the camera grind, a low chattering sound that ended in a quick series of clacks.

Damn.

Connie turned her head and looked up. "Do you hear—"

She didn't get to finish her sentence. I feel my rage cauldron boil over, and I lifted the slingshot, pulled back the rock, and fired without even lining it up.

Ping, whir!

The second rope uncoiled, whipping down the side of the building like an electric eel leaping at its prey. I slid out of the way at the very last moment, so of course, Edgar got the knotted end of it right on top of his head.

It clunked. He smiled.

"You did that on purpose to screw me, didn't you?"

"No! No, dude, I would never—"

"Chill, I'm kidding," he said and gave me a big smile. "Did it look funny? I bet it looked funny."

Connie brushed the top of his head softly. "You okay?"

"I'm fine." He shrugged. "I heard it coming down. Thought it might be funny if I got the bonk again."

Despite how nervous she was, Connie smiled. "Do you take anything seriously?" she asked her friend as she threaded the second rope through our harness.

"Nope," he said.

As Connie secured the cords into the battery-operated winch, I flicked my eyes up to the camera that had moved only a minute earlier. It was jerking in a tiny flicking and clicking motion. As if someone were leaning on the controls, and it had reached its range limit.

We needed to get up the wall. Fast.

Connie stared at our target. Then she stepped forward and looked at Edgar. "You ready?"

I answered, "Yes."

She grabbed my hand and put it on the winch lever. "Pull up to go up. In the middle is stop. For down, just—"

"I got it," I said, yanked on the red handle, and we jerked upward in lurching, bouncing motions. Edgar and I were cinched together. It might have been easier if we were face to face, but Connie had insisted he face away from me because it was more secure. I wondered who it might be more secure for.

I eased off on the speed.

Standing on the ground and gazing up, it didn't seem like a long way, but when you're clinging to a rope looking down, the second floor looked like we were ten stories high.

Slowly, we crept upward, inch by inch. My hands were already damp on the controls. The winch hummed louder than I felt comfortable with, but there wasn't anything I could do about that. Then it began to make an odd, throaty noise.

No. That wasn't coming from the winch.

When I slowed our ascent, I heard endless barking. Kane. Was that part of his distraction, or was he calling for help?

"Emelda," Edgar whispered, "I could walk up the side of this building faster."

I lightly thumped him with my heel. "That sounds like a challenge. You wanna race to the top?"

"However fast we go, I reckon it'll end in a tie," he said, and I could hear the smile in his voice. "But maybe we could give it a bit of juice. Not too much."

I flipped the lever to full.

The nylon rope within the electronic winch started smoking. We stopped moving and banged against the wall again. I could hear Connie gasp below us as the smoke billowed across my chest. My sweaty fingers fumbled for the controls, and when I got ahold of the lever, I pushed it all the way to stop.

But all the way? That wasn't stop.

We fell.

Chapter Seventeen

Kane

The beast, it fights me, but it is a fight it will not win!

Growling, tearing, shaking my tiny head, I battle with its eyes. Well, not eyes so much as its eyebrows. The eyes are glass, headlights, so a confrontation with those would lead to cuts and slices across my tiny mouth.

Not good.

Instead, I am waging my small dog war upon these blades of rubber and metal. The rubber strips away easily, and I am emboldened by this small victory. I chew one of the wiper blades in triumph, showing my dominance. Then I toss it aside and spit out the taste.

"Is bad," I mumble to myself, my tongue lolling out.

Boom, boom, boom!

This noise comes from the building. I turn to it and see a large man is at a window. He is yelling, his face contorted and red.

"What? What is it you are saying in a loud, rageful manner?" I say at him. "I cannot hear you with the thick glass between us! Should you not come down and admonish me? Yes, yes."

I turn back to the windshield. Of course he cannot hear me, and the sound of a man's voice would only confuse coming from this animal. A dog name I cannot pronounce. Schanitzel? Schanozzle?

"Hasenpfeffer Incorporated!" I shout and laugh. Such fond memories of watching the old TV show with ma mère. The feisty lady with the letter stitched to her sweaters. The other with the very tiny head. Such funny ladies.

Such wonderful times with my human mother. I miss her so. Moroseness threatens to overtake me, so I push the bittersweet memories aside.

Above, the man continues to rage upon the window, so I return to my ruthless attack upon his car.

Of course, this is for show. I must remember that I am attacking the vehicle not to defeat it but to distract the security people inside. To garner their attention while Emelda and Edgar climb up the rear side of the building.

Emelda and Edgar. Sounds like a Hollywood couple.

Emelgar.

Hmm. Now, this sounds like a dragon from a Throne Games novel. Not that I could read them, but I saw one of the shows. I liked the brutal violence but too much baby making. So much baby making. Yet so few babies.

I do love babies. They are innocent and sweet. Prey animal babies are also innocent and sweet but savory as well.

This is making me think of my pack. My wolf wife. Will I have babies of my own one day? I do hope so. I think I would make a good père, like the human one I was blessed to have. At least, I will try my best. And if I get it wrong on the first one, well, there is always another spring to make a new baby.

I think this is why some human families have so many babies. They keep going until they get it right. I admire their tenacity. Don't focus on those early mistakes, no, make the next one better. Obviously, it must be working for them, because they keep doing it.

Twisting the windshield wiper in my mouth, I feel the flimsy metal bend and hear a crackle.

Wait, no.

That crackle did not come from the wiper. Nearby. Behind me.

In the bushes, I see a shimmy. Something moving. Am I being stalked? A gray fuzz darts within the bramble.

Fever flushes through my canine body. A desperate yearning. However, it is a desire I must ignore. I turn away, but another flash of gray. My mouth waters. My heartbeat quickens.

"I-I-I can-not," I say, but now, my mouth has gone dry. Out of the corner of my eye, I see it.

Its tiny beady eyes regard me from the bush. Those little rat hands hold something as it chews, watching me like *I* am some television show. I am not entertainment for a squirrel!

And within me, a building lust. Not a baby-making lust like on the Throne Games show. This is a lust for its blood.

No! I must do my job to keep Emelda and Edgar safe. And the man at the window...

He is gone. I should have paid better attention.

Hmm. I know that they also watch on the cameras but, for now, I cannot see the large, red-faced man. Cannot hear his booming as his fleshy fist impotently bangs against the window.

So, I have... a moment, then, yes?

Slowly, I turn toward my new prey. I take a tentative step forward and bare my teeth at the squirrel. The stupid creature continues eating whatever foul bit of refuse it has discovered. This inferior creature, eating rubbish!

Yet it sits there, taunting me! Indifferent, as if I am just some silly creature to watch while one snacks on a discarded burger wrapper.

I leap from the vehicle's hood and land on all fours, my legs spread wide and menacing. Stupid creature only twitches its fuzzy tail. *Swish, swish, swish.*

"I will rip that tail from your fuzzy gray Disney Tiny Toons body!"

The moment I launch forward, it stops its incessant, chubby-cheek chewing. Ah ha! It sees me coming for it. Be afraid, little squirrel. Be very afraid.

Its stupid pinhead twitches to its right, toward the building. Good, it is distracted. Or looking for the best way to flee. But I will—

Ping!

Bits of rock spit out of the ground, but I push through that stone dust. Did the fuzzy rat creature throw a stone at me? Ha, ha! It will take more than that—

Crack, ping!

Stone shards bite into my flank, and now, I turn in the same direction the stupid squirrel is looking. The large red-faced man has exited the building and is running toward me. Then he stops and raises his hands toward me. Fingers interlaced, he is pointing something at me.

Oh, schanozzle.

This is not good.

Chapter Eighteen

Izzy stared at the camera feed pointed at the rear lot, forcing himself to not blink. His eyes watered, but he'd been so sure he'd seen *something* flutter a second time. Leaves? The wind?

There wasn't a cloud in the night sky, and the forecast hadn't said a damn thing about rain or storms. How bad could the wind have gotten to blow leaves halfway up the building?

The cameras had needed maintenance for a long time now. Dirty lenses, bad motors, frayed wires. Odd flickers. He'd contacted the bosses, but since the building had cleared out, they'd stopped answering his messages. Probably focused on other issues, whatever those might be.

Didn't matter.

Watching over an empty building was easy money. But he still did good work. And that meant making sure people didn't get inside the empty building he was watching.

Mike had yelled curses all the way to the elevators. Dumb monkey was losing his shit over a dog who'd taken a particular dislike to one of their company cars.

"Never much did like the nighttime," Izzy said as he pecked at the security bunker's computer with two index fingers. "World is an odd enough place without putting blinders on it."

He'd tried to get another of the cameras out back to get a shot of the wall. Where he'd seen that flutter. Or thought he'd seen the flutter. But it just did that jerky thing again.

"Probably a damn bird's nest in the way."

Eyes burning, he finally blinked, and of course, the moment he opened them, in that fraction of a second, he would have sworn he saw something move just out of frame. Or was that just the night playing tricks on his mind?

Then he did see movement. But not on the screen pointed out back.

The lower-left monitor showed that crazy dog, the one Mike had been bewitched by. Good word for it, he thought. The damn car didn't even belong to him!

His frustration lightened when he zoomed in to the car's front window. All across the hood were bits of black rubber and bent metal. Izzy smiled and chuckled.

"Damn dog chewed the windshield wipers right off the car. That is one determined poochy-pup right there."

When he zoomed out again, he saw the dog on a tear, racing toward the far side of the parking lot.

"Nothing there but bushes."

Then he saw the flash. And the burst of dust just in front of the dog. He panned the camera and saw Mike stalking toward the animal with his arms extended.

That moron is shooting at the dog!

Izzy was a dog lover, but he had to admit the little mutt had probably brought all that on himself. Not worth dying over, but Darwin had his plan.

Another flash, and this time the dog leaped away. Lightning fast, a fraction of a second before the ground beneath him burst into dust. No, it hadn't *just* leaped away.

"What in the hell?" Izzy mumbled. "Did that dog just backflip?"

When it landed, it was facing in the camera's direction. Izzy stared, transfixed, and licked his lips. He shook his head slowly, his eyes locked onto the screen. *What in the blazes is it doing?*

At the bottom of the screen, he saw Mike stalking forward, arms raised, gun out. The man's hands were trembling. All that rage and steroid juice running through his system was making the dumb bastard even more dumb.

The dog stood motionless. Staring intently at the man advancing toward it. Thirty feet away. Then twenty-five.

He didn't want to watch this. Sure, he'd seen some awful shit in his life, and a lot he didn't want to remember. This would be a part of that file once Mike fired. He didn't want to watch some little dog get gunned down. He'd seen enough humans go that way, but they'd brought it on themselves.

Usually, anyway.

A flicker on the screen showing the rear of the building. Something black flew from the top to the bottom. Like a bag of garbage tumbling off the roof! It moved so fast, he only caught the last fraction of a second.

"What in the hell is going—?"

The panic from the bottom-left screen drew his eyes back. Chaos. And chaos had to be addressed before it became bedlam.

Izzy checked the weapon on his belt and flicked open the safety strap.

On the screen, the tiny dog had leaped left and right as comically silent bursts of blacktop exploded around it. Mike bobbed from side to side as if he was trying to use a speed gun on an angry wasp.

Then the dog had jumped in the air, *landing on Mike's face*, and the big man stumbled out of the frame.

Izzy ran for the elevator.

Chapter Nineteen

"Son-of-a—" I said as we dropped like a rock. Luckily, a part of my brain reserved for *not dying* nudged me and went, "Hey. Don't do that."

Hurtling toward the ground, I flicked the winch's lever back to the middle spot. The brakes kicked in, and we stopped like a yo-yo at the end of its string, bounced once, then the back of my head banged into the wall. Edgar's head smashed against mine.

Stars burst into my brain, but I clenched the rope with one hand.

"Stupid, stupid, stupid," I muttered to myself.

That got a laugh out of Edgar. "That earned me three stupids? I don't even know what I did, but man, high marks from the lady."

"No," I said, exhaling and trying to make the world stop spinning. "I flicked the wrong thing. Then the other thing couldn't do its thing, so the cord thingy shifted over. I think it's jammed."

Edgar reached up behind his head and found the other rope with his fingers. Pulling the cord into his hands, he gripped and pulled. "Get it back onto its track," he said, grunting with the exertion. "We need to get movin'."

The man wasn't a large guy, but he was lifting *both* of us up. Arms over his head, hands bent at a queer angle, Edgar had us suspended in midair.

I stared up. "Do you work out or something?"

His arms trembled, but he still managed a laugh. "Chat after?"

"Right, right!"

Pushing the nylon rope through from behind, I gave it some slack and threaded it back over the pulley. I clamped the winch's cover down into place so the gear was tight against the rope again.

Looked good. At least, I thought it did.

I didn't want to look down. Not because I was afraid of heights; I just didn't need to see Connie giving me the double bird, demanding I bring her friend back to terra firma. Dangling there, I wondered if that was the best idea anyhow.

No.

We had to get inside to find out where Doc Hammer and Marata had gone to launch their "animals first" plan. Not a lot of labs around the country to facilitate that. I just needed to find a list of Covenant black sites and go from there.

"Okay, let go of your rope," I whispered. When the slack had gone taut, I pressed the lever to get us climbing again and took a deep breath. Well, as deep as I could take with a dude strapped to me.

"Don't worry," Edgar said. "We'll find what you're looking for."

I gave the electronic winch a bit more juice and, close to my new friend's ear, I whispered, "You might be the most optimistic guy I've ever met."

"That just tells me you've been hanging around with the wrong people."

"You ain't lying," I said as we passed the fourth floor. And he was right. Before I'd met Kane, I found every loser and asshole and burnout Minneapolis had to offer. Guys and girls. For years, everyone I hung around was pissed off at the world and looking to even the score.

Kane was different.

Edgar was different.

And in her own way, I had to admit, Connie was different.

If I got done with all this madness and didn't die, I'd have to change up the scenery.

The window cleaner's harness finished its upward journey and banged against the extended rails of the descender with a thunk. The winch's gearbox groaned. I shifted it to Off and locked the lever in place.

Edgar spun for a moment until his right foot touched the building. He raised his arms and gripped the two overhanging bars then pulled us toward the roof with his feet. His arms were shaking, so I grabbed the two metal braces and helped.

"Just walk with your hands toward the building, and once we're close enough, I'll roll us forward," he said.

"It's like you've done this before."

"That's because I have."

I looked down the side of the building but couldn't tell if the windows were dirty or clean. "How does someone wash windows he can't see?"

Edgar grunted as he pulled us closer to the edge.

"I probably clean better than most people," he said. "I don't look for the parts that are dirty. I get an idea of the area I'm supposed to clean and take care of the whole thing as if it's all dirty. The grubby parts get clean, and the clean parts get cleaner."

In an odd way, that made total sense.

"Hold on," he said as he pulled us and twisted, which rolled us onto the roof. Once over the ankle-high guard rail, we landed on our sides, back to back. Edgar grabbed a clasp on his vest and yanked it. We separated.

He stood quicker than I did and with far more confidence. Maybe there was an advantage to not seeing you were this high up.

Edgar waved his hands behind him, tilted his head, and pointed toward the middle of the building.

"That roof door will be in the center, a little toward the back," he said. "You should see the top of the hand braces. You know, like on the side of a swimming pool."

"Yep. I see them."

As he pulled his telescopic cane off his belt, I spun around to let Connie know we'd made it up just fine. And, yeah, to kind of throw that in her face a little.

But when I looked down, she was gone.

She'd bolted. We'd made so much noise, she'd freaked out and bolted.

"Nice."

Chapter Twenty

Kane

The red-faced guard is now very red faced.

This is due, in part, because I have split some of his skin by his eyebrow. I was still in my car-attack mode and went for what had worked only a minute earlier. However, "worked" may be a generous description.

"Get off of me!" the man screams so loud it makes my fuzzy ears ring.

But I have defeated much larger beasts before. Once you get ahold of them, you must not let go. Large creatures have an advantage at range and can strike with overwhelming force. However, when you remove that distance, it is a winnable battle.

Smaller creatures also have an advantage. They know fear well. And while wolf is a ruler in the wild, he still knows fear. Too often, much larger creatures become accustomed to dominating others. Besting all challengers.

To them, fear is an alien. And not like the bug-eyed ET alien with early-onset diabetes from its candy fetish. More like ones that spring from plant-like pods and face hug. Nasty.

What was my point?

Ah, yes. When confronted by fear, colossal beasts do not have what the Dr. Phil TV person calls "coping mechanisms."

I must cease the pop-culture analogies and focus on my attack, so I bite down on a shirt collar, hard, as Mike the guard tries to strip me from his bulging body.

He raises his hand, gripping his pistol like a club, but he is not striking as hard as he might. Even in his panic, he knows the weapon could fire, and holding it such could mean the bullet would strike him in the man tackle.

Admittedly, that would be convenient.

I feel a rush of wind as we fall, my teeth loosening as my legs dangle in the air. The large man lands, flat on his back, his feet kicking at the pavement, trying to throw me aside. I hold on and growl at his neck. I can sense his heart quicken. Feel the dampness rise on his skin.

His fear grows.

The neck, yes. This is where the vulnerability lies for so many animals. The threat, my growl, even from such a small creature, is palpable.

He can feel my rage.

He can sense my voracious appetite for his blood.

He can hear me preparing to unleash teeth that slash and claws that tear.

"Push the dog off, and I'll shoot it!"

He can throw his voice?

No, this is another man. When I look up, I see determination upon his wizened face. Not panic. This is a man who has dealt with violence before. He has faced fear and not blinked.

I cannot defeat both of these men.

Extricating myself from the collar of the guard below me may be a simple task, but it would take a few seconds to run. In those seconds, I would have not one but two men shooting at me. I do not think I can outrun that.

But I must.

This new man moves closer, his weapon trained upon me. The expression twisting his face tells me he is preparing to fire. The man below me has a vest on. I can feel it as my feet scrabble across his chest. Plating.

Would he risk hitting a man, even with protection, at such a range? Maybe this other man is a very good shot. Or just not a big fan of Mike the security guard.

Surrender is death. I know this. So I growl louder, trying to think of a plan.

I must confuse. Yes. This is my only salvation.

A talking dog would confuse. But it could also raise other questions. It may put Emelda in danger. Animals that speak? They may think we are part of Covenant. Or their enemies who also experimented with Enhanced creatures.

I cannot decide, which is a strange sensation. My instincts have failed.

The large man below me makes the decision for me. He grips the sides of my hairy body and tears me from the thick fabric of his shirt. I fly through the air, end over end, my mind swirling and spinning.

When I land, I leap up quickly and try to run, but I stumble.

"No, no! Sorry, sorry, sorry!"

That was not what I wanted to say. So it is a good thing I did not say it.

When I rise to my feet, my head is foggy from the impact. I flop back down onto the parking lot. Resting now. I do need rest. But two men with guns. And the voice?

A shadow passes over me. The tall figure blocks the dim moonlight above. I recognize the way she stands, the way her arms move. The twist of the shoulder as she speaks.

"I'm sorry, he just got loose," Connie says to the men. "I was taking him for a walk, and he just started running. I am so sorry."

The large man on the ground rolls to his feet. On his face, I can read his thoughts. The fear I instilled is all gone, replaced with the rage.

"Your stupid dog attacked me, lady!" he screams at her. His face is no longer red. More purple. "You need to have that thing put down. Better yet—" he steps over and grabs his pistol off the ground—"why don't I do that for you?"

"No, I'm sorry," Connie says and takes a step closer to me. I realize this woman has put herself between me and two men with guns. She is not brazen about this. I can see her fingers trembling. "He didn't mean it."

"He didn't mean to bite my face?" the big guard says, spittle flying from his lips.

The other guard turns to him and examines the gash. Then this other man... laughs.

"Aw, hell. You got a tiny cut on your damn eyebrow, Mike. It's nothing."

"Tiny cut?" I mumble, indignant. I attacked that man, and it was *not* a tiny cut!

The two men turn toward us, their eyes drifting between me and the woman protecting me. A question forms on the lips of both men, but neither knows how to ask.

Thankfully, Connie speaks first.

"Tiny cut?" she says as if repeating the words.

The men look at her, unsure.

"Tiny cut? You want to shoot my lovely dog over a tiny cut?"

"No, no," the older man says. "We don't—"

"Yes, we do, Izzy!" purple Mike says, raising his pistol but not yet pointing it.

The look on the second man's face tells me he is considering what may happen next. I can read it as if he were speaking aloud.

"If he shoots the dog, you will call the police. The only way to prevent this is to kill you as well. This will only bring more questions, and those answers will bring people here. I cannot let that happen."

The calmer man reaches out and presses the gun's barrel back toward the ground.

"Put that away," the man called Izzy says. "No one needs the trouble."

Connie spins and hoists me up with a grunt. Is she saying I am fat? I am not fat.

Holding me to her chest may be the bravest thing I have seen. If the purple-faced man shoots me, it will kill her as well.

"He... he's a rescue dog," Connie says, her voice shaking. "His former owners were terrible. Large, muscular men who look like you."

"Oh?" Mike the guard says, perking up a little at the unwieldy use of flattery.

"Yes," Connie says, petting my head. Her hands are sweaty. She is getting human sweat all over my fur. Nasty. "They were very cruel and beat him every chance they got."

"Good," says the guard with the massive, life-threatening gash above his eyebrow. He holsters his weapon.

Chapter Twenty-One

As treacherous as it had been to climb the building, it was almost a letdown to find the hatch open. Of course, there'd be no reason to lock the roof access so people outside couldn't get in. Who would be up there you didn't want coming down?

My damp hands slid easily on the rails as I climbed to the bottom of the ladder. I'd heard the gunshots and knew, just knew those bits of lead had been chasing Kane. Sure, he could heal from injury, but that unique ability required a very particular high-iron diet.

Blood.

Where would we get that from? He'd probably have to chomp down a few neighborhood cats, which he'd be just fine with. But I liked cats. Well, Kane did, too, but only when they were fresh. Blech.

"You gonna move out of the way?" Edgar called from above.

I'd felt his foot sweep against the top of my head but brushed it off like a bug, lost in thought.

"Sorry," I said and slid back.

Just like he had said, we'd dropped into a tiny room between the north and south wings of the building.

"What's on either side of these doors?"

He dropped down, pulled his telescopic cane from under his arm, and let out a long breath. Had his unbreakable resolve been shaken?

"From here..." He spread his arms and pointed in opposite directions. "There's five offices on the left. Each of those has a PA position."

"PA?" I said and ran it over in my head. "You mean like personal assistant? A secretary?"

"Ha, don't let the PAs hear you say that. They do everything and the job of the exec they are assisting. It sounds like a lowly gig, but from what I know of it, the PAs just might have the most powerful role in any company."

I looked at the door to the execs' wing. Just below the handle was the punch-code lock he'd mentioned. We could just go have a look around. From what Connie and Edgar had said on the way over, there was a security station on the bottom floor and another on the third. We'd be two floors away from dudes with guns, so we shouldn't have to worry about anyone hearing footsteps on their ceiling.

But.

I didn't know if the doors would set off alerts when we opened them. If we popped open door number one, we might have about a minute before the security monkeys came swinging out of the elevator.

The executive wing to the left might hold the secrets we needed. The problem would be finding them. Had all the high-up muckety-mucks taken their top-secret papers and power ties with them? I would have.

Unless they were coming back.

That was a possibility, too. We didn't know Covenant's plans. Maybe after all the blood and gore got rinsed out of the first-floor atrium, they'd all return to finishing their evil to-do lists.

"What about on the right side?"

Edgar swung both arms dramatically in that direction. "Over here, you've got twelve desks in the middle, all attached into cubicles."

"Okay."

He spread his arms in a V. "On either side of the cubbies, you've got four offices on the right and three on the left. Those on the left are bigger."

"Do you know what kind of work they did over there?"

Edgar dropped his arms and shrugged. "A lot of pushpins inside those cubbies. Ten-key calculators. More pens and pen holders in there than an Office Max. The first week, I knocked every damn one of them on the floor. By Friday, I got a better feel for it."

I looked at him. The dude was actually smiling, proud. Like working out the room had been some personal challenge, and he'd beaten it. Until they'd both gotten fired because Kane and I had gone *Full Metal Jacket* downstairs.

"My guess is that is the administration part. There's some of that downstairs, but since these pushpin folks are across from the cologne- and perfume-wearing folks..." He jammed two thumbs over his shoulders pointing at the executive side. "I'm thinking they probably work on the finer details of whatever the big shots come up with."

That made sense.

Covenant treated their dark business, well, like a business. Maybe the people downstairs made sure the bills got paid for the paper towels in various evil lairs around the country. Probably never knew it.

But the door to my right?

They might have been privy to the higher-level stuff. And since it was more admin, they'd have been less likely to hide it all away.

If you broke into Darth Vader's tank room, you probably wouldn't find the plans for the Death Star. But if you found where his accountants worked, well, you might find a requisition order for diet sodas for the Death Star vending machines. Who knew?

We were on borrowed time, so I rolled the dice.

"Let's do the right side," I said and took a step back. "I'll search the admin offices and cubbies. If we find nothing, we'll try the exec side."

"What do you want me to do?"

"You be the lookout," I said with a smile I hoped he would hear.

"Emelda," he said, his face serious, "I'm really starting to like you."

When he broke into a big, beaming grin, I said, "Thank you, Edgar."

"Get in and go fast."

"You got it," I said. "You wanna punch in the code?"

"Three, seven, nine, one," he said. "You'll hear a click, and the handle should turn."

I stared at him, my chin hanging down. "You knew the code?"

"Yeah. I got it from the woman who hired me."

Blinking quickly, I was confused. "Wait. You said you needed to feel the numbers because you didn't know them. Didn't you?"

"Did I say that?" He shrugged. "I mean, if I had told you the code, I'd have probably been left sitting in the van. This is way more fun."

Chapter Twenty-Two

Of course the offices were locked.

But I'd been in places like this before. And, sure, by "been in," I meant I'd broken into similar buildings with Roy to steal stuff. I wasn't proud of it and assured myself I'd left that world far behind.

Well, not too far. I was technically planning on stealing something now.

However, having that sort of stuff on my CV gave me keen insight into how to get through locked doors.

It only took searching the cubicle farm to find the drawer with the keys. The lords and ladies of the office always entrusted some brown-noser with a copy of them. Something that said brown-noser would be pretty damn smug about.

"How's it going?" Edgar whispered as I came out of the third office. "Anything good?"

"Not yet. It's weird," I said, crossing by the rows of cubicles. "The offices are pretty cleared out."

"Maybe they were doing one of those corporate reshuffles," he said with a smile.

I slipped a key into office four. It didn't work, so I tried another. "But the cubby area has a bunch of personal items. Potted plants, tiny stuffed animals, pictures of kids."

"Isn't that what office people do?"

"I dunno. I've never worked in an office." I kept my voice low as I tried a third key. "It's all so horrifyingly normal."

The lock clicked, and I yanked open the door.

Like in the previous offices, the drawers were basically empty. The odd file folder with nothing inside. Tiny piles of rubber bands and paper clips.

The only signs anyone had even been there were the multiple coffee rings on the wood desks and a few framed posters on the wall.

Of course, that meant I could search them quickly. I'd come up empty each time until office number six. That one hadn't been totally cleared out and, most importantly, someone had locked their top desk drawer.

That felt promising. And it was no challenge for a skilled thief with access to a couple of paper clips and a dirty coffee spoon.

When the drawer popped open, it separated from the desk and, naturally, clattered loudly to the floor. Coins and pens and batteries flew everywhere.

"Holy cow, Emelda," Edgar said in a whisper from his spot by the entrance. "Can you be a little more quiet? Haven't you ever sneaked into a place?"

"Yes," I said but did not clarify.

Nothing in the drawer. No maps or lists. Not even obscene doodles. The only thing of vague interest was a flip phone.

Why would someone lock up a flip phone?

I looked at the desktop. A family portrait of some woman with a lot of makeup and a dude in his thirties with a hairline in its fifties. Another photo of just the guy. And two smaller ones of the kids.

"Chicka has a booty phone," I said.

Edgar had heard me. "What?"

"Nothing," I said and pocketed the phone. If I got desperate, I could go through the contacts later. Maybe a little blackmail might get me a list of Covenant dark-site locations.

When I stood up, I saw something on the opposite wall that piqued my interest.

"This is promising," I said. I crossed the room and stared at a map of the world. A map with little pushpins in it.

"Okay," I muttered, looking from spot to spot. There were seven green pins and about a dozen red pins. Did colors designate which sites were up and running? Or give some indication of what might be at each one?

The scale of Covenant's operation was bigger than I could have imagined. A green pin in London, another in Paris. A few more in Asia—Taiwan and Vietnam. The red pins were everywhere. Japan, Australia, South Africa, Brazil.

"Holy cow."

As I leaned forward to see the cities, my hand rested on a large, flat book on a table. My heart fluttered as I opened it.

Some woman standing by Big Ben. Another of her and a group of friends by the big arch in Paris. She even had the obligatory shot of the Leaning Tower of Pisa, where she's holding it up.

Disappointment hit me. These weren't super-secret Covenant sites.

As I angrily flipped through the big scrapbook, the truth was laid before me in snapshot after snapshot.

The green pins are where she'd been in the world. The red? Those were the places she wanted to visit next.

I was frustrated. Annoyed. And jealous.

Not sure if it was just my worldview, but my world was pretty small. And recently, it had been a lot of running, driving fast, and trying not to get killed. All this time, millions of people around me were just... living. Going about their lives.

Janet Fuzzyhead, whatever her name was, had mapped out her bucket list and was ticking off the places one by one. I didn't have a map. Or push pins.

Me?

I had a moon app to tell me when it wasn't safe for my friend to go outside so he didn't turn into a dog.

"I need a life," I said to the wall.

"Hey, Emelda?"

I sighed. A wave of dreary, black emotion rolled over me. What was I doing? This was all so crazy.

"Emelda?"

"Yeah, yeah," I said and trudged out of Janet the World Traveler's office. "I was just—"

"Stand right there and, slowly, empty all your pockets," said the dour man in the rumpled security uniform. The expression on his face told me I needed to do exactly what he'd said.

Well, that and the pistol in his hand.

Chapter Twenty-Three

I pulled out the booty phone and dropped it onto the cluttered desk. As I did, I scanned the cubicle in front of me. There had to be something I could use as a weapon. Maybe a fistful of pens?

"Keep your eyes up here where I can see them, ma'am," the guard said.

He held his gun at his side. Not pointing it at me or Edgar.

At least not yet.

His gnarled finger lay parallel to the barrel. At least the old dude had some trigger discipline.

I patted my front pockets to show they were empty then held my hands up. He rose on his tiptoes to get a better view.

He flipped on the light. The fluorescents plinked to life, and I got a good look at him. He'd been handsome years earlier, a bit like Denzel Washington. Now he looked like Denzel's dad. Actually, these days, Denzel looks like Denzel's dad.

The guard motioned me toward the aisle where he and Edgar were standing.

"You okay, Edgar?"

"Sure," he said, the corner of his mouth tweaking upward. "Except for the part where I got a dude next to me with a gun pointed at my shoe."

The guard shifted his weight, knitted his brow, and looked down. Then he glared at Edgar. "I remember you. The cleaner," he said, his voice deep and raspy. "Blind cleaner. Unless that was some bullshit."

Edgar shook his head. "If it was bullcrap, I wouldn't be cleaning offices. I'd be a pilot." He held up his telescopic cane. "But they don't let you fly with these."

I'd been creeping forward as Edgar spoke, shifting my eyes from desk to desk. I saw a plastic cube full of Post-it notes. Sure, given some time,

I could bleed the guy out with paper cuts. Then I saw a glimmer. And a metal looped handle sticking out of a green plastic cup.

At first, I thought it might be a knife, but these were bean counters. Why would they bring a knife? A gun, maybe, for when they'd finally had enough. But a knife? No. It was a letter opener. It looked old, so less for function and more for a "my dad gave this to me" aesthetic.

Better than nothing.

I took a half step toward it, and the gun came up a little higher. Again, not pointing at me. The guy had some restraint. He'd done this sort of thing before.

"Stand still and put your hands on the wall of that far cubicle," he said then pointed to the workspace in front of me with his pistol.

"This is all just a big misunderstanding," I said as I reached toward the letter opener. "I just forgot some files I need to—"

"Hands on the cubby wall, now!" The guard slowly shook his head. "This is going to go one way. You're going to do what I tell you to, or you're gonna fall down and never get up."

Edgar raised his arms in the air, his white cane dangling from his fingertips. "Just do what he says. I don't think he wants to shoot anybody."

The guard clicked a shoulder mic and called for his partner. He groaned and tried again.

"Mike? I need you up on the top floor!" he yelled into it. Then he pointed his weapon to the door I'd just come out of. "Move that way. Into that office, but stay where I can see you. Walk while facing me."

I did what he said, stepping across the threshold in reverse. My heel caught on the metal runner pinning the carpet to the floor. When I stumbled, he *did* point the gun at me. A scowl creased his face.

Was this guy going to shoot me in an office and close the door?

"Hey, we don't want any trouble," I said as he rounded the cubicles. He pointed the pistol down again, but with a flick of the wrist, I'd be dead.

"Go to the window," he said. "Overlooking the front lot."

I did, scanning the windowsill. I saw a snow globe with a tiny Sydney Opera House tipped on its side. It looked heavy.

The guard appeared at the office door. Edgar waited on the other side of the cubicle farm, his head tilted as if he was listening to something. Probably trying to work out what was happening by the sound.

The man asked me, "What do you see down there?"

I had no idea what the hell he was asking me, so I told him the truth. "A place I'd rather be much more than up here."

"That can still happen," he said, but I read the look on his face. He didn't believe the lie either. "How many cars are in the lot?

"Cars," I said, slapping a palm on the window and leaning forward. The glass was cold, tracing my fingers with a thin mist of condensation. My other hand gripped the snow globe. "One car. You worried someone stole your ride?"

The guard hissed and shook his head. He mumbled. "What a puss. Went to the damn hospital over a dog bite."

Dog bite?

The gun came up as he entered the room. He pushed the cushy leather chair aside and went to the window three panes away. He glanced down, back at me, then cursed under his breath.

Behind my back, I palmed the snow globe. If I had just a moment, I could smash it over his head. That might be enough to knock him down. He was older but in fighting shape. I'd have to smash hard and keep smashing.

The guard must have seen the determination on my face. Slowly, he backed toward the door with the gun pointed at my chest.

"Come on out," he said. "Slowly. I don't have any problems shooting you. People I work for would probably give me a bonus."

I started moving. I just needed him to turn around! But he walked backward, facing me as he went to the door.

As he stepped into the hall, he said, "Now, here's how this is going to—"

The guard pitched forward, his head thrusting downward. Disoriented, he spun around unevenly and banged his gun hand against the door. Then his knees buckled. I stood frozen in place. Was the guy having a heart attack?

I heard a crack, and he fell backward into the office.

When he dropped, Edgar was standing there and holding his telescopic walking stick like a skinny baseball bat. He stood over the man, his cane raised in the air, breathing heavily, mouth open in a fierce grimace.

The guard had banged the back of his head as he landed hard on the thin carpet. I heard the thunk of his skull against the concrete beneath it.

Dude was out cold.

I looked up at Edgar. Then I came to life, rushing past the prone and possibly dead guy on the floor. Standing next to my friend, I just gawked.

"How did you do that?"

He spun the cane in his hand and smiled. "Cane fu."

Chapter Twenty-Four

"We should just get out of here," Edgar said for what had to be the tenth time.

I'd run around the office space and grabbed as many cords as I could in about a minute. Fear and frustration spilled a dark sludge across my brain, so I'd been happy to smash a few lamps to get them.

With Edgar's help, I'd hefted the guard into the wingback chair. I'd wrapped the cords around his ankles and wrists. Another good thing I'd learned from second-story work? How to make good knots. We often had to use rope to get up to the higher floors, and we didn't want to ruin a sweet payday with a plummet to our deaths.

I'd jammed his pistol into the back of my waistband. The weight of it felt good there. And yes, I had the safety on. It wasn't the first time I'd had a gun stuffed into my pants.

The guard's head lolled forward. A line of spittle dribbled from his mouth, leaving a darkening stain on his uniform.

"I think we need to get this guy to a hospital," Edgar whispered to me. "His breathing sounds bad."

Palming Mr. Sleepytime on the forehead, I lifted the guy's face. "Better now?"

"What's the plan here, Emelda? This guy—"

The guard grumbled, coming to again. A second later, he was awake in a snap, as if his mind had played the night's season one recap on fifty-times speed. He shifted his arms back and forth, attempting to free himself from his bonds. He tried kicking his feet but only ended up bobbing his knees up and down as if he was trying to put out a very tiny fire beneath his feet.

Laughing, I said, "There he is!"

I felt exhilarated. Powerful. And I needed to make him feel powerless.

"My partner is going to be back here in about a minute," he said, glancing between the two of us. "Now, I was being gentle with y'all earlier. If—when Mike gets here, he ain't the gentle type. He'll be happy to shoot you both."

"Good thing he's not here, then, yeah?" I said, leaning against the office wall. "Nope. It's just you and us."

The guard blinked then squinted. "I'm having a hard time seeing out of my right eye. I think I've got a concussion."

From the doorway, Edgar pleaded with me. "Emelda."

I held a hand up. Sure, I couldn't count on Mike the Shooty Guard not showing up at any moment, but I'd found nothing useful in the offices. In fact, I hadn't found much of anything in the offices.

"We're looking for some former employees," I said. "Covenant's already written them off. Probably thinks they're dead."

"None of my business," the guard said. "My name is Ezekiel. Izzy. I'm just one of their security crew. I have nothing to do with whatever they did here. Don't need to take it—"

I smashed the snow globe down onto his knee. Not full force, but he still wailed in pain.

"Izzy, I don't need your resume. I ain't hiring."

Edgar pitched his chin to the side and frowned. He closed his eyes, slowly shaking his head.

"I need to know where the people we're looking for might have gone," I said. "What other sites do these guys have?"

Izzy stared down at his knee, frowning. He blinked and looked at me then Edgar. Then back to me. He screwed his face up and looked at my friend again.

"You ain't a blind guy at all, are you?"

"I am not defined by my ability to *not* see," Edgar said, his quirky smile returning. "But yes, I have full visual impairment."

"You bashed me with your cane," Izzy said, squinting and trying to rub his right eye with his shoulder. "You must be able to see."

Edgar shrugged. "Gray eyes staring out at a dark-gray world, man."

"Then how'd you know where to hit me?"

"If I told you, you wouldn't believe me."

"But—"

I raised the snow globe again, and Izzy winced.

"Okay, okay," the guard said. "You're the boss. But I don't know anything that might help you find your friends."

I laughed again. "They are not my friends. One tried to kill me, and the other watched as a group of Enhanced zoo animals tried to make me their dinner."

Ah ha.

At the mention of the Enhanced, I saw the man's eyes twitch. He knew about them.

"If it helps, we're not planning on hurting them," I said, then rolled my eyes. "Okay, that's not true. But *they* are planning on releasing hell, and I cannot abide."

Clearly in my mind, I could see the words Marata had scrawled onto the wall at the derelict factory: "Animals first."

"They'd need access to whatever voodoo Covenant has. Some old lab," I said, rolling the snow globe from hand to hand. A tiny blizzard for tiny Sydney music lovers. "Where in here can I find a list of sites?"

Izzy chuckled. "Like I would know that? My job is to just keep people out of places like this."

"And how's that going for you?" I frowned at him. This guy just wasn't taking me seriously enough. I held up a finger and brushed past Edgar.

He called after me. "Where are you going?"

When I returned, I had the old letter opener in my hand. I placed the tip on Izzy's thigh and held the snow globe above it.

"Where can I find the list of sites?" I said as his eyes locked onto the tip of the dull blade nipping at his nylon slacks. "Probably an old one. One they're not using anymore, with nobody around."

The guard shook his head rapidly. "From what I've heard, they're not using *any* of them anymore."

"Bullshit!"

My anger got the best of me, and I smashed the letter opener's handle with the ball of thick glass. It split the fabric and dug in about an inch. Izzy wailed in pain. Edgar's hands flew to his ears.

I raised the snow globe. "I'm not playing here."

"I ain't either," the guard said, licking his lips. "This whole place, this building, will be razed to the ground in a few days. If you woulda tried to break in here next week, you'd be sifting through ash."

I was ready to call bullshit on that, too, but I looked around. All the offices had been cleared out. Whatever was left behind probably got left in the rush. That did track.

Leaning back, I crossed my arms. I stared at him then nodded for him to continue.

He sighed. "They shift us around a lot and change crews, so nobody can get up to any foolishness. Any plans. I worked with Mike before, like six rotations back," Izzy said. "Before I got here last week, I spent a month at a warehouse in Texas. Before that, a big packing and distribution center in the Carolinas. Been doing that for the better part of a year."

I shrugged.

"But when I left Texas, they were already bringing in the wrecking crew. The place is gone by now," he said, his words coming fast. "Just before I left San Antonio, the new guys said the sites they'd come from were being shut down. Not just shut down but turned to rubble. They don't want anyone to know what they've been up to."

"Cool story, bro," I said. "But I still need that list."

Izzy caught the look on my face and struggled against his cords again.

I raised the snow globe higher.

"Wait, wait!" he shouted. "I *might* know where the guy who runs all this is. At least, that's what the other guards told me. If there's a list, it would be there."

"Where is that?"

His eyes drifted to the glass ball in my hand. "I don't know."

"Now, Izzy."

"When we get transported from job to job, they put us on charters. Planes, right?" he said. "Except for one site. We flew into an airport in Boise and got loaded, about ten of us, into the back of some military helicopter. No windows."

"Where did it take you?"

"That's what I'm saying," Izzy said with a bit of spit spraying. "They didn't want us to know. And when the helicopter doors opened, concrete walls surrounded us on all sides. Stars above."

"You had to guard empty walls?"

"That was the roof. Crazy looking because it was about as wide as a four-lane highway and long as two football fields. We went down some stairs and got split into teams," Izzy said. "Me and this other guard got assigned to one set of hallways. Twelve-hour shifts. I was there a week and slept on a cot in a maintenance closet. We traded off the whole time like that."

"And?"

"Nothing! Nobody even came down those halls, but..."

I rolled my hand impatiently.

"I heard things on the floor above," he said, his voice hollow. "Never saw them."

"They had Enhanced there," I said.

He shook his head slowly. "Not like that. But you could hear things moving around up there. Heavy. A bunch of them. I prayed none of them ever came down the steps, and somebody was listening. Never saw them."

For the next few minutes, I continued to question Izzy and only had to whack the snow globe once more. Just a little one. Despite that, he didn't offer any more than he already had.

So I pulled my phone from my back pocket and made a call.

Denny picked up. "Emelda! Twice in one day!"

"Can't really talk right now," I said to him. "How far can a helicopter travel in about an hour?"

"What?"

I growled into the phone. "Come on, you know these things, right?"

"Why would I know these things?"

"I dunno. Because you're a data guy. A hacker."

"I am *not* a hacker, Emelda," he said, and I heard some clicking on the other end. "But, okay, according to Google, you'd go, on average, about a hundred miles. But it depends on the size of the helicopter."

"Big."

"Big? Just big?"

"That's what I've got." I shrugged. "I need to know where it might have gone."

He sighed. "Do you have a starting point?"

"Boise," I said. "That's in Idaho."

"I know where Boise is!" More keyboard tapping on the other end. "Man, not much. A few towns. A lot of Native American reservations. It's pretty desolate. You need to give me more."

I turned to Izzy. "Do you know the direction you guys went? Did you hear traffic or anything?"

The guard shook his head and winced. Maybe he did have a mild head injury. "Naw, no direction. We were inside, no windows. But I think the place was out in the sticks."

"You've got to give me something, Izzy."

He ran the tip of his tongue over his lips as he eyed the glass ball in my hand. His face suddenly lit up. "When we landed, like I said, the sky was clear. But for the whole week, all week long, it stormed. The whole time."

"Okay, that's... something."

I asked Denny to look up what area in that one-hour radius might have a lot of storms. It didn't take long to get an answer.

"None of it. The place is dry as bone. Some towns there don't even get ten inches of rain a year."

I pulled the gun out, put it on the desk, and spun the barrel toward my captive. "Izzy, you're lying to me."

"I'm not! Why would I lie to you?" he said, his words tripping over his dry lips. "Clear skies when we went in and stormy all week long. Even when we left to get on the helicopter, clear skies. Down inside, though, storms rumbling the whole time."

Denny chimed in. "What about ocean waves? Those sound like storms."

"It's Idaho," I said into the phone. "There ain't any oceans nearby."

"No, you're right," Denny said. More clicking of keys. "There's rivers all over, but I can't imagine you'd get big crashing waves out of those."

I wished Kane was there. I could think better when he was around. He'd tell me to puzzle it out. Take a look at the pieces and look for a fit.

Long concrete roof. High walls. Sky above. Nonstop storms. Or waves.

A lever flipped in my brain. "Is there a dam in the area? Like some hydroelectric dam?"

"Um... *yes*," Denny said. "A bunch, actually."

I thumped my foot against the guard's leg. "Could it have been a dam?"

Izzy looked up to the ceiling for a moment then nodded. "Yeah, I suppose."

"Okay," I said to my tech nerd. "Any of them, um, not working or whatever? Or privately owned?"

The other end of the line went quiet for a long moment. I thought he might have hung up.

"Denny?"

"I'm googling, Emelda," he said. "Which is something you could do instead of me."

"No, I'll wait."

I turned and looked at Edgar. Again, he had his head tilted to the side like he was listening to some song in the distance and was trying to remember the name of it. Before I could ask him what the hell he was doing, Denny cut back in.

"I found this YouTube guy talking about an old dam on the Snake River. Right in your zone," he said. "The transcript says he'd visited it years earlier, but that was before he had the channel. When he went back to go film it, he couldn't get to it."

"Why?"

A pause. "It was shut down. Needed repairs the state didn't want to pay for, and the whole place was cordoned off. He couldn't get near it."

"That's less than helpful."

"Hold on, hold on. Gimme a sec," Denny said and couldn't hide the excitement in his voice. He sounded like he was getting a thrill from the sleuth work. "Okay, so an article from last year says some private outfit bought it from the local government. The deal only went through because they'd committed to getting it back up to scratch. After they're finished, they'll sell the power back to the region."

Right. That bit of the puzzle fit. Or maybe I was jamming pieces together to make them fit. Me and puzzles had always had a mutually abusive relationship.

"What's the name of the buyer?" I knew Covenant wouldn't make it that easy, but a girl could hope.

More clicking. "Here it is. Apsu Industries. They're pouring money into the dam, but from what I can tell, it's not up and running yet."

"Apsu?" I wrinkled my nose. "Is that like an acronym for something?"

More clicking, then "Not that I can see. Only results I got say Apsu was the 'primordial deity of fresh water.' Also not helpful."

"Actually, it is." I smiled. "That's the guys I'm looking for."

"How do you know that?"

Tech Sergeant Gregor had told me his old bosses always used the names of old gods for their companies. Probably some alpha-dog Wall Street thing.

The dam was owned by Covenant. According to Izzy, the big boss, Steve Janus, was holed up inside. He'd have all the company data right there, including a complete list of their sites. And at one of *those* sites, we'd find Doc Hammer and Marata.

Maybe I didn't hate puzzles so much after all.

Chapter Twenty-Five

Kane sat next to me in the van's rear seat. Connie had wanted her friend up front, but Edgar hopped in the back too. He said he'd be happier sitting next to the "magic dog."

Connie *hadn't* been happy when I told her we couldn't go back to her apartment, but I'd never seen her happy. The guard had recognized Edgar, so their places were no-go zones. Likely forever.

I hadn't mentioned that last part yet.

As we headed to a hotel on the outskirts of town, Connie's eyes darted up to the mirror and met mine. I guessed she'd rather look at me than the talking dog, but since I'd been the one who'd brought all this weirdness into her life, I likely appeared as alien as he was. She probably took comfort in the dimensional barrier offered by the rear-view mirror. As if the tiny lettering on it might read, *Objects in mirror are only a figment of your imagination.*

"This is a world," she said and blew out a long breath. "This is a world I am not emotionally prepared for."

I laughed. "Hell, that's the first thing I say when I open my eyes every morning."

"No, you do not," Kane said, raising his fuzzy head off his fuzzy paws. "I do not recall you one time saying this thing."

"Right," Connie said. "So he knows what you do first thing in the morning?"

I had no interest in *her* interest in making me uncomfortable, so I quickly changed the subject.

"Hey, so how *did* you know where to hit the guard?" I asked Edgar. "You smacked him three times, perfectly placed, and knocked him right on his butt."

Our driver piped in. She'd gotten far more chatty now that the chances of us getting killed had dropped a few notches. "Did the voices tell you how to do that, Ed?"

"Emelda here hangs out with a talking dog," Edgar said to her. "So when you put it in that context, my thing ain't so crazy."

"Oh no, you *are* crazy," Connie said. "Ask your voices what they think. They'll tell you you're crazy too."

Edgar grinned. "Nah, I don't want to start talking to them. They'd never shut the hell up." He arched his chin to the left and sighed.

"Emelda, there is something we must discuss," Kane said, pawing at my leg, but I raised a finger to him, telling him to hold on for a moment.

I asked Edgar, "What the hell are you talking about?"

He cocked his head toward me. "Are you talking to me or Kane the dog?"

"Ah ha!" Connie said, putting a fist in the air. "So the ghosts didn't tell you that, did they? See, it's all B.S."

I snapped my head toward her. "Ghosts?" Then I turned to the man sitting on the other side of my talking dog. "Are you saying ghosts talk to you?"

"No, I believe that's what you just said." He chuckled at his own joke, spinning the retracted cane between his fingers. "But yeah."

"Wait, so you're saying you knew where to hit Izzy because some ghost voices told you?"

"I'm only working with what the world has given me," Edgar said and coughed into his hand. He cleared his throat and continued. "But the way you say it, this makes me sound like I believe in bizarre supernatural beings. What do you think, magic dog man?"

Kane didn't answer the question. Instead, he asked me, "Did you hurt the building's guard?"

"I needed information," I said, feeling heat on my cheeks. "And you bit the other guy, so why are—"

"Yes, this is true. However, this was to keep you and Edgar safe," he said, his voice low. "Not torturing for information."

"*Mild* torture," I said with a smile, but I didn't get one in return. "He'll need a few stitches, and once he wriggles out of those cords, ol' Izzy will probably end up sitting next to the guy you put in the E.R."

My friend shuffled his paws. "It was necessary, but I do not feel good about my part in Mike the guard's injury."

"Here's something you can feel good about," I said and scratched his head. "I used that thing you always talk about to work out where we're going next. Puzzle logic can be quite handy."

Kane sighed. "I am glad. But puzzle thinking is not just to use for torture."

"Can we stop saying the torture word?"

"Sure," he said. "Puzzle thinking is not just to use for violent questioning."

"Not much better."

"More important is to work out your life puzzle," Kane said and rested his chin on my leg. "This is not like a puzzle with the kittens and flowers on it. Very difficult because all the petals bend into the puzzle piece edge. So hard to tell color. And the kittens, they look so tasty, this is a distraction."

"Kane?"

"Yes?"

"You had a point?"

He raised his doggy head and regarded me with those soft amber eyes. "A single piece cannot make a complete puzzle. This requires two. Or three or four or more, yes?"

"You mean I gotta find my pack," I said, nodding.

"If you cannot fit into the surroundings, find surroundings where your piece will fit. You may have to smooth some edges, but this is okay. That takes not just the will to do this but the bravery as well."

We were all quiet for a moment. The only sounds were of the tires whirring along the road and a gentle rain tapping the roof.

"Damn," Connie said, breaking the silence. "How is it the only one in this car who's got life worked out is a dog?"

For the first time, she laughed. Edgar did, too, and I couldn't help but smile.

Not Kane. I could tell by the look on his face that he was really troubled that I'd intentionally hurt someone. He was worried about me.

Maybe I wasn't worried enough.

Chapter Twenty-Six

Connie took a drag of her bent cigarette and blew the smoke into the night sky. The wind grabbed it and, as if offended, shoved all that haze right through the sliding glass door of my room. I let it slide.

Everyone deals with an anxiety hangover differently.

Obviously, for Connie, this meant lying slumped in a hotel lounger and blowing cancer fog into the rooms of people she didn't like very much.

For me?

In the past, my anxiety response had been to make some really, really bad choices. To paraphrase Kane, stress-fueled ideas are bad ideas.

There are healthy ways to ease anxiety. A good cry can often bleed all that black ink right out of your eyes. No shame in that.

Some people find exercise a good stress reliever. The problem with that is, of course, it involves exercise.

But I certainly wasn't going to start ugly crying in front of Connie. Or do crunches.

Instead, I'd raided our hotel room's minibar and made me a tumbler of what we used to call "Three Mile Island iced tea." Everyone's got their own recipe. In the last dive bar I'd worked at, this meant just dumping every alcohol available into a tumbler over ice. Add sour mix, some Coke or Sprite. Whatever you've got. But no garnish because, given the alcohol content, it could instantaneously combust. Flaming lime wedges singe eyebrows.

Draped across our lounge chairs, Connie and I brooded in our own private ways. Not Edgar and his trusty canine Kane.

The rooftop pool had only one other couple there, two middle-aged women who'd wobbled over to declare that dogs were definitely not allowed in the hot tub. Connie blew a big plume of smoke and informed them that her friend was blind and the dog was, in fact, a service dog.

That had them clutching their towels and trotting down the stairs, muttering to one another. I had to give it to Connie—that was a pretty decent move.

We lay back quietly, looking up at the stars. And listening to a guy and a dog having a blast. Something about it was off-putting. Annoying. Maybe because I was here and not over there. But I couldn't bring myself to go over and join them.

For one thing, I didn't have a bathing suit.

Neither had Edgar, so he'd gone in his boxers. Kane, of course, didn't have any clothes. He was covered in fur. But even if he had been human at that moment, I was sure he'd have still gone without clothes.

All that splashing and unbridled joy hurt my head, so I broke our silence.

"I'm sorry for all the trouble, Connie," I said. "You helped us out. I feel like we've made your bad situation worse."

She waved a hand through the smoke, pushing it toward the pool. "Nah, I didn't like that apartment much. And your boy delivered. Kane must be loaded."

It had been a sizable chunk of money, so I'd called Denny and asked him to do the bank transfer. After I gave him all the details, he'd let out a low whistle.

After a month of running around the country, crossing borders, hiring cars and hotels, I'd wondered how much we'd depleted the money Kane's human parents had left behind. According to Denny? Not much. All totaled, the dude still had six figures in there. *High* six figures.

That confirmed for me that life wasn't fair. I'd worked my butt off for a decade and had about eighty-seven bucks to my name. Kane had been a human for just one year and had more dough than I would make in a lifetime.

And it wasn't just the money.

"Are you going to take Kane up on his offer?" I asked Connie. "His hum—um—his parents had a property in Canada. The house is gone after a fire. But there's a barn and a tiny cottage, from what he said."

Connie shrugged. "Maybe. If we do, it'll be just to put the world on hold for a few weeks. Or months. But we've got to plan for the future. That cash is great, but it won't last forever."

"What are you going to do? I mean, are you guys...?"

She tilted her head at me. "Together?"

"Yeah."

"We're friends. Edgar's the best friend I've ever had," she said, shrugging. "Why would I want to screw that up with joy, sex, and lifelong commitment?"

"Makes sense, I guess."

"He's also gay, so..."

"That does put a wrinkle into plans."

"Yeah, especially when the guy you like ain't into your particular wrinkle."

I turned to look at her, but she was stone faced. Arching my head around, I tried to catch her eye. When she finally did glance toward me, she burst out laughing.

"You nasty," I said, chuckling, and felt lighter for it.

She gave me a nod and flicked her cigarette. The ember glowed like a tiny red star as it floated past the pool deck, over the rail, and disappeared in the darkness beyond.

"Hey, do you want a bit of advice?" Connie said, still smiling.

"Not really."

That got a chuckle out of her. "Fair enough, but I'm going to give it anyhow. Whatever this thing is with you and that guy over there... or that dog over there... you can't keep it up."

"We're doing just fine."

Connie shifted in her seat to face me. "Y'all told us a little about what you're doing. And what you're planning on doing. Maybe you've lost sight of it, but do you realize just how dangerous all this shit is?"

It was my turn to chuckle. "Every day. And every time I get chased by some monster, face off against someone trying to kill me, and get chucked out of a window."

Connie blinked. "You've been chucked out of a window?"

"Well, I got *dragged* out of a window," I said nonchalantly. "Landed in a pool."

"This is what I'm talking about, Emelda," she said, dropping her feet to the cool concrete deck and leaning forward. "All this stuff. You could get killed at any moment. And then again the moment after that."

The human psyche is strange and amazing. The thing that feels impossible or otherworldly eventually just feels normal.

"That's probably true."

"It is."

"Okay," I said, pursing my lips. "And in the middle of all this almost dying, I've never felt more alive."

Connie shook her head. "Until you're dead."

"Who knows? Maybe I'm immortal," I said and pointed over at Kane as he cavorted on a towel next to the hot tub. He was rolling around, trying to dry himself off. He looked like an idiot. An idiot having fun. "I mean, I hang out with a dude that turns into dogs when the moon's out."

She eyeballed me then looked over at Kane. "Edgar told me that when he first met your friend, he'd been hanging on a wall for a few days," Connie said. "And that he would swear he sounded like he was eighty."

"He probably sounded old. Dehydration and starvation will do that."

"I think there's a whole lot about that boy you ain't telling me," she said, then held up both hands. "And I don't wanna know. I can't even get my head around the man-dog thing."

"Edgar doesn't seem to have a problem with it."

She smiled as she watched her friend. "Yeah. He sees life different from anyone else I know. Maybe because he sees with his heart, not his eyes."

"Poetic."

Connie lit another cigarette and took a deep drag before continuing. "After we checked in and me and him went to the room, he told me about what happened up in that building. That he'd been guided by voices. He's convinced he can hear ghosts."

"My best friend is a dude who becomes dogs. Yours is crazy."

She shook her head. "I hate to admit it, but you've kind of helped me out."

"Do tell. It's rare that someone tells me I got something right."

Connie shrugged. "You know, you two brought a ton of shit our way. Turned our lives upside down."

"You mentioned that," I said. "Where's the part that I did good? I'm waitin'."

"But," she continued, the corner of her lip bending upward. "The good thing you did is that you proved to me the universe does have its secrets. I don't know the world as well as I thought. Maybe there is a bit of magic in it after all."

I looked over and watched Kane the schnauzer shake his body, splattering water all over his new friend.

Chapter Twenty-Seven

I awoke to Kane elbowing me in the ribs. The harsh overhead lights of the airliner stung my eyes. My ears buzzed with a faint, hollow tinnitus that made me feel underwater.

He turned in his seat and whispered, "You are supposed to listen to the lady with the swinging arms."

When I tried to lick my lips, the tip of my tongue just sorta stuck there. The bone-dry atmosphere inside planes always felt like air pumped in from the rundown house of an old woman who'd died in her bed six weeks earlier.

I closed my eyes again. Kane had begged to sit at the window, so I got stuck on the aisle. Easier bathroom access, sure, but I knew when that drink cart shot by, I'd end up with a smashed knee or busted toe.

"Nobody listens to those people," I said. "Look around."

After a pause, he said. "This is not true. That man over there is watching her very closely. He is not even blinking."

"Can you see his hands?"

He shuffled in his seat. "Not from here."

"Yeah," I said, sliding lower to get comfortable. "Probably a good thing."

We'd parted ways with Edgar and Connie at the airport. I'd asked them where they were headed, but just as he'd opened his mouth, she'd jumped in.

"Parts unknown," Connie said with a crooked smile. "You guys are trouble magnets. I think it's better if you don't know."

I sighed. "Just being polite."

Shuffling away, I gave them both a quick wave but noticed Kane wasn't walking next to me. When I looked over my shoulder, I saw him breaking away from an embrace with Connie and then bending down to wrap Edgar in a hug.

I kept walking.

A minute later, Kane came trotting up. "I hope they will be okay."

"Them?" I laughed. "We're heading into the lion's den, wolfman."

"Yes, but you have me to protect you."

Cocking an eyebrow at him, I shrugged. "They'll be fine."

"I do hope so."

I sneaked a quick glance back to see the two of them disappearing into a sea of aimless travelers. "I knew you and Edgar were getting buddy-buddy, but how'd you crack the ice queen?"

Kane jutted his bearded chin toward me. "I do not know this term. It is not a nice thing to say, though, yes?"

"There are worse versions of it."

He laughed. "Consuela and I bonded much like you and I did, I suppose."

"How's that?"

"She saved me from getting killed." Kane nodded. "It is like this in the wolf world as well. Not spoken, of course. But gratitude. And trust. An enemy would not risk their lives for you. So when someone does, the only other choice is friend."

We'd reached the tail of the snaking security line as it dragged hopeful and despondent travelers in equal measure toward the next line they'd have to stand in.

"You've got a very simple vision of life. Must be a wolf thing."

"It is life thing,' he'd said. "Only humans make it complicated."

The flight to Idaho had taken us five hours. I'd planned on sleeping the whole way, but in the end, I got about seventeen seconds of actual shut-eye.

Despite my repeatedly asking him not to, Kane pointed out clouds and mountains and houses and shopping malls and farms as we passed over them. His mood had soured after witnessing a bird bounce off the wing and leave a red smear. That had kept him quiet for about two minutes.

And, of course, he'd been a favorite of the flight crew. One of them even brought him a free beer wrapped in a cloth napkin.

"Don't tell anyone," the young man in the snug uniform said. "I lifted it from first class. The guy in 2B has been pounding brews for the past two hours. I'll say it was his."

When the dude walked away, Kane dropped my tray table and put the can on top. He smiled at me and looked out the window again.

"Such a peaceful world from up here," he said. "I have seen television shows where people fly, but that is watching someone watching something. Different when your eyes experience this. Beautiful."

"I wouldn't know. I got a beefy dude blocking the window."

"Beefy? Who is beefy?" His eyes got big. He raised his arms and sniffed both pits. "Do I smell like meat?"

When we finally landed and exited the plane, our journey was far from over. We had to get another hundred miles northeast. But before that, we had to pick up yet another car, because we'd left the one we'd rented in Mexico at the Atlanta airport. I wondered how long it might just sit there. Probably weeks.

Shuffling toward the rental-car cluster—with all their stark reds, brilliant blues, and painful-to-look-at yellows, Kane put a hand on my shoulder. "We will buy a vehicle."

"We're at the airport," I said. "No car lots around here."

He shrugged. "Maybe rental car place will let us buy."

I stopped walking and turned to him. "Just how much dough do you have? I mean, I know you had a huge chunk of change the first time I looked, but we've been draining it."

"More than one account. My human parents had much savings, and there was more money when house burned."

"Insurance? How did you even file a claim? You can't read, dude."

I felt shitty for saying that the moment his eyes hit the floor. "Help from the family doctor. Dr. Fineman. A good man. I will miss him when I return to the forest."

"Maybe you could pay him a visit after you get your wolf on again."

He grinned at me with both sets of teeth. "Yes, I will do this."

Seeing that big all-the-better-to-eat-you-with smile, I regretted the suggestion. Fineman would probably crap his drawers if he saw a big gray wolf knocking on his door. Hopefully, his house was made of brick.

We tried a few rental counters and asked about buying a vehicle and got the same strange looks and pointing fingers at each. Some sold cars but from lots in the city. Or we could buy online.

"I know a dude selling his car," a voice behind us said. It was one of the maintenance crew, trading full trash bags for empty ones. Securing a new liner in the bin, she nodded toward the baggage area. "Barry has been trying to unload his ride for months."

"Unload?" I said, crinkling up my nose. "I dunno if we want a car someone's trying to unload onto someone else."

The fireplug of a woman chuckled and coughed. Smoker. "They raised rents near the airport, and he had to move farther out of town. Car's fine but a real gas guzzler."

"Right."

"Like the sort that you gotta make sure the engine's off when you pull up to the pump, otherwise you'll never totally fill the tank."

She belted out a gut-busting laugh as if this was the funniest thing in the world. I wondered if Barry hadn't sold his car because his coworker spent the past few months submarining him.

The squat woman pointed out Barry, and that got a grin out of Kane. Barry was damn near as tall as he was, so maybe, for the first time, whatever car we might get would fit him.

Chapter Twenty-Eight

"How did Barry drive in such a car?" Kane said, pressing his legs into the footwell to push the seat back farther. I shot a hand out to stop him.

"Don't do that! The last time you messed with a seat, you busted it and ended up staring at the ceiling."

Kane looked up and pointed. "It has window on roof."

And it did.

Barry's car had been both a curse and a blessing. First off, it was a classic. Or rather, old enough to get registered as a classic.

Kane had agreed to buy it the moment he saw the big red bird on the hood.

I tried to hide my disgust. I was pretty sure that the body had more Bondo than steel. The driver's door hung oddly, like the car had once gotten into a drunken bar fight.

"That came off another vehicle after I smashed into a light pole," Barry had said.

"How did you smash sideways into a light pole?"

Barry scratched a tuft of rat hair on his chin. "Really, really hard."

Nice.

Kane was already running around the car to take it all in. At night, it was probably a beauty, but in the midday sun, it looked like it should be in a junkyard. No, it looked like it should be on a crane in a junkyard, ready to be crushed into a cube.

I looked over at Barry. "What do you call it?"

"What?"

I rolled my eyes. "Gimme a break." I'd met many, many Barrys over the years. "What's her name?"

"Scooby." He turned to me, his eyes damp. "Because, you know, it looks like a dog with those two big eyes in front."

And it did. Barry's car was a 1976 Pontiac Firebird Trans Am. A 455c V8 engine. Edelbrock carburetor and intake manifold, a Hurst shifter, and a Kenwood cassette stereo.

Yep. A *cassette* stereo.

Why not?

Of course, it had fallen into some disrepair. It needed shocks, tires, brakes, struts, new headers, and, most likely, a raging bonfire to drop it into.

"She's fast, and she'll run," Barry assured us. He had to sell the car, but his heart wasn't in it. "Sometimes, she keeps running even after you turn her off, though, so you gotta keep an eye on it."

It did have a manual transmission. For me, that sold it.

We transferred the money, and Barry signed the title over to me. I promised to file the paperwork the first chance we got. Which would be, yeah, never. Better to leave it in Barry's name.

As we drove down Interstate 84, I fiddled with the radio. It was dead. Of course.

"This may not have been the wisest purchase," I said and went to roll the window down. The knob came off in my hand, so I threw it into the back seat. "I'm sure it isn't, actually."

Kane pushed open the sunroof and dangled his fingers out of the gap.

"I like it," he said. "Same type of vehicle my human brother once had. The purple car, yes?"

Right. That had been the one Cal Davis had *stolen*. Kane was buzzing out on the memory, so I didn't bring that up.

"Yeah, it's like we've come full circle," I said.

"I can drive safely in circles."

"Uh uh," I said and gripped the padded wheel tighter. "You'd still find a way to crash. No driving for you."

I'd exchanged emails with Denny while we'd been on the plane. He'd moaned a bit about it, reminding me he wasn't my tech guy, but I think he secretly got a kick out of it.

When we landed, he'd sent me a note to take 84 north and give him a call from the road. Apparently, we weren't the only ones with the dam in our crosshairs. A group of green-loving locals wanted it gone.

"Their petition says, 'A demand to stop the desecration of our land and waters on Snake River,'" he read from a change.org listing. "'The foolish plans to restart this one-hundred-year-old dam will kill countless fish and wildlife and create deposits that will leach methane into the—'"

"Yeah, yeah, yeah," I said to the phone stuffed into the open slot of the broken cassette player. "Anything that's useful in there?"

"Yeah, you can't get to it."

"What does that mean?"

"All access to the dam is blocked off," Denny said as he clacked on his keyboard. "If you dig into their charter, there's a clause that would allow them to set up a half-mile cordon around the dam because of the insurance liabilities."

"Is that normal?"

"How would I know? I'm not some dam expert."

I frowned at the phone. Yeah, I should have given him a laugh for that, but I would not stand for pun shenanigans. Unless I was the one doing the punning, of course.

"Izzy the guard said the top of it is like some concrete shoebox with big walls on all sides. Can you hack into somewhere and get satellite imagery to see if there's a way in?"

"Not a hacker." Denny sighed again. "But, yeah, I don't see an easy way inside. Google Earth has images."

"Hacker."

"And so does Wikipedia and even Tripadvisor."

"Ah, the true professional. Verifying sources," I said and grinned at the phone. "Super hacker."

"I'm hanging up now," he said and then was gone.

***

The three-hour drive took us from 84 up into the boonies of Idaho.

Kane started snoring twenty minutes into the trip. But without a radio, it was kind of soothing. Like ocean waves on one of those sleep apps. Just as long as I didn't fall asleep too.

We rolled past towns with cute names like Fruitvale. And the airport woman had been right. By the time we rolled into the town of Rolleston, I was on fumes.

I pulled into a gas station and got out to stretch my legs. I fired up my phone's moon-phase app and updated our location.

"We got about four hours before we have to get indoors," I called over to Kane as he headed inside the gas station. "Grab me a drink, will ya?"

The best thing about Scooby the car was, unquestionably, the cupholders. I expected they were the only parts on the car that actually worked properly. Barry had pulled out the original center console and put in four massive cupholders, enough for everyone in the car to drop their Big Gulps into.

Or forty-ounce beers. I never got a full read on Barry.

After I filled up, I hung up the hose and screwed the cap back on. One thing I did love about the old car was that access to the gas tank was tucked behind the license plate. You had to flip it down on its spring to get to it.

Inside, I hit the bathroom and came out as Kane was paying for the fuel and drinks. We'd need to grab some food but not at the gas station.

"Anywhere you recommend we can grab a late lunch?"

The guy behind the counter looked up at the clock on the far wall. "More like an early dinner, right?"

"Unless you haven't had lunch, right?"

With a noncommittal shrug, he told us that there were a few diners on the main drag, Spring Street. We were only about ten minutes away.

"You won't find much town outside of that street," he said. "Some houses and stuff around the edges. Nice square where they have holiday celebrations and stuff."

When I asked about the dam, he let out a long breath. "Been here since my granddad's dad was a boy. That's how this town got started, all the workers. That and the gold rush."

"Gold rush?"

"Yeah, wasn't just California, you know?" He said, pronouncing the word Cal-ee-forn-ee-ah. "Back in the day, they had tens of thousands of folks pour into the area. Most left broke. Some never left at all."

"Grim."

“Well, I mentioned the gold rush because it’s called the Dolly Pot dam. A Dolly Pot is what they used to smash up stone to get the gold out of the rock. Like one of those deals they use to grind up pills and stuff.”

“Mortar and pestle?” Kane said, grinning widely and very pleased with himself.

“Nah, but we got a Walmart. Nothing fancy,” the guy said.

“Great.” I nodded and forced a smile onto my face. “How do we get to the dam?”

“You don’t.”

“There’s got to be roads that lead there, right?”

Station Guy laughed. “You guys roll in for some romantic holiday to go make a wish?”

I blinked. “Make a wish?”

“Yeah, yeah. When the dam was shut down, it became popular as a tourist spot after some Instagrammer showed that people were putting padlocks on the metal gate up top. You’re supposed to write your initials on the lock and chuck the key in the water.” He snickered. “The hippies hated that, but they’re always mad about something.”

“Yeah, sure,” I said, shrugging. “We’re here to profess our undying love on a century-old hunk of concrete, so—”

“Limestone.”

“Whatever. How do we get there?”

“Like I said, you don’t.” He walked over to the window and pointed into the distance. “There was one main road to get there, but now they’re bringing the dam online again, they blocked it off.”

“Okay,” I said. “It’s blocked off. No biggie.”

“It was blocked,” Gas Dude said. “But people kept going around the gates.”

“To put up locks?”

He bobbed his head side to side. “Some of that. But mainly because the greenies were messing with it all the time. When you get into Rolleston, it’s a lot of basket weavers and incense makers. Real hippie town. I don’t live there, but they sell the best weed.”

“Why would you buy weeds?” Kane said and looked at me.

I tweaked my head at him. *I’ll explain later.*

“So to stop people from going around the barriers, they went and blew up the bridge,” he said and laughed. “Hard-core.”

"But there's workers up there, right? How do they get there?"

Gas Dude started to answer, then he stopped, smiled, and pointed to the ceiling. It took a moment, but I finally heard it.

"Helicopter?" I asked.

"Whoever's working the dam, they got some money," he said, looking out the window. "But to quote the old song, '*You* can't get there from here.'"

Chapter Twenty-Nine

A carved wooden sign said "Rolleston" with a bunch of icons, denoting they had places to sleep, eat, and shop. Each offering had a white icon. Almost as if to say, "Yeah, you've seen a million towns like this. Here's the stuff we've got, just like everyone else."

"I bet when they put this big highway in here, a lot of the people who used to stop by just started wheeling through."

Kane nodded. "Looks like a nice, quiet town."

"Is quiet a good thing?"

"Yes." He put his elbow out the window and let the wind tousle his long hair. Closing his eyes, he continued. "With babies. Fire alarms. And the dead."

I laughed. Then I recalled the claims of our friend, the Cane Fu expert. "Do you really think Edgar believes that ghosts talk to him?"

"He says it is true, and this is enough."

"I don't know if I buy it."

Kane nodded slowly. "You do not have to. That is Edgar's path, not yours. His view of life does not rely on your interpretation or acceptance. You just have to accept Edgar."

About a mile past the sign, we saw rows of homes, then shops sprang up.

People walked in pairs. Families out for a stroll, heading somewhere or coming back from somewhere else. I didn't see anyone by themselves.

A group of middle-aged men and women were all seated outside a small cafe. A few of them sat at tables set for one, but even they were talking to the others nearby.

"It's like some town hall meeting all spread out," I said, eying them one by one, trying to read their expressions and mannerisms like Kane had taught me. "It's kind of strange."

"Is not strange," he said. "Only seems strange to you because they look happy."

"Harsh."

"Is true."

At a four-way stop, I pressed on the brake, looked left and right, and realized there were no other cars on the road. It seemed Rolleston was a big walkin' town.

On the main drag, I spotted a place we could stay that night, a bar-and-motel combo. Turning down a side street, I drove half a block and parked the car. I clicked off the ignition. The engine rumbled and rattled and coughed for a few seconds until, finally, it shut down.

I yanked on the handle and had to jam my shoulder into the heavy door to force it open. The metal hinges squawked, complaining like I'd woken them up from a comfy nap.

Kane had climbed out the window on his side. I know this because I saw the top of his head bob up then heard him collapse to the sidewalk with an "oof!"

I put my hands on my hips and waited.

He popped up, brushed off his jeans, and rubbed his hands together.

"That always seems so much cooler on television when people do that," he said, looking at some scrapes on his palms. "It is rather challenging."

"Yeah, don't do that."

We rounded the corner and got friendly nods from people walking by. Above us was a sign that read "The Lodge." I pulled open the heavy wooden door, ready for the stank of stale beer and sweat to hit me in the face. Instead, it smelled like... lilies?

Not what I expected.

"Just sit anywhere," the woman behind the bar said. "Anywhere where nobody is already sitting. Unless that's your thing."

She gave us a pleasant laugh. A joke, I expected, she'd told a thousand times.

Kane laughed with her and offered a thumbs-up.

She smiled back and cocked an eyebrow, looking him up and down. "You're a big fella," she said with a crooked smile. "Momma must have fed you a lot as a tyke."

"I nursed from the teat I could," Kane said, looking down at his hands, "but I was rather small. Sometimes, I had to fight for a teat."

The woman said, "We get a fair bit of that around here. You'll fit right in."

Pulling Kane toward a booth, I pointed at one side and went up to the bar. He was happy to wedge himself in.

It took a little convincing, but I asked for a very, very rare steak for my friend. I picked the cheeseburger.

The bartender, who'd introduced herself as Lilly, asked me, "What kind?"

"Just a burger with a slice of cheese."

She pointed to the back wall of the bar. Between two racks of liquor bottles, a chalkboard listed at least a dozen different burgers, all with the names of countries ahead of them.

"What's an Aussie burger?"

"Burger with beets on it."

I wrinkled up my nose. "Beets? That sounds awful."

"You can get them pickled or roasted. Pretty good, actually."

"I'll never know," I said. "The Yorkshire burger? What's that?"

"It's a Yorkshire pudding with a slab of meat inside," she said and put a beer in front of a tired-looking man in painter coveralls. Streaked with hundreds of colors, he looked like a piñata at a Pride parade. She smiled at him pleasantly then turned back to me. "And no, it's not real pudding. British thing."

"Uh-huh," I said and nodded at the list. "The grilled-cheese cheeseburger is two grilled cheese sandwiches and a meat patty, then?"

"No," Lilly said, shaking her head. "Four grilled cheese sandwiches—two on either end, two more in the middle. Double decker."

I saw a spaghetti burger, hot fudge sundae burger, and frog burger on offer as well. I asked her for something called the Hellfire Burger.

"That's just a burger with hot sauce or chilies, yeah?"

"Yeah, it's good. Especially if you've got a cold."

"I don't."

Lilly grinned. "Then it might give you one."

I thanked her, started to walk to the booth, then turned back. "Hey, you've got rooms available?"

She told me they did. With a wry smile, she asked if I needed two rooms or one. I told her one room with two beds. Slowly, she shook her head. "What a waste," she muttered softly and gave me a wink.

"We're just travel buddies," I told her. "And we're hoping to find someone who does river tours."

"Sure," she said and pointed deeper into the bar. "There's a couple of guys who do fishing charters and sight-seeing. Ask around, and somebody will help you out."

I didn't miss the trick that she'd raised her voice just a little so that the "guys" who offered those particular services would hear that a potential client had rolled in. Small-town marketing.

And sure enough, a couple of faces turned my way.

I walked over to one of the smilers. He had graying hair that was slightly yellowed and teeth to match. He wiped red sauce from his mouth and salt-and-pepper beard, perking up as I approached.

I introduced myself as Heather Thomas. Why not? I told him we were hoping to get out on the water the next day. He said he ran a medium-sized fishing boat twice a day, once at dawn and the other midafternoon.

He asked, "What you fishing for?"

"Instagram photos," I said, and a part of me died inside when I added, "We're influencers."

"There's beauty shots all up and down the river. A couple of rotten old boat docks that your kind of people like."

Your kind of people. Another flickering light in my soul snuffed out.

"What about the old dam?" I asked, trying to sound casual. "It would make a great backdrop."

That darkened the old guy's face. "We don't go near that abomination," he said. "They shoulda tore it down years ago."

"Still, it'd be a good shot. Maybe just a swing by?"

He shook his head. "Can't."

"We can give you some grief pay for it," I said with a chuckle, trying to keep it light.

Waving me in, he lowered his head and voice. "The new outfit that took over has the place barred up. Two bends before the dam, on this side, there's a big metal grate from bank to bank. Can't get a boat past it."

I shrugged. The disappointed social media influencer.

"What about from the other side?"

Again, he shook his head. "No, ma'am. They tore up all the landings, even the concrete ones that had been there for years. A line of buoys blocks that side."

I blinked at him. "That's pretty hard-core."

"Well, they had to, I reckon," he said, taking a sip of his beer. "We got a lot of nuts in town. Environmental types. I heard you asking Lilly for a steak. You're lucky you came here, because some other places would have run you right out. Or thrown red dye at your pretty blouse."

I was wearing a plain white T-shirt and a leather jacket. But sure, I got his point.

"So no one goes near the dam?"

"The kooks did all the time. The dam folks put a stop to that with extreme prejudice," he said, his fuzzy-caterpillar eyebrows dancing to the sound of those last two words.

"What does that mean?"

He sighed. "Do you want a boat tomorrow or no?"

"Maybe," I said. "I'll have to talk with my friend. He's a big dam fan and really wanted to get a look at it."

"Never gonna happen."

I thanked him and took his card. He gave me a limp wave as I walked away.

When I got back to the table, Lilly the bartender was there, one hand on her hip, head thrown back in an exaggerated laugh.

Sister, please.

I'd told her Kane and I weren't an item. And a town this size probably did not have a vibrant crop of eligible men. Eligible for what, I didn't yet know. But I had an idea.

I slid into the booth across from my friend with, admittedly, a bit more flourish than I would normally. Gliding to the far end of my side, I bumped slightly against the wall and put my feet up on the vinyl seat. Kane glanced slowly toward me, and I saw the tiniest tweak of a smile.

"Your friend is funny," Lilly said, shifting her weight and cocking the hip in my direction. A month ago, I'd have thought very little about that motion. After hanging out with a wolf dude, it felt like I had a starter-pack on the language of animals.

Twitch and furrow.

Or, in this case, hip thrust and booty shake.

"Yeah, he's a barrel of monkeys without the barrel," I said, dipping a french fry into the sauce oozing off my Hellfire Burger.

Kane arched an eyebrow. "This is just monkeys."

"Got it in one," I said, pointing the chip at him, then I popped it into my mouth. Holy. Hell. *Fire*.

I blinked as my eyes watered. I smiled—or at least, I hoped I'd smiled—trying to force my tongue to the roof of my mouth as I swallowed.

"What does this mean? That I am many monkeys?" Kane asked, turning toward me.

I shrugged and squinted at him. This was one of my go-to "ain't I cute" facial expressions, but really, I couldn't speak. I was pretty sure my throat had seized up. I could still breathe, but if I'd have opened my mouth when I did, I probably woulda whistled.

Lilly leaned forward on the table, pressing her elbows to either side of her chest. She said, "I like monkeys. They're fun."

"I have seen a monkey at a reserve in Nanaimo," Kane said, tweaking his head as he tried to read my expression. "They fling excrement."

Lilly laughed again. "Hell, I'm willing to try anything once."

I looked around for a glass of water to put out the fire in my throat. Nice. She hadn't brought any over. I poured ketchup onto my plate, dipped a chip into the red gelatinous mass, and put a glob three times the size of the fry into my mouth.

Kane nodded to me, looked down at his very bloody steak, and smiled at Lilly.

"May we have some drinks to go with this delightful meal?"

"We got every kind of beer you can imagine, darlin'."

"I do not like beer very much. Makes my head quite fuzzy."

Lilly slapped the table with her palm. "That's the best part!"

He asked for some alternatives. Lilly suggested we try some local kombucha.

"I think half the town makes the stuff," she said, rolling her eyes. "We're up to our eyes in old hippies around here."

Kane nodded thoughtfully. "This must make it very hard to get around."

Lilly tilted her head and chuckled. I gave her a thumbs-up, pretending to be chewing. Kane asked for two of the weird brews, her choice.

After she walked away, I grabbed the ketchup bottle and squeezed it into my mouth until I felt sauce dribbling down my chin.

"You must be very thirsty."

I pointed at the burger and rasped, "It's so spicy."

He smiled. "Ah. That was what the expression was. I didn't know if this was anger or sadness with the crying."

"I wasn't crying," I croaked.

"No, yes, I did not mean crying," Kane said, throwing his hands up. "I mean water coming from your eyes and nose but *not* crying."

As I recovered, Kane picked up a knife and fork and gingerly cut his steak. Sure, he took some pretty huge bites, but he looked like the perfect little gentleman. You'd never know a year ago, he was a wolf. Then he lifted the plate and poured the bloody drippings into his mouth.

Well, you might know.

"I will miss this world, I think," he said. He licked his lips and seasoned his baked potato. "Especially salt. This makes food taste better."

"And it can spike your blood pressure so high you'll pop the top of your head off."

Taking a big forkful of potato, he chewed. "This is worth the risk."

He was being light, but he'd brought up leaving for a reason.

"We'll get you back home, Kane."

"And how is this?" He jammed in more potato. Talking with his mouth half full, he added, "With the Covenant syrup gone—"

"Serum."

"Yes. I said this."

"Uh-huh."

"With this gone, what is the idea to become wolf once more?"

I tried to keep a neutral expression on my face but had no idea how we'd work it out.

"We'll definitely work it out," I said, wiping my nose with a paper napkin. "We already know that the new moon can transform you into a wolf, right?"

He nodded. "This is true. But next day, I am this fleshy human riding a moped naked through the Mexican desert."

I heard a crash next to me and jumped. When I turned, Lilly was staring wide-eyed with bits of glass and kombucha splattered across her tennis shoes.

"Sorry, sorry," she said and put the surviving bottle down. In front of Kane. "I'll clean that up."

"Not a problem," I said.

"Garrick!" Lilly yelled at a volume I would have not thought possible, or recommended, for someone so small. "Cleanup by booth four!"

Our bartender apologized again and went to get a nonbroken bottle. Kane, the gentleman wolf, slid his beverage toward me. I guzzled half of it down. It felt like I was French kissing a glacier, and it was wonderful.

"Thank you." I pushed the bottle toward him.

He poked back to me with one of his sausage fingers. "I can smell the alcohol. You drink it."

A tiny man in a dirty apron scuttled over with a brush and dustpan to sweep up the broken bottle. Without a word, he bent down and got to cleaning up the mess.

I put a finger to my lips and looked over at Garrick. "We'll work it out, Kane. Trust me."

"I do trust you."

"First, though, we need to find a way to get into that dam."

Kane rubbed his scruffy chin and nodded. "We could get a hang glider, fly over, and jump to the very top."

"No."

"I have seen this work," he said, getting excited. "But it is very important to roll as you land. This is key."

"We're not making plans based on the crappy TV you've seen."

He threw his hands up. "Then I am out of good ideas."

Glancing at Garrick, I saw he was picking a glass shard out of his hand. Poor Garrick.

I leaned toward my friend and spoke more quietly. "I bet we can hike down the bank."

"Road blocked, yes?" he said, chewing a huge mouthful of food.

"Yeah, but roadblocks never stopped us before. Once we do that—"

"Can't do that," a voice from the floor said. Garrick held up a sliver of glass and chucked it under our booth. "You won't get anywhere near that place."

I looked at Kane. He shrugged then nodded.

"We just want some good photos," I said to Garrick. "We're social media influencers."

He went back to his glass sweeping. "Yeah, heard you say that to the boss. Don't matter if you're the pope getting a piggyback from Jesus, you ain't getting near that dam. Definitely not on foot."

"Oh?"

Head down, he said, "Some brave souls in town made it their mission to cause a bit a ruckus up there now and again. Bit of spray paint, snipping wires. They even mucked with the penstock, where the water flows through."

"Nice," I said.

"The new owners didn't think so," he said, still not looking up. Just slowly dragging his hand sweeper through the dark liquid and broken glass on the floor. "The powers that be gave them carte blanche to protect their investment."

"Right," I said and leaned closer to the guy. "And how do they do that?"

Garrick looked left and right. "They've got flying machines that guard the whole area."

"Flying machines?" I said, a bit too loudly for him. Garrick shrank back and scanned around. But, I mean, flying machines? Was this guy from the 1920s?

He spoke just above a whisper. "You know, like drones and stuff."

"Drones?"

For the first time, Garrick looked right at me. He gave me a crooked smile. "You just gonna repeat what I say as a question each time?"

"Each time?" I said and stuck my tongue out at him. He blushed. Hey, I can work a dude too. Lilly the trollop bartender didn't have a monopoly on that business model.

Garrick used his knees to slide closer, soaking his apron in the spill. "I think they're hiding something up there, and I ain't the only one who thinks that."

"Nah," I said. "They're just protecting their investment, like you said, right?"

Garrick slid so close he almost went under our table.

"You know, the water carries sound real good. All the way up the river," he whispered. "People say they've heard things."

"Like what?"

Before he could answer, Lilly came up and held out the new bottle of kombucha. She looked at mine then at the kombucha-less spot next to Kane. She put it down and shoved Garrick slightly with her knee. "You almost done down there? I got orders up."

"Yes, ma'am," Garrick said. He stood, gathered up his dustpan and hand brush, and headed back to the kitchen.

"How's the st—" she started, but then saw Kane's plate. "How *was* the steak?"

"Good but slightly overcooked," Kane said, shrugging.

"It was damn near raw."

"Yes. Next time," he said, pointing at me. "Raw next time. Yes. Thank you."

"Mmm," our bartender cooed. "He likes it raw."

Ugh, what-*ever*.

I slid out of my seat, stood up, and asked where I could find the bathroom. It was like I wasn't even there, so I snapped my fingers between the two of them.

"Yo, where is the ba—"

I got bumped from behind and had to throw my hands out so I didn't face-plant on the table. When I did, I knocked another bottle of kumbawhatchucallit over. It spilled into Kane's empty plate. I looked up at Lilly, ready to growl at her, but she'd been in *front* of me.

Just beyond our thirsty bartender, I saw the front door closing. Whoever had bumped into me had left in a hurry.

"Jerk," I muttered.

Lilly pointed down to the plateful of bubbling brown liquid mixing with blood. "You need another?"

"No, thank you." When I'd looked to the door, I'd seen that the daylight was turning orange. "If we could get the check, that'd be great."

"I'll make sure your room's set up," she said. "I hope you're not rolling it up already."

"We might poke around for a bit, but we've got a big day in the morning."

"Too bad. This place lights up real pretty in the dark."

I pointed at Kane. "So does he."

Lilly gave me a half smile, dropped our bill on the table, and walked back to her bar, where two women were very loudly requesting another round of shots.

Reaching into my pocket, I went to grab Kane's passport wallet. I patted the right pocket and the left. It wasn't there. Then I looked to the door.

"Holy shit," I said. "Did you see who bumped into me?"

"Yes."

"Who?"

He shrugged. "A lady with very wrinkly skin and a winter hat."

"Why didn't you say something?"

"About what?"

I stared at the front door. "I think she bumped into me and snatched the wallet. Your bank card's in there."

"You can get me another," he said. He stirred the bubbling blood liquid with his finger then put it in his mouth. "You are very resourceful."

Jamming my hands into my pockets, I couldn't believe *I* had gotten pickpocketed. "Does this look like a town with a big banking system?" My fingers felt a wad of paper, and I pulled a napkin out of my pocket. "What the hell is this?"

"Maybe it is IOU."

Unfolding the napkin, I read the words written there.

Three blocks to the east, turn right. Down to the end. House on the corner next to the eyeball. You want the wallet, come get it.

Chapter Thirty

Kane asked me, "Should we be taking evening plan advice from a soiled napkin?"

Three blocks east, we hooked away from the main drag and headed down a street that was both residential and retail. Many of the large homes had been sectioned off and converted into small businesses. A real estate office. Dentist. Pharmacy.

The echoes of those former homes remained. Long, square-paver sidewalks beckoned passersby to the door. Wrap-around porches with swings that once offered respite after a long day became display cases lazily swaying in the breeze.

On the next block, one home had both a gift shop and a tarot card reader. I supposed that if you got bad news about your aunt's impending illness, you could go right next door and get her a preemptive get-well-soon card.

And stenciled upon the window of the tarot card shop: a giant, all-seeing eye.

I pointed to the corner house, where the pickpocket had taken our wallet. We'd have to cross the street to get there, but I wanted to case the place first. I stepped onto a lawn of an actual home and hid in the shadow of a massive Norway maple tree .

The home in front of us, like many of the others, was a dual business. Ryland's Machine Shop in the back. In the front, it was harder to tell. The sign on the lawn was too far away to read. Actually, there were a bunch of signs in the front yard.

Thin white curtains had been drawn across the trifold glass of the front windows. Many years ago, that might have been some family's Sunday-morning breakfast nook. Now, it served a den of thieves. Or thief. I didn't know if the wrinkly lady with the winter cap had friends.

Doubtful.

Kane hadn't followed me into my hiding spot. He stood in the middle of the sidewalk, staring at the houses we'd already passed. I whispered his name so he'd join me under cover of the late-afternoon shade. I repeated it twice, and when he didn't come over, I gave up and walked over.

I asked him, "What do you think that place even is?"

"Which?"

I rolled my eyes. "The we-took-your-wallet-come-get-it house."

"I do not know," he said. Then, he looked back, one house over. "Why does that window have a big eye on it?"

"The what now?"

Kane shuffled back and forth, bent down, and stood again. "Everywhere I move, the eye watches me," he said. "Is very spooky."

"Will you pay attention?" I lightly shoved him. "We don't know what's waiting in there, and I need your head in the game."

He looked toward the thief house but then tilted his head and whispered, "The eye. It never blinks."

"That's because it's painted on the glass! It's a fortune teller."

"Oh?" Kane lit up. "I have seen these in shows. They know the future."

"No. They know how to get money out of desperate people looking for answers."

"This is us, yes?" Kane said, pointing at the eye. "Looking for answers. Maybe we go—"

I held a single finger up and shook my head. I pointed to the house on the corner. Kane was huge, so I decided if we were about to walk into some coven of wallet-stealing grannies, he could take them.

"Let's go."

Crossing the street, I heard his clomping feet behind me. A moment later, he raced past. That got a laugh out of me.

"Are you hiding from the eye?"

"Still looking at me."

As I walked the corner home's stone path, I read aloud the hand-painted signs jammed into the lush front lawn.

"Stop the damn dam." I pointed at another. "Save our local flora and fauna." The next: "Vote for Jeanette Fracus." Another: "Save the whales."

"For what?"

"What?"

"Save whales for what?" Kane said, staring at the words. I saw his lips move as he tried to read it himself. "Save for dinner? Save for substitute player on kickball team?"

I slammed my hands over my ears. "You're in a weird mood, dude. I need you to focus."

Kane took a deep breath and let it out slowly. "I am centered. I am focused. I am calm with the world."

"Good to hear," I said, and as we approached the door, I nodded to my left. "I think the eye just winked at you."

Chapter Thirty-One

A hand-carved wooden sign hanging from the eaves by rusted chains identified the home as the headquarters of the Rolleston Environmental Protection Party.

Whatever the hell that meant.

We climbed up the creaky steps, and before we got to the porch, the door opened a crack. A man with slicked-back gray hair peeked through the gap.

His eyes darted left and right. "You come alone?"

I shrugged. "Usually."

"What?"

"No," Kane said and took a protective step forward. "I am with her."

The gray man's eyes rose to take my friend in. He swallowed. "No, I mean did you bring anyone with you?"

Kane pointed at me. "I brought her. Or, rather, she brought me."

The guy peeking through the door looked at me. "Is your boy a bit touched or something?"

"First off, nobody says someone is 'touched' anymore, yeah? That's pretty awful," I said, hands on my hips. "And understand one thing. Y'all stole our shit. We're here to get it, so if anyone's gonna get touched, it'll be you. Um, by him."

Damn. I'd started out kinda badass but then kind of lost my train of thought. Damn.

The old guy waved his hands above his head. "This is a hostility-free safe zone! Can you understand that?"

"I understand it's not a redundancy-free zone, sure."

The guy turned his head and whispered something to someone hidden by the door. A moment later, a hand appeared over his head. It was waving Kane's wallet.

He said, "We just wanted to talk is all."

"So you robbed us?"

"Borrowed it." His eyes shifted downward. "So you would come."

Gray Guy started to speak again, then stopped. Someone was feeding him lines. He said, "We didn't want to be seen approaching you in public. This is a secret meeting."

"We have already been spotted," Kane said, pointing to his left. "Still now, she watches. Unblinking."

The man in the doorway grimaced. "What?"

"Why don't you want people to know we're meeting?" I asked, trying to get us back on track.

That got a self-satisfied smile out of the old fella. "Well, to find that out, you'll have to come in." He opened the door wider, revealing a sea of faces behind him. "Do you like kombucha?"

***

We sat in the living room on the most uncomfortable love seat ever constructed. I could feel the springs on my side violating me in ways that probably would require filing a police report.

Across from us was a long couch that looked like it had been upholstered with the hair of an angry orange cat. On either side of that, two big sofa chairs. Behind those, a couple of wooden chairs pulled from a nearby dining table, which was still loaded down with the remains of the day's lunch.

Filling the couch, the sofa chairs, and table chairs sat about a dozen people. Between them, others stood. All watched us intently.

Before us, sitting in the middle, was the woman in the winter cap from the bar. Jeanette Fracus, she of the "vote for" signs out front. A local politician with, my best guess, a shady past. She'd pickpocketed a thief, and I'd never noticed a thing.

"Who are you?" she asked.

I frowned. "If we only had our ID, we could show you."

With a flick of her bony wrist, Jeannette chucked the wallet at Kane. He'd been staring at a forest of papier-mâché art hanging from the ceiling but snatched the wallet out of the air like a third baseman. Didn't even look.

"Kane Davis," Janette said. "Born in British Columbia, and that's a positive sign. Canadians are a good sort."

"This is true," Kane said.

Jeannette scowled. "Except it's a fake."

That got a hearty guffaw out of me. "Wait, wait," I said, waving my hand in the air. "You guys steal our money. Scribble a threat on a dirty napkin. And accuse *us* of being untrustworthy. That's high-larious."

Kane grunted. "I do not find it as funny."

A woman in her thirties, sporting a bob of pink hair, cleared her throat.

Jeannette waved her hand in the air. "Go ahead, Caley."

"The passport says Kane Davis was born in Terrace, BC, but he didn't go to school anywhere. Never had a job. You don't have a Social Security number because, well, Canadian, but you don't have one of their Social Insurance numbers either."

I looked at my friend next to me on the love seat. "Why the hell are we being interrogated?"

"I think this is how hippie people make friends, maybe," Kane said.

That got the whole group agitated. Apparently, they weren't big fans of the h-word. Fingers pointed, voices rose.

Jeanette calmly raised a hand, quieting the rabble. "We don't allow labels in here," Jeannette said, lowering her frail hand to her lap. "And I find those sorts of slurs tiring."

Kane nodded. "Is this because you are vegan?"

"Um, what?" she said.

"Mon père would say vegan people had low energy because they eat grass and fungus spores. No meat."

I stood from the couch to get a look at their afternoon's meal. Caley, the resident tech nerd, slid over to block my view, but she was rail thin, so I got a good view of the table. Yep, all vegetables.

"Animals deserve respect, not a frying pan," Jeannette said from her perch in the middle of the couch. "We never eat anything that has a face on it."

"I do not either," Kane said.

"Then we agree."

"Yes," my friend said. "I pull off face and eat first because this is often most tender."

She hooked her finger at Kane, ready to fire another volley.

I jumped in. "Enough, enough," I said, raising my hands. "We got our wallet back, so we're gonna go. You got ten seconds to tell us why all the subterfuge to get us here."

"Such a good word," Kane said and flashed me a big, bearded smile.

Jeannette sighed, closed her eyes for a moment, then took a deep breath. "I got some intel about you from one of our associates," she said. "We have eyes and ears all over this—"

"Garrick told you," I said. "The cook and kombucha cleanup dude."

The old woman's mouth hung open for a moment. She shrugged. "I cannot reveal my sources. However, it was passed on to me—"

"By Garrick," I said and couldn't stop my grin from sharpening at its edges.

"—that you're trying quite hard to get to the dam."

I shrugged. "My followers expect me to get shots other people can't. It's kinda my brand."

Caley snort-laughed. "You are *not* a social media influencer."

"Says you," I said.

"That doesn't matter," Jeannette said, waving her underling back. "You seem very determined to get to that monstrosity."

Smiling, I said, "We just need a way there. Up close." It was true, and I felt it had been a cleverly deceptive answer. Just enough info to get what we needed and nothing more.

"Yes," Kane added. "So we can break in."

Instantly, the mood in the room changed. Fist pumping. Big smiles. Cheers and high fives. My jaw dropped.

These people are lunatics.

"Advocates! I knew it!" Jeannette declared, raising a single bony finger in the air and looking to her people. She turned back to me. "I could just tell."

"Because Garrick told you?" I said and squinted at her. "He told *us* about the drones protecting the place."

"They've got face recognition," Caley said, running a thumb across her brow to shift a lock of pink hair. "Any of us get close, and we'll go to jail."

"We've *gone* to jail," Jeannette said. "Nobody cared."

"Because our elected leaders are puppets," one man shouted.

"Vote Jeannette," another woman said, pumping a fist in the air.

I felt a tap on my shoulder and turned to see the old guy who'd met us at the door earlier. With a kind smile, he handed me a brown bottle with no label. He handed a second one to Kane, who put it on the end table next to him.

Taking a slug, I swallowed. Then the aftertaste hit. And the grit. I put my bottle down on the coffee table and sat down again.

"Now, I don't know what you two want with the dam," Jeanette said. "I will only ask you this: Is your interest in the dam to disrupt? Cause discord?"

To buy a few seconds to think, I looked around the room. At the far side of the room, I saw an open door leading deeper into the house. On one side, a clutter of picket signs leaned against a wall. On the other side of the door, boxes had been stacked halfway to the ceiling. Bumper stickers on their exterior suggested more stickers were inside.

All bore protest slogans.

Disrupt.

Discord.

Bring the Change.

Stop the Dam.

I said, "I think we can help each other."

Chapter Thirty-Two

The organization of disrupters and discorders was the most disorganized group of people I'd ever met. Everyone was allowed a say, which was great. It was also chaos.

"They could ram it with a big boat," one young woman dressed in multicolored scarves said.

"Let's parachute them in!" another one suggested.

A deep voice from the back said, "Explosives. Blow it to hell and be done with it."

This prompted Jeannette to stand and face her group. "All fine suggestions, and I thank you for the input." She turned to the scarf woman. "We can't damage a concrete dam with a boat."

"A big boat!"

"Not even with a big boat," she said and waved her hand in the air. "And we don't have parachutes. Or a plane."

"Bomb time," the deep voice chimed in again.

Their leader smiled gently. "We're not blowing it up."

Thank god for that, I thought.

"We can't buy the bomb-making materials." She pointed to a squat man digging at the dinner table for scraps. "Joseph has warrants in three states because he tried to do that."

"Four!" Joseph said proudly as he chewed on something leafy and wilted.

I tried to calm the roar in my brain. All we needed was to get inside and find out where Marata and Doc Hammer had gone to prepare for their attack. This crazy group of disruptors was veering us off course.

"Hey," I said. Then I repeated it louder. "Hey!"

The look on Jeannette's face made me think she'd forgotten we were even in the room.

"We're not blowing up the damn dam," I said, scowling. "We just need to get inside. No explosions or parachutes or ram raids."

Their leader crossed her arms. "If we're helping you, we'll need something in return."

"We're not blowing anything up. That's an awful idea," I said, remembering our time in Mexico. When the river next to the convent burst its banks, it had destroyed everything in its path. "All the stuff downstream would get wiped out."

"It's an abomination that's disrupted fish and wildlife for a century," Jeannette said. "There's nothing downriver that would be harmed if it were gone."

"Except maybe a few pleasure boats," Caley said with a glint in her eye. "No big loss."

"Listen to me closely," I said, looking over the group. "No bombs. No guns. No flamethrowers."

"Ooo," a balding man said as he leaned against the couch's armrest. "Flamethrowers!"

"No, no. I think we've got just the thing," Jeannette said and nodded to the man of four warrants, Joseph. He burst from the room and was back within a half minute. When he returned, he handed me a cardboard shoebox.

"What's this?"

Jeannette tapped it with a long fingernail. "Open it up."

I did and stared at two cylinders. "Tiny soup cans?"

"Those are electromagnetic field disruptors," Joseph said. He reached over and gently stroked their smooth metal skins. "Israeli spooks designed them to screw up nuclear centrifuges in Iran."

"Bullshit," I said and snatched one, which was the size of a hockey puck and three times as heavy. "How could you possibly get your hands on something like this?"

Grinning smugly, Joseph tapped his temple. "I know people."

"He ordered them off eBay," Jeannette said. She took the device from me and grabbed the other from the box. "Put these on opposite sides of one of the dam's turbines, and it'll disrupt the magnetic field. The turbine spins out of control and causes a power spike that'll fry the breakers. That monster on the river will be out of commission for days. Maybe a week." She placed them back gently and closed the lid.

I looked down and saw the return address was somewhere in Florida.

I frowned. "How do you know these things will work? They could just be junk."

"We checked, of course!" Joseph whined. "Me and Amos tested them out on the vacuum cleaner."

I looked down at the carpet. Yep. Dirty as hell.

"We lost a damn good vacuum." Jeanne said, bitterly.

Joseph added, "And Amos."

"*What?*" I shouted.

"Oh, right. Important safety tip," Jeannette said, tapping the box. "Don't stand between the field disruptors when you turn them on. "

I pushed the box toward her. "A guy *died* using these?"

"No, no." She shoved it back at me. "It was Amos's vacuum. He left."

This was all too much, and I was too tired from a long day of travel. "I gotta think about this. And I need sleep if—"

"Emelda, no," Jeannette said, hints of panic on her face. "If we're doing this, it has to be tonight."

I gasped. "What? Tonight? Are you insane? We can't—"

Caley stepped forward, shaking her head. "They've got ears all over town. Spies. Listening devices and cameras," she said. "They'll already know someone's asking about the dam. You don't have days to do this."

"It needs to be tonight," Jeannette added, nodding.

Covenant was paranoid and probably did have cameras around the town. And Izzy would be free of the fifth floor by now. Would he tell his bosses we were headed here? I quietly cursed myself for having had the conversation in front of the guard.

Maybe Covenant had gotten overconfident? But a corporation that spanned the planet with billions in the bank could be overconfident. A lot of confidence building right there.

However, a night raid would be a problem.

"Kane has a condition," I said. "Moonlight makes him break out in hives." What was I saying? "Very itchy."

"Affected by the moonlight, yeah?" The balding man sitting next to Jeanette laughed. "We call those werewolves."

"Ha, no. What?" I said, awkwardly crossing my arms. "There's no such thing."

The man glared at me with hooded eyes. "I knew a werewolf. Used to live around here. His name... was Mundy Wilcoxson."

"Mundy was *not* a werewolf, Blake," Jeannette said, rolling her eyes. "Just very hairy."

"If it's got to be tonight, I'm not going without Kane. But I'll need something to cover him up. Or keep him inside whatever boat we've got. That's nonnegotiable."

Blake broke away and squeezed through the throng of people. "I may have something."

I watched him go into the next room. "What does that mean?"

"Blake used to work on film sets," Jeannette said. "He's collected so much junk over the years, he probably *does* have something."

"Right," I said, looking at the empty doorway. "And by 'collected' you mean stole stuff?"

"Tomato, toe-mah-toe."

"This is ludicrous." I jumped up, frustrated and having second thoughts about the plan. Because there was no plan. "We can't even get to the dam, right? The one road leading there has no bridge. There are barriers both up- and downriver."

I saw the woman from earlier about to speak and put my hand up to her. "And we're not parachuting in!"

The room fell silent.

"I maybe have something," a grizzled voice said. The group looked past me, so I turned to see a man step into the kitchen. Grease-stained from his denim overalls up to his silver crew cut, he could have been in his thirties or sixties. Impossible to tell.

He scanned our faces as he stood at the open door, which served as a connector between the two sides of the massive house.

When he stepped forward, I saw the innards of a crammed workshop behind him. Steel shelves stuffed with oily boxes of all sizes. Workbenches and tools and cutters and sheets of metal. This was the machine shop I'd seen earlier from outside.

As he washed his hands in the sink, Jeannette said, "Ryland is an unofficial member of our group. He fixes stuff for us and pays twice the rent anyone else would in this town. Without that support, we would not have made it this far."

Ryland elbowed the faucet and rubbed his hands dry on his dirty overalls. He turned to the group. "You know I support you lot—and I've been honest about this—I don't like any of ya."

"Yes," Jeannette said and bristled. "You mention that every chance you get."

I whispered to her, "What a nice guy."

She turned so only I could hear her. "Australian. It's just their way."

"I've been listening in on your conversation." The man in the overalls pointed at Kane. "I saw the big bloke walk up earlier. Caught my eye when he started dancing all weird in the street."

I shrugged. "He needed to use the bathroom."

"*You* are definitely intriguing, mate," Ryland said to me, stepping closer but staying on the tiled floor. "But something about your friend. Just so... unusual. I can't put a finger on it."

Still chilling on the couch, Kane nodded. "I am wolf."

"Oh?" Ryland cocked an eyebrow. "Yeah, that'll be it, then."

Before Kane could elaborate, Blake the film-set thief strode triumphantly back into the room. "Look what I found!" he said, waving what looked like a deflated balloon man. "An old green morph suit!"

"What the hell is that?" I asked.

Blake strode up to Kane and waved my friend up to stand. When he did, the film dude unfurled the garment, holding it by the shoulders. He pressed the nylon fabric up against Kane.

"Thankfully, it stretches quite a bit," he said. "They use these for green screens so the person wearing it can wander around in the shot and not be seen on camera."

Kane wrapped his arms around the green skin. "I would be invisible!"

"No, in the dark, you'd look like a dude wearing a green neon sign," I said then turned to Blake. "We'll need to dye it black."

He snatched it back, clutching the green onesie to his chest. "No way. This is a valuable film prop. Worth a lot of money."

I saw a flash of pink hair as Caley came up and put a soothing hand on Blake's shoulder. "I've got water-soluble dye. Tint it black, and it'll wash right out."

The film dude frowned. Then, squeezing his eyes closed, he handed it to her.

"Great. Stellar," I said. "But we still don't have a way to *get* to the dam."

Jeannette's eyes sparkled, and she pointed to the man in her kitchen. "I believe Ryland said he had an idea."

He stared intently at Kane and slowly shook his head. A smile crept up his face.

"I do," he said.

Jeannette actually gasped. She took a half step forward then stopped. Clutching her hands to her chest, she asked, "Now? Why now?"

Ryland shrugged.

"But we've asked for weeks. *Months*, Ryland! And these two walk in, and suddenly, it's okay," she said. "Why?"

With a widening grin, he pointed at Kane. "Something special about this one."

"What are you two talking about?" I asked. "*What's* okay?"

Ryland turned to me and nodded slowly. "You can use Willie."

Chapter Thirty-Three

I stared out the huge round window and saw nothing. Utter blackness slithered through the glass, its icy tendrils worming into my skin, making my muscles stiff and bones ache.

We were thirty feet below the inky surface of Snake River, heading toward the dam. To stop my shivering, I pulled my knees in to my chest.

"Don't wiggle around so much," Ryland said, his voice hollow as it echoed off the curved hull. "She's a bit dodgy with the controls sometimes, and I don't want to hit anything that'll spring us a leak."

"A leak?" I went to swallow and only felt my tongue curl closer to the back of my throat. "You never said anything about leaks."

"Don't fret. Ol' Willie is a tank."

"Ol' Willie" was not a tank but a submarine. Yep. A frickin' minisub.

After he'd given the okay for us to use the submersible, we'd split into groups to get ready.

Kane had gone with the Onesie Team. Not that they'd officially been called that, but nothing about this plan was official. It was gonzo.

As Caley had promised, she had some temporary hair dye to morph the morph suit from green to black. When Kane strode back in to model it, I saw swirls of lime color and uneven black streaks. He looked like a dill pickle that had gotten jumped in a dark alley.

While he stood in the living room, arms outstretched, Caley led a team of three others to sponge the green parts with more dye. Because Kane was so much larger than anyone who might have worn it before, he'd had to strip off his clothes just to get into it.

The suit was skintight and left little to the imagination.

"Emelda, can you see me? Can you tell I am here?" Kane asked, the fabric over his mouth bending into a shallow curve.

"Kane, I can tell what sort of *mood* you're in," I said, covering my mouth with my fist. "I mean, it's not an invisibility cloak."

"Yes, but this is to make movie people disappear," he said, his smooth head tilted to the side. "When I go through the forest, it will be like the trees have swallowed me."

Caley made a coughing sound then cleared her throat. She cut me a glance, and we shared a private smile.

"Let's see if we can find you some shoes," Caley said, wrapping her arm through Kane's jet-black limb. "You go running in that and you'll tear holes in the feet, and we'll never hear the end of it from Blake."

When he disappeared into the next room, my mood darkened. Kane would be too big to get into the minisub with me and Ryland. So he would take the scenic route on foot. In a black onesie. But the forest was his home, and if anyone could pull it off, it was Kane.

"I reckon the waters may have shifted a bit since these charts but not heaps," Ryland said, using a grease pencil to mark our path across a computer-generated map of the river bottom. He'd lived in the area for decades and had taken Willie out on dozens of dives. All the way up to the dam and back many times.

That had ended when Covenant had taken over. He hadn't wanted to risk his forty-thousand-dollar sub getting impounded. Or worse.

Somehow, Kane and me showing up had changed his mind.

Originally, Willie had belonged to a university research crew out of Australia who'd used it to monitor bleaching along the Great Barrier Reef. After that, some enviro-kiwis bought her for their rather aggressive anti-whaling efforts.

"She got clipped by an anchor line, which took off one of her fins," Ryland explained. "Willie also got hit with a bloody harpoon!"

"Are you sure it's still safe?"

"Willie's been patched up so many times, she's mostly patch," he'd said to me with a reverent smile. "Her scars only make her stronger."

Now, inside the minisub, I watched Ryland use a penlight to navigate his underwater charts. I ran my hand over the submersible's cold, smooth interior. The vibration from the electric motor made it feel like Willie was purring.

"There are a few wrecks down here, but I've charted them," my pilot said, looking between the map and a monitor that was making a dent in my right thigh. The sub hadn't really been made for two, so it was a tight squeeze.

He'd tried to convince me the device was a "single-beam echosounder, topographical navigation sonar" of his own design. But now and then, the screen would light up with excited text like *Possible Trout!*

Yeah, I was pretty sure it was a fish finder, but I kept that to myself.

"I guess people have been out on this river for more than a century, so you'd expect a few sunken boats."

"Sure," he said, reaching up and twisting a lever on one of the four valves above his head. I heard a hiss, then my stomach soured as fat bubbles rose across the big porthole in front of me.

"What do those do?"

"These are what makes her fly, mate."

Smiling, he pressed his fingers into a bird's nest of wires above his head. I heard a click, and a ring around the porthole lit the murky water ahead of us. He then wiggled one valve, and tiny silver bubbles raced through the light, zooming for the surface.

My tummy tweaked but not as bad as before. "We went down."

"Just a wee bit," he said, nodding to a manic crisscross of tubing above us. "She's got four tanks of air. You want to surface, squidge some into the ballast tanks, and that pushes the heavy water out, which makes you lighter, and you float up."

"Makes sense, sure."

"To dive, let air out of the ballast. The water rushes in, making you heavier, and you go down." He tweaked a valve, and another cough of bubbles rose.

I felt my chest tighten. "And we got plenty of air for the tanks? To breathe?"

"Sure." Ryland scratched his throat. "I'd have to account for an extra person, more weight, but we've got heaps to get us back to the surface."

"Cool," I said, looking up at the tempting allure of dangerous PVC fittings. "Can I try?"

"Not a chance." Ryland playfully covered the pipes with his arms. "You look like a daredevil."

I laughed. "Only a little."

"No touching," he said, gazing at his maps again. "One big burp, and it's a one-way race to the bottom."

The fish finder blinked: *Possible wreck!*

I leaned forward, and sure enough, through the green water haze below us, I could see what looked like a toppled mast and part of a busted hull. Most of the boat had either broken apart or sunk into the muck. Seaweed and silt draped the bones that remained.

I asked Ryland, “How old are those boats there on the bottom?”

“Some old, some new. I reckon some of those could be folks in the past year who got too close to the dam. The corporate assholes who run that place might have put them in the deep.”

“Are you serious?”

“Jeannette’s people think so.” Ryland’s eyes went from the tiny monitor to the map to the illuminated porthole then back to the map. “We just passed under the barrier without a hitch. We’ll be at the meet-up point in about fifteen minutes. I might just take a piss on the dam when we’re there.”

“Now who’s the daredevil?”

“Nah, we’re on the upstream side. The angry bit’s on the other side.”

It was so quiet. Peaceful. The only sound was the purr of Willie and the chattering of my teeth. I should have brought my jacket.

“You got a heater in here somewhere?”

Ryland shook his head, and his face glowed as he stared out into the water beyond the window. Instead of answering, he grinned and pointed at the glass.

When I turned, I saw a river monster staring at us. Glassy black eyes. Crazy long body that shimmered silver in the porthole’s light. A swath of dark, irregular circles down its flank that looked like leopard print.

“What the hell is that?”

“Garfish,” he said. “Been around since prehistoric times.”

The fish lifted its head, brandishing a long snout—yes, snout—lined with jagged white bits. Teeth.

I pressed my back against the cold hull. “Does it bite?”

He laughed. “Not people usually. Those jaws don’t go very wide. Beautiful, isn’t it?”

“Beautiful” wasn’t the first word that came to mind. “Terrifying.” “Horrifying.” “Pants-wettingly freaky.” Words like that came to mind.

The fish tugged its enormous snout upward then casually swam in circles. Every circuit, it seemed to give us a sideways glance.

Ryland looked back at the chart on his knees. He pointed at some snaking lines. "This is where we may have to drop a bit deeper," he said and looked up at the tubing. "Going up and down isn't ideal for our air supply, but Jeannette's convinced the river's got listening devices to detect motors. She *claims* that's how they lost two boats."

"Lost?"

He eyeballed me. "Sunk."

"Oh. Wow."

Ryland shrugged. "Don't know if it's hogwash, but we're not taking chances. We'll go low so that if they're listening for boats, they'll never hear us."

Out the big circular window, I saw a flash of silver tail. Apparently, the garfish had either gotten bored with the two humans in the hamster ball, or it had picked up the scent of prey.

I watched it for a moment. For as monstrous as the chompy fish was, it did have a certain grace about it.

Reminds me of someone I know.

Chapter Thirty-Four

Kane

I am shadow.

A dark hole in the night. I am the night hole.

Hmm, "night hole" does not sound so appealing. This conjures images of a hastily conceived superhero character. I will have to think of a better name.

As I stride confidently through the crisp, cool forest, the evening air kisses my near naked skin. The man sock fits so snugly, this is like wearing nothing at all. Naturally, this I prefer.

The hippie people also seemed to favor my appearance despite their fastidious blotting of the black dye. Apparently, some areas required far more blotting than others. Even now, I feel a slickness dribble down my thigh.

Ah! The Slick Shadow!

Not quite. Closer.

I stand still, a slick shadow within in the shadows, wearing only torn black Reebok shoes. Torn because they had to cut the toes out, for my feet were far too large. In fact, there was much conversation about the size of my feet while I endured the enthusiastic blotting.

No matter.

A wolf focuses on his present, not the past. And also the future but not too far ahead. Just enough to plan for what will be the present very soon. So, in that way, also in the present. Future present.

I peer through the trees to see the river, only thirty meters to my left. When I raise my hand to the water, which sparkles with starlight, I can sense Emelda is below. This is how it is with a pack.

My eyes quickly adjust to the darkness, for this is the hunter's way.

The moon above lights my path. Unable to get at my skin, she is now an advocate, not an adversary. But I know this is a perilous relationship. Alas, so many are.

I am not alone in the woods.

Motionless, I stare through the darkened fabric, looking left and right. Yes, I could see better if I tore a very tiny hole to see, but I promised Film Rick I will be careful with his illicitly obtained treasure.

Raising my hands, I feel vibrations ripple toward me. I sweep my arms back and forth as the cool night air whispers her secrets. What is this mysterious presence I sense?

A head swivels toward me. Large yellow eyes shine brightly from a branch above.

"Who?"

Frowning, I put a finger up to my lips. But the stupid owl does not seem to understand.

"Who?"

With expression, I try to tell it that this is no time for inquisition. No time for mindless monosyllabic chatter.

"Who?"

Ah. I am covered in the man sock. The owl cannot hear my expressions. And, of course, would not understand the human words. The creature shifts its weight, the body twisting to face the same direction as the head.

Quite creepy.

And big. I have seen many owls in the British Columbia forests. This one is a disturbingly enormous owl. As big as a chubby human toddler. How does the branch hold up such a meaty fowl?

"Who?"

I yearn to shake a fist at the creature, but this inquisitiveness is not its fault. They are very curious. And I remember one on television, some old commercial, that revealed how fascinated they can be by candies on sticks and how many—

The owl snaps its gaze ahead and freezes. Slowly, the head turns back toward me. Then I read its expression, not listening to its words. Or word.

"Danger," the creature emotes to me. "There is danger here."

That is when I hear a lone buzzing sound. No, wait. Not one but two. Could this second be an echo of the first?

I do not think so, for one source of the noise is directly ahead, hiding in the dark. The other, much quieter, seems to be coming from my left.

From the river.

Chapter Thirty-Five

"It's a *what*?" I shouted for the third time and got the same answer: grim silence from Ryland.

One minute earlier, we were floating along and creeping closer to our target. An almost leisurely trek, and I'd felt a bit like Jacques Cousteau as we glided through the black water.

The fish finder beeped excitedly. It had been tracking the inquisitive garfish, a single blip on its screen, until it found something new.

Possible trout!

The new blip appeared three times the size of our toothy friend. My pilot had looked at it, curious. Not because of its size.

"That's moving rather fast," he said. "And, um, toward us."

Then the fish finder confessed it had no idea what was out there. That admission had changed everything.

Unknown object.

Ryland began twisting the valves and levers above his head, and my stomach lurched. He'd angled Willie sharply to the left then right. He seemed unsure which way to turn to avoid the missile.

Yep.

"Did you say that's a missile?" I shouted, my voice ringing off Willie's metal hull. Again, no answer from Ryland. His hands were moving fast, like he was fighting off invisible seagulls.

Never in my life had I thought the word "missile" would be a factor.

"Going down!" Ryland shouted. "Hold on."

"I thought you said we couldn't go lower than thirty feet."

He barked out a laugh, but his eyes? Zero joy there.

"Ryland?" I yanked at his overalls. "A thirty-foot floor, right? That's what you said!"

"I'll take my chances with the bottom." His eyes widened as he looked out the big window ahead. Once we'd moved away from a sandbar, the river water had turned clear as glass. I wrapped my arms around my chest.

The light from our window cast its beam ahead, revealing an underwater forest. Long-dead trees, swishing seaweed, rocks, and wreckage. The latter punched me in the gut. It felt like we were diving toward a graveyard.

Ahead, a curious sight: bubbles.

When I pointed them out, Ryland froze for a moment then once again became a chaos of limbs. Sweat flew off his brow and streaked the inside of the window.

How the hell is this guy sweating? It's freezing down here!

The fish finder pinged enthusiastically: *Possible bass!*

As if realizing its mistake, it sheepishly switched back to *Unknown object*, but this time, the letters glowed red. And flashed.

Reluctantly, I lifted my gaze from the tiny screen to the porthole and saw something shimmer. A silver streak growing larger.

Willie the minisub began to groan, and we went deeper and deeper. My throat constricted and could only draw in shallow gasps. My heartbeat throbbed in my ears. It felt like the metal walls were closing in.

"Pressure's going up," Ryland said. "Move your jaw to pop your ears."

I shouted at him, "What can I do to help?"

"Nothing," Ryland said as we tipped forward. The porthole filled with images of a murky brown moonscape. He'd pointed Willie at the river bottom, and I had to throw a hand out to not tumble into the illuminated window.

At this angle, I couldn't see the silver streak anymore. "Where is the missile?"

"I misspoke. It's not a missile." Ryland choked out a laugh, drawing the back of his hand across his brow. "It'll be a sonar-guided underwater drone."

"What's the difference?"

Shrugging, he said, "'Drone' sounds less scary."

"*Does it?*"

Ryland flipped open the plastic cover of a square box and twisted a wire, snapping it. We lurched forward.

"What'd you do?" I asked.

"That was a governor," he said. "To prevent too much juice coming from the battery. You don't want to fry the electric motor. These subs are not meant to go fast."

"And you broke it?"

"We *need* to go fast. I'll take my chances."

Through the window, shadows below formed into structures. Massive boulders and what appeared to be concrete chunks and rebar jutting out like ribs of a long-dead sea creature.

I put my hand on the glass. "On the left," I said. "Those look like they'd slice us."

"Port side. Not left."

"Now? You want to teach me nautical terms *now*?"

He shrugged. "Might be your last chance to learn."

"Don't say shit like that!"

I flinched as something silver flashed in front of us. The garfish had picked that moment to whiz past our viewport, its tail whipping back and forth like my mother's hand after I'd gotten mud on the couch. What a weird time for that memory to pop up.

Panicked, I shouted, "Fish!"

Ryland didn't take any notice of the outburst because he probably thought I was losing my mind. But the fish reminded me we had something that might help track the miss—err—drone.

I reached over and flipped the screen of the fish finder toward the two of us.

When Ryland saw the light of it, he growled. "No time to mess with that, Emelda. We need to—"

"It might be able to show us where the drone is!"

Ryland sucked a breath through his teeth and nodded. The monochromatic screen displayed a jagged outline of the bottom. The massive boulder's vague shape appeared, a green line against a black background with a tiny word: *Rock.*

A series of jagged vertical lines warbled back and forth on the screen. When I looked through the porthole, I saw a field of seaweed undulating on the river bottom.

But I couldn't see the drone.

When I wiped condensation from the screen, my fingers bumped against something on the side—a rubber wand with an accordion base like a stick shift in a car. When I moved this around, the green-lined objects on the screen shifted to the left then downward. I was moving the sensor.

I saw a thick circle heading toward us. And growing.

The screen of the fish finder rolled a few times as it processed this new data. As the circle grew larger, its analysis was complete. *Possible trout!*

Not likely.

On the edge of the screen, I saw the double flash as a new object appeared. I moved the joystick to get a better view of it.

Instead of warbling lines like the rocks and weeds, this had hard edges. It looked like a tiny city skyline. As we got closer, I could make out areas of smooth lines with chunks missing.

The device came to the same conclusion I had: *Possible wreck!*

Leaning forward, I thumped the glass of the porthole. "Out there. Just beyond the weed bed, there's a sunken boat on the bottom. Can you hide behind that?"

"Maybe."

Ryland put his foot up next to the window and leaned as he twisted the levers on the left side—port side—of the sub. We tilted so fast, I thought we were going to roll.

"Holy shit, Ry!"

I fell back and smacked the top of my head against the inner hull. Stars filled my vision. Hands on my head, I bent forward again to see Ryland staring intently at the tiny screen.

Nodding, he gave me a thumbs-up. "Nice! Good thinking," he said. When he manipulated the device's joystick to move the sensor, his smile turned to a grimace. "Is the trout what I think it is?"

"I think so."

He drew in a huge breath. "I don't think we're going to make it."

"Go faster!"

"This is faster."

Watching the green display, I prayed for the trout circle to move higher on the screen. It didn't.

"How is it following us?"

"Sonar. Once it locked onto us, damn thing will follow Willie until it hits."

My eyes widened as the circle grew.

Ryland shook his head and squeezed his eyes shut. "Dammit, dammit," he shouted. He grabbed two of the valve handles above his head and threw them forward. The sub filled with the sound of hissing, and the nose pointed upward.

I tumbled again, this time hitting the back of my head. Matching lumps.

"New plan," he said. "If that thing hits, we need to be closer to the surface so we can get out."

The circle on the screen was beginning to block out everything else around it, filling about a third of the display. No way we'd make it to the surface.

"Wait, wait," I said.

"Can't."

A thick white line briefly filled the screen, and I saw a massive fin cross the window out front. The ugly-ass gar was rocketing away, heading for the bottom.

On the display, I saw the fat circle bobble. For the past minute, it had just grown and grown. Steady as a rock. But when the huge dinosaur fish crossed its path, it shifted after it then reacquired our signal.

The gar had bought us a few seconds. But the drone was back on track.

Kane's voice came to my mind: *"One cannot think with panic juices running through brain."*

My whole body was bursting with panic juices. My mind was chaos.

"Calm heart, calm mind. Observe and act."

I forced myself to take a deep breath. Calm. Ryland had closed his eyes and gone spread eagle—a foot on each wall, one arm to the ceiling and an elbow on the floor. He was bracing for impact.

The circle grew faster, now filling half the screen.

I breathed slowly. If I were smarter, I would have told Ryland what I was about to do. But I was about to do something really, really stupid.

Chapter Thirty-Six

Kane

The sparkling entrails of my foe lie scattered across the forest floor.

Scanning the darkness, I reach down and grab another stone in case a second metal bee is close. The inquisitive owl blinks at me.

I nod to the creature.

"Thank you for the warning, friend," I say aloud, but owls do not speak human. With my expression, I try to convey the same. However, I am covered in the man sock. The creature cannot see my face.

I decide on an alternative. Universal language.

The owl stares at me blankly as I give it a thumbs-up.

Actually, I do not think this is a universal language. Many animals do not have thumbs. When I am wolf again, I will miss them. Maybe there is an animal equivalent of thumbs-up?

Moving closer to a gigantic tree, a mother oak, I align my black body with its trunk. I am now a shadow within shadow hiding in shadow. I am the Super Shadow!

The oak is my ally. Together, we will defeat the buzzing menace.

For I do hear another.

Its insectile song rises and falls as it searches for me, and I hear disappointment in its electric tones. I know it seeks me, but Super Shadow cannot be found. Ha ha!

Hmm. Buzzing grows louder. Closer.

I frown at the owl as it continues to stare at me.

Do not stare at me, toddler bird! I am thankful for your earlier alert, but continued staring will betray my position.

Unless this is its game. Yes. Yes. This is why it quizzed me so. *Who are you to walk through the woods in a black man sock? A creature such as you does not belong here.* I wish to tell it, the forest, the woods, this is where I belong!

It is in the world of humans that I do not fit.

But I cannot relay this to the owl. And they are implacable creatures. Once their mind is set, it is very hard to change them. Any plea would fall upon deaf ears. And those creepy bubble eyes.

With eyes that big, can the owl see through the mesh covering my face? I furrow my brow and scowl at it to present my displeasure at its current betrayal.

"Who."

"Hush!" I hiss at it.

This is a mistake. The buzzy tones rise and quickly grow louder. It picked up the sound of my voice. I shake my head, disheartened by the turncoat owl.

When I peek around the trunk of the mother oak, I see a tiny, bouncing red light. Kneeling, I hear my knees crack. At this sound of this, the flying machine stops. It whirs and spins as it hovers unnaturally.

The red dot of light grows and casts a beam to the ground. A cone-shaped glow scans the forest floor. I pull back behind the tree and grip the stone tighter in my hand. I hear the wavering sounds of the menacing flying machine as it jerks to one side and the other.

What is it finding? I am head to toe a shadow.

Ah.

I stare down at my Reebok shoes then look next to the tree. I have left Reebok prints in the loamy earth. Once again betrayed by footwear! I do not know why humans love it so.

Wait, no. The red beam crawls across the forest floor and stops as its light glitters on the ground. It has discovered the remains of the first mechanical bee, which I took out with a rock much like the one in my hand now.

Have I killed its brother or sister?

Oh, yes. Yes, yes! This excites me so. Super Shadow has killed the kin of the evil bee, and as it stares upon the shattered remains, my archenemy pledges a life oath to destroy me. This is Vengeance Bee!

Origin story. Totally.

The buzzing rises in tone, but I cannot see my new mechanical foe, so I slide my head around the tree to look. The red light blinds me. It is shining its glow-cone ray directly at my eyes.

I shout at it, "Curse you, Vengeance Bee!"

Another sound, clicking and clacking, and I raise my hand to block the beam. When I do, I see two armatures extend from either side of the drone. Both hold... sausages?

Wait, is it planning to throw sausages at me?

Maybe I was too quick to judge.

Sausages would be good.

"Who!"

I shrink back at the sound of the owl, and I am about to admonish it for the utterance, but I cannot. Because the owl explodes.

Bits of feather and inquisitive fowl shower down upon me as I whip back behind the tree while hurling the rock at the angry bee. Down to one sausage, for it launched the other at the owl, I see the left armature tweak, readying to fire.

Before it can, my stone connects with its face, and it explodes into a shower of sparks and drops to the ground. The sausage explodes in its hand. I spin back behind the mother oak as projectiles impact the bark on the other side.

The truth is evident. I had it so very wrong! I now know this with certainty.

Those were not sausages.

I take a tentative step forward to ensure my archenemy is dead. When I look to the nearby tree to offer an apology to the owl, of course, it is not there. Only its claws remain, still clutching the branch.

The mechanical bee makes a sudden low, rumbling sound like distant thunder. Then it stops. But no, that did not come from the mess of wires and metal before me. Not the dead Vengeance Bee.

It came from the river. I turn to see a spray of water glistening in the moonlight. From an explosion.

My heart sinks to my stomach.

"Emelda."

Chapter Thirty-Seven

Ryland screamed, "We're hit!"

Bubbles exploded around us. Our world spun off its axis. He tumbled into me, and I crashed against the hull. We were sinking like a stone, bottom first.

Dude was heavy and crushing me into the rear bulkhead of the sub. Couldn't move. I felt his head swivel left and right, wiping cold sweat across my shirt.

"Do you see a leak?" he shouted. "Where's the leak?"

I put my shoulder into his back, trying to push him off me because I couldn't breathe. The porthole turned white, bathing us in blinding light as if some feral god had snatched us up and angrily peered inside.

The minisub shuddered from the shock wave of an explosion just twenty feet above us.

"Did..." Ryland said, leaning forward to get a better look. "Did it miss? How did it miss?"

Twisting to suck a breath in, I said, "I burped Willie."

That had been my very bad, no-good idea, but I'd had no doubt the missile would have blown us to hell. Seconds before it hit, I'd reached up and yanked the valves open full. We dropped as all that air burst from the sub.

"The missile..." His voice trailed off. When it returned, it was just a whisper. "The missile chased the bubbles."

"Not a missile," I said with a moan. My entire body felt bruised and broken. "Drone."

Ryland coughed out a laugh. "Did you see that explosion? *That* was a missile. Technically, since we're underwater, more like a torpe—"

Willie's tail section banged against the river bottom, and Ryland's head bashed against mine. If we ever got out of the damn sub, I'd need a new skull.

Ryland shouted, "Hold on!"

Pressed against the ice-cold metal, my ear filled with the roar of sand and rock grinding against the outside hull as we tipped forward. With a jarring impact, we smashed flat to the riverbed, and everything went quiet. The ring light around the porthole winked out.

"How far down are we?" I asked, my thin voice ringing off the tin walls.

"Uh, I can't see the chart, but the deepest part—"

A spray of water hit him in the chest. Then another burst from his right. The metal all around us began to *tick-tick-tick*.

I swallowed hard. "Do we need power to get back to the surface?"

"No."

Letting out a breath, I said, "Thank God for that."

Ryland put his hands in his lap, letting the spray of cold water dribble through his fingers. "But we need air to do that."

I closed my eyes. "And I let it all out."

"Yep." He nodded slowly. "We won't blow up, so that's a good thing."

"Right."

Ryland shrugged. "Don't know if drowning is much better."

Willie groaned loudly, and I heard a bang next to me. I ran my hand over the hull and felt a dent, like a prizefighter had punched us from outside.

"Maybe you should hold onto something," he said, a soft voice in the darkness.

"We're not moving anymore," I said. "Hold onto what?"

He laughed darkly. "Your breath."

Outside the porthole, I saw something flitting in the black water. Likely the garfish taking one last look. Maybe a *Possible trout!*

Then the glass cracked.

"Of course," I said. "Why not?"

The fish finder's tiny screen, our only light source now, cast everything in an eerie green glow. Eerie turned horrifying once the light hit the circular window. The crack was growing, and once it finished its snaking trek across the glass, a punishing blast of water would rush in.

I felt dizzy and numb from the cold. And I was pretty sure my heart had stopped beating.

"Nope," I muttered, putting my hand to my chest. "She's pumpin' like mad."

"What?"

Waving off Ryland, I looked up at the hatch above us. I'd been sitting for nearly half an hour, so when I rose into a crouching position, my knees cracked. I shot a look at the glass. Nope, just my knees. For the moment, the glass fissure was contemplating its next move.

I gripped the hatch wheel. "We can open this and swim to the surface, right?"

Ryland was lying against the curved hull, splashing his hand in the pooling water.

Willie moaned. The sub sounded like it was in pain.

"You'll never get that open with the water pressure."

"But, um," I said, twisting the wheel enough to free it, "when the water rises in here, we'll be able to push it open."

"Maybe. Some of the shallower parts of this part of the river are only fifty feet."

I let go of the wheel and crab walked over to the big bay window. Without touching the glass, I craned my neck to look up.

"It's too dark to see the surface."

Ryland nodded. "The deeper parts of the river are more like a hundred feet," he said. "But you take a big breath, kick off hard, and—"

The sub shifted, and Ryland shouted, "Hold on!"

"Do you think screaming that *ever* helps?" I shouted back then fell against the hull, which tipped us even farther. Another bang to the head. Then another as I flipped again. I felt like I was in a tumble dryer that was high on a roll of quarters. Over and over and over.

At one rotation, Ryland lost his grip and came crashing next to me. Blood burst from his forehead. I lay on top of him and pressed my feet and hands to the walls of the sub, trying to hold him steady.

Finally, after what felt like a dozen rotations, we stopped. The very woozy Ryland, *once again*, ended up on top of me. By some metrics, I believe that now qualified us as officially dating.

I shoved him aside as gently as I could, and when I put my head back, exhausted, my vision blurred. I lifted myself from the rising water and found Ryland on his side, half of his face submerged.

Grunting with the effort, I dragged him by his sodden overalls and propped him against a crisscross of white PVC tubes. Where had the tubing on the floor come from? That didn't make sense. Until it did.

Right. The floor wasn't the floor.

When I looked at the middle of our cramped space, I saw the hatch wheel peeking out of the water. We'd capsized. Our only way out was now buried in dirt, sand, and silt.

By some miracle, the glass hadn't busted during our roll. Outside the window, I saw a flicker of dark green.

On the ceiling, Ryland's "sonar" lit up: *Possible trout!*

If nothing else, we were putting on a hell of a show for the garfish. With nothing but seaweed to stare at all day, it was now binge-watching the *Stupid Humans* program. And it obviously found us endlessly entertaining.

Well, not endlessly.

If we couldn't find a way out in the next minute, it would come to an end pretty quick.

"We've rolled onto the hatch," I shouted over the sound of the water rushing in. The leak in our hull had torn wider. Then I looked at Ryland. *Why isn't he answering me?*

Blood from his hairline drizzled down his face. When I shook him, his eyes flickered tiny white smiles at me then closed again.

Dammit!

Okay, just breathe, I thought to myself.

Just not too deeply.

Twisting around to grab the hatch, I tried spinning the wheel. No good. It was buried in mud.

"Okay, okay. I can fix that," I said. "How do I fix that?"

I sloshed through the freezing water to look out the window. A pure black void. Except a tiny flicker of dark green in the distance. The curious fish had either gotten bored with our show or didn't like sad endings.

"You're missing out, fish," I whispered. "Gonna be epic."

My words were much bolder than I felt. With water rising higher and higher around me, I stared out the porthole toward the surface and said a quiet prayer, then added, "From here to there."

I picked a spot on the wall next to Ryland. I took a deep breath. Then I launched forward and smashed my shoulder into the thick metal. As the sub rocked, I leaned onto the upper part of the wall to keep it going. Nothing doing. It rolled back, and I fell into the water.

I needed to roll the sub one-hundred-eighty degrees. Or, hell, just ninety degrees. Enough to get the hatch out of the sand. Then I could open it and get us out.

If I could roll it.

Dripping with ice water, I got back up, raised my leg, and kicked the wall.

The wall shook, and Willie moaned.

"Oh, shit."

Okay, no more kicking. Crawling, maybe? I wove my feet between the air pipes and leaned forward, but all the water was making the sub bottom-heavy. It didn't budge. I reached up, wrapping my arms around the fish finder, and lifted myself higher on the sub's wall.

The screen flickered. *Possible trout!*

Ignoring the device, I pulled myself even higher, my arms straining and shaking. I screamed as loud as I could, "Come on!"

The only answer I got was another tiny flutter of green through the glass. The fish had returned for what was gonna be a hell of a series finale.

"*Season* finale," I said, coughing as I corrected myself. "Season one. Season two, already renewed."

With all the strength I had left, I lifted myself up, and, caution be damned, kicked at the wall. I screamed and screamed and kicked again. Harder and harder. If nothing else, I was going to tear the fucking sub apart and swim through the gap.

The sub twisted. Shifted. Moved.

Dammit, we were rolling down another hill!

"Come *on*!" I shouted and ended up on my back again as I flipped over. I braced for the next rotation, but instead, Ryland rolled from the front of the sub and smashed into me. Then we both fell and landed hard on the hull.

"Oh, shi—"

A biblical flood of water rushed toward us, and everything went dark. We were submerged. I reached around to find my unconscious friend, grabbed him under the chin, and lifted both of us to the surface.

Not easy to do. The water had risen so high I had to stand on my tiptoes.

Wait.

How was I standing in the cramped sub?

Looking up, I got my answer. Blinking away water, I saw a circle of dull green-gray light. The porthole. I was standing on the rear hull. The sub had flipped onto its tail end. Had an air pocket lifted the bow?

Before me, the glow of the porthole grew brighter. We weren't on the river bed. We were moving up!

For a moment, bright green filled the window. Not garfish green; this was like neon. Then it was gone, and in its place was an impossible sight.

The stars.

The dark sky.

The beautiful grin of the crescent moon.

I watched the pinpricked night as waves sloshed over the cracked glass. A minute later, the silhouettes of treetops eclipsed the night sky. Sand ground against the hull, and then the sub tipped, gently this time, until we were flat once again. There was a roar from the rush of water, but this time, it was rushing out, not in.

The hatch had opened, and an enormous figure in a green onesie poked its head in.

"Emelda?" the green man said. "Is this you?"

I laughed. Water streamed down my face, but it wasn't from the river. "Did you think there might be another sunken sub out there?"

"I hope not." He bobbed his head left. "I believe I got a tiny cramp from the swimming."

Chapter Thirty-Eight

"I'm okay, I'm okay," I said to the massive green man, as I rolled out of the minisub and onto the hard-packed sand. Sucking in deep breaths, I waved my hand toward the open hatch. "Get him. Get Ryland."

Kane pulled the sub onto its side and poked his head in.

"Careful!" I said and coughed. "He's hurt."

Kane disappeared into the open hatch up to his calves then dragged Ryland out with his hands hooked under the man's armpits. Not that they looked like hands. They looked like cartoon oven mitts. A surreal situation made more surreal.

Gently, Kane loaded the half-conscious Ryland onto his shoulder. My mind was spinning. Loopy. The green figure carried the much-smaller human as if he was trying to get an infant to sleep. He was even gently rubbing the man's back. He'd make a great daddy.

Why in the world did that come to mind?

Kane carried Ryland to the tree line and laid him softly in a patch of grass. The moment the man hit the earthen bed, his eyes popped open.

He blinked and stared at the big green creature. "Am I dead?"

"I hope you are not," Kane said. "Because that would mean I am also dead. I do not see my wolf ancestors here. Only a man dressed as if he were in a jug band. And I am wearing a man sock."

Ryland put his fingers to his wound and winced. "I thought... wasn't that suit black?"

Kane nodded his neon-green matchstick head. "All the black has washed off in my heroic river rescue. Except for Reeboks. They are still black. But very sloshy when I walk."

The man on the ground put the heels of his hands to his eyes. "I'm still not convinced I'm not dead. I understand ten percent of what you're saying."

"That's about par," I said, getting up to my knees and brushing off sand. "How's the head?"

Ryland assured us he was fine, and when he washed his face in the river, he seemed okay. Dazed and damp, with a two-inch gash at his hairline, but fine.

When I looked up, a dark void blotted out half the northern night sky.

"We're about a hundred yards from the foot of the dam," I said, uneasily getting to my feet. The cold-water bath had made my muscles feel creaky. I looked at the minisub lying on its side. "You know, Kane, I woulda made it. I just had to roll her a bit to get the hatch open."

"Yes, of course," he said and pumped his fists in the air. "You were doing very well. And I thank you for allowing me to rescue you both."

He turned to Ryland, who was kneeling by the shore, and put his meaty hand on the man's shoulder.

Ryland tipped over. "I'm fine. Just resting."

I asked Kane, "You're thanking me... for you rescuing us?"

"Yes, I feel fuzzy feelings by helping. So while I help you, I also get emotional, heart-happy gift from this," my friend said. "You are welcome. And thank you!"

"Well, you are welcome," I said, smiling. "And thank you."

Ryland got back up, sat atop a log, and stared at his minisub. Half beached on the shoreline, it lay on its side, looking like a sea creature that had crawled out of the water and died.

"Willie is all banged to hell," he said, slurring his words a little. "Holes in the hull. Dents across the bow and stern. The front glass is spiderweb cracked."

I nodded to him. "I'm sorry we killed your boat, Ryland."

"Ha, killed?" he said, put his hands on his knees, and pushed himself to his feet. "It'll take a hell of a lot more than a few cuts and scrapes to put her down."

"Her? I thought Willie was a he?"

He cocked an eyebrow. "Wilhelmina is most definitely a she. All boats are shes. Named after my first wife."

"First?" I raised an eyebrow. "How many times have you been married?"

"Never been," he said as he inspected his baby. "I haven't found the right Wilhelmina yet."

"Do you meet a lot of Wilhelminas?"

"Not a one." He grinned at me. "Probably why I'm still single."

The guy had just been shot at by a missile, nearly drowned, and his pride and joy had been beat up like a boy band at a motorcycle rally. And he was still smiling.

"She can't go back into the drink like this," he said and nodded toward the woods. "I'll head back and grab Willie in the morning."

"The road's out," I said.

Kane added, "There is also angry buzzy bees with exploding sausages."

Ryland looked at my big green friend and furrowed his brow. "I can't see your face, so it's hard to work out if you're kidding."

"Don't mind him. He's French Canadian," I said. "How you gonna get back?"

The sub pilot shrugged. "I've spent my life on the water. And below it," he said, walking toward the shoreline. "Current's not fast, so I can swim my way back. And she'll be fine here because that lot in the dam will have other things to deal with."

I looked back toward the massive concrete wall straddling the river. "Oh?"

"You're going in, yeah?" he said. "Grab those disruptors out of the sub. After you slap those on one of their turbines, they'll be too busy to worry about my broken Willie."

***

Kane and I stalked in and out of the trees and stayed low, trying our best to keep out of sight. Not easy with a device as big as a tuna can stuffed into each front pocket. And while sneaking around with a guy who looked like a life-size version of the green "Walk" dude you see at intersections.

About fifty feet from the base of the dam, massive chunks of limestone, slippery rocks, and uneven terrain made the trek increasingly difficult. Kane tweaked his head left and went to a long bulge covered in decaying leaves and moss. I'd thought it was a hill, but he brushed away the muck and exposed smooth concrete.

We traced it back and discovered this was like one of those huge cement sewer pipes they bury underground.

"It just stops," I said, staring at the spot where the "hill" ended in a thicket of bushes and the remains of trees that had tumbled down the slope heading to the river. When Kane yanked out the shrubs and dead branches, he found something odd. A door.

"How did you know this was here?" I said, inspecting the entry. "It's all covered in rotting wood."

He pointed to brown splotches across the metal door. "Smelled of rust. Unusual aroma for the forest."

"You think you can bust it open?"

"Perhaps," he said, taking a step back. "However, it looks like it goes under the dam, yes?"

Peering around it, I nodded. "Not under the dam, but it does go into the earth. But I bet it's some old maintenance entrance from when it was first built."

"Hmm. Underground tunnel," Kane said, lowering his head. "I am not a fan."

Chapter Thirty-Nine

We sloshed through the tunnel, trying to keep as quiet as possible. Since it was as dark as a tomb, I had to use my phone's light to see where we were going. Near the entrance, a sludge covered the walls, swallowing most of the light. Sad rainbows shimmered off the ankle-high water. The oily smell made my nose twitch.

As we walked further, the interior turned gray, much of it flecked with peeling red paint. Every few feet, rusted machinery hung from the walls like old battleship barnacles. Cloth frayed from thick wires that led to busted gears and long-dead motors.

Ribbed glass couplings poked out below metal boxes. I'd seen similar devices on top of power poles in my old neighborhood. Glass insulators whose wiring had crumbled away after a century of disuse.

Kane pointed his big green nose up and sniffed the air. I pointed the light ahead. It looked like a black hole.

"I can't see the end of this thing," I said.

He looked forward. "The end is near."

"Don't say stuff like that."

Kane motioned to writing on the concrete walls where they weren't slathered with grime and dark-yellow streaks. Some of it appeared to be stenciled instructions indicating maximum current loads. Others were warnings I didn't understand like, "Look at your disconnects" and, more ominous, "Keep your mind on your business."

Every few feet, we could see where someone had hand-painted a name with dates. I'd seen writing like that before. On tombstones.

"What do these say? Numbers with words."

I flashed my light ahead and saw the hint of horizontal lines rising from the floor. Stairs. From what I could estimate of our progress, we should have been close to the base of the dam.

I stopped and inspected one of the names and dates. "Big construction projects like this don't just cost money, they cost lives," I said, feeling tightness in my chest. "Especially a hundred years ago. They weren't big on safety."

Kane ran his finger over one name. "This is a person, yes?"

"Was," I said, tapping the writing. "I'm guessing ol' Alister Gualtieri got crushed or fell. Damn. Alister was just twenty-two years old."

"Why would they put this here?"

Shrugging, I pointed the light farther down the tunnel. "Might just be to remember the guy. And there were always rumors—don't know if they're true—that when men died on big projects like this, they dropped the body into the wet concrete."

Kane flinched and backed away from the wall.

"Rebar bones." I popped my eyebrows up and down. "It's just a legend. I doubt it's true."

He turned his big green head toward the names. "So dead bodies may be within these walls?"

"Best not to think about it."

Ignoring my own advice, I couldn't stop thinking about it as we walked in silence for the next few minutes.

Just twenty-two. And he'd spend an eternity encased in rock.

The horizontal lines did turn out to be a short stack of concrete steps. I shined the light up and could see a massive slab of iron on a track.

I read aloud the faded stenciled words on the front of it. "Fire Door."

"Fire?" he said as his damp Reeboks slapped up the steps. He traced his finger over the word. "Water is everywhere. Why would they worry about fire?"

"Probably because if there was a fire, you didn't want it to spread through the tunnels," I said and pushed on the door. It wobbled just a little. "And they might have stored the fuel for the machines in here."

"This would explain the petrol smell."

"Right." I quickly checked behind us because I was getting paranoid, then joined him at the top of the stairs. "Looks like this door can be tripped to shut quickly. Once fire gets going on fuel, it's hard to put out."

Kane lowered his head. "I have seen such a thing. My human parents died in such a fire."

I put a hand on his green shoulder. "They seemed like very kind people."

"The best," he said, nodding. "I think of them often, for they are always with me. I hear their words in my head."

"Now, you're starting to sound like Edgar." I pointed at the door. "See if you can get that open."

Kane gripped the door, wrapping his fingertips around the big metal slab.

"Don't just yank it off," I whispered. "I think it slides open."

He repositioned his feet and shoved.

Crrreeekkk!

The rusty wheels ground and screeched against the rusty track, and the sound pierced my soul to the core. My hands shot to my ears. I wanted to pull one away to wave him off, it was so crazy loud, but I worried the squeal of it could split an eardrum.

Finally, it stopped. When Kane let go, the grinding started again as the door began to slide back. Kane grabbed a busted cement block and placed it in front of the door.

"Yeah," I said. "So much for sneaking in quietly."

"Door is open," he said. Nodding forward, he added, "More stairs go up."

"Yes, they do." I patted the two devices in my pockets. Sure, that didn't do anything, but it felt like I was at least doing something. Like getting geared up for battle. "You ready for this?"

"For what?"

I laughed. "I don't know. Whatever is up those stairs."

Kane turned to me and stared. Or at least, I thought he stared. Hard to tell.

"Listen, you're gonna have to at least pull your head outta that thing." I looked up at the door. "And we'll have to be pretty quiet. It might mean 'furrow and frown' will be the only way we can talk with each other."

His goofy green face pointed down at his cartoon body. "I did tell Rick the movie man that I would not damage man sock."

"Right," I said. I bent down and searched for something sharp. "But it'll be a lot more damaged if you get torn up by any monsters in there because we can't communicate quietly."

"This is true."

Digging through a wooden bucket next to the stairs, I found a rusty cement trowel. It would have to do. Kane grabbed the fabric on either side of his chest and held it toward me.

I spun him around. "I'll do it on the back, so Rick doesn't see it right away."

With the edge of the trowel, I split the fabric down the center, exposing his broad shoulders. I cut it down to just above his tailbone.

Kane tried to pull his arms in, but the skin-tight fabric clung to his fingers. I laughed. It was totally ludicrous.

"Bow your head," I said. He did, and I frowned. "I still can't reach. Get on one knee, my knave." Once he did, I reached around to the gap and lifted the sock material over his head. His face just inches away from mine, he gave me a big grin.

"Hello to you, Emelda."

"Hi, baby Kane," I said and chuckled. "It is like being reborn."

"I have done this already."

"You wanna sound cool?" I said and gave him a conspiratorial look. "You say, 'Been there, done that, got the T-shirt.'"

He nodded then quickly got to his feet.

I still had my hands wrapped in the suit, so when he did, it stripped him down to his stomach, showing off, I'll admit, a finely sculpted chest.

Uh-uh. Don't get distracted.

With the two of us working the clingy green fabric, we got it down around his waist. From there, I took the two floppy arms and wrapped them around his midsection. He looked ridiculous, but I wasn't going to tell him that.

Over the years, I have learned that it doesn't matter how confident a guy might appear. With just a word, a girl can lift a dude up or bring him down with a simple comment about his appearance. And with great power comes great responsibility.

"That's a good look for you," I lied. "You kind of look like a superhero."

He grinned ear to ear. "I do?"

"Yeah," I nodded and put my hand over my mouth. "A bit more DC than Marvel, but you're making it work."

"I do make it work," he said, lifting his chin. "For I have been there, done that, and have acquired the T-shirt." He looked down at his outfit. "Or rather, a green onesie."

"Close enough."

Kane's shoes were so waterlogged, each step sounded like he was stomping fish. Mine weren't much better after my sub bath and trudging through the tunnel. I held onto the bent handrail at first, then pulled away when I felt gook.

The stairs were made of rough concrete, but when I shined the flashlight down, I could see where a green sludge had grown, died, and regrown over the years, turning it black in places. All I could think of was that every time I breathed, I was sucking down spores.

I stopped thinking about it.

At the top, another door, more modern than the one we'd just been through. I gave him a look, and he nodded. Unlocked. That was promising.

I pushed the door open slightly and saw a brightly lit hall straight ahead and another to our right. Then I heard the low rumble, a long, rolling sound that rose and fell.

"The guard said it sounded like storms in here," I whispered.

"From the waterfall outside, yes?"

I nodded. "Must be."

He grinned at me. It was nice to finally see his face again. "I like waterfalls. Good place to find fish."

"You fished? How the hell does a wolf fish?"

"Not as wolf," he said, poking his head out and looking down the empty corridors. "Mon père taught me this as a boy. He liked to go fishing, but I do not know why he called it this. It was sitting and talking and not catching fish."

I patted Kane on the shoulder. "It wasn't about the fish," I said, pushing the door open wider. No one in sight, but that wouldn't last long.

"Then what is the purpose of this?"

"Probably because he was hanging out with you," I said, steeling myself to go through the door.

He furrowed his brow. "He also drank very much beer. Very much."

"Uh-huh," I said, slipping into the bright hallway beyond. "Also probably because he was hanging out with you."

Chapter Forty

This level of the dam had old-school incandescent lighting. Brushed-steel poles extended from the ceiling every ten feet. Circular caps above the bulbs reflected their cold white glare onto bare concrete floors. The hallways ahead and to my right reminded me of a hospital, sterile and uninviting.

"What do you think?" I closed the tunnel door slowly so it didn't make a sound. "Ahead or right?"

He looked both ways. "Both seem equally perilous."

Straight ahead, then. I started forward, and like Izzy the guard had said, I heard the dull, rolling echo of a storm in the distance. I imagined how many workers had walked these halls over the years, listening to the threat of a hundred-foot waterfall just outside. Death murmuring its dark promises.

Behind me, Kane drew in long breaths. Was he nervous?

"I do not smell them," he finally said.

"Smell who?"

"The Enhanced. Machine oil and rust. Very much mold. And tea."

"Tea?"

About twenty feet from the next door, I turned and looked at him. "What do you mean, tea?"

"Is like coffee but with—"

"I know what tea is, man."

He shrugged. "Tea is what I smell. English Breakfast, I think."

I reached up and tapped him on his nose. "Maybe this place is guarded by British aristocracy. I'd rather take on people than monsters."

"Sometimes, they are one and the same," he said. I looked at him and he gave me a sad smile. "No offense to your species. However, I have found that the scariest monsters are the ones that don't look like monsters."

"You are not making me calm, here, dude."

"Sorry."

When we reached the end of the hallway, I tried the door, and the handle wouldn't turn. I saw a panel to the right about the size of an iPad.

I crossed my arms. "I bet this is for some kind of key card pass."

"No, no, nothing as banal as that," a voice buzzed from an unseen speaker. The screen came to life, and a floating head appeared on the display. I recognized it.

"Janus," I said and took a half step back. "We were just talking about you. Why am I not surprised to see your spongy face?"

His head tilted back as he laughed, and the jowls under his chin wobbled like a slug struggling with a dump. I couldn't put my finger on it, but it didn't look right. When he faced me again, the warbling fat there just kept moving. Weird.

"No surprise, of course," he said. "You're in my house, but I expect you already knew that."

I leaned forward. "So you're *here*? In this building?"

"My dear, I am everywhere. And nowhere."

Kane harrumphed as he leaned against the wall next to the screen. "This makes no sense."

Janus's head bobbled left and right. "Oh, delightful. You've got your bizarre giant with you. Good. Yes, yes. Two birds and one stone and all that."

I've disliked many people in my life but prided myself on not outright hating anyone. As a kid, my grandmother used to say hate stains you, not them. "It darkens your heart while the focus of your rage is happily going about their day, paying you no mind."

Didn't matter. The liquid fire coursing through my veins reached my brain, and tiny explosions burst in my peripheral vision. I *hated* this Steve Janus. Dude was all kinds of evil. Wrong, awful, and vile. And not just the parts that wobbled.

"Listen, I'm a very busy man," Janus said, rubbing his bulbous nose. "But I don't want you to think I've forgotten about you and your pet. In the next few—"

I smashed the device with my fist. The darkened screen shifted and hung by one corner as the storm's muzzled growl seemed to grow louder around us. Or that just might have been in my brain. The rage felt intoxicating.

"He has a grating voice, yes?" Kane said, eyeballing the busted tablet.

The screen fell, and bits of glass sprinkled across the floor. I stared at its electronic wreckage. "Janus is somewhere in this dam."

Kane scratched his beard. "I am glad he is no longer talking. However, it did seem like he was about to say something of vital importance that may influence the outcome of the next few minutes."

"Doesn't matter."

My friend stepped up to the door, avoiding the glass on the floor. He sniffed the air. Then he got a queer look on his face.

I asked him, "What is it?"

"I do not know. No organic smell other than damp and rot. But I still do not smell any of the Enhanced creatures."

"That's good news."

He gave me a single-shoulder shrug and then nodded.

"What?"

"It is hard to describe. A scent of frying."

I chuckled. "Maybe they're cooking us breakfast."

Kane shook his head, looked behind him, and took a few steps back. "Not bacon frying. That is a good smell. This is more like before a storm."

He reached down and tied the two floppy green arms a little tighter then flexed his biceps and banged his fists together.

I asked him, "Does punching your own hands help?"

"Fist banging helps me focus."

"Uh-huh," I said, moving another step back. "Some thoughts are best not said out loud."

Kane rushed forward and threw his side into the door. Any other dude? That would have cracked his shoulder blade and his arm and probably rattled several teeth out of his head.

The door buckled, and the handle flew down the hall.

When he stepped back, I could see that his shoulder was red. Then a trickle of blood ran down his arm. He eyed it for a moment and wiped it with his fingers. He licked them.

"Gross," I said.

He took a few more steps back, and I held up a hand. If he went at it with the same force, he'd probably crash through the door and out the other side of the next room.

Examining the busted frame, I could see inside. No lights within, but I saw what looked like tiny, upside-down smiles. Whatever was inside was reflecting the light from our side. But nothing moved. Nothing snarled. Nothing raced toward me with gnashing teeth and swiping claws.

I put my fingers through the gap and gave it a tug. The door rattled. I lifted my leg and let out a yell, smashing my heel into it. The door spun sideways and fell to the floor.

We stood there staring into the dark room.

Pointing at the door on the floor, Kane said, "I loosened it."

The weirdest feeling rippled through me despite nothing moving in the room. Despite no sounds of creatures or threats. Despite the quiet after the door slammed to the ground, one word screamed in my mind.

Run.

Before us, lights flickered to life, fluorescents buzz-blinking awake. The first images I saw reminded me of walking into a bar's cooler. CO2 tanks. Rounded at the top then fatter below.

The room was at least three times longer than it was wide, the size of a cargo container. The bases of the tank things lit up with spots of light that glowed brighter and brighter. First, they appeared red, then they flipped to white in unison.

"Oh darn," I said.

In the room's two upper corners, large screens rolled, and once again, we saw the face of Steve Janus. Bigger this time. And a much bigger smile than before.

"You've saved me some time, so thank you for that," he said, tapping away at an unseen keyboard. "Meet my PETs."

As he said the last word, a piercing two-tone alarm filled the air so loudly I had to slam my hands to my ears. The fluorescents flickered out, and a red light spun in the middle of the ceiling. When I looked down, I saw the cylindrical tops of each of the machines rise a few inches then clank into place. An oval that looked like a pupilless white eye glowed in the middle of every one of them.

"Personnel-eradicating semiautonomous tanks," Janus said, leaning back and putting his hands behind his head. "Quite proud of that little acronym. Paid a consultant millions for it."

The PETs rose from the floor as wheels popped out from their bases. The doorway lifted. No, the entire *wall* was lifting.

Then the robots advanced.

Chapter Forty-One

I raced past Kane and had to shout his name to get him moving. What the hell was he staring at?

Then it occurred to me.

Janus's killer robots were predators, but they were *machines*, not animals. Kane's experience with creatures who wanted him dead would have shown aggression in either facial expression or body posture.

These had neither.

"Run!" I shouted.

That was all it took. The half-green man breezed past then spun to face me. Dude was running as fast as I was while doing it backward. I needed to get back into shape.

"Why are we running from vacuum cleaners?"

Struggling to catch my breath, I pointed to the corner ahead, and he ran into the next hall. *Still* running backward.

Between breaths, I shouted at him, "How close are they?"

"I cannot see them anymore," he said. "They are in other hall."

"We gotta get out of this one."

Pointing ahead to another door, I nodded. I was too out of breath to actually form words. Kane spun on a heel, and his Reeboks squish-stomped toward it. He tried the handle. It didn't budge. When I saw him lift a knee, I shouted for him to stop.

"Wait," I said, catching up to him. I put my hands on my thighs and sucked in deep breaths. "Last time we bashed down a door, we got a swarm of killer robots after us."

"*No, please! Do come in!*"

The voice had come from another tablet mounted on the wall. I hadn't even noticed it. We heard a click of the door lock. Kane reached for the handle, and I smacked his arm.

"Why would you open it?"

He blinked and pointed. "It is now unlocked, no?"

"Right. And the guy who wants us dead opened it."

"Hmm," he said and rubbed his chin. "This does seem out of character. Maybe he feels bad."

That got a laugh from the floating head on the screen. "I love this guy! I wish all my adversaries were as dumb as he."

Smash.

This time, Kane had bashed the tablet, and it had disintegrated into a million pieces. He looked down at his knuckles as a trickle of blood dribbled between his fingers. He put his hand behind his back.

"Apologies. Knee-jerk reaction," he said then furrowed his brow. "Or rather, fist-jerk reaction."

Behind us came the squeal of tires across polished concrete. We turned. The PETs were rounding the corner. And even though they were just machines, the silver tanks seemed to clamor to get to us like a pack of hungry dogs vying for their prey.

I considered our options: try the next hallway to our left and hope for another way out or take the door Janus had opened. Neither seemed like a great idea.

Kane squared off against our hunters and raised his fists. The front line was three machines across. The rest of them, maybe thirty, trailed in neat rows.

"They are just metal," he said, grinning wildly. "I believe I can take them."

Almost as if on cue, compartments slid open on either side of the three nearest to us. From one side, metal claws came out and snapped in the air. From the other opening protruded a long spike that looked like a titanium pool cue sharped to a point.

Kane licked his lips. "I believe I can take some of them."

The corner turn had slowed the robots, but now, on the straightaway, they were picking up speed.

I slapped Kane in the arm and ran down the next corridor. After a few panicked steps, I realized I couldn't hear him behind me. I spun around, still running, but not as fast as he could like that.

"Kane! Let's go."

He looked at me, looked at the killer robots coming for him, then shook his head.

"You must find out where Marata and Doc Hammer have gone," he shouted to me. "Do this."

"We'll do it together!" I said as I got to the next corner. To the right was another hall much longer than the others. At the end, I could see a large red door. Through its vertical window, I could see a set of stairs.

"I found a way off this floor," I shouted to him.

"You go. I will draw the angry vacuums away," he said. Before I could say another word, he elbowed the door behind him and slipped through.

Dammit!

I bolted down the hall.

When I reached the door, I tried pulling it open, but it only rattled. Then I looked up. Like the one at the top of the outside tunnel, this was from the original design. The door was on a spring-loaded track.

I grabbed the fire door's iron handle and pulled sideways. It started to slide, its wheels complaining as they ground along the track in the floor.

A huge *crash* echoed down the hall. Then more crashes and the sound of metal colliding into metal. Under the cover of all that racket, I got the heavy fire door open enough to slip through. I spun around and pushed it back then ducked low.

I knew what that noise had been. Janus's PETs had smashed through the other entryway, chasing Kane.

Shit, shit, shit!

In my stomach, I felt acid churn. I couldn't let him—

Something metallic clanked upon the vertical window above my head. I pressed myself against the door, flattening my body as much as I could. A beam shone through the glass, a spotlight illuminating the stairs. When I craned my neck up to look, I saw that one of the evil robots had extended its pill-shaped head and was scanning the area on my side.

I held my breath.

Squeezing my legs, my stomach, and my arms rigid, I didn't move. If it didn't see me, it might leave. Then I did move but not on purpose. The PET had slid its long spike under the door and was dragging it open.

Stunned, I watched it. Frozen.

I had to hide, but I didn't know where to go. The spike brushed up against my leg, and the spring-loaded door slid back. The metallic appendage then reappeared as it punched a hole in the door inches from my shoulder. A blinding light shone through it then winked out.

A throaty buzz emitted from the other side of the door. With nowhere else to go, I rolled forward.

Before I hit the floor, a second hole burst open in the exact spot where I'd been hiding. If I'd still been there, the spike would have skewered me like a shrimp kabob.

Whirring and buzzing and scraping rang through the stairwell. The machine's other arm hit the door. Was it trying to punch through?

No. The spike had gotten stuck in the door.

The machine shook and banged until it had wiggled itself free. One tip of its claw poked through the hole, and it began pulling the door aside again.

"Ah, nope."

I jumped up and crab walked to the stairs then stood and began taking them two at a time. The door slammed against the wall. The PET stood in the entryway. With its claw and metal spike raised like arms, the machine's white eye darted around until it found me. A panel opened on its chest, and behind it, I saw... a waffle?

Something in my brain screamed for me to duck. I did.

A metal dart cut through the air and stuck in the gray concrete wall above my head. Not a waffle, then. The robot was shooting projectiles out of some honeycomb-like device in its chest.

I clambered up to the landing and bolted to the next set of stairs as another dart struck the wall behind me, spitting bits of rock and dust into the air. Blinded by the debris, I hit the first step wrong, tripped, and fell sideways.

"Ow!" I screamed as my ribs felt like they'd folded inward.

The eye shifted, blinding me with its piercing white light. The dart launcher swiveled toward me and rotated. A new deadly dart locked into place.

I ducked, covering my head.

Then I heard a crash. When I opened my eyes, I saw the light wobble as the spike shot wildly into the base of the stairs, missing me by just inches.

Stuck, the machine spun its wheels on the stone floor, and it sounded like the thing was screaming in frustration. The fire door had sprung back, smashed into the robot, and pinned it against the doorframe.

The PET shot its claw arm out and shoved so hard, I heard the massive fire door fly off its track and smash against the opposite wall. But by that time, I was already rounding the corner on the next set of stairs. I heard the *thwack-thwack-thwack* of more darts hitting the bottom of the stairs.

At the second landing, another door. I tried the handle. Locked from the inside.

The echoes of skidding wheels filled the corridor below. Then they stopped, and I could hear just the whirring sound of servos. What was it doing?

In the dim light of the stairwell, I carefully peeked below. I watched as its wheels turned and articulated to manage the incline. The front two rollers gripped the first step, then it raised its metal body. Another set of two wheels landed next to the first, then the initial set advanced upward.

Huh. Killer robot has trouble with stairs. What a stupid design.

Its eye whirred upward, but I snapped my head back before it spotted me. Splinters of light glittered across the wall. I heard more whirring, and the wheels skidded and bumped. Then came the sounds of the machine rolling away at high speed as it raced back into the hall.

I spun and looked at the locked door. No tablet on this side. Hmm. Maybe the stairwells were Janus free? That would be something to keep in the back of my mind.

Above, I could see two more floors. Hopefully, one of those doors would open, or I'd have to go back. At least for now, I was leaving the scary robots behind.

Halfway up from the second floor to the third, I had a chilling thought.

The machine would have *eventually* made it up the stairs, but it had stopped. Either it had gotten a signal from its metal brethren, or it knew I couldn't get away regardless of which floor I went to.

Because each level had an army of killer robots waiting for me.

Chapter Forty-Two

Kane

As I run very fast, the crash behind me makes the hairs on the back of my neck arise.

I do not know why this happens. Mon père once explained to me that the human body has responses born from its transition from prey to predator.

"Most important of these," he'd told me, speaking French, as this was always his preference, "is the fight-or-flight response. The blood pumps hard enough to make your arms throb. Your brain fires with electricity. The vision sharpens. Your muscles prime to run toward or away from a challenger."

I asked him, "How do you know which path to take? Run away or attack?"

He shrugged and chuckled. "Your feet will decide that, young man. If you look up and you are running away, then you are in flight. If you are running toward, you must be ready to fight."

"What if you are frozen in place?" I asked, remembering a time when a family of starving bears had surrounded me as a cub. "Your feet unmoving as if roots have grown into the ground."

He'd tousled my hair. "Then you are dinner, my boy."

Alas, my feet have taken me to a dead end. The Reebok shoes may be confusing them.

Breathing heavily, I stand in a cold, dark room with a lone metal table. One wall is covered in writing. Just scribbles to me. On the opposite side, I see a door.

This opens to a smaller room, but within, another passage is open to my right. A second turn to my left, and my feet are now taking me down a short hall with a low ceiling.

My human father never actually explained why the neck hairs arise. What purpose does this have? Was this a trait bestowed by the chaos of evolution or the human god?

It is not like I can shoot the hairs out like a porcupine. Unless this is an ancestor I do not recall. I doubt this. I have seen my predecessors during my moonstruck transformations. New ones each time, but never have I seen a fat, spiky rodent.

Behind me, a clatter and clash of metal. Wood breaking and splintering. Something glass falls and shatters. The angry robot vacuums are following my circuitous path and getting closer.

Ahead, I see another door and reach for it as I run. The hair on my arm rises. Why is this? It serves no purpose!

Just before I get to the handle, a fist flies toward my face. Where did this flying fist come from, I wonder?

Too much wondering. I lost focus.

The fist connects with my jaw, and I stumble, hitting the wall to the left of the door. Quickly, I push off with my powerful bare arms and turn to my new foe. Alas, my Reebok laces have freed themselves. I trip on them and land face first on the floor.

"Who the hell are you?" the large bald man says. His eyes fill with bloodlust and rage. Bulging arms burst from a navy-blue work shirt. On his lapel, it has a word I cannot read, so I decide it says Earl.

Earl yells, which is unnecessary because he is standing over me, "What in the hell are you wearing, boy? Are those green tights?"

My head snaps toward the hall from which I came.

The man above me leans toward his shoulder radio and depresses a button. "Hey, Wyatt. I think some ballet dancers have broken in."

The radio crackles. "What?"

Laughing, Earl slaps the wall with an open palm. I hear the machines clattering closer, their wheels skidding across the concrete. The huge man stares at me, hands rolled into fists. He is so focused on me, he does not hear the machines. This does not matter, for they are on the same side. That side, of course, is the "kill Kane" side.

I dislike people on that side. Or killer robot vacuums on that side.

Too eager to wait for my response, he throws a second fist at me, which I easily roll away from. His hand smacks the wall and crunches masonry beneath it. I am happy to have escaped the blow, but I did not escape the smell of the man's exposed armpit. Chemicals and sweat. And very much meat.

As he cradles his fist in his hand, I leap up and consider the open door behind him. Instead, I turn the handle on the closed door.

Before slipping into the next room, I make a suggestion. "You should reconsider your dietary choices. Occasionally, maybe a leafy salad."

He goes to punch me with his uninjured fist, but I am faster, of course. I am wolf. Well, a wolf who currently looks like an upside-down lime Popsicle.

Faster than a lightning strike, I swing my arm around and smash my fist into his. The man retracts the hand, yelping in pain, as he stumbles back through his open door.

There is a time to fight, but there is also a time to plan. To consider options. Abscond from a current location to find another so one might strategize.

Some may see this as hiding. This is not hiding. No, no. Wolves do not hide. Not even wolves who are green Popsicle people.

Now I am thinking about Popsicles. So good. I prefer the grape ones.

Leaping through the open door, I realize I may have made an error in judgment. A better plan may have been to go through the door Earl entered through. Alas, that way, there be Wyatts.

But at least there may have been a way out. Not so here. In this room, I smell solvents, soaps, and bleach. Possibly some type of storage area for cleaning supplies.

Good! I can fashion an incendiary device from all of these chemicals and melt my metal foes into gelatinous slag!

My heart darkens. I do not even know how to make spaghetti, so firebomb construction would be outside my skill set.

Weaving around mop buckets and white plastic drums, I pass by three stainless steel tanks. An arm's length away, I can feel their heat. My animal-tuned ears pick up on the rush of water and the hiss of steam.

The hairs on my arms bristle at this. Am I cold? Why do they stand erect so?

To my left, there are five lockers, side by side, nearly cutting the room in two. Behind these could be a fine place to come up with a plan. As I round them, my instincts trigger, and I raise my fists to five new foes!

Who are these oh-so-silent and stealthy men?

I relax. Not men. They are what mon père would have called rain slickers. A fancy word for raincoats.

Pain scorches my shoulder, and a blast echoes around the room. I leap behind the lockers and feel a warmth spreading down my back. When I reach my hand around, it comes back red.

"You've run out of room in the room, moron," the angry voice of Earl shouts at me.

Rising to one knee, I see a mirror next to the lockers. An angry red gash gapes across my shoulder blade, blood dribbling out. A pipe from the boilers I saw earlier wraps along the back wall, so I rip away the insulation and press my wound to the hot metal. The skin sizzles and burns.

There is pain, but I endure it with ease. Actually, quite a bit of pain. Wow. That is more pain than I expected. My eyes water slightly. But at least the bleeding has stopped.

Another shot rings out, and my foot kicks out toward the wall. *Alors!* He has shot me in my exposed foot! I look down and see a hole in the Reebok. I wince. I am not taking very good care of borrowed clothing.

I must focus!

Okay, if television is correct, he only has four more bullets. Can my body take four more bullets?

In need of intel, I peek around the side of the lockers but pull back quickly. A slug whizzes past my cheek and sparks upon the wall. Very close. But just three more bullets.

Hmm. I worry this may only apply to those in western shows. Six-shooters, yes? Earl sounds like an old-time western name, yes, but it is one I assigned to him. He could be a Chuck.

The man laughs. "You got nowhere to go, asshole," he says, and I hear him take a step forward.

"Yes, admittedly, this was a poor choice," I say then go for more intel. "You would not happen to be a cowboy, yes?"

Oddly, the man does not answer with words. He *barks*. Barks?

Carefully peering around the corner, I see Earl (possibly Chuck) with his arms at his sides. His gun falls from his fingers, and he stares at me with a queer expression upon his face. However, the face is not the most interesting part. It is the spike sticking out of his throat. A pointy, metal shard-like thing. Another pierces his shoulder, and he convulses.

Slowly, the man half turns, and another four strike his body.

Thut-thut-thut-thut.

His head turns back to me as if in a plea for help. There is nothing I can do. And I do not think I would help. This is a man who shot me twice. That does not engender a desire to help.

He falls against the doorframe, crumpling in the gap. Just beyond, I see six then eight then twelve angry Janus robots heading toward me. I pull my head back and survey my surroundings. Very quick survey because there is little to look at.

Why did they kill the large man?

Were they not on the same side? The angry vacuums shot him as if he were my ally. Hmm. I believe they see all humans as enemy. This is possibly why Steve Janus had them secured in the room.

The hairs on my arms and neck grow straighter. *Why is this happening?* Do they say I am cold?

I hear the scrape of metal arms and claws as the tenacious robots push the man from the door. Once they are through, they will easily overtake me. They now search for more humans to kill with flying spikes. For not the first time, my wish is to not be human.

Gears grind. Rubber tires squeal. A battle cry of a kind.

I stare at my backs of my hands, where all the hairs stand. My teeth chatter. I feel a shiver and wrap my bare arms around my chest.

I must be cold. I will die alone and cold.

I cannot do anything about the former, but the latter...

I untie the flappy arms from around my waist, another useless move. My vision blurs. I will have failed Emelda. This is what hurts most. I am not afraid to die, because my ancestors await me. If they watch me now, they will see me as a disappointment. But this is not the first time they would judge me so.

I will deal with the shame. I cannot deal with failing my friend.

I slip the man-sock sleeves onto my arms and feel... warmer. The machines smash into buckets and knock mops to the floor. I hear the crunch of wood beneath their scrabbling wheels.

Pulling the green nylon over my shoulders, I feel better. I do not understand why. How could this thin nylon provide the warmth my body desires?

A chill, like a breath of icy wind, spreads across my face and skull. My neck hairs twitch and prickle.

This must be fear. An odd way for my mind to express it.

Pulling the stretchy sock over my head, I am instantly comforted. My vision takes on a green hue once again. I can feel the split in the fabric across my back, but why does this exposure not evoke the strange, cold-air chill? This gap is where we made the cut in Film Rick's man sock. My heart darkens further. I promised to return the suit unharmed. I dislike promises broken.

Like the one I made to Emelda.

Alas, there is little I can do. I rise to my feet. A wolf does not die on his knees. Standing, I feel the rain slickers at my back, as if they reach out to weakly console me.

The manic clattering of the Steve Janus robots is chaotic. One smashes into the lockers, which tilt toward me. I wait for them to round the corner. I will give them my fiercest scowl! Ah, yes. They cannot see through the man sock. Maybe they will feel my intent.

The first shiny wheel appears, and I feel fear.

This is strange for me. But this is what it is. I want to raise my arms and fight! But something grips me, something within. A fear that I was unworthy of her kindness. Fear that this human risks her life for *me*, and I can do nothing to fulfill my promise to protect her.

Fear that I have failed her.

The first machine is here, its appendages whirling and spinning. Claws snapping. It shifts as another bumps it from behind. Two machines face me. Then three.

They are here.

And, pitifully, I am frozen in fear.

Chapter Forty-Three

On the top level, I crept down the hall, but each step echoed like I was shouting, "Hi, it's just me, Emelda, sneaking around. Come get me!"

The concrete floor looked like it had once had those carpet runners down the middle years earlier. The areas along the walls were faded, dusty, and worn. Down the middle was a strip of clean floor.

Or did the evil, stabby-stabby robots not do so well on the carpet, so they ripped it up?

The one thing going for me, I supposed, was that the constant "storm" outside masked my footfalls a little. However, that made it impossible to hear anyone who might be lurking around a corner. But each turn I took, nobody. Just another spooky hallway.

That was odd.

There were no people milling around. I didn't hear the everyday chatter of voices. Down each passageway, there were rooms, two or three on each side, but no doors. I leaned into the first few and pulled out my phone to shine the flashlight inside. Storage areas with busted wood crates and packing material strewn all around. Tarps bunched along the walls that looked like lazy gray ghosts sitting around, watching an invisible television.

I chided myself. "Do *not* start thinking about ghosts." I was freaked out enough already.

But this was strange—I didn't see any cameras. And Janus *loved* his cameras.

In the Covenant HQ, where Doc Hammer and her lackeys had held Kane. Throughout his Greek mansion in Mexico, and even in the tunnel system beneath the old convent.

Here?

Nada.

Of course, he had a friggin' robot army that could likely feed him video. And the doorway tablet pads I'd seen on the first floor obviously had cameras.

Back in the hall, I looked up. The dam was built like a concrete fortress. Maybe the solid walls were too much of a pain to drill cables through.

The one difference on this top floor was that fire doors had been installed, breaking the corridors into thirds. I cautiously stepped through each, anticipating that clamps would release, and a door would slice me in two. That didn't happen.

I got to a T-junction. Left or right? Both passages looked identical.

Standing in the middle of it, I outstretched my hands. Closed my eyes. I really didn't have time to divine where I should go next. Kane was probably running through halls and jumping boxes and diving around corners to avoid the evil robots on the lower floors.

The sooner I got where I needed to go, some records room, the better. Get the hell out of this tomb.

I cracked an eye open and stared down the passageway to my left. Something tickled my brain about that direction.

Like on the first floor, fat bulbs hung from the ceiling on short cords. Dull metal covers cast their light below. Who had incandescent lights these days? Could you even buy them?

As I walked down the hall, I balled my fists, frustrated. I felt like there were these puzzle pieces floating around me—no people, no cameras, and old-timey lights.

Like something about all those clues was screaming some truth at me I just couldn't hear.

At the next corner, I peeked down the hall.

A dull red glow came from a slash in the wall at the very end. Slowly, I walked toward it, passing cautiously through two more open fire doors. As I got closer, I heard murmuring. Or was that my imagination trying to pull something tangible from the storm's din?

Within ten feet of the door, the murmurs began to coalesce into voices.

There were people inside.

Chapter Forty-Four

Lance looked over at his coworker. Alaina appeared to be just as perplexed as he was.

"Why aren't they attacking him?" Lance asked, pulling at his fingers as he watched the images on the screen. Unlike the drones outside, they had no control of the PETs. Steve Janus had never allowed that. He treated his PETs like pets.

Alaina watched over Lance's shoulder. She then looked at her console. Another of the tiny screens had gone dark. Two more sites left. For her, those screens couldn't go black fast enough. Once they did, the two engineers would take the express car and get the hell out.

It felt like things were spinning out of control. They'd *always* felt a bit out of control, but now, that spin was wobbling more and more.

"I don't..." Alaina said, her mouth hanging open. She watched as the fuzzy camera feeds from the PETs passed right over the enormous man then kept going. "They're just ignoring him. Can you turn the cameras back?"

Lance pushed away from the desk and threw his hands up. "The only reason we've even got that feed is because it's a carrier signal buried inside the boss's watts cast. I can't send commands to them at all."

Alaina leaned forward and pressed her index finger to the screen so hard the tip turned white.

"He's right there!"

Lance sighed. "They're looking for people. They're programmed to attack anyone they see," he said and winced as the camera feed passed over the crumpled body of the big bald guard on the floor. "Which is why they skewered what's-his-face."

"How did they even get out?" Alaina said and shot a quick look at their door. Had she heard something in the hall? "Aren't we supposed to get an alert when he releases his PETs so we can keep to the safe halls?"

"Who knows? Not like Janus has ever had any concern for the people here. All he cares about is the power for his broadcasts. No power, no Steve Janus."

Alaina dropped into her chair and reached for her cup, but she'd already drained it. Nothing left but a damp tea bag. "This whole damn dam just so a guy can run his empire from some little room."

"It's a *lot* of power," Lance said, looking around the room and swallowing hard. "Probably giving us all cancer or something."

"The watts cast powers *those* things,' she said, nodding at the images on the screen. "And look how dumb they are. They eviscerated one of our guys, but some asshole in a green suit? I bet he could walk through this place, and they wouldn't blink an eye. The eye."

Lance shook his head. "The bots target body heat. I bet in that green suit, he's a ghost."

The two of them watched the screen as the PETs pulled out of the old locker room and began racing down the hall. Concrete flooring and white walls whipped past the display. The big green man was no longer in view.

"Unreal! They just bailed and left him behind!" Lance was finding it hard to swallow. Their last night at the dam, so close, and now this. "You think that guy is from The Organization?"

"The Org?" She laughed. "They're ancient history."

"Then who is that guy? Why is he in here?" Lance said then voiced a theory. "Obviously, he knows about the PETs and wore that suit to infiltrate this place. You know what that means?"

"He's coming up here."

"Exactly," Lance said. He flipped his wrist and checked his watch. "You saw the size of him. That guy is a trained killer. And if Brooks is down—"

"There's still Wyatt."

Lance laughed darkly. "They had two guys guarding this whole place? We used to have twenty."

"The boss has more faith in his new robots than humans now."

"Janus is paranoid."

"Wouldn't you be?" Alaina said as she sat back down at her console. "Covenant is crumbling. Just the two sites left."

"Once those are dark, we're out of here." Lance looked at the screen, which showed the fuzzy image of the PETs searching for the intruder. The one they'd *left* back in the storeroom. "Screw it. I'm not waiting for the Green Man to get up here."

"What's that supposed to mean?"

"We're only supposed to keep this place going until all the other sites are down, right?"

"Yeah."

"Then we're done." He slid the chair over and tapped the second-to-last screen on her console. "The Atlanta site will be burning wreckage in the next few minutes."

"But it's not the last one," Ałaina protested, but her heart wasn't in it. Like her partner, she was eager to bail.

Lance shook his head. "That's been a dead site for ages."

"Maybe." She leaned in and stared at the camera feed. "I can't get it to respond to any of the self-destruct commands."

"It's long *dead*. No one can even get to it, and there's nothing more we can do from here," Lance said and jumped from his seat. "I don't know about you, but I'm leaving before that big green dude gets up here. Time to fire up the express car to freedom."

She needed no more convincing.

They ran toward the far corner of the room, pulled open the gate, and got into the century-old elevator. Just as they slammed the mesh door closed, they saw a shadowy figure step into the doorway.

"Have I caught you guys at a bad time?"

Chapter Forty-Five

The room looked so bizarre.

If I'd seen it on a top-secret aircraft carrier or in a spaceship? Yeah, it woulda fit right in.

But this dam was a century old. People who'd been dead before my grandfather was born had written on its walls.

So at the end of a dark and damp hall in the relic of a building, seeing dozens of monitors, computer servers, blinky lights all over the place, and two people inside what looked like an over-sized birdcage?

Seemed outta place.

"Have I caught you guys at a bad time?"

Instead of answering, one of them threw a hand lever, and they started dropping into a square cutout in the floor.

Not a cage. An elevator.

"Wait!" I shouted.

Through the wire mesh, their eyes grew enormous. Chains passing through a hole in the ceiling rattled as the cage slipped lower and lower.

I went to step forward, and the woman pointed something at me. "Stay back!"

In the darkness, I couldn't see what she was holding. So I stood back. "I'm not here to hurt you."

"Right," the man said, now only visible from the chest up. "Tell that to Brooks!"

"Okay, sure. Where is he?"

The woman shouted, "Dead!"

Raising my hands, I pleaded with them. "I only have a few questions. I'm looking for—"

Screens around the room lit up, and I slipped into the darkness of the hallway. Then I heard a familiar voice.

"Oh, no, no, no. That will not do," Steve Janus said. "Returning to your quarters already when there is so much work to be done?"

From the hall, staring through the control room door, I could see the thick chains of the elevator rattle as the car jerked to a stop. The two people inside gawked, only visible from the chin up. I had horrible visions of blades slicing out from the floor and their heads rolling toward me.

"You are contracted until all the sites have been shut down," Janus said.

The two sets of panicked eyes flicked to an area to their right. A screen with his image had to be there.

"If that job is not done, neither are you."

The guy nodded frantically. "The final two sites are both gone. Job's done. And we've got..." He turned his head toward me.

I mouthed, *Don't.*

"There are intruders in the building," he said, his eyes still focused on me. "One guard is already dead, and we don't want to be next."

I stood in the shadows, unsure of what to do. I felt like I was listening in on a corporate Zoom call to the bowels of Hell.

"Ah, yes," Janus's voice piped up with a bit of pep. "I see one of those final locations is fully engulfed, right you are. But the other—the feed is just dark."

The two heads poking out of the floor looked at each other. The woman spoke first. "An explosion probably took out the video link."

Steve Janus laughed. "Probably? I don't do business with 'probably.' I need facts... um, other person."

"Alaina, sir."

"Don't bother telling me your name, because I don't care." Janus sighed audibly. "I need confirmation. A job done right is a job well done. We need to clean up that mess before I can roll out phase two."

This apparently was news to the two heads.

The guy asked, "Phase two?"

"Yes, yes! What do you think my PETs are for? Of course, these are just the Mach One version. You should see Mach Two. Very exciting," Janus said. "But first, those old sites need to be gone. No loose ends."

The woman's fingers hooked through the mesh. "They're dead, sir. There's nothing more we can do here."

"Oh?" Janus said, clearly enjoying the distress he was causing them. "Are you entirely sure?"

"Yes, sir!" the man said, nodding emphatically. "One hundred percent."

"Well, if you are one hundred percent sure..."

The woman said, "Yes!"

"Okay, then. Very good," Janus said in a sing-song voice. "Well, I'm a busy man, so I'll leave you to it."

That got a confused look from the heads. "Leave what to us, sir?"

"Dying," their boss said. "If you would just wait there, I'll have my PETs come up from the lower floors."

"But—"

"As I said, no loose ends and all that," he said. "I'm shutting down phase one, and you are part of phase one. With those sites dead, now it's your turn."

"Sir, please don't—"

"Thank you, bye," the voice said, and the blue glow in the room winked out.

Standing at the door, I stared at the two people poking out of the floor. They stared back. Then they ducked.

"Didn't you hear him?" I shouted, running into the room. "He's got those damn robots tromping up the stairs. When they get here, you're both toast!"

Actually, we were *all* toast if they came. I bolted out of the room and ran to each of the fire doors. It took me a few seconds, but I found their release handles. I flipped the first then the second. Both slammed shut.

When I stepped back into the control room, the two heads ducked again.

"Stop that! I know you're there," I said. I strode over and looked down through the top of the cage elevator. When I crouched, they looked up at me like baby birds. Pitiful.

They stood again, and I knelt to meet their eyes.

"Looks like you guys are in a bad spot," I said. "I'm the only one around here that can help."

The guy frowned at me. "Why would you help us after we tried to blow you up? You were in the sub, weren't you?"

"*That was you?*"

The woman growled and smacked him on the shoulder. She turned to me. "Nothing personal. Just part of the job. Sorry."

Sorry? I rolled my eyes and shrugged.

"Alaina, right?" I asked, and she nodded. "We're looking for two people. Former co-workers of yours, and they're hiding out at one of your sites."

The guy shook his head. "They're all gone. Your friends are toast."

"Friends?" I'd almost shouted the word. "They're *not* friends. Those two are gearing up to release an army of Enhanced animals on the world, and they'll need one of your labs to do that."

"The old animal lab beneath the zoo is gone," the guy said. "Flattened by a gas leak."

"Are you sure?"

"Yes! I helped her do it," he said, pointing at the woman. "Like we told Mr. Janus, all the sites are gone."

The woman frowned at her friend then leaned back on the far side of the cage.

"That's not entirely true," she said, nodding to a bank of screens behind me. "The video feed cut out on the last one. The island."

"It's a dead site," the guy said. "You said so yourself."

"Maybe," Alaina said to him while pointing at me. "But if she thinks someone's trying to restart the program or something, I mean, that would be the place."

I stood and towered over them. "Hold on. What's on the island now?"

"Nothing," he said. "Ilsa Hammer shut it down more than—"

"Wait! Doc Hammer was *there*?"

He nodded. "That's where she first brought the data when she defected from The Organization. The island is where Covenant's Enhanced program began."

I had my answer. Now we just had to get there in time. "I need to know how far off the coast that island is so I can..."

I stopped speaking because the woman was slowly shaking her head.

"What?"

"It's not way out in the ocean," she said, glancing at the man next to her. "It's much, much closer."

Chapter Forty-Six

Kane

Okay. So that was weird.

Where have the stupid robot vacuums gone? Did they sense my power and fieriness and flee with unbridled fear? Not run but roll. But roll so very quickly, yes!

However, I had been the fearful one. Ashamedly so.

When they discovered my hiding spot, the robot predators had taunted me as if playing with their prey.

This is what cats do. Such cold-blooded creatures. Toying with a mouse as it desperately clings to life, hopelessness its only companion. Tiny mouse eyes begging for mercy but finding none.

This was me as three of the machines rounded the lockers to discover me, their soulless eyes twitching. Judging me. As cats do. Very judgy.

In a moment of false bravado, I considered striking first. But beyond those three, the room filled with their murderous kin and deep into the corridor beyond. Each with claws to strike and scrape. My brave front crumbled, and I was left craven.

Immobilized by an icy fear that froze my muscles solid.

The first of the machines twitched then spun its head to the sizzle of flesh on the boiler pipe. The moment it raised a claw to attack, its companions did the same. Ready to kill.

But it was merely a remnant of my skin and blood. A wisp of smoke and steam. The machines retracted their claws. Their eyes spun back to regard me once again. Staring. Unsure.

In unison, their orbs shone left then right. They were looking at the raincoats?

I wanted to shout at them, *Take your best shot, robot carpet cleaners!* But they did not take their best shot. Or any shot. Instead, their eye-lights focused to the floor where I had been kneeling. Then back to the dead guard.

But not looking at me.

Why is...

They were searching for a human. My year-long prayer, in some small way, had been answered. I did not want to be human, and to their eyes, or eye, I was not. I was a green thing. Like the rain slickers.

A ripple of electricity flowed through the robots.

Their metallic pill heads swiveled, and I heard a rumbling and a squealing of wheels. In waves of three, those in the hall began racing away. Soon, all of them were rocketing down the corridor.

For the first time in many minutes, I could move and peek around the dented lockers. I saw the final robot slow and peer into the doorway where the meat-smelling man had leaped at me from. Then it sped up and joined the group.

I am frozen once again but this time in shock.

As I watch the last machine round the passageway corner ahead, my arms slacken. I lift them to strip off the sock head so I can see better. No, my eyes did not fool me. They have left. Searching for more humans to shoot their spikes at.

But that, for now, is not me.

When I pull my arms from the suit, my shoulder complains, but I can handle pain. It sharpens the mind. And each time I move, the mind gets very sharp. Razor sharp. So sharp.

And in that clarity, I know where the robots have sped off to. Emelda. I must go help my friend. They now hunt her.

I take a step forward, and my Reebok burns, which I believe is uncommon for footwear. No, it is *my* foot. When I look down, I see blood spurt from the shoe's black material. Earl's bullet pierced my skin, and only now that I am moving does the blood flow. Each step grows more painful.

Pulling the body sock down to my waist ignites a fire in my shoulder. Tying the arms again is very painful, but I do this.

I hobble through the locker room and step over dead Earl to peer down the corridor from where he came at me with his fist only minutes earlier. A short hallway lined with brick leads to stairs. That is where I must go.

However, my next step falters as my trailing foot does not comply. I look down and see a blood-smeared shoe print on the concrete. The bullet sliced something vital to its movement.

By some grace, I have been given a second chance. A gift.

And I will need another if I am to help Emelda. I turn back to the dead man, whose blood pools across the floor. I need to repair my human body.

And in death, his offering is the gift I need.

Chapter Forty-Seven

The two heads poking out of the floor were nattering at me, both at the same time. Just panicky noise, so I ignored them. I crossed the room and slid into a chair facing an array of monitors. The ones that interested me, though, were the tiny ones all in a row.

All of them were dark. Except the last two.

One showed a scene of chaos. From a high vantage point, it displayed angry flames, black smoke, and collapsing floors. I recognized the roof because it had an apparatus hanging over the side that looked like the rounded stairs of a swimming pool.

"That's the building we were at yesterday," I muttered. I turned to the two people, still talking over each other. I told them to hush. "Why is that office complex burning?"

"You heard Janus," the guy said, his voice somber. "He's moving on to his phase two."

"Okay, but he poured a fortune into the Enhanced program," I said. "Why end it now?"

The woman spoke up. "Lance dug into some intracompany messaging when we got the order to shut down. Apparently, someone's been sabotaging everything. A big dude and a woman."

I smiled.

"That's you?" she said, her eyes wide.

Their blathering started again, but I was more interested in that last monitor. The one that showed the island where Doc Hammer and Marata had gone. The screen looked dead, but in the upper corner, I saw the words "Cam 3."

Poking around the keyboard for a moment, I found the menu that let me toggle through the feeds. As I did, each tiny screen illuminated with a green border. I tabbed over until I got to the last monitor.

The options on the main screen let me choose which camera to view. Cam four was also dead. But cam two told a different story. Dark, but I could see shadows. I spotted white arrows on the screen and tapped them with the mouse.

The display on the monitor changed.

As the camera's lens lifted higher, I saw the trunks of trees. Beyond their tapestry of leaves, I could make out what looked like a large barracks. No door on this side, but it was hard to see with all the static in the image. On the corners of the building, two huge floodlights poured pools of white onto dried mud below.

Not people. Or anything else. At least, not at first.

On the lower corner of the feed, I saw something twitch. Insectile legs that *glowed*. No, not glowing. The background lighting was creating a halo effect on the spindly hair of its appendages. Some bug had crawled across the lens, making it look gigantic. Then I swallowed.

The bug crossed from the left side of the screen to the right, skittering limbs and a fat body. When its legs hit the ground, puffs of dirt flew up. *Not* on the lens. And so many legs! When it disappeared off the screen, I repeatedly hit the arrows to follow it. The camera chased the giant bug then started lifting skyward. But I had been frantically tapping the move-right button.

That was when I saw a human face staring into the lens.

Well, not exactly human.

The figure scowled and appeared to reach around the back of the camera. The feed went black. But I'd recognized the elongated face. And the dirty lab coat. It was Marata.

She'd heard the whirring motors of the camera.

"Damn," I muttered and checked the last feed. The top half of cam one displayed the night sky with a few thin clouds obscuring the stars. The bottom half shimmered. Water. In the middle of the image was a void. But, sitting on the water, that void could only be one thing.

Doc Hammer and Marata had a boat. That was how they were going to get their Enhanced animal army off the island.

I pulled a black marker out of a dirty coffee cup and wrote the coordinates at the top of the screen on my bare arm.

"Yeah, so the island is *not* a dead site," I said and turned back to Lance and Alaina. "There are people there. The people we're looking for."

"Good for you!" Alaina wrapped her fingers around the cage. "Now, get us out of here!"

"Wait, hold on. No one is supposed to be there," Lance said, furrowing his brow. "The island is under quarantine. Covenant faked an industrial accident so no one would go near it."

I laughed. "How do you fake an industrial accident?"

Lance pulled at his lip. "Not that hard, actually. Before we bought it, it had been a dumping ground for construction equipment. The bosses filed paperwork that some old machines had leaked toxins into the soil. I think they even got a payout to clean it up."

An explosion from the hallway shook the room, and I jumped, not from the blast, but from a scream that had erupted from the stuck elevator poking out of the floor. High pitched. I didn't know if the dude or the chick had made that sound, but it frightened me more than the boom outside.

The robots had gotten through the first fire door. It sounded like they'd blown the damn thing up!

"Yep, so I'm out," I said as I leaped from the chair and ran to the door.

"Wait, wait, wait!"

Groaning, I turned back.

"You got what you needed," the woman said as I stepped back into the room. "Release the clamp so we can get out of here too!"

I rolled my hands into fists and took a slow, calming breath. "How do I do that?"

The guy spun around and pointed to the other side of the cage. "You'll see a silver panel on that pole. We can't reach it from in here."

"Fine."

I took one quick look behind me then ran across the room. The thick chains attached to the top of the old elevator passed through a set of huge pulleys. A metal conduit ran from those, across the floor, and up a concrete pole. Where it ended was a shiny, flat button. Obviously not a part of the original design.

"Hold tight," I said and hit it.

They braced as if they might plummet to the bottom. The clamp didn't release.

"Dammit," Alaina said, shifting a metal lever inside the cage up then down. A motor whirred and complained, but the cage didn't move. "It's stuck."

Lance turned white. Or rather, whiter. "Janus locked it down."

Backing away, I shook my head. "Listen, you put yourselves in this mess. I don't—"

"No, hold on," Lance said, pleading with me. "You need to interrupt the dam's power, just for a second, and it'll reset the connection. Then you can open the clamp."

Alaina buried her face in her hands. "How the hell is she supposed to do that?"

Well...

I ran my hands over the hockey puck–sized devices in my pockets. "If I disabled one of the turbines, would that do it?"

The woman lifted her head, her red eyes staring at her coworker. He nodded.

"It'll trip the entire system into a reboot." He looked at her. "Everything will reset."

That sounded promising. "Including those murder bots?"

"Maybe," Lance said. Then, more confidently, he added, "But if it doesn't, you could try using the safe word."

Alaina shook her head. "It doesn't work anymore, Lance."

"Early on," he said, waving her off, "there was a word we could use to stop the PETs so they didn't attack us. You'd say *merimna*, and they'd freeze for sixty seconds, so you could get to a safe zone."

I frowned. "Mana-what?"

"Merimna," Lance said. "I looked it up. It's Greek for worry or panic. Fitting because it was a verbal panic button."

"It doesn't *work* anymore. Janus decided it was a security risk," the woman said. "You need to reset the power, or we will die in here!"

"You'll still have to come back and hit the clamp release!" Lance shouted as I bolted from the control room.

Back in the hallway, I couldn't go left. The fire door was holding, but beyond that waited the killer robots. To the right were another door and a set of stairs.

As I raced down the steps, I pulled out my phone and called my tech guy.

"I am *not* your tech guy," Denny said over the line as he crunched on some snack. Dude was always eating. "And I don't want to be involved in anything you're doing. I'm sure it's criminal."

"It's not."

He sighed. "Good."

"Well, we did sort of break in."

"See!" he shouted over the phone. "I don't wanna—"

"Hush, nerd. I've got some coordinates here," I said, running down the stairs as I read the numbers off my arm. "Can you tell me where they are?"

"Why don't you just plug them into your map app on your phone?"

"A bit busy," I said, making a turn on the next landing. "That's why I've got a tech guy."

He went quiet for a moment just as I passed a stairwell door. I doubled back and reached for the handle. Before I turned it, I put my eye to the window. Dark. I slowly turned the knob, sweat prickling all across my skull.

"Those are wrong."

His voice startled me, and I actually yelped.

He said, "What?"

"Nothing, you just..." I said and pushed the door open. The air felt ten degrees colder. "What did you find?"

"Those coordinates are in the middle of a lake."

"Great. That's right."

"Hold on," he said. "Oh, it's an island. Commercial property."

"We need to go there," I said and ran my fingers along the interior wall. I felt a switch. "Where is it?"

"You can't *go* there. There's a flashy warning thing that says it's under quarantine because of a toxic spill."

"Don't worry about that."

"Toxins? Of all the things to worry about, yes, toxins are one of those things, Emelda!"

"It'll be fine," I said and swallowed dryly, willing my fingers to flip the light on. "Uh, where is the island?"

He sighed down the phone. "Way, way out. Like thirty miles off a place called Copper Harbor."

"Where's that?"

"Michigan," he said. "Your island is in the middle of Lake Superior."

Of course it was.

I flipped the switch, expecting to see another bare corridor. Instead, I saw a long room. It looked like it had once been a hallway but had been converted into storage. All along each wall were metal monsters, dozens of them. More at the end and in cases extended into the next hallways. Not dozens. Hundreds.

They looked like mechanical versions of the Enhanced creatures. Thick metal skins, impenetrable to bullets. And machines never tired.

These were the upgrades to the PET robots. Janus's Mach Two army.

I flipped off the light and ran down the stairs as fast as I could.

Chapter Forty-Eight

Kane

When I am wolf once again, I believe I will miss television. So much you can learn from the wonderful device.

Such a valuable gift humans have given to themselves. Or have been inspired by their television god to create such a conduit of knowledge and learning.

I still do not wholly comprehend the human relationship with their divine.

Often, ma mère would try to help me understand, but we really do not have the same in wolf world. Our ancestors speak to us. In fact, it is like a television of the mind in some ways. Pictures, words, ideas. No diet soda commercials, so maybe we are better at this than they.

But I will allow that our ancestral inspiration could be similar to human spirituality. Where they have a deity, we have our dead who relay such inspiration, guidance, and council. However, I do worry that in my lineage of those wizened mentors, I may have an idiot or two.

I have made many "inspired" errors. I blame them.

And it is now that I may be following their suggestions. A voice within tells me to head down, deeper into the dam.

Rounding the corner, wiping Earl blood from my mouth, I have readjusted the green man sock so it covers my body. If I encounter any machines, I may go unnoticed.

I nearly fall backward when I see another large man coming at me. Huge. Powerful. And green.

Ah. Yes.

As a man, I am muscular and lean. It only took a moment to recognize that such a fine human form before me had to be my own, reflected in brushed steel. I can see why others struggle to resist it.

I break away from the enchanting image and continue my trek. I find stairs and am compelled to travel further downward. Like a wolf to the safety of his den, but it is not safety I seek. If the angry machines are not pursuing me, they are pursuing Emelda.

Above all else, this cannot happen.

Like a panther, I prowl the steps, my senses alert. The slower pace has me reflecting on my life as a human. And the regrets.

I will miss spicy tacos. However, I will not miss getting pepper juices on my fingers and then using the lavatory.

I will miss the sound of a baby's laughter, even though most did not get my very best jokes.

I will miss all the things I did not do. Like jumping from a plane to escape the authorities after an overly complicated bank heist. This looked like such great fun in movies.

Below, deep in the bowels of the water dam, a queer whining and grinding noise grows louder. I stalk toward it.

Singing in a choir. This I wish I would have done. Wolves have something similar. A call to protect, yes. A call to find others, this too. But also a howl of celebration and gratitude. What ma mère might have called prayer. I would have liked to try this as a human, joining my voice with others. That joy.

When I reach the very bottom, I fling open the door and immediately realize that I should have been paying more attention to my surroundings before the flinging. Flinging might not have been the best choice.

"Who the hell are you?" the large man with the tiny head says to me. It is an angry face, pinched and damning. "*What* the hell are you?"

I had been mid-run when he yelled and came to a squeaking halt thanks to the Reebok shoes. Stopping so quickly, however, I nearly tumble over.

The guard in blue coveralls with *so many pockets* hesitates at first, seeing a strange green man, but then he runs toward me. I must prepare to fight, but I am entranced by his garment's abundance of places to put one's things.

Focus!

I try to distract him with charm. "Hello, yes," I shout down the hall as he barrels toward me. "Wyatt, it is you! How are things with the family and also pets, if you have them?"

He does not fall for my clever deception.

Sadly, I must resort to physical force, but as I raise my fist, something within me hesitates. I am overcome by grief.

I know this man is an enemy of mine. And it's not just because he is effectively wearing a onesie like me, but a different color, thus denoting him as a foe. Also, the rifle he has swung around from his back as he runs. Another clue that we will not be besties.

However, something inside my soul does not want me to injure this human. I know from where this comes. The canines I become, these stay with me. Their thoughts and desires and instincts.

Could it be the terrier that wishes to climb into laps and get ear scratches? Ear scratches do not get offered when you punch humans.

Could it be the pug dog, a compact force of nature, who seeks approval from the humans even when this desire seems contradictory to his actions? However, this approval-seeking does not prevent a very off-putting form of self-hygiene.

Could my hesitation be born of the golden retriever that wants to embrace this man and tell him all will be fine?

Just five strides away, the man points his rifle at my chest, and the desire to comfort and hug evaporates. The wolf within takes over.

Crouching, I launch myself at the guard, twisting in the air so that his rifle fire whizzes harmlessly past me. When I connect with his soft chest, we tumble and roll. Wyatt has indulged in much confectionery, which I can smell on his skin. This has given him a somewhat rounder shape, nothing to be ashamed of, for the internet reminds me all bodies are beautiful.

Our two beautiful bodies smash into a metal door frame, and we tumble into a secondary room halfway down the hall. This space is alight with the buzz of electronics. Computer monitors align one entire wall. The hum of it makes my head dizzy.

Or it could have been the smash into the door frame.

And also that Wyatt is now on top of me, gasping for air. He is a chunky monkey. A beautiful chunky monkey, still.

"Gah!" he screams as I kick out my legs and flip the man over my head. Up on a knee, I spin around and see he has smashed into a second door, which comes off its hinges and falls into the room beyond. He lies flat on his stomach.

I gasp. "You also have pockets on the back? So many places for keys and wallets and loose change!"

Wyatt bellows angrily as he staggers to his feet and grips his rifle, but I am faster. My hands are on the barrel before he can lift it toward me. I yank the weapon with my right hand and raise my left knee and feel a crunch. An exhalation bursts from his lungs, and he gasps for air.

My heart sinks. I grab him by the shoulders and tilt my head down to look him in the eyes. He struggles, but I am taller, stronger. My hands are like iron vises.

"It does not have to be like this, my friend," I say in a calm voice.

His eyes darken, and he spits blood onto my face. "What the hell are you wearing?" he says with a slight lisp.

I glance around him and see a bloodied tooth on the floor.

"You supposed to be some kinda ninja?"

I release the man and step back, my hands outstretched. "I do not approve of such language. My human parents taught me to respect all people, for all are the same beneath the skin."

"You're mental," he screams at me and throws a punch, which I dodge.

I lunge and smash the man across his pinched face, which is now less pinched. Bloody and flappy in parts.

Again, my heart aches. I am causing this man pain. He stumbles to his feet, fist flying, but I easily move away. He lowers his head and smashes his shoulder into my midsection, lifting me off the floor.

Good move.

My back collides with a wall, and air bursts from my lungs. He reaches up and grabs my head for leverage but only succeeds in stripping the man sock off my head. Another good move, since I am temporarily blinded as he yanks the material across my face and down to my shoulders. He swivels from beneath me, and I droop forward, my brain fuzzy and spinning. Breaths are hard to take.

He reaches for the rifle. I want to leap at him, but there are sparkles in my vision. Lights flicker just beyond Wyatt, but I know this is because I have been winded. And these weeks of killing have made me weary. Hesitant. Can I attack and not kill? Not hurt?

The large man, blood streaming from his nose, spins the rifle toward me. He points at me as a realization dawns on his face. "You're here with that bitch, aren't you?"

Hmm.

The desire to not hurt snaps away. Replaced by anger. Rage. This is a feeling I know well. My ancestors howl in approval. I hear them. See their wolfen faces.

The barrel is slicing through the air, slowly, and I once again grasp it with both hands. When I drop to a knee and rotate, I strip it from his clutches. Using my momentum, I continue my spin and connect with the side of Wyatt's head.

He begins to fall, and I twist my body and bash the other side of his skull. I strike again, and the rifle stock splits.

The man crumples in a heap. Not dead. I could kill, yes, but I choose not to. Wyatt has been injured, but he will not die this day. No, not today.

I suddenly feel pain, but it is not emotional. Physical. Have I injured myself? Another wave of pain explodes in my shoulder. Then another pain in my chest. One more in my arm. When I look down, I see metal spikes.

Distracted. Yes. I was distracted.

Beyond the broken door ahead, a vast space with strange, bulbous machines. These are the turbines the hippie people spoke of. Very loud. Spinning with electric arc light. But all along the walls, the catwalks, to the left and ahead?

Rows upon rows upon rows of Steve Janus's robot machines. Their white, illuminated eyes are all locked onto me.

Their spikes fly, and I grab Wyatt to use him as a shield. He shutters and twitches as the darts pierce him all up and down his body. Then he goes limp and lets out a final sigh.

I was wrong. He did die this day.

"Aargh!" I bellow as another wave of spikes connects, piercing my thighs. I roll to the floor. Sparks fly, and the metal darts rain down upon me. I am nearly buried in them.

The hungry grinding of gears and spinning wheels fills the room of electronics, so I twist my injured body back into the hallway, using my Wyatt shield for protection. I punch the door closed and hear the *fap-fap-fap* against it as a new barrage of spikes lands. Some tips poke through.

Something else, too.

Something beneath that sound. Within that din and clatter and cacophony, I hear a voice.

"Kane?"

Emelda is here.

Chapter Forty-Nine

"Kane!" I shouted over the deafening roar of sixteen massive turbines. I hadn't seen him. Just a flash of green. But I knew that when all of Steve Janus's PETs swarmed toward the room one level lower on the opposite wall, they could only be hunting my friend.

I stared down into the massive turbine room. "Room" wasn't the right word. The cement cavern was as big as an indoor stadium. The catwalk I stood on wrapped along the wall and hung from the ceiling by iron poles that looked more rust than metal.

Grabbing the rail, I leaned down and screamed his name as loud as I could.

He might not have heard me, but the evil robots did. At first, just the one cylindrical head spun toward me, its white oval eye searching. Jerking left. Twitching right. It looked like a nervous bowling pin out in the forest that had just heard the stony roll of a sixteen-pound predator.

A brilliant white light blinded me, and I thew my hands up to shield my eyes. Right. It found me. The robots that had been piling into the room stopped. From far to near, each of their cylindrical heads spun, angling up at my perch.

"Uh-huh," I said, then dropped flat, putting the catwalk floor between me and them.

Thunk.

Thunk-thunk-thunk.

"Emelda!"

The damn robots were shooting at me through the catwalk. The floor shuddered, my own personal earthquake, as a shiny metal forest burst to the surface all around me. I had to get moving. Crawling, I hugged the wall, my knees scraping against the grated flooring.

"Emelda!"

I dared a quick peek over the edge to spot Kane and braced for the volley. They did not disappoint.

Thunk-clank, spark!

Forty, maybe fifty of the evil robots were rolling down both sides of the lower catwalk, some thirty feet below me. I jerked back to the wall as more spikes flew. Behind then in front.

The catwalk had a grated layer so that workers had grip when they walked. You didn't want your engineers plummeting one hundred feet to their deaths. Hard on morale.

Just below that first layer was a thick plate. The robots couldn't find me and were punching holes into that plate to see where the fleshy human might have scurried to.

Thunk-thunk-thunk.

Dammit! Too close.

Pressing my back against the cold concrete wall, I fought off the panic building in my chest. I looked back to the open door at the end of the catwalk I'd come through a minute earlier. In that darkness, I could find temporary safety. But if I did, Janus's PETs would only start hunting Kane again.

I felt a hard edge press into my thigh and patted my pockets.

Could I throw the disruptors from here? Jeannette had said they were magnetic, but what if they clung to the catwalk instead? Or fell down past the turbines and out of view? Out of range?

In a dark corner of my mind, a small voice doubted whether the disruptors would actually work. Internally, I scowled at this little voice and told it to shut the hell up.

They had to work.

I'd slap them onto a turbine. It would spin out of control and seize up the robots long enough for me and Kane to escape. I was sure it would work. I was *mostly* sure it would work.

When I started crawling again, my movement shifted the catwalk, and it banged against the wall.

Thunk-thunk-thunk!

Only a foot ahead of me, three more danger darts burst through the floor. Could they sense when I moved? No. They'd heard me.

I pulled off a shoe and threw it backward over my head as far as I could. It bounced once then—

Bap-bap-bap-bap-bap-bap!

Looking under my arm, I saw spikes pierce the catwalk, sending my shoe jumping around like a popcorn kernel in a hot pan. It ended up hanging on one metal tip. Me? I wouldn't have fared so well.

"Emelda!" Kane called out.

I crouched close to the floor and found a hole where one spike had slipped and fallen out. I could see a gap in the door where Kane was hiding. The machines were buzzing below me like angry ants, weaving between each other all along the catwalk below.

At the sound of the big man's voice, a few of them spun their white eyes back toward his spot.

I chucked my last shoe in the other direction, which triggered another volley of projectiles.

"Close your door, Kane!" I shouted toward the ceiling and, a half second later, spikes bounced off the wall thirty feet above. Thankfully, Kane didn't question my direction, and I heard the door slam below.

Then I had a thought.

During that last burst of metal darts, they'd shot them not near me but farther down the wall. Way above, up in the corner.

Hmm.

Cupping my hands around my mouth, I shouted toward the open door at the end of the catwalk but, once again, up at the ceiling. "Do you remember laughter?"

A burst of whirring and clanking below. Then, just as before, came another punishing barrage of spikes. All directed at the ceiling's corner. Some stuck in the concrete while the rest fell and clattered to the catwalk.

Twisting my body around, I turned to shout again. Then I remembered the safe word Lance had mentioned. Alaina had thought it was now ineffective, but the *word* I yelled wouldn't matter. It was worth a shot.

As loud as I could, I screamed, "Merimna!"

Clank, spark, bling!

Then, from his hiding spot down below, I heard Kane sing back, "*Be-doo-be-doo-doo.*"

Clunk, clunk, clunk!

They'd targeted his door when he'd said... whatever that was. But the machines had been fooled by my voice in the huge, cavernous room. They couldn't work out where it had originated.

So they'd chased the echo.

Lifting my head up to the ceiling, I shouted the useless word again, drawing the syllables out: "Meri-meh-nah!"

"*Be-doo-be-doo.*"

"Cut that out, Kane!"

More spikes, this time flying in all directions. Sparks flew above me, above the wall across from me. Just spikes going everywhere like mad. I had to drop low and cover my head as a few of them rained down onto my body. And they just kept coming.

The bots were chasing the echo, shooting any wall it bounced off of. At this rate, they might even run out of metal darts.

That flicker of joy didn't last. I felt a queer sensation in the pit of my stomach. Then my body spasmed. No, not my body. The catwalk I was lying on *moved*.

Spikes lit up the turbine room like it was the Fourth of July, and I wrapped my fingers through the grated metal as I shook and jerked and jumped.

They weren't chasing the echo anymore.

A spike split the metal between my hands, and when it fell away, I could see through the hole. Below me, all up and down the path, fifty of the bastards were just shooting blindly.

No.

Not blindly. They were shooting at the rusted metal braces above.

I heard the rip-scream of metal, and my world tilted violently as the catwalk and I fell to the predators below.

Chapter Fifty

Tumbling down the steep incline, I ground my teeth together, waiting for the inevitable crash. One end of the catwalk had broken away while the other held on by a thread, and I rolled and flipped uncontrollably as the metal grating took bites out of my skin each time I bounced.

As a kid, I had never like roller-coaster rides or flumes or any of that stuff. I'd been terrified by that helpless feeling of falling. Out of control.

Now?

It enraged me. Time did that bizarre slow-mo thing while my mind raced through the possibilities. Do I tense up and brace for impact? Or go loose?

I'd heard years ago that they did a study on drunk-driving accidents, looking into why the drunks so often lived and the victims didn't. According to a few people claiming to have read the study, during the impact, the drunks were loose and limp, which reduced injury.

Was that actual science? Or just what assholes had told me when they were trying to get a drink after I'd cut them off?

Like any good fighter, I went for the combo.

I arched my head forward and wrapped my arms behind my neck while I loosened my lower body. When I hit the wall, the catwalk broke into its individual parts. Ten-foot squares of rusted metal rained down onto the robot army like four-hundred-pound Scrabble pieces.

My square of rusted flying carpet shifted sideways. My red-raw fingers couldn't hold on to the grate flooring, and I fell backward. Watching the ceiling above compress into a circle, it felt like I was falling into an open mouth.

I got the wind knocked out of me when I landed. The impact shot dust and debris into the air, creating columns of hazy light that reached out of the O-shaped lips above. Stunned witless, I braced, waiting to be swallowed whole.

I wasn't in a mouth. When I moved, I felt cloth and rubber and thick wire and strands of shredded rope, and all of it smelled awful. Some of it was damp. Moist.

"Gross," I whispered to myself.

Pushing myself up, I bashed my elbow on an old pallet. I cursed, stumbled to my feet, and saw that I'd fallen into one of the enormous steel drums in the turbine room's corners. Tattered old rags and rotting boxes lay out like a moldy floor below me. I'd ended up in the trash.

"Oh, there you are," Steve Janus's voice boomed. "Fitting, I think. You getting thrown out like so much garbage."

"Screw you," I muttered, getting up to my knees and brushing the muck off my clothes. All it did was spread the muck around, so I stopped. Foul goop squished up between my bare toes.

When I stared out the opening, I saw his floating head once again. Not on a screen this time. It had been projected in the air and was *huge*, filling half the space above the turbines.

"Listen, I'm very busy, so if we could get on with the killing, it would be most helpful. I've got a ten o'clock that..." His gaze turned from me, focusing somewhere just outside my barrel. "No, stop it!"

I could hear the spinning of small rubber tires and the clanging of metal. When I looked up, I saw one edge of my catwalk floor leaning up against the lip of the barrel. It shook violently.

"You can't all fit up the ramp, no, *no*," he said. The guy was talking to his PETs like, well, pets. "You there. Cut through the barrel and end all this. The rest of you, go and finish the big moron in the green suit."

"Damn," I swore softly. "Damn. Damn."

The loud bang against the drum told me the robot had smacked into it. A sizzling noise fired up as an orange spot grew larger and larger on the curved wall. Nice. Robots with lasers. This dude was right out of a Bond movie.

Beneath his peals of laughter, I could hear the robot horde racing down both sides of the lower catwalk. Heading toward Kane. Of course, that meant they wouldn't be looking at me.

I lifted the wooden shipping pallet and leaned it up against the barrel interior. Using the slats to climb up to the lip, I peeked out. Janus, of course, saw this. His eyes flickered, and one of the Kane-hunting robots spun its white eye toward me.

A half second after I ducked back down, a spike shot over the barrel and embedded itself in the wall.

Not going to do that again, but I had seen what I needed to.

A row of turbines spinning and humming. The closest was only about fifteen feet from where I was standing. I dug into my left front pocket, praying that the disruptors hadn't gotten smashed when I'd tumbled down the catwalk.

I pulled the first out, and it looked fine. But what did I know? I pulled the second out.

In my past, I'd chucked beer bottles the length of a bar, so hurling the little metal puck fifteen feet? I could do that. But it wouldn't be as simple as just throwing it.

I had to lob the device so it hit that nearest turbine. Then chuck number two on the other side. If I'd been outside the barrel, easy. But I wasn't. I closed my eyes to picture what I'd seen when I peeked over the lip. I turned to line up my throw.

"No, no, you morons," Janus said, looking toward the far wall. Why would he move his image to look around the room? Surely, the guy was monitoring from somewhere using cameras. "Single file. Single file!"

I gripped the first disruptor in my hand, said a small prayer, then, for luck, kissed it. Why not? I extended my arm back and, in one smooth motion, arched the device up and over the lip of the barrel. I held my breath.

Clank!

"What was that?" Janus said, his head snapping toward me. "Don't throw trash on my turbines!"

Holy shit! That worked!

A burst of red light cut my celebration short, and liquid metal spluttered from a tiny hole. The laser grew wider as it melted through the thick barrel wall. Now through, it moved upward. I watched as the beam cut a ten-inch line then made a right angle. It was cutting a hole.

I rolled the second disruptor in my hands and edged away from the laser. I really needed another look, but when I gazed upward, I nearly tumbled back into the beam.

Janus had lowered his video image to where his eye was the size of the barrel's opening.

"Oh, Emelda Thorne. You didn't think that I would protect my power source?" Janus said, his voice booming into the barrel. He pulled back slightly and looked down at me like a disappointed parent. "That you could just come in here and flip a switch and turn me off?"

The what, now?

A loud crash drew his attention, and he turned and smiled. "Good, good. Now move it out of the way and kill that troublesome man."

Again, he had *turned* to look. He wasn't connecting from some high-rise penthouse on some next-level Zoom call. Janus *was* that big, floating head.

The laser had cut three sides of its hole. Once it had number four, spikes would come flying.

"You're *here*," I said, my mouth hanging open with the realization. I pointed at the head. "*That* is you."

His face bent into a giant-sized frown. "I don't buy into all that self-actualization business. 'I am me and I am worthy.' I don't have any need for it."

"You're a friggin' computer! Artificial intelligence or something."

That got another huge laugh out of him and sent the head spinning with glee. When it stopped, he was wiping away digital tears. "You couldn't be more wrong. I am a god!"

"That's why you needed the dam's power," I said, my voice barely above a whisper. "It's what powers you."

He raised a few fingers and flitted them in the air. "Not even close, but none of that matters. You will be dead—" he tilted his massive head toward the robot carving the hole in my hiding spot "—in about five seconds."

"The Enhanced program you stole. The Next-Gen program. That evil shit came from you," I said, drawing his attention to me. "You did that from here."

"I am beyond your comprehension. Don't even try," Janus said, tapping his head with a single floating finger. "You'll sprain something."

Gripping the device, I kept one eye on the laser. Almost there. "How about I kill you instead?"

"That is technically not possible," he said, grinning.

I pulled my arm back, staring at the glowing square on the drum's interior wall. I just needed a quick look.

The glowing metal square fell away. Through the hole, I could see the exact spot I needed to hit, and I hurled the second disruptor like a skipping stone.

My world fell into that slow-motion pace once again. The device rocketed out the hole on its upward arc, and I knew—I could see it in my mind—that it was right on target.

The turbine would fail. The PETs would seize up. Janus would blink away. Sure, it would only be temporary, but that was all Kane and I needed to get the hell out of there.

Kane. I hoped he was okay.

Then I remembered that I wasn't okay. Not yet. Flattening myself against the side of the barrel, I heard the thunk of the disruptor hitting the turbine, and my heart sang. I punched the air. "Yes!"

Now, I just needed to hold out for the disruptor to spin out the turbine. I readied myself to dodge any spikes about to fly through the hole.

But they didn't come.

Instead, the floating head appeared above me once again. The asshole's electronic smile was so large it was obscene.

"Yes, hide, little girl," he said. "It's what you're best at."

I gave him my own smug grin. "We'll see about that!"

To my right, I heard a scraping and flinched. Backing away, I watched as the robot's claw pushed through the hole. In its hand, it held my device. The disruptor.

My limbs felt weak, and I sank down the side of the barrel. I felt like all the other thrown-away shit around me. Trash. I'd failed.

Another claw pushed through the gap and began bending the sides of the hole, making it larger. It wasn't going to shoot spikes at me. The thing was going to reach inside and crush my skull. I looked around the debris for a weapon. Anything. Digging around, I came out with half a broom handle.

It would have to do.

A foot of the metal bent away from the hole. The machine's bulbous white eye stared in at me. It looked hungry. When it went to bend the other side, to make the hole wider so it could grip and crush and tear, it still had the disruptor in its hand.

It stared at the device for a second and threw it to the floor. When it went to peel back the metal, it stopped and stared at the hand again. The disruptor was magnetic. It had stuck to the PETs claw. The robot shook its hand up and down, trying to dislodge it.

"Stop that playing with it," Janus bellowed. "Just throw it against the wall, you moron."

I stole a glance out of the hole. The robot was trying to get rid of the device. Throwing didn't work. Neither did shaking it. The PET used another claw to scrape the device off, but then it stuck to that appendage.

It looked like some toddler trying to get glue off their fingers.

Janus rolled his eyes. "Just crush the damn thing!"

The gigantic white eye looked toward me, up at the head, then back at the disruptor. Its servos made grinding sounds as the claw squeezed. The device's metal case dented. A tiny spark danced between two fingers of the metal claw.

The robot shuddered and then froze. On the other side of the barrel wall, I heard humming. Arc light burst around the room, and I backed away from the hole. A bolt of electricity struck the PET, but it didn't strike and stop. A thick vein of energy pumped and writhed like a snake, its teeth deep into its victim's flesh.

"Throw it away, throw it away," Janus shouted, the head zooming away from me and out of sight. "Get rid of it."

The arc light got brighter and brighter, and the robot's metal body began to glow red.

Okay. Time to move.

I scurried up the slats of the wooden pallet and tumbled over the edge of the barrel, falling right at the feet of the trembling robot. It ignored me and smelled like it was burning from the inside out.

Above, another thick vein of electricity crackled in the air. I rolled to my right to get clear. When I looked up again, I saw that the robot's white eye was flickering. Then it turned red.

The other robots turned away from the open door and began racing toward me, their claws in the air, snapping. On the ones in front, I saw compartments on their chests open. They were readying their spikes.

More arc light flew around the room, this time from the red-eyed robot. The bolts struck its comrades, one then another. Then each of those passed a vein of light to the next. Each of their white eyes, in turn, turned red.

"Kane!" I shouted as I stood. "Kane, we gotta get the hell out of here!"

All around me, the robot army was shaking and smoking, red eyes cutting through the fog. The only way out was behind Kane, but there was no way I could get past the shaking machines all piled together.

Through the smoke, I saw the strangest sight in as long as I could remember. And I'd seen a ton of weird shit in the past month.

A huge blue figure burst from the smoke, flying through the air. Blue?

Kane landed a few feet in front of me, one knee to the floor, his fists extended to stop his fall. He raised his head to me.

"Did I look cool?"

"Yes, yes," I said and ran to him. As he stood, I wrapped my arms around his midsection, and when I pulled away, I was covered in blood. Kane had somehow managed a costume change into blue overalls. They were soaked red. "Are you okay?"

"I am fine," he said. "Wyatt helped. And I got this!" He motioned to his new outfit with pride.

I asked, "Where's the green suit?"

Excitedly, he tapped a bulge on his chest. "In a pocket! So many pockets, it took a while to choose one. Let me show you."

I grabbed his arm, lowering it as I shook my head. "Later, wolfman. We gotta go."

We ran toward the closest door. I wanted to be gone before the PETs were able to reset.

"That was a very good idea," Kane said, looking around at the robots shuddering and shaking. "How did you know it would do this?"

"While you've been updating your wardrobe, I've been making friends," I said as I checked the door. Through its window, I could see a corridor and, best of all, no killer robots. "A couple of Janus's worker bees gave me the idea."

I yanked open the door. Ahead, the hallway appeared to lead in the direction where we'd first come in. To my right, a staircase led up. Yeah, no thanks.

Kane clapped my shoulder. "You must have been very fearsome for them to tell you this."

"Something like that," I said, pointing down the hall. When I turned back to him, my own furrow or frown betrayed me. It didn't matter. He read the expression on my face.

He put his hand on the door. "You promised to help them?"

"We don't have time, Kane!" I shouted at him and punched his coveralls. "We'll be lucky to get out of here ourselves. You've taught me all about animal instinct, right? My instinct says we gotta go, now!"

Kane shook his head slowly then dropped to one knee.

"You have become strong, Emelda," he said, looking into my eyes. "You would make a formidable ally in the forest."

I frowned, staring at the robots as they shuddered and danced in a haze of sparks and smoke.

"But as you have embraced your animal, you have left some of your human behind. Empathy. Compassion."

"My human trait of self-preservation is fully intact," I shouted at him. "We have to—"

"If you leave them to die, you will endure another human trait. One that will never leave you." He put a gentle hand on my shoulder. "Regret. You will carry that burden for the rest of your life."

I growled at him. "Which is about ten seconds from this moment, Kane."

"Then spend it as a human would," he said.

I wanted to yell at him. I wanted to scream. Hell, I wanted to punch him in his beautiful face. But he was right. For all my bluster and bravado, I would never forgive myself if I left Lance and Alaina behind. Once Janus recovered and found them, they'd be dead.

Sighing, I looked around at the chaos behind us. The robots were racing along the catwalks, out of control. Above, the massive floating head of Steve Janus spun faster and faster, shrinking and inflating.

Then a few of his PETs, their now-red eyes blazing bright, started moving toward us.

"Ah, hell," I said and ran up the stairs.

Chapter Fifty-One

We raced up to the second floor and had to cross down a corridor to get to the next set of stairs. The place was like a tomb, but thankfully, a well-lit tomb.

A thundering boom from below nearly knocked us off our feet, and all the lights went out.

No, not all of them.

Oval red lights appeared at the ends of two hallways, whizzing left and right. The PETS were going haywire but were still on the hunt for Kane and me. We hit the next set of steps and ran up to the next floor, which was illuminated by dim emergency lighting.

At the next level, five robots spotted us and squealed their wheels in hot pursuit. How they were going to manage the stairs quickly, I didn't know and didn't want to find out.

With a swoop of his arm, Kane picked me up and carried me two flights up. At the top floor, I shimmied out of his grasp and pointed ahead. "Through that door, but we've got to—"

The building shook again, this time more violently, and it felt like the entire structure was crumbling beneath our feet.

"That's not good," I said. I pulled out my phone and flicked on the flashlight. There was a sea of red-eyed robots between us and the control room, but they weren't interested in us. We wove around quivering machines, which were shaking and smoking and hot to the touch.

Another boom, deep below.

Ten feet from the door, Kane yelped. I spun around to see one of the PETs had pierced its claw through his coveralls, which was drawing blood. My friend tried to pull his leg away, which only dragged the machine along with him, leaving two long scrapes in the concrete. Its red eye flickered as its pill-shaped head twitched from side to side.

A tinny voice burst from the robot: "N-n-not g-g-going any-any-any..."

With his free leg, he kicked the machine, but it only wobbled.

"Very sturdy," he said and smashed the metal arm into the side of its head. Sparks filled the air. The red eye flickered out.

"Stop playing with the robot,' I said, yanking at his arm. I ran into the control room. He was much slower because, of course, he was now dragging the machine still attached to his leg.

I shouted, and the two faces sticking out of the floor looked at me through the cage's mesh. Their eyes betrayed relief at the sight of me. That darkened when they saw the big stranger in coveralls.

"What the hell did you do?" Lance said. I pointed the light at his face, and he had his hands on the sides of his head. "Everything went dark. Did you knock out the power?"

"Um, yeah," I said, running around to the side of the cage. "That's part of it."

"What's the rest?"

They flinched as Kane stepped closer. He said, "Some of the robots are exploding."

"What?" Alaina said and pushed back to the cage's far wall.

Lance pointed at my friend's leg. "W-what about that one?"

"It seems harmless," Kane said with a shrug. He punched the cylindrical head, and it bobbled back and forth.

"It's stuck to your leg!" Lance said, his eyes wide.

"No time for chat," I shouted, pointing to the pole near the stuck elevator car. "Power's out, so I can release the clamp, and we can get the hell out of here." I ran toward it.

Both of the people inside shouted, "Don't do that!"

Another blast, much closer, shot dust and shards of metal and concrete into the control room. One of the robots in the hall had exploded. I grabbed onto the elevator's chains so I didn't fall down the hole in the floor.

I groaned. "We gotta go!"

Alaina shook her head, squeezing her eyes shut. "With *no* power, the motor won't work. If you release the brake, we could fall straight to the bottom."

I turned toward Kane. “There’s nothing we can do.”

That wasn’t the sort of news either of them wanted to hear. “What?”

“You were helping Steve Janus,” I shouted at them through the mesh. “This is your problem, not mine.”

Alaina shouted back, “It was just a job. We were doing our jobs!”

“Right,” I said. “I bet that’s what the Nazi guards said on the stand.”

Kane backed away, dragging the dead robot across the floor. “We are going straight to the Nazis with the analogy? That happened very fast.”

“No time!” I shouted.

As the two in the stuck elevator pleaded for help, Kane tried to lift the entire car up, but the massive iron cage wouldn’t budge with the brake engaged. As he struggled, I looked up to where the chains disappeared into the ceiling.

“What’s at the top?”

Lance stared the same direction I was. “It goes to the roof. A platform at the very top. But without power, we can’t get it up there.”

I nodded. Izzy the guard had told me that was where he and the others had landed in the helicopter. I got a sudden pang in my chest. I really hoped Izzy had gotten out before they’d blown the building to bits.

Kane growled and stepped back again, dragging the dead robot with him. “I cannot move this troublesome cage.”

Craning my neck around, I tried to get a better view through the ceiling. A long shaft with some sort of cover at the top. Around that, I could see the hints of dark clouds. No stars. No moon.

Damn. If Kane could transform into the wolfwere, then he’d have the strength to throw the damn thing up *through* the hole. Of course, it wasn’t a full moon, so I’d have more likely gotten an English sheepdog. Not much good there. Cuddle-worthy, sure, but nothing that would help with the people stuck in the elevator.

We needed another way.

“If we got you to the bottom, is there a way out?”

“How?”

Another explosion. The entire building shifted, and computer monitors crashed to the floor. I asked again: “Can you get out from the bottom?”

Alaina nodded quickly. “There’s a door that leads to a ramp that will take us to the shore.”

Kane pointed at me. “You have a plan.”

I laughed. "Not a very good one."

"Those," Kane said and rubbed his hands together, "are my very favorite plans!"

Chapter Fifty-Two

Kane

I do not like this plan anymore.

When Emelda reexplained her plan, I liked it even less. Mainly because I felt she could get very hurt. I very much dislike this idea.

Emelda climbs atop the cage and waves me up.

"You can do this, for you are powerful, Kane," she tells me with words and expression. "Only you have such strength. I believe in you."

Alas, I sometimes have trouble believing in myself. The second-best always feels this way.

This is her plan, though, and I trust her. She is a very smart human. Although her plan does not seem so smart.

Dragging the dead robot, which I believe is gripping a leg bone, I climb on top of the cage next to her and test the thick iron chain. "Do you think—"

Another explosion. Then another. Then another. The building groans and rumbles.

"No time to think," she says. When I turn to her, she grins at me. "There is no think. Only do."

My weakness! She is quoting old movies at me. Alas, she has misquoted, something I find very frustrating.

"It is not 'do' the little green man says. It is—"

"This does not matter!" she says. "Give me one of your Reebok shoes."

I gasp. "*Alors*, why is this?" I look down.

"Just do it, man," she says.

I reluctantly comply. I hate this plan even more now. As she instructed, I grip the thick chain of the elevator car.

This is her plan. It will work. Or it won't.

If we were to release the car, as the nervous people say, it would fall too fast. They would smash at the bottom, and sad family and friends would attend their funerals. And also because of the smashing, they would have very tiny caskets.

However, if the cage elevator had a counterweight, then it would not fall so fast.

As Emelda has explained it, she and I are the counterweight. Well, she, me, and my robot leg barnacle. I take one last look at my friend. She nods, and her expression emboldens me. This will work!

She throws my Reebok shoe at a silver square, and I feel the chain break free.

This will not work!

The screams of the people beneath us get swallowed into the darkness below as we shoot upward through the distressingly skinny tunnel. Faster and faster, we rocket through the cement tube like a torpedo in an old war film.

We shudder back and forth. My shoulder hits the wall and bursts with pain.

"Too fast! Too fast!" shouts my friend.

I must slow our ascent, but we are accelerating so quickly if I try to touch the shaft, it would take off my skin. Ah ha! Then I will not use *my* skin.

Lifting my leg, I press the dead robot against the concrete wall. A shower of sparks lights up our vertical tunnel. Still very fast, but we have slowed.

"Oh shit," Emelda cries out. "There's a metal housing up there blocking the top!"

"Hold on to me," I bravely say to her. "Grab my neck."

Once she does, I tense my powerful and enviable abdominal muscles. Gripping the chain, I thrust my hip upward until I flip upside down. This is a move I learned from a movie about a magical young man named Mike. Ma mère watched this film many, many times, so I know this move well.

A second later, I feel the busted robot collide with the metal plate. The impact rattles my entire body, and cool air blasts my skin.

I hear the chain clatter to a stop.

However, we do not.

Our momentum carries us upward, and Emelda, me, and a very busted robot soar into the night sky.

Chapter Fifty-Three

It would take Kane an entire day to recover. Hell, it would take me most of the day to recover, and I didn't have a half dozen holes in me and a two-hundred-pound robot piercing my calf muscle. The injuries from the robot spikes had mostly healed, and I didn't need to ask my friend how that had transpired. I already knew it had to do with a dude named Wyatt.

A name I wouldn't soon forget because Kane was wearing the guy's blue coveralls, which had "Wyatt" embroidered on the front pocket. *One* of the front pockets. Wyatt certainly had loved pockets.

My friend's clothing benefactor obviously had been a foot shorter, because the bottom cuff came up to just below Kane's knee. The overalls looked silly on him, but once he'd taken the morph suit off, he'd insisted on wearing them.

Ah. The morph suit. After we'd given it back to Rick the film guy, he'd gone into something resembling a fugue state. Jeannette guessed that would probably last a few days.

For her part, she and the others had been elated. *Cheering* when we'd returned after our long trek through the woods. Even Ryland was smiling and had opened his workshop to help get the busted robot off of Kane's leg. This despite his beloved Willie getting washed downstream about ten miles after a massive rush of water had come out of nowhere.

Well, not nowhere.

A third of the dam had disintegrated after "an incident." Local crews would be hired to clear the rest of it away, which meant a few hundred folks who had been out of work no longer were.

Jeannette had graciously offered to let us crash at her group home, but I wanted to get a good night's sleep at our motel. Couldn't do that at her place because the phone—and yep, she had a landline phone—had been ringing off the hook the whole time we were there.

The entire town had been convinced Jeannette's crew had something to do with the explosions at the Dolly Pot dam. She had done nothing to dissuade callers from that opinion and was eagerly preparing her next mayoral campaign.

She'd even offered to help with Kane's injuries.

"One of our ladies knows some ancient healing techniques," she'd said. "Did I introduce you to Maven?"

"No. I don't think so. You have a lot of people here."

"She makes a bit of money as a cobbler, but she does some hexes and stuff on the side." She nodded to me as if this somehow explained everything. It hadn't, so she clarified. "For extra cash. She's a part-time witch."

"Part-time?"

Jeannette sighed. "Can't get full-time witch work in a town our size."

"Right."

"And that said, it's lovely to have you here, but there'll be a lot of questions," she said to me conspiratorially. "People would have heard you asking about the dam yesterday, so you may want to think about getting out of Dodge."

"Yeah, we gotta be somewhere." I sighed. "One last adventure."

"Oh, darling, if there's one thing I've learned, it's that the adventures never end. There's always a new one right around the corner. Usually one you never even planned."

Back at the motel bar, I found our key in an envelope with the name Heather Thomas written across it. One day, I'd have to look the old actress up.

We'd headed into the back and found our room. Kane slumped into the sheets and was out the moment his head hit the pillow. I crawled in next to him. Not *in* bed, mind you. I slept on top of the covers. I got a rep to uphold. Okay, I don't have a rep to uphold. But I knew after our upcoming visit to the island, Kane and I would be parting ways.

That had stirred up a roiling cauldron of emotions in my head. The last thing I needed was to put myself into the arms of temptation. Know thyself and all that. I knew that if I cuddled up next to Kane, I mean... what would that be like?

I tried not to think about it. Thankfully, exhaustion shut my imagination down, and I fell asleep.

When I awoke a couple hours later, I saw that my big friend had gotten up during the night and strung his locket around his neck. Despite it being silver, albeit tarnished so much it was bone white, it didn't appear to be hurting him.

We'd never gotten him a tiny Emelda picture to put in it. I wondered if we'd have time now.

Downstairs in the bar, I got a burger. It was still technically morning, so a breakfast burger that had two poached eggs instead of meat. I'd been famished and eaten the entire thing. With fries. I'd even asked the bartender to put gravy on them. Not bad. Not great, but not bad.

We only had a few hours before we'd have to hit the road. First, I needed to get my backpack from Jeannette's house because I'd been so tired, I'd forgotten to grab it when I left. I also had a particular problem and thought if anyone might have a solution, it might be them.

I stepped out and let the warm sun gently kiss my cheeks. That moment of peace didn't last. The tiny town was buzzing over last night's news. Keeping my head low, I hurried down the street, hooked right, and only looked up when I passed the property with the big eyeball out front.

Part of me wanted to ask the shop owner what my future looked like. But then I wondered if that was where Jeannette's witch friend worked. I had enough spooky shit in my life. I didn't need to bring witches into the mix. I didn't even believe in witches, but after what I'd seen over the past month, why not?

A month.

Had it really been just a month? Felt like a *lifetime*. No. It felt like coming *alive*.

Now, I just hoped I wasn't about to die with our last adventure on the island. That would have been some pretty shitty timing.

The door to the hippie headquarters opened before I could even knock. Of course, they'd been watching. Caley stood in front of me with a welcoming grin. At least more welcoming than the day before.

I pointed inside. "I forgot my backpack here. I hope I'm not disturbing anything."

"You're not."

I was surprised to see she was the only one there. At least downstairs. When she noticed my gaze, she laughed.

"Even antagonists have to have jobs," she said and motioned me to the sofa. I spotted my backpack on the table but felt it would be rude to grab it and go.

She went into the kitchen area and began clanking cups, so I looked around and tried to picture one day living in a home like this. Warm. Inviting. Fewer anarchist placards, sure, but something cozy. One day.

When she returned, she offered me some tea, but peering into the cup, I saw what looked like sticks and dirt. I pretended to take a sip, put it on the end table, and sat on the love seat. She sat right next to me and stared at my feet.

"Oh," I said and wiggled my new kicks. "Thanks for the shoes."

A shrug. "You needed them."

"Yeah. I don't think I've had moccasins before," I said, unsure what to say. "Um, that stuff last night... nobody got hurt or anything, did they?"

"You mean downriver?" she asked, and I nodded. She shook her head. "A few boats ended up in the next county, but no one's ever been allowed to build any homes down that way. And it's not like it was a very big dam."

"Oh, good."

"I mean, the river has a few new routes it's taking now," she said and shrugged, "but it'll all work itself out in the end. As the universe intended it."

I thanked her and fiddled with my hands.

She noticed this and smiled at me. "What do you need?"

Letting out a long breath, I said, "It's just... we've got this thing to do."

"Your 'last adventure.' Jeannette mentioned that."

I nodded. "So I was wondering if, I mean, you guys probably know where to get explosives, right?"

"Oh. Oh wow."

"Right," I said and tried to smile. I failed. "Just enough, you know, to kind of blow up an island."

"An island?" Caley said and laughed. That faded away pretty quick when she realized I wasn't kidding. "Emelda, even if we could once get that level of ordinance, we couldn't now."

"Sure, I understand."

"After what happened last night, even just an inquiry would set off red flags. And we're already under the microscope. I'm sorry."

I sighed. "No, I totally understand. Had to ask. I just... last night, I really didn't think it through, and we got lucky. I have to have a better plan for what's next, and I just don't know what to do."

She leaned forward and took my hands in hers. "Put it out to the universe."

"Right," I said and smiled. "I don't think the universe is on my side right now."

Squeezing my fingers, she said, "It is. Even when you don't know it. You just have to open your eyes. I mean, like your big friend. How did that man ever come into your life?"

"I was in my apartment. And..." My voice trailed off. I remember feeling as low as I ever had. A busted beer bottle hovering over my wrist. Would I have done that? Could I have done that? But then I'd heard a little dog yapping outside.

The next morning, my life had changed forever.

She looked at the expression shift on my face and nodded. She sat back, still holding my hand. "You get it. You get it."

I shrugged. "Maybe. I just—"

A voice interrupted me. "What do you want to do with this thing?"

Ryland had stepped out of his shop, wheeling out the robot that had been gripping Kane's leg. He stood there sporting fresh overalls. He got a sheepish look on his face.

"Sorry," he said and waved from the kitchen. "Good morning, Emelda. How are you?"

"Fine."

"Good to hear. A farmer called me about my minisub, so I'm going to head out in a few minutes with my trailer," he said, tapping the busted-up PET with a wrench. "You want this thing, or should I dump it along the way?"

Before I could answer, Caley gently grabbed my chin and turned my head toward her. "Emelda, I know it might seem bleak right now, but a solution will present itself."

"Yeah, I just don't know."

Ryland cleared his throat. "I don't want to keep it here if the Feds come poking around. It's incriminating evidence."

"Open yourself to divine inspiration, Emelda," Caley said, drawing my attention again. She leaned against the armrest, closed her eyes, and pressed her palms together. She took a deep breath and let it out slowly. "The universe will provide."

"I've always had to provide for myself," I said far more bitterly than I'd planned.

"I mean, this hunk of metal is dead as a doornail, but I could run some power through it," the man in the kitchen said. "I just don't think that would be a good idea."

Caley opened her eyes slowly. "You have trust issues, don't you, Emelda?"

I shrugged. "Doesn't everybody?"

"Sure, but you trust Kane, don't you?"

"With my life."

She smiled at me. "And think of the gifts that trust has brought you!"

I thought about getting shot at, chased, nearly drowned, nearly blown up, kidnapped... but also, sure, some bad stuff too.

I smiled.

She tugged her ear, making it wiggle. "Listen to the universe. It's speaking to you."

"*I'm* trying to speak to you two," Ryland said with an edge in his voice. "I don't want this thing in my shop."

To Caley, I said, "I'll try. I just don't know if the universe has got anything to say."

Ryland cleared his throat dramatically and spoke louder. "Because when I cracked it open, I saw that reactor, and I don't want the damn thing to blow up like the other ones."

Patting Caley's knee, I then stood. "I promise I'll try to, I dunno, leave myself open to inspiration."

I walked over to the table and grabbed my backpack. I slung it over my shoulder and saw Ryland staring at me as he leaned on a handcart. Sitting on the platform was the last PET of Steve Janus.

"I don't need this headache. If it blew, a blast like that would probably take out this entire block." He pushed the handcart deeper into their kitchen, tipped it, and dumped the robot onto the floor. He retreated into his shop, closing the door behind him.

I stared dreamily at it for a long, long moment, lost in thought. Then I realized something. Oh wow! How could I have been so dumb?

"Thanks for the tea, Caley," I said. "I just realized I'd forgotten to pay my check at the bar for the eggburger."

She stood and held her arms out to me. I didn't know if she was asking for a hug or what it was. I repeated the gesture. One hand on the doorknob, I pointed at her head. "I used to have hair like that," I said, pointing to her pink coif. "Purple, though."

"That would look great. Why don't you have it anymore?"

Unsure what to say, I just shrugged. I had no good answer for that. We promised to keep in touch, but everyone says that and never does.

Back outside, I looked at the beautiful late-summer day and breathed in the lily-scented air. I was overwhelmed. We knew where we needed to go. We knew what we had to do.

But we couldn't just show up to the Island of Doctor Hammer without a plan. Without something to level the entire place and end the threat forever.

I turned and saw the big eye in the window of the home-turned-swami-shop next door. I glared back at it. But it didn't appear to be gazing at me. From my angle on the porch, it seemed to be staring at the house I'd just left.

Intrigued, I turned and looked in the direction it was looking.

The window.

Through the window, I saw the kitchen. And in the middle of the kitchen, the dead robot.

Just sitting there. A hunk of metal and...

Oh. Yeah, right.

Chapter Fifty-Four

"It is not safe to phone talk while operating a motor vehicle," Kane said, reaching over and running a finger across the chipped leather steering wheel cover. I pushed his probing digits away. "I think I should drive."

I shook my head and put a finger to my lips.

Sure, driving while on the phone, even in hands-free mode, was dangerous, but Kane driving was very dangerous. He knew this. I knew this. Anyone within a hundred yards of him at the wheel would know it and would have plenty of time to consider this fact later while adjusting the traction straps of their hospital bed.

A day earlier, we'd left the tiny town behind arguably in better shape than we'd arrived. Well, that depended on your perspective, of course.

Now, we had a destination.

We had a mission.

We had a busted-up robot in the back seat of a 1976 black Trans Am. Our bomb to level Hammer and Marata's new science project.

One tiny issue: we had to get to an island in the middle of Lake Superior. That wasn't proving easy.

"We'll pay you double," I said when the skipper of Snapper Trapper Fishing Charters got back on the line. I had him on speaker so Kane could hear. "It's just my friend has never been on—"

The man sighed down the line. "It don't matter how much you wanna pay, ma'am. The owners won't let us anywhere near the island."

"Did you call them?"

"Don't have to call them," he said and chuckled. "Margey runs the tackle shop just outside my door. I asked nicely, and she gave me her mean Margey look."

"Can you ask again?"

He sighed. "I knew you were going to insist, so yeah, I asked her twice. When I asked the second time, she threw a Belgian pink wiggler at me."

Kane let out a small gasp and popped his eyebrows. "This sound like an HR violation."

I shushed my friend and tried again. "Listen, I know—"

"I'm sorry, there's nothing I can do for you," the man said. "If'n you wanna take your friend up the north shore, there's some beautiful spots all around there. We can even weave into Canadian waters a bit, so it becomes an international voyage."

I eased the beast of a car into the left lane to pass a van so stuffed with bags, I couldn't see in the rear window. As we went by, two kids in the backseat pressed their faces against the glass. They got a look at Kane, and their eyes got big. He made faces at them. They smiled and waved.

"You're the third charter we've called," I said, trying to sound pitiful. It came easily. "It's really important."

"Ma'am, you're just not going to find anyone willing to risk their license because you wanna go to an island that's quarantined off. It ain't safe anyhow."

I thanked the guy and pushed End on my phone.

We drove in silence for a moment, which was good because I needed to think. Of course, that quiet didn't last.

"That is last call you will make to fishing people, yes?"

"We need to find some way to the island, Kane."

"Yes, this I know," he said and shifted his bare feet in the well below the glove compartment. "But three tries then stop, yes? This is standard."

"Not necessarily."

"Always how they do it on TV."

We had another day or so of driving. My plan was to head to a town on the shore close to the island. Maybe if we saw some people heading out, we could ask them for a lift.

The clock was ticking on Hammer and Marata's "animals first" initiative. We had to get to the island and shut it down before they could do whatever that was.

I'd called my tech guy for ideas. Straight to voicemail.

Hi, this is Denny. If you're calling to book Staff Infection or Mothers of Confection, please leave a message, and I'll get right back to you. If you're calling for some sort of technical advice, please know that I am not a tech person and cannot solve whatever issue you might have.

He was avoiding me. And not being subtle about it.

I grabbed my phone off the dash and flipped through my contact list. This earned me another barrage of complaints—and some choice words in French—but it wasn't like going through my contacts was a long process.

"That's kinda sad," I said and put the phone back onto the dash. "I'm twenty-five years old, and my contact list is three people."

"I do not know what this means."

Stretching, I scanned the side of the road for signs about diners or rest stops. I needed to get out of the car and think.

"I dunno," I said. "Being a grown-up means you've got a crew of people you can call when you need someone to help you move or bury a body."

"Body?"

"It's just a human expression."

Kane grabbed my phone and poked at the screen. He didn't know much about the devices and mainly watched YouTube clips. Old shows he used to watch with his human mother. It killed my battery, but the smile on his face would linger for hours, so I'd let it slide.

"Who do we have in contact list?"

I snatched the phone from him and put it back on the dash. "My grandmother."

"She is wise. Our elders know things we do not," he said. "We should call her."

I shook my head. "That would only lead to questions I don't wanna answer. Besides, she wouldn't know anyone who could help."

"She might."

"Not happening," I said. Number two on my list had been Denny, and that was out. Number three was just a number. I hadn't given it a name and couldn't remember who it belonged to.

Out of options, I thumbed contact three and put it on speaker.

"Pine Valley Motel, this is Olivia," the voice answered. "How can I get you tucked in today?"

That brought a big smile to my face. I lowered my voice, trying to disguise it.

"Hello, I'm organizing a hot fireman's convention and was wondering if we could book out your motel."

A laugh bubbled down the line. "Do not tease me like that, Emelda."

"How'd you know it was me?"

"Because life doesn't just hand you paradise like that," she said, chuckling.

I'd missed the sound of her laugh.

"And I'd know my friend's voice anywhere."

Friend. That hit me right in the blood pumper. "How are things going at the motel?"

For the next few minutes, she got me up to speed on the gossip. Not that I cared too much about any of that, but she was happy to gush about the local happenings. She told me how since they'd unofficially been declared a monster town, bookings had been up. News crews and a documentary team. Some ghost-hunter show filmed there for a week, even though no one had said a thing about ghosts. Just monsters. Close enough, I supposed.

Then her tone changed. "Oh, right. I haven't talked with you in a while," she said, her voice shaking a little. "You remember Dock, right?"

"Of course. How is he?"

Silence for a moment. "He died."

"What?"

"It's all the strangers we got rolling in and out of town. Most are great, but you'll always get the troublemakers and opportunists."

Olivia explained that he'd been in his camper just outside his townhouse when he got attacked. Police thought it had been a robbery that had gotten out of hand.

"Not like he had a lot to take. Just that old wooden motorcycle, but even if someone did steal that, they couldn't sell it. Everyone for three states would know it was Dock's."

"So who did it?"

A brief pause. "Open investigation. No one knows."

I knew. It had to have been Doc Hammer's Covenant team. And I knew, somehow, *we* had gotten a good man killed.

"It's nothing you did, ya hear?" Olivia said as if she could read my mind. "Things happen. And Dock's wife died a while back, so now, they're together."

That didn't make me feel better. I didn't know what to say.

"And no kids or anything, so he'd left all his stuff to the church, which was what he wanted," she continued. "They're selling his camper and the bike. Dock would have been happy about that."

"Yeah, I suppose," I said, my voice distant. My heart ached knowing I might have had something to do with his death. "I'm sorry."

"Not your fault, Emelda."

"Is there," I said, searching for something to say, "um, anything I can do to help?"

She chuckled. "Not really. Unless you know someone who wants to buy a 1982 Marinette Flybridge."

I looked over at Kane, who had poked his head out the window to let the wind take his hair. I tapped the wheel, thinking. We had to find a place to bunk for the night and work out what to do next.

"Nah, we got a car," I said. "Not the jeep. You wouldn't believe—"

"The Flybridge ain't a car, Emelda," she said. "It's a boat. Remember, he had a boat?"

I blinked. "Right, that's how he got the nickname."

"But the ol' heap is more than forty years old, so they won't get much for it," Olivia said and breathed out a long sigh. "He'd been planning a trip and had it way up in Duluth. They gotta get it out of the water and haul it down. Hell, that might cost more than they'll get for wreck like that."

"Duluth?"

"Good fishing up that way. Some of the deepest waters in the Midwest, or so I've heard," she said. "But they gotta find someone to bring it down from Lake Gitche Gumee."

I licked my dry lips and turned to Kane, who was leaning way too far out the window. If I got close to a mile marker, it'd take off his head. I looked at his newly acquired blue coveralls and could still see the stitching on the back where Jeannette's people had sewn them up. They'd kindly run them through the wash too. A few times.

When I tugged at his outfit, he looked back at me. I mouthed: *Boat.* Kane drew himself back into the car and listened to our conversation.

I asked Olivia, "Um... how far is it from Lake Gitche Gumee to Lake Superior?"

She laughed. "What?"

"Well. I might buy it."

"You mean *Kane* might buy it," she said, knowing how happy I was to wave around my friend's bank card.

Kane shrugged, and I smiled. "Of course."

"Emelda!" Olivia said in her lovely, teasing voice. "You know, Lake Gitche Gumee, like the song? The old Canadian guy sang it."

I shook my head even though she couldn't see me. "No."

"Lake Gitche Gumee *is* Lake Superior, hun. It's the Ojibwe name for it."

My mouth hanging open, I nearly drifted off the road. Again, I looked at Kane.

He grinned and stuck his head out the window again. Into the wind, he yelled, "The universe provides."

Chapter Fifty-Five

"I think she's sleeping," I said and rapped on the glass again, this time harder.

When we'd rolled into Duluth, Minnesota, the next day, I'd stopped at a gas station and asked where the marina was. That got me a good laugh. Apparently, they had a few of them.

Olivia hadn't known where Dock's old boat might be, but she gave me the number of the church that had inherited it.

"Why d'you want that old boat?" the pastor had said, his voice far too chipper for a Wednesday morning. Or maybe Thursday. I'd lost track. "The camper is the hot item. But you'll have to put a bid in quick. Auction closes this weekend."

"No, we're looking for the boat specifically. Dock had taken us out a few times, and he'd always said he wanted someone who loved it to take over the helm one day," I said and felt shitty for lying to a man of the cloth. "I'd always felt like he was talking directly to me."

"I see."

I cleared my throat. "How much do you want for it?"

"Well, not much." A sigh gurgled down the line. "She's not exactly seaworthy."

"Oh."

"You'd have to get that up to scratch. And she needs the proper permits."

"Right, right," I said. "I can take care of all of that. What's your price?"

"Well, we're using this as a fundraiser for the church, so really, it's about how much you'd like to pay."

Dammit. Now if I lowballed the guy, I'd be stealing from God? For a preacher, dude was a hard sell.

"Okay," I said. "How much would it take to make it seaworthy? Um, lakeworthy, I guess."

The pastor laughed. "I'm not a boat person, but I think that could cost more than the boat!"

After a few minutes of back and forth, we'd agreed to pay them ten grand. Once I transferred the cash, the pastor told me we could come by to fill out the paperwork at his rectory behind the church. I told him yes, no problem. Again, I felt like crap for lying to the guy.

We wouldn't be going by for the paperwork. He'd given me the address on file for where we could find the boat.

I cupped my hands to block the sun and peeked in the marina office's windows. The interior was as spacious as your average CVS *if* you piled in the contents of five CVS stores. Shelves on every wall and boxes stacked upon boxes, most of those open with a boater's bounty spilling out. Life jackets and paddles and lanterns and anchors and lights and ropes of every size you can imagine and a few you can't.

Outside, a massive C-shaped wood and concrete dock held about thirty boats. Some were small fishing vessels. Others looked like single-family homes on the water.

Blinded by the sunlight sparkling off the water, I squinted, trying to work out which one Dock might have owned.

Finally, the door swung open wide, and a tall, rail-thin woman leaned up against the jamb.

"Sorry," she said, thumbing a lock of greasy gray hair from her eye. "I was doing the books."

"You looked like you were sleeping."

She looked down her nose at me and frowned. "Always happens when I'm doing the books."

The woman appeared to be one of those tall people who always hunched over. She looked like the bent ash of a cigarette that would vanish with a sneeze.

After she introduced herself as Al, we'd told her we'd bought a boat that belonged to a friend who'd recently died. She knew who I'd been talking about.

"Dock is a good man," she said, then corrected herself. "Was a good man. He's had a berth up here for longer than I been around."

Back when they navigated by the stars? I did not say out loud. I told her we'd bought the boat.

"We're in town to just visit some friends, but we'd like to look at it," I said as casually as I could. "Maybe take it for a quick spin around the harbor."

That got a laugh out of her.

"Nothing quick about the *Glenora*," she said. "She's a thirty-two-foot Marinette Flybridge. Twin V8s at the back. Aluminum hull should make her light, but ol' Dock loaded her down a fair bit."

"That sounds, um, fast enough."

"She was," the woman said. "Back in the eighties. Today, you take that up past twenty knots and she'll split off into tinder."

I nodded. "Okay. We'll go slow."

Al gave us a sideways glance. "Been a few months since I fired *Glenora* up. Part of what I do around here. But she'll need permits and licenses before anyone takes her anywhere. I know a guy who—"

"My heart broke when he died." I rubbed my eye and sniffed. Wrapping my arm through Kane's, I said. "Our fondest memories were with him on the *Glenora*."

My friend nodded slowly. "I have never been on boat."

I frowned at him, then turned it into a sad smile. "You're right. *Glenora* will be very different without Dock there." I aimed my heartbroken expression at Al. "But it's a chance to say goodbye in the place he loved most."

Eyeballing me, she stretched her back and let out a sigh that smelled like stale cigarettes and staler whiskey.

"I'll need to see your watercraft operator's permit before anything," she said.

Smiling, I nodded at her. "It's back at the hotel. Maybe you could take us out?"

"I'm a bit busy."

"You were sleeping when we arrived, Al."

She shrugged. "I was napping between the busy parts."

"I would very much appreciate a ride on the boat," Kane said with a warm smile. "And it would be lovely if someone who was a friend of our friend were the person to do this with us. I think that person is you, my dear lady."

Al blinked a few times then stretched a smile across her sun-kissed face. She nodded and went to find the key.

***

As Kane sat up by the bow, leaning back and stretching his legs, I watched everything Al was doing while trying to not look like I was memorizing all the steps she took to fire up the boat.

After a few minutes, she dropped a handle next to the pilot's chair, and we putted in reverse. Slowly, she turned the wheel, and the boat's rear slid to the left. Al shifted again, and *Glenora* let out a massive belch of black smoke.

Then died.

"She's temperamental," Al said and tugged on what looked like a cigarette lighter you might see in an old car. "Gotta get the mix right."

She piloted the boat into the small bay on the other side of one leg of the marina's docks and took us in a few circles. She saw me looking at the speedometer.

"No wakes near the marina," she said then nodded to an inlet. "Not until you get out into the open water. Five knots max, or they'll fine you something fierce."

"Can we take it out a bit?"

Al shook her head. "We better head back in."

Face to the sun, Kane spoke softly, a deep timbre making his voice sound like distant ocean waves.

"If you could, please," he said. "A little while longer. This is a precious moment of peace, and I wish not to disturb the quiet."

Al laughed. "Yeah, boatin' is a kick, ain't it?"

My friend turned to her with a solemn expression. "We are with Dale Brubaker when we visit a place he once loved. His love is still here. It is woven into the fabric. A patina that warms the hull against the wind. His love fortifies the riggings and fuels the *Glenora* boat into unknown waters."

The other woman and I looked at Kane, both at a loss for words. Al cleared her throat.

"Actually, she takes diesel. But one more circuit won't hurt no one."

Kane faced the sun once again, his hands threaded behind his head. When the marina boss turned back toward the berth, I stepped close to the big wheel. "Can I pull it in?"

Al shrugged, stood from the pilot's chair, and theatrically waved a hand toward the seat. It didn't seem all that hard. I just had to put the boat between the two walkways on either side. Lined it up perfectly.

"Great," she said and cleared her throat. Then she looked at me. "You gonna slow it down? This boat don't have brakes."

Ah, right. I dropped the lever down a few notches into neutral. Twisting the key, I cut the engine.

"Too fast," she said, her words stumbling over one another. "Chuck it up into reverse to slow it."

I returned the stick to the R position, but nothing happened. When I looked at Al, she just stared back with a flat expression.

"You wanna fire the engines back up?"

When I reached for the key, she put her hand over my hand. "In neutral, doll! Don't start 'er in reverse. You sure you've piloted a boat before?"

"Yes, of course. You're just making me nervous."

I looked up and saw the dock coming up way too fast. Jamming the stick into the neutral position, I went to pull on the cigarette lighter thing.

She batted my hand away. "Don't need to choke it, she's good and primed. Just—"

I twisted the key, and the boat came alive, coughing out another big black cloud of smoke. I dropped it into reverse about fifteen feet from the dock and gave it some gas. The boat shifted, and Kane tumbled forward, his arms outstretched.

Al gasped at seeing Kane go over the rail and disappear to the deck below. "Oh lord!"

"He's fine," I said, eyeballing my landing. "But the boat's probably got a new dent."

I'd given the motor enough gas to slow us down, so when we did berth, we only tapped the wooden dock. Al shrugged and fluttered her hand in the air in a so-so gesture.

"It's been a little while," I said, grabbing the key and stuffing it into my pocket.

We watched as Al tied the boat up to the cleats in a complicated knot and then followed her back to the office. She opened the door, stepped in, then spun back toward us before we could follow. Guess we weren't invited in.

"I'll need to see the ownership papers come across the fax machine."

Fax machine?

"And I can call our mechanic, Sammy, about getting the permits reinstated," Al said and sighed. "Probably get you back on the water within a few weeks."

I gave her a big smile and thanked her. She held out her hand. I went to go shake it, and she pulled it away.

"The key?"

"Whoops," I said. "Sorry." Laughing, I dug into my pocket and held up the key. Its tiny foam life preserver key chain dangled in front of her nose.

She snatched it, turned, and closed the office door behind her. As we walked back toward our car, Kane turned and waved at Al. She nodded back and hung the key up in a lock box by her cluttered desk.

"We cannot wait so long for the *Glenora* boat to be ready," he whispered.

"We won't," I said. "We're going tonight."

He nodded. "You are going to break and enter the stuffy office to steal key, yes?"

"That's a few million bucks of boats out there," I said, shaking my head. "I got a peek at their alarm system, and it's pretty good."

"Your former life of crime taught you many lessons. But it is good you have left that world behind."

We stepped into the parking lot, and he headed for our car. I looked down the sidewalk, trying to find a place we could hole up for a few hours. Kane stood at the sleek black door of the Trans Am.

"Are we not going?"

I shook my head. "Can't."

"Can't why?"

Digging into my pocket, I grabbed my little treasure and held it out in an open palm. "I don't have the key for it."

"*Quoi?*"

"Because I switched the car key for the boat key when they were in my pocket." I tucked my pilfered prize back in my pants and headed up the path. "So I haven't *entirely* left that world behind."

Chapter Fifty-Six

We'd spent the rest of the day wandering around the city of Duluth. I'd been a bit frustrated watching the clock, willing it to move faster with harsh glares and muttering.

Not Kane. He found everything and everyone around us endlessly fascinating. He'd start conversations with complete strangers. He asked endless questions about what they did, where they were going, their kids, all sorts of banal shit. And those people lapped it up.

After he'd gone up to a couple getting out of a camper—"Yes, I would like to inquire about your honor student!"—I dragged him over to a nearby bench facing the water and sat him down.

"You're treating this like we're on holiday," I said. "You gotta have your head in the game. Tonight is going to be hell."

"Yes," he said and waved at a little boy on a swing. The kid stared for a moment, smiled, and fell off the swing. "And, right now, you have done all you can do, no?"

"Right, but—"

"But nothing. You cannot do anything more. So now, you enjoy the world of people."

"I don't like people."

Kane laughed. "You just have not met the right ones. And you cannot meet the right ones if you do not talk to people."

"People are cruel and mean and—"

"And kind and loving and generous. The right kind."

I crossed my arms. "I've just been hurt too many times."

"Yet tonight, we are going to do something that may hurt much. Risk our lives, yes?"

"Yeah."

"This after risking our lives in Mexico. And many times before," he said, shrugging his broad shoulders. "Yes, you are willing to do this dangerous thing, but talking to people is too scary for you?"

"It's not scary," I said and leaned against the bench. "I just don't see the point."

"People is life. Friend and family. Not any of the other things. You are robbing yourself of joy."

"Well, I am a thief."

Kane turned to me with a broad smile that warmed up the graying day. "You are much more than this. Emelda Thorne is a warrior and loving grandchild. A fierce protector. And you are my very best friend."

I swallowed, unsure how to respond.

"But yes, also a thief," he said, standing. "So let's go steal a boat."

***

I slowly piloted the *Glenora* out of the marina with the lights off. Mainly because I hadn't found them yet. We'd met a security guard on the deck, but once I'd shown him my pilfered key, he'd allowed us to pass. Kane had asked him what the job was like, did he enjoy it, and what was it like working nights, and I had to eventually drag him away.

In my experience, nighttime was the best time to take things that didn't exactly belong to you. The Duluth morning sun got blotted out by a slate-gray sky all afternoon, and my weather app assured me it would last most of the night.

I looked up at the thick blanket of clouds. We didn't have to worry that the moon would transform Kane at the wrong time, but we *did* have to worry that it also wouldn't transform him at the right time. We couldn't wait. On the video feed at the dam, I'd seen a boat moored at the island's shoreline.

Instead of calling my noncompliant tech guy for directions, I used the GPS on my phone to find the island. I could have fired up some of the onboard navigation equipment, but Al hadn't shown us how to use any of that stuff.

From the copilot seat, Kane tapped me with his foot. "I would like to drive."

"You are the worst driver ever."

"What would I hit?" he said, laughing. "It is boat. Nothing to hit but water."

"You would find something." I said and shrugged the comment off. "Okay, if we live through this, you can have a turn on the way back."

He wagged a finger at me. "This is because you have a stolen boat! You would prefer I am holding the wheel when we return."

"You know me too well," I said and gave him a squinty-eyed smile.

***

The water had been choppy the entire trip over. Now that we were close to the island, it had calmed, which only made me more nervous. Would the sound of our boat's motor give us away?

About a half mile out, we'd passed quarantine buoys warning that no one was permitted beyond. I read them to Kane.

"What is toxic hazard?" he asked me.

"It's just a way to keep people from stepping foot on the island," I said, hoping that was true. Of course, Doc Hammer and Marata were doing all kinds of gonzo shit in their huge lab. There likely *was* a toxic hazard, just not the one advertised.

I squinted as our destination came into view. From a distance, the island looked like a pie out on the water. The top of it, all the trees and foliage, clawed at the dark sky. It had a rise in the middle and another on the far eastern side. But the pie shell looked odd.

It was only when we got close that I realized why. A barrier surrounded the entire island. Six-foot poles with orange material stretched between them.

I slowed the boat and spun the wheel. As we bobbed up and down in the wake, I scanned the rocky beach.

"You think that orange ribbon goes all the way around?"

"I do not know," Kane said, staring across the ink-black water. "If only we had a way to circumnavigate this island to find this out."

"Yeah, it..." I stopped and softly kicked his leg with a moccasin. "Sarcasm? This is what you learned from humans?"

He gave me a big grin. "It is very handy."

"And 'circumnavigate.' You're like a word-of-the-day calendar."

Kane smiled big. "Calendars are very popular with humans. Your friend the motel owner asked if I wanted to be in one."

"Oh?"

"Yes. Olivia said I would make a good July, but I declined because I do not understand what this means."

"Big firecracker month. I bet it had something to do with strategically placed roman candles." I leaned into the accelerator, moving us along the island. "Probably best you turned it down."

For five minutes, we slowly putted around the island. Kane sat quietly, staring deep into the woods and occasionally sniffing the air. When he put his nose up the third time, I asked him what he was smelling.

"Very many different scents. Hard to pick out with feeble human nose."

"Like what kinda smells?"

He scratched his beard. "Dirt and sand and saltwater and—"

"Ah, okay, okay," I said, holding up a hand to him. "What do you smell that you did not expect?"

Kane thought about this for a moment. "I have been to islands before during my travels. Big and small."

"You have?"

He nodded. "Yes. Do you want island stories or smells list?"

I rolled my hand and my eyes.

"Okay. Very much chemical smells. I do not know what they are, but some are spicy."

"Spicy? You mean like food?"

"No, not food. Burns a little in back of the nose."

Staring ahead as I piloted the boat, I noticed a dark blotch jutting out into the water. I had a feeling what that might be.

"Burning. Okay. Maybe something caustic," I said, shrugging. "Well, this was Covenant's first experimental site. Probably solvents and cleaning agents and all sorts of stuff."

"Yes."

"And before that, it had been a dumping ground for construction projects. Who knows what kind of toxic crap there might be spilled all around?" Squinting into the darkness, I slowed us down. "Anything else?"

"Perspiration. Body excretions like urine. Much of this."

I cast a glance at the dark island. "Well, there's a lot of sand. And with all the creatures they had here in the early days, it was probably like a big cat box."

"This may be the case, but after some time, such smells fade," Kane said and looked in the direction I was looking. He saw the object too. "These are fresh."

"Great," I said and turned the wheel slightly away from the shoreline to avoid a massive boulder. "And I think that's the boat."

Chapter Fifty-Seven

The boat was a long industrial barge with a massive metal shed over the top of it. It looked like something you'd use to haul cargo down an old-timey canal.

"I can't tell if they're loading or unloading," I whispered as we walked the rocky shoreline. I looked down at the comfy footwear I'd gotten from Jeannette. "I wish I had hiking boots or something."

Proudly, Kane said, "I have the Reebok shoe. I should have been wearing these all along."

"You got *one* shoe." I'd used his other to flip the push plate back at the dam. "How can you walk with one shoe?"

"It is better than two potato-sack shoes."

"Moccasins," I said, defensively. "But yeah, if I'd been thinking right, I'd have picked something up in town more suitable for an island assault. Too late now."

We stopped and ducked down where the barrier had been flattened. Whoever had been piloting the boat had rammed it right over the orange ribbon when they'd beached the massive barge.

Kane poked one of my moccasins. "When we return to the mainland, I will get you better footwear."

"I've got expensive taste in shoes," I said. "I'll drain the cash you've got left."

"I do have other money accounts," he said. "I will buy you the boots you require."

Ramps had been attached to the barge's bow for loading or unloading cargo. I cast a quick glance to my left, staring into the creepy darkness, to be sure no one was coming. Then, as if on some seven-second delay, I finally heard what my big friend had said.

"What do you mean, you have other accounts?"

"My human parents split their money into three. When you spend our money, you are taking from just the one."

"Huh," I said and turned back to the boat. "How much is there in the others?"

He shrugged. "More."

"More than what's in the main one or just, um, more?"

He shrugged again. "I am wolf. What do I know of math?"

I jabbed him in the chest with the tip of my finger. "I think you know much more than you let on."

Kane stared at me for a moment, then his face lit up.

"Ah, yes," he said, clasping his hands. "This is how your species procreates. Women think men are more than they are. Otherwise, you would probably not have babies."

We'd anchored the *Glenora* offshore in a bay about a hundred feet away from the barge. That, of course, had come after searching ten minutes for the anchor release, which was not easy to do in the dark. The gentleman wolf, Kane had carried me to shore.

Treading lightly over the crunchy orange barrier, I ducked low and hopped onto the barge. This made the boat bob in the dark water, and its metal hull banged against the ramps. Flinching, I looked back to the island and spotted a short path that got swallowed by trees.

No movement there.

Sliding past the piloting station, I eased down into the cargo area and slipped into the darkness beneath the metal awning. I turned around and did not see Kane. A moment later, I heard him *clop-thunk-clop* across the bow.

When he dropped behind me with a soft thud, the entire barge rocked and banged against the steel ramp.

"Quiet!" I whispered hoarsely.

Kane lifted his shoulders. "Damp Reebok shoe is not so good for sneaking, I do not think."

The flat cargo bay revealed itself to be much larger up close. A dozen thick braces held the metal canopy up over an area that looked half the size of a soccer field.

"There's not much here," I said, creeping along silently. Well, the hippie shoes were good for stealth if nothing else. I pointed to the stern. "Some stuff under a tarp at the end, but you could hold a dance contest here and have room for spectators and a bar."

"Very sad," Kane huffed behind me. "Using the beauty of dance to unleash horrors upon humans? Have they no shame?"

Turning to him, I held a flat palm up this face. I didn't have time for weirdness. I wound around my friend to check out the piloting station.

A single high chair and some simple controls. A few small rectangular boxes that might have been radios or some radar readouts that told the pilot where the sandbars and rocks were. Or *Possible trout!*

I turned to go investigate what was under the tarp and felt a large hand on my tiny shoulder.

"What?" I looked at Kane and did not like the expression on his face.

Pressing my shoulder down, he bent his knees. I did the same. Then he put a finger to his lips. With my expression, I repeated the question. *What?*

His eyes slid toward the bow then back to me. *Someone is coming.*

Breathing slowly, I searched for a weapon but saw nothing. We needed to hide, and our only option was at the far end of the barge. I dropped to a knee then spun back and pointed at his shoe.

Frowning, he slipped off his precious Reebok. I quickly tied the laces and hung it around his neck. When I did, I saw he was wearing the tarnished locket. For good luck, I tapped it a few times. He smiled, then he did the same to mine.

On all fours, we hurried through the dark cargo area until we got to the tarp. I ran my hand along its side and felt rounded edges. Barrels? I waved him around to the other side, and the moment we crouched, the barge wobbled. At first, I thought we'd caused that. But we'd been lifted *up* slightly, not gone down.

Someone had just stepped onto the boat.

We heard the jangling of metal against metal and the squeak of wheels. A loud bang caught the breath in my throat. The squeaking began again. A cart of some sort, and it was getting closer.

I spun and looked at the back of the barge. We could make a run for it and dive off the back, but if the person with the cart was armed, we'd get bullets in the ass. Not the way I wanted to go.

The *screet-screet-screet* of the wheels came closer, and my heart pounded, matching its rhythm.

Then silence. I held my breath.

Behind our heads, the tarp shifted. I heard a triple *thunk.* Then the cover was fitted back into place. All of that in about two seconds. They'd moved the tarp, added three items, and fixed the covering again.

When the wheels began squeaking again, I started to stand, but Kane held my arm firm. He shook his head and again put a finger to his lips. I nodded.

The cart clattered as the stranger lifted it from the cargo area to the front of the barge. Kane was close to the edge of our hiding place, so he slowly leaned over to get a better look.

Watching his expression, I tried to work out what he was seeing. His eyes went wide. His lips parted slightly. He glared at me with those enormous amber eyes, and I looked back, puzzled: *What?*

Extending a hand, he helped me up. With his other, he kept a finger to his lips.

At the end of the ramp, I could see two gouges in the sand and rock where the cart had come through and the glint of the metal from the cart itself. But with the cloud cover, it was too dark to see the guy pushing it.

He appeared to be dressed all in black. But I couldn't make out the shape of his body. One black-clothed arm was wrapped around the red handle of a trolley. Then, the cart got jammed into a rock or in the sand, and it stopped.

The worker struggled with it for a moment then wrapped another arm under the crossbar handle.

Then another.

Lifting the cart, the flat metal surface briefly reflected the light, and I saw him. Not a him. An *it.*

My body tensed, and I nearly let out a cry. I felt Kane's steadying hand on my back, and I knew what that meant. *Don't move.*

I didn't know much about the creatures, but I assumed they could be alerted by movement or vibrations. That was how they knew they had food in their webs.

Because it was spider. A big fucking spider.

Chapter Fifty-Eight

My stomach somersaulted, punching me in the lungs with each flip, as we watched the creature scurry down the path. Six legs for walking while two gripped the wheeled cart. I could almost feel those thick appendages creeping up and down my spine.

When it disappeared in the trees, I slid down the crates, bunching the blue tarp as I did.

"Why spiders? Of all the damn things."

"*Giant* spiders," Kane whispered as he fitted his shoe back on. "That one is as big as ma mère's kitchen table."

"Not helping," I growled at him.

He tapped his lips with a finger. "We must be quiet. Spiders have excellent hearing. I think giant spiders have, um, giant hearing."

I frowned. "Why would you know that?"

"Nature shows," he said. "Ma mère used to have me watch them."

"Why?"

"Because I missed home."

Through the darkness, I could see the tops of small trees shifting as the insanely enormous spider made its way down the path to... where? I had no idea. But not here, so that was a good start.

"Great," I said, looking down at the tarp. "My all-time biggest phobia, and she's made an island of them."

"I also do not like spiders," Kane said. "Very shifty. Hard to read. Too many eyes."

"Still not helping!"

When I'd slid down, I'd lifted the tarp on the far side, exposing what was beneath it. The spi—I couldn't keep calling it that. I got more freaked out each time I just thought the word.

"Look," I said, getting to my knees and pointing at a collection of red cylinders. "These look like the same sort of drums we had at restaurants to dump old grease in."

"A sweet odor." Kane sniffed the air and frowned. "Ethanol. Possibly methanol or both mixed together."

"Why would they put..."

Then I realized it. They were loading the barge up with fuel. I yanked off the tarp entirely, and I counted two dozen barrels of the stuff.

"They plan on taking this barge a long, long way," I said and pulled out my phone. I had one flickering bar but was able to do a simple Google search. "The Lake Superior coastline is nearly three thousand miles."

"Very far."

I flicked a finger on one of the barrels. "That's their plan. They're going to take this barge all around the coast. The US and Canada. That's why they need all the fuel."

Kane turned slowly and stared at the vast space beneath the canopy. "Why do this?"

"They're going to release their Enhanced creepy-crawlies all along the way," I said and blinked. "How many do you think could fit here?"

"One hundred forty-seven."

"That's a pretty specific guess."

He shrugged. "It is number that came to my head. But this is one gigantic spider every nineteen miles."

"Kane," I said and shook my head. "Is that right? How are you doing math?"

"Nineteen-point-zero-four, actually," he said and shrugged. "Wolves are very good at math."

"But that's like Rain Man good. I didn't know—"

"Does this matter?" He frowned. "Is one hundred forty-seven enough for what they want to do?"

I walked forward and surveyed the empty platform. Spinning around, my arms outstretched, I tried to think. "If they're planning on crawling across the continent and killing all us humans—"

"I am wolf."

"—then I don't think so. One hundred fifty killers for hundreds of millions of people doesn't seem enough."

Kane nodded. "Then this is not their plan, maybe?"

"Maybe," I said. I stared into the woods where the thing had skittered away with its handcart. "When I was at that zoo in Atlanta, I nearly got eaten by Enhanced animals. Meerkat. Chimp. A hippo named Hugo."

"But they are using table-sized spiders here, yes?" Kane said. "What is different about spider—"

"Ugh, please don't even say that word. Say, um... Charlottes. Less scary."

Kane grinned. "Like the book with the pig, yes?"

"Yep."

He looked downcast. "Very sad when Charlotte died at the end. I cried much."

"Dude!" I said, my hands on my hips. "I never read it. You totally spoiled the ending."

Kane put his hands to his mouth and inhaled quickly. "*Mon dieu!* I am so—"

"Don't worry about it. Not really on my list," I said. "But you were going somewhere. Why would they want Charlottes?"

The big man dropped to a sitting position and crossed his legs, pulling his feet up onto his knees. He took a deep breath and closed his eyes. "If killing people, then she would need big cats. Not like tabby cats or Maine coon cats."

"Yep, got it."

"Lions. And also bears," he said, nodding to himself. "And sharks."

"Okay, this isn't help—"

"But this is not what they have done." Kane opened his eyes. "But Charlottes can be deadly, yes?"

"In Australia, sure. But everything in Australia is deadly."

Kane extended his legs and stood. "But how do they kill?"

"Uh, they're poisonous," I said, then my eyes went wide. "Venom."

Kane tapped the side of his nose.

"Oh, wow. Their plan isn't to kill humans," I said and looked at the space that would soon be writhing with the horrifying creatures. "The Charlottes are carriers. Like Covenant's Enhanced program on eight legs, spreading across the country."

"Two countries."

"It won't stop there." I walked toward him. "Each person they infect will infect others. As those things crawl all the way from shore to shore."

***

"Can't you get them to move the satellites or something?"

"What?" Denny said, his voice incredulous. "No! I have zero abilities with tech. None, Emelda."

I chewed on a nail. It had taken three attempts to dial up Miss Florida's son because, this far out, my cell reception was dreadful. To even get a call out, I'd had to sit up on Kane's shoulders to get any sort of signal.

"It's pitch-dark out here," I said, staring across the piloting area of the barge. "We can't just go traipsing around the place. Not with those things out there."

"What things?"

"You don't want to know."

"You're right. I don't wanna know," he said. "I don't want to be a part of whatever any of this is. If someone's doing shady shit on that island, call the police."

"And say what?" I said, chuckling. "There's two crazy people with an army of giant spiders that will infect every man, woman, and child?"

The line went silent. I looked at the phone then put it back to my ear.

"Th—wh—nd?"

"Hello? Denny?"

After a few seconds, he said, "You there? It's a horrible connection. I missed the last thing you said."

"Don't worry about it." I sighed. "We just need a basic idea of what's here. Are there any plans or anything. Blueprints?"

"Blueprints? Jeez, man," he said. "Look, Google Earth has some shots, but they're a few years old."

"Okay. That'll do. What do you see?"

"Hold on," he said, and I heard him crunching something. I pulled the phone away from my ear as he chewed. "Okay, this is from a while back... but there's a building on the east side. Something big, like a massive storage shed."

"Storage?"

"Yeah, but... hold on..." he said. More crunching. "I'm trying to work out the scale. It's big. Roof peaks in the center. It looks as big as, I dunno, a Cub Foods."

"The grocery store?"

"Yeah, maybe."

"So like a warehouse or something?"

"Impossible to tell," he said, and then slurped from his drink. "And just down fr... is some ar... I can see."

I held the phone out and saw the solitary bar was having a fit. The call was about to drop. "Hey, you there?"

After a moment, his voice came back. "Yes. Hello, I'm here."

"Great," I said, grinning. "Thank you, tech guy."

"I'm not, Emelda," he said, then his voice softened. "You know, I'd love it if you'd call sometime and you weren't minutes from doing something dangerous."

"Right."

"Or deadly."

"Same sort of thing."

He sighed. "I mean, maybe next time, you just call to chat. See how I'm doing. Tell me how you're doing. As long as it's not 'I'm about to storm a castle.' I would love to hear about you having a normal day."

I laughed. "What's that?"

"You know, going to work. Complaining about a roommate who drinks all the milk. How much you love the cupholders on your new car."

"I can't imagine a life like that anymore."

"Can't? Or won't?" Before I could answer, I heard the line go dead.

***

We followed the winding path through the woods. Branches and leaves blocked my view, so I didn't know what was beyond a few feet ahead of me. When I reached out to move a thick branch aside, Kane gently put his hand on my wrist.

He whispered in my ear. "We must be quiet. Stealthy. Moving branches makes the trees sing out. Leaves flutter."

I lowered my arm.

"Then how the hell am I supposed to get through?"

Kane pointed down and crouched. I went to my knees and crawled under the branches, feeling like an idiot.

"It'll take an hour to get anywhere on hands and knees."

"Not so long," Kane said, keeping his voice low as I bent around the twiggy vines and brush. "For most of my life, this is how I walked through woods. Stalking prey or avoiding predator."

Right. I stared ahead. As a wolf, this was how Kane saw the world.

"That must have been terrifying."

He grunted as he bent around the same branches I had. "I do not remember fear as such. Just life. Aggression and caution in varying measures."

Once we'd passed the clutch of foliage, I stood upright and wiped off my pants. Staring ahead, I sighed. In ten feet, I'd be right back down again. No use dusting off the pants.

"Your view down there would be like two feet ahead of you. All the time," I said, my eyes rising as he stood to tower above me. "You never know what's around the bend."

"Now I am way up here. So tall, yes?" He pointed ahead, urging me to walk forward. "But still, we do not know what is coming. Down low or high."

"Makes it hard to plan."

"We have plan," he said. "We are going to building in the east."

"No, I mean, hard to plan for what's next. And what's after that."

"Then do not worry about all the far-ahead plans. Only now."

"Sound stressful," I said and reluctantly dropped to my knees again to slither under a branch. "Never knowing what's next."

He let out a breath as he dropped to his hands. "Once you accept that you do not know what is next, this is not so stressful. Only that you have the skill within to deal with whatever is revealed along the way to where you are going."

I chuckled. "And that gets you through the forest?"

"That's what gets me through life. As a wolf or a man," he said then grunted. "Or dog. Or scary beast."

When I felt the tug on the waistband of my jeans, I froze. Kane had heard something. Or smelled something. Or just sensed something.

A moment later, I saw the fluttering of wispy branches ahead, dancing above the path. Kane tapped my left thigh, so I rolled off the path to the right and quietly slithered into the underbrush. He'd done the same on the other side, crab walking over a downed log.

We waited for half a minute in silence. My heart raced. Sweat trickled off my head and dripped off my nose. But what could I do from here? Jump up and punch whatever was coming through the bush? No. Just wait. No more choices to be made.

So I closed my eyes, took a deep breath, and exhaled slowly.

Whatever would happen next would happen. It was out of my hands.

I opened my eyes and saw *many* hands. Or legs, rather. The giant spid—err—Charlotte was pushing its cart through the bush, big knobby tires chewing at the dry mud of the path. I held my breath and lay there, motionless. After a minute, it had passed with another load of fuel drums.

I crawled back to the path with Kane right behind me.

"We got about five minutes before that creepy-crawly comes back this way," I said, then I looked ahead. "Unless there are more coming."

He nudged me forward. "If there are, we will handle it. There is little use in worrying about monsters on the path we do not yet see."

"I think there's use!"

We moved faster through the woods, winding left and right. A few times, I lost sight of the path, and each time I turned to Kane, he would shrug with a tiny smile on his face. Ugh.

Scanning for the ruts carved out by the cart's wheels eventually got me back on track.

Finally, we got to the building on the east side of the island. I turned around to look in the direction we'd come. The tops of the trees weren't swaying. At least, not yet.

"We need to get off of this path," I whispered to him and motioned to my left, where I saw another clearing, much wider. Hunched over, I crossed in front of the bushes, keeping as quiet as I could.

Tucked into the woods again, Kane slid behind me. I could feel him at my back. He wasn't touching me, but I could feel him. An odd sensation.

I pointed to the building. "Doc Hammer and Marta will be in there. Time to end this nightmare."

"How do we do this? I do not see a door."

I spun and looked at him. "We don't need a door. We got a robot bomb, right?"

When he went to go around me, I threw out my arm. Shaking my head, I said, "Can't go back that way. Eight Legs will be coming back."

He looked around and pointed to a clearing next to us. "What about this here?"

I looked over and saw another path. Much wider but chopped up like crazy. Dried mud with grooves and valleys. I bristled at the thought of what sort of creature might have done that.

"No branches to slow you down," I said quietly. "But it's like running across a cheese grater."

"I will be fine," he said and stepped onto the wide path. "I am not cheese."

I grinned at him. "That is not one hundred percent true."

"Hurtful."

I took a quick glance back at the original path. Waving treetops about fifty yards out. The Charlotte was heading back with its empty cart.

Raising my eyebrows at my friend, I pointed two fingers at the ground. *Go get the robot and meet me back here.*

He nodded and ran down the path, leaping from ridge to ridge of the dried, caked mud. Silent as an angel's wing.

"Must be the Reeboks," I mumbled to myself. "Or Reebok, I guess." As he disappeared in the darkness beyond, I got a strange pang in my chest. I couldn't shake it.

Maybe my nervousness had returned now that I'd been crouching there alone. My crazy fears and worries slammed back into me like waves bashing against rocks at the beginning of a storm.

I got the queerest feeling that I'd never see him again.

Chapter Fifty-Nine

Kane

This is far easier. We should have taken this path instead of the spider path. I can run very fast now I am out of earshot of that creature. I do not have to moderate my steps to keep silent.

Unless there are more creatures down this path as well?

I sniff the air.

Animal and insectile scents masked by chemical. Oils and dirt and grease. More of the petrol smell like back at the flat boat. Is this part of their plan? To hide themselves behind industrial musk?

To my right is a rusted gate, but this does not lead back to the beach. I peer into that area as I pass, but shadows hide its pungent secrets. When I look up, I see clouds above have thickened. The mistress moon hides from me.

Ahead, I see the troublesome orange barrier and bank left. From here, the flat boat should be only a few hundred meters along the stony beach, which I can traverse easily enough. Yes, I fall twice. Three times, but the third I did not fall all the way, so this does not count.

At the docking area, I stop and listen. No spider monster.

I slip around the orange barrier and run to our boat. Careful not to splash, I climb back aboard to grab the robot. Shiny black tape secures bare wires. Ryland told Emelda twisting these wires together should reengage the robot bomb.

I make sure that the tape is tight so it does not slip off as I run back. I can handle many things, many challenges. However, exploding is not one of them.

Despite the weight of the robot vacuum, my return is faster because I am now familiar with the terrain. I race down the rocky beach outside of the orange barrier. Then, at the optimal spot, I grip the bomb tighter and leap over the barrier.

Halfway down the wide path, the powerful petrochemical smell again assaults my nostrils, but I ignore this. I slow as I return to where I left Emelda. She has moved.

Of course she has.

I feel a growl building within. No, must not! She is her own person and will do what she must. I just wish, sometimes, she didn't.

But where has she gone?

I look left and right. I want to whisper, call out. But this would be a bad idea, I know this. No movement down the spider path.

Where, then?

I hear a woman's scream.

"Emelda?"

My heart races. Is she in trouble? Another scream. And then some very aggressive and suggestive cursing. Yes, Emelda for sure.

The sound of her is coming from above me. No, not above. I see that just below the roofline of the building is a grating. No windows, so this may be for ventilation. Possibly to hang Christmas lights but more likely for adequate air flow. I race up to the concrete side of the structure.

Putting the dead robot down, I jump up to peer inside. But with the overhang threatening a concussion, I cannot. I need something to stand on.

"Yes, of course."

I lay the robot on its side and step on top. The metal bends slightly under my weight, but I can just get my fingertips to the bottom of the grated slit and see inside. My body tingles as I take in the sight.

A massive space filled with tables and workstations. Computer screens fill an entire wall. There sits a naked Doc Hammer typing on a keyboard. I frown.

I do not see Marata, but it may be because of the massive spider army crawling all over the floor. Over tables, over fuel barrels that line the wall. There are so many. And so very huge. Some larger than others, but none smaller than me. I shudder as I am overcome by a punishing case of the willies.

So gross!

I look at the night sky. More clouds have come in, and I curse my evasive tormentor.

"This is now when I need you, moon," I whisper to her. But she does not answer. I turn back to the awful sight.

When the cluster of creepy-crawlies shifts, I can clearly see the far wall. Two long rows of thick Plexiglass cages, one atop the other. This is where Covenant held their captives as they conducted the animal experiments. A small machine moves up and down, a tiny car of sorts, and unlocks cages to free newly created creatures.

The second row on the far left, this cage does not hold an Enhanced spider.

It is Emelda.

Chapter Sixty

I threw my shoulder into the cage door, but the thick plastic didn't budge an inch. The impact shot tremors up my arm and across my back and made my spine twitch like a rattlesnake tail. I didn't care.

"Get me out of here, Hammer!" I shouted, but she continued to ignore me. Just tapping away on her keyboard like she was posting a Facebook update.

Going to unleash an army of mutant spiders. Then a Glee *marathon! Living my best life, lol.*

Slumping against the dirty cement wall behind me, I could only blame myself. Well, not just myself. That sneaky damn Charlotte had skittered around me when I'd been staring down the path, waiting for Kane. Thump to the back of the head, then lights out. Another kick to the skull, and I awoke just in time to see the cage door slam and lock.

Some seriously awful bedside manner.

My blood boiling, I leaped forward and pounded my fists on the cage, leaving sweaty smears across the glass. Just looking below made me shiver violently.

These things had always freaked me out, but I'd never gotten a really good look because I'd been running the other direction. And this Enhanced version inspired nightmares.

Huge, hairy, horrible creatures crawled all across the floor. All over each other. Thick legs, furry black carapaces, oil-black eyes.

"I stomped on your cousins!" I shouted. "Every chance I got."

That finally got a reaction out of Ilsa Hammer. She stood up from her desk, her nude body gliding through the roiling sea of monsters like she was their mother, her hands gently caressing them as she passed. When she stepped closer to the wall of cages, I saw how she'd changed. Not just changed. Deformed. Grotesquely longer limbs. Distended jaw. Her tight black ponytail long gone, she had a patchwork of fuzz across her head.

And, now Enhanced, she had eyes as black as those of the Charlottes.

"Th-th-they don't speak human, Emel... da!" She said, and it sounded throaty and strained. "But-t-t, if they did... I'm sure they would l-laugh!"

"Screw you," I said, looking down from my perch.

"It is your kind who are ab-bout to be screwed," she said, her voice rising in pitch. "My children will scrabble across this country, spreading the g-g-good cheer."

"Never happen," I said. "You'll have the armies of two countries blowing them to pieces. I'd like to see your *children* go up against a tank!"

Doc Hammer spun in a circle, elongated arms spread wide. "By the time they respond, it w-won't matter. The Enhanced hu-humans will join *our* army. They will be the second wave."

"You are human! You would do this to your own species?"

"Oh, but I am no longer just human," she said and rose on the toes of her bare feet. Her yellowed nails scratched at the concrete. "I have evolved! And I will lead a new species that is b-b-better than human."

I forced a laugh that I didn't feel. "Better? You're literally a monster."

"And that is the point! The delicious, d-delicious point!" Hammer said, taking a few steps back as she lovingly stroked the creatures around her. "We have always been m-monsters! All this governing of emotions, the false self-regulation, and so-ci-etal norms? I will smash that f-facade and release our true nature. A vile anarchy like the world has never seen!"

"You haven't spent much time on social media, have you?"

On a roll, she ignored me. "Once infected, the new breed of humans will devour the weak among you. Their soft flesh will empower my race of Enhanced people. And I will be their queen!"

Where the hell was Kane? I couldn't wait for him and had to find a way out of the damn cage.

I scanned my plastic box. Rotting wood chips and straw partially hid the cell below me. In the upper corner hung a camera with its wires ripped and frayed. My eyes fell to the next compartment over. The body on the floor was broken and bloodied, her dark hair matted with viscous gray sludge.

"No room on the throne for two, huh?" I pointed at the dead woman. "Or did she have reservations about your 'animals first' plan?"

Hammer laughed, and the sound of it made my skin crawl.

"Marata ins-s-spired me! A brilliant w-woman."

I shook my head. "She don't look brilliant now. She looks like a dog threw up a boiled ham."

"How d-dare you!" the Enhanced woman's face stretched into a ghoulish scowl. Hammer stepped closer, placed her palms on the lower level of the glass cages, and stared up at her dead partner. "She made them perfect killers. Too perfect."

"Good," I said, scanning the cage. Could I break the lock? *Come on, universe, a little help!* For the moment, I needed to keep Hammer distracted. "Then I'll have a front-row seat when they turn on you."

Her eyes still on the dead woman, the corners of her mouth hooked up so high, it looked like her head might split in two. Damn, she was hideous.

"Only humans now." Hammer shrugged and stepped back. "A tiny edit in their genetic code, and now they only attack your weak species." To make her point, she reached out and stroked one of her creatures as it skittered by.

Frustrated, I kicked at the lock on the cage door but only ended up smashing my foot. Instead of loosening the lock, I'd split the top of my moccasin and probably broken a toe. Hurt like hell. I dropped to the floor and cradled my foot.

"D-don't worry, my dear," the Enhanced woman said almost soothingly. "Soon, injuries like that will not bother you. You will be our first convert." She reached down and traced her fingers across a passing creature. It stopped and pivoted its carapace toward her. Hammer looked back to me. "It's time for you to join the new race, Emelda Thorne."

Then the creature's legs scrabbled over its brothers and sisters. As a thick, milky liquid began to drip from its mandibles, it raced toward the cages.

Chapter Sixty-One

Kane

They caged my friend like an animal. I wish to call out but must find a way inside the building.

I rise upon Reebok toes to get a better view but lose my footing and fall. As I tumble, my knee smashes into the robot, and I land hard on the ground. An odd light washes over me.

The moon! I lift my hand to the light and await the beast. Or powerful canine. What will I become? But I do not change. I stare at the bloodred glow of my fingers.

"What a moron," a voice says. "Hold on. Yes, yes... accessing the data from the network. New location. Ah, good. Up to speed and now adjusting my assessment." On its side, the robot's red eye shifts, momentarily blinding me. "A total moron."

Strange. Why does robot bomb talk now? It is supposed to explode.

"How do I make you blow up?" I say to it. "This would be more helpful than derisive comments."

"*Help* you?" The eye blinks. "You destroyed my power source and ruined my program and all my lovely machines!"

"Hmm," I say to it and roll up to my knees. "This does not sound like the work of a moron. Maybe you were too quick to judge."

"Shut it, moron," the robot vacuum says. "All my brilliance is now relegated to this one device! But at least I can still watch you die."

I stand and regard the wall. I look up at the sky and see only clouds. The moon evades me still. Inside, I hear Emelda scream out once again. I leap upon my robot footstool again.

"Get off me, moron!"

Recalling its claws and darts, I warily glance down, but the robot body is immobile. Just the pill head swivels from side to side. I give it a kick, and the light flickers. I kick again, harder. The head snaps off, bounces against the wall, and lands somewhere behind me.

Good.

But inside the building? Not good. I can see a spider crawling toward my friend's transparent cage. But she is not cowering, for a hunter does not. She is attacking and lashing out with tiny but fierce fists. Interesting plan. She is striking a camera in the corner of her cage. It comes loose and falls.

Good thinking! She can use it as a weapon against… the wall. She attacks the wall.

My eyes are drawn to a discarded pile of rumpled clothing in the cage next to her. Soiled and soaked with blood. My mind whirls when I recognize the garment as a lab coat, shredded to ribbons. And it is not empty. Marata. She is dead.

I cannot let the same happen to Emelda!

Hopping down again, I hook around the side of the building. When watching the horror within, I noticed a large bay door. With all my strength, I swing a fist at it, but it only rattles. I smash it again.

"You can't get through that, moron," a voice behind me says. "It was designed to keep the Enhanced creatures from escaping. Reinforced steel! Keep punching, though. I am so enjoying your futility."

I spin around.

Steven Janus robot is now just Steve Janus robot head. Laying on the rutted dirt path, he is the size of the thermos mon père used to take when we would drive the car into town. When *he* would drive. I was never allowed to drive into town.

"Punch it again!" the Janus head says, and its red eye flickers with glee.

Stepping back, I plead with the sky to clear. Nothing.

"Ha, no help from on high, my big friend," the head says. "But you can listen here while she's torn apart."

Rage overtakes me. I run over, pick up the head, and shake it.

"Oh, please. Don't shake me. I'm just a solid-state device that can't be *whooaaahh—*"

I have thrown the robot head deep into the forest. With a small amount of joy, I watch it arc down the wide path and disappear into the dark.

Before I can turn back, I hear a clank sound in the distance.

Clank?

How does a robot head clank in the woods?

I look back to the sky. No moon but maybe something else. Ma mère used to say there is something more, and she would point up. Emelda alluded to such a thing when describing her conversation with the pink-haired hippie girl.

"*Listen to the universe*," Caley told her. "*It's speaking to you*."

Does the universe speak in clanking sounds? I think this would be a very limited conversation. But with no other choice, I choose to listen.

I sprint down the path, traversing the gouges and grooves in the dried mud with ease, for a wolf is a skilled runner. Even more so in one high-top sneaker.

Stopping when my keen eyes find the faint red light, I have returned to the long, rusted gate I saw earlier. I leap over it and scan my surroundings. Before me, the robot head lies on the ground, and its eye lights a vision incongruous to the island forest.

Ah, yes. The source of the petrol and oil smell.

Denny, the nontech person, said to Emelda this island was once a disposal for construction equipment. This is what I see. Tractors and dump trucks. Backhoes and front-loaders. Possibly fronthoes and back-loaders as well, but I cannot be sure.

However, I now have a plan! And hoes and loaders are not what I need.

It does not take long searching before I find it— a massive, yellow beast with the wide, earth-chewing tracks of a tank. A powerful barrel-chested engine. And a big scoop.

Since I was a boy, last year, this was my favorite of all machines.

"The bulldozer."

I run toward it, jump onto its mud-caked tracks, and slide into the cab. When I see the key dangling from the ignition, my heart sings, and I recall again what Caley told Emelda.

"*The universe will provide*."

Confidence buoys my spirit and flows through me like a raging river. I nod gratefully and whisper, "Thank you, universe."

I grin because I need not trouble with the building's reinforced door. Bulldozer makes its own doors!

"Here I come, Emelda."

I turn the key. Nothing happens. I try again. Nothing. Not even the *clickety-click* sound.

"Hmm," I say. "Bad universe."

Outside in the dirt, the stupid robot head laughs at me. "That piece of junk's been sitting there for ages! The battery is long, long dead," it says and *giggles*. Very unbecoming. "Did you bring a spare battery, moron? *I don't think so!*"

The robot head laughs and laughs and laughs and...

How is such an endless laugh powered? Its light?

I jump out of the cab, snatch the robot head from the dirt, and examine it. Wires dangle from its neck. When I pull on these, an electric spark singes my fingertips.

"Stop that!"

I run back to the tractor and lift the side to reveal the engine. Attaching the wires from the Janus robot's neck to the battery terminals, I see a spark. Good!

As I reach for the lid of the engine compartment, the red eye squints at me. "A minor setback. I can—"

I slam the lid closed.

Back in the cab, I put my fingers on the key. Then I ask my wolf ancestors for their blessing. Their strength and their love. I twist the key. The bulldozer roars to life.

Yes, yes!

Ah. No steering wheel. Two joysticks like video game. I must puzzle it out. Left joystick is for moving. I turn a dial with the turtle and rabbit to rabbit. I know this story.

I push the left joystick, and the machine bounces and bucks. I try the right joystick, and this moves the scoop up. I raise it slightly then try the left once more.

The bulldozer leaps forward, jerking. I see the Janus robot head bounce out of the engine compartment, complaining the entire time, but I do not listen.

Slamming the left joystick forward to its max, I turn toward the exit. The engine growls like a beast of prey and belches out black smoke. I lower the scoop, and when it hits the gate, the powerful machine does not even slow.

"Yes!" I cry out. "I am bulldozing!"

I turn left down the path toward the building. Toward Emelda.

Everyone has always told me, "Kane, you cannot drive. You are the worst driver of all the drivers who have come before."

This may be true. In fact, yes, it is probably true.

But I can do one thing very well. I am an expert at this one thing.

I can crash.

Chapter Sixty-Two

In the cage's corner, I dug through the remains of the camera. My fingers moved slowly because beating the device had shredded my knuckles. But I had to work fast. To my right, the enhanced monster crawled through the cells on my level.

Hammer had used a remote to slide the first cage wall open, and it had greedily scrambled through. Grinning her horrific smile, she opened the next, relishing the moment. Only two cages between me and the creature. Even from here, I could see the poison, the mutated virus, dripping from its mouth.

Another cell wall swiveled open, and it pushed through.

Turning toward Hammer, I held the broken camera lens in my hand. She watched me, still smiling but curious. I couldn't defeat an army of monsters. This was the only way. I held the sharp glass above my arm.

"I won't let you turn me into one of those things," I told her and drew the shard across my skin. I winced but kept cutting.

"The coward's way out?" she said, shaking her head. "Why am I not surprised?

Hammer thumbed her remote, and another cage wall popped open. The creature's eyes locked onto me, then it looked at the woman on the floor. It bent down.

It poked at Marata's lifeless body as if checking to see whether any tasty bits might remain. Then it raised its gaze to me. My greatest fear was literally staring me in the face. I'd hated the damn things my entire life.

My grandfather used to brag about how he used to smash black widows as a kid. With his thumb! I recalled when one had climbed up onto his beer can, and he'd flicked it off and crushed it. Then he wiped the gook on the couch. In that instant, eyes wide, he looked around the room. Looking for my mother.

Dude was cool with smashing spiders, but getting caught wiping spider goo on the couch by his daughter? That frightened him.

"Just the name of them is scary, Grandpa," I said, squeezing my eyes shut. "I can't even say it."

"Spider?"

"Yes!" I said and buried my face in the sofa cushion. "The word feels like it is crawling across my neck."

"Try another, yes?" He said and snapped his fingers so that I would look up. "*Araña*."

I frowned and shook my head, unsure.

"This is what we call the little beast in our language, Emelda. Your language."

I sounded the word out: "Aran-ya."

"*Si*," he said. "*Araña*. It almost sounds sweet."

Blinking away tears, I said, "It sounds like a bitchy mean girl," I said then blanched. "Sorry. I'm not supposed to say 'bitch.'" I covered my eyes.

"And yet you say it again," my grandfather had said and, with a rare smile for me, finished his beer and crushed the can.

I blinked as the monster put one leg then another on the wall of my prison. Its mandibles flickered, spraying thin strands of the gray poison across the glass.

"Back off, *araña*!"

It retracted one of its legs. Weird. Did spiders speak Spanish? No. Of course not. Maybe German. I dunno why, but that seemed to track.

When I'd said the word, I hadn't pictured a creepy-crawly. I'd envisioned some mean girl in class. Pigtails and a white-and-blue dress. Shiny black shoes. Sneering at me. A creep.

Had the spi—*araña* read something off my face? Some micro expression?

It didn't matter. I turned back to Hammer and extended my arm, which was red with blood.

She shook her head. "You won't b-b-bleed out before my child gets to you," she said. "And th-then you will feed and be healed. A p-p-part of my army."

"Don't count on it," I said and kicked the cage door.

The self-anointed queen laughed. "No, you'll have to wait," she said and raised the remote. "There's no getting out—"

I kicked again, and this time, the door flew open and slammed against the front of the cage. Hammer stared, her mouth hanging open. Then she spotted the tiny wire sticking out of the lock. A wire that had been in the seam of my moccasin.

"Part of my skill set," I said as she looked up at me. I tapped a thumb to my chest. "Ex-thief."

Scowling, she pointed the remote at the spider and thumbed the button. I heard the click of the wall behind me but ignored it. I whipped my hand toward her, spraying the blood from my arm onto her face and chest.

I spun to the glass wall just as it began opening and shoved it back with all my strength. I looked over at the naked woman, who was wiping red smears from her cheeks.

"Hammer!" I shouted as I grunted, holding the entryway closed. "Welcome back to the human race."

The monsters surrounding her stopped moving. The creature nearest me halted its press on the wall, then turned and scrambled out the other side of the glass cages.

They'd picked up the scent and, in unison, turned on their queen. Their ex-queen.

"No! My childr—"

A writhing mass of creatures enveloped the woman and swallowed her words. A muffled scream rose and suddenly stopped.

Then the wall exploded.

Chunks of cement and metal flew across the room, smashing into walls, the floor, and the scurrying monsters. A worker spider pushing its cart had been right where a big yellow machine had busted through. It got crunched under the tracks while its load of barrels was launched to the concrete wall. A mixture of fuel and blood pooled on the floor.

As the dust settled, I saw the nose of the machine had a big scoop for lifting dirt.

"A bulldozer?"

The cab door to the bulldozer flew open, and a gigantic man leaned out.

I shouted across the room, "Kane!"

He turned to me and hooked a thumb back at the wall. "I drove!"

"You did!"

"I crashed!"

Laughing, I shouted back, "You did! Now, get me out of here!"

The spiders began creeping toward the bulldozer. The pile in front of my cage moved away, leaving a dead, bloodied woman on the floor, her eyes wide and her face twisted in a frozen scream.

Kane leaped onto the hood of his machine, looked down at the insect army, and raised his fists. They stalked forward. The closest lifted a tentative leg toward him.

Then it stopped.

Chapter Sixty-Three

Kane

Not a monstrous beast. Not a fierce wolf. Not even a fluffy poodle dog. Just a human man, but I am prepared for a fight.

After crashing through the wall, chunks of concrete raining down upon my bulldozer, I swagger up onto the tank tracks with my fists in the air. Rock dust drifts down upon my body, accentuating my bulging muscles. This is because I rolled up the sleeves of my coveralls before exiting.

I knew, for this fight, I would have to bring the gun show.

More than one hundred of the spiders crouch, immobilized. Their shiny black eyes stare at me. *Wuff.* Many, many eyes. Both collectively and individually. It would be very expensive to take a spider to a movie because of the cost of additional 3D glasses.

When I leap from the bulldozer, they skitter back to make a space. I raise my clenched hands higher and bare my teeth, but they do not attack. They do not advance.

I turn to the one nearest me.

Never before have I communicated with tiny spider creatures. Mainly because they are very creepy, and I never wanted to hear what they might say. Likely something about which bugs are most juicy.

But this is not tiny. Large like a forest animal, and thus, I can read its expressions. The twitch of its eyes. The flick of a mandible. The leg that bends in a manner that appears almost deferential.

A question comes to mind when I stare at its face.

Us?

Like a current, dark bodies flow toward me. From the middle, I see a bulbous shape emerge and creep closer. The others part, giving it a path. She regards me with those soulless eyes.

When this spider, the largest of them, reaches me, her front legs rise. The hairs extend and quiver. The hooked mandibles glide through the air. She tenses for a moment as the fangs come close to me. My instincts tell me to do nothing. That also may be fear. Part instinct, part fear. Fifty-fifty.

"*Heee*," the creature intones. "*Heee.*"

Okay. Maybe thirty-seventy.

The creature's eyes press closer to my face. "*Heee.*"

Spider legs drape over my arms—two then four. With the creature's carapace upturned, a curved stinger distends from its belly as long as my arm. When it twitches, venom splatters to the floor.

I could strike it, but surely, it would be faster than me. Stronger than me. But I am not compelled to. Not yet.

"Heee," the creature says as if using this voice for the first time. It regards me strangely. Confused. "Heee isss weee."

The giant spider's mandibles flicker in the air again, quicker than before. Then her legs scrabble down my body, and she shudders. Crawling away from me, she tentatively reaches for something beneath my bulldozer.

When I turn, I see it brush away some rubble, exposing one of its kind beneath the tracks. It shrinks back.

An odor lifts off the broken carapace of the lifeless creature. The foul scent of death. The rest of the spiders react to it, crouching low, agitated by the smell.

"That wasn't me." I put my hands up and point to the enormous creature inspecting the bulldozer. "She did it."

The spiders rise at the release of some pheromone. Some message. It has come from the alpha female as she inspected the fallen. The one I crushed beneath my tracks upon entry.

She turns to me, and I see her expression has changed. A new, unspoken word is there. And when I turn, I see it reflected upon the insectile faces of the spider horde around me.

Enemy.

In a tidal-wave rush, they attack. Thick legs and snapping mandibles and so many raven-black eyes, coming for me. So fast, I cannot escape. Light turns to dark as I am surrounded, covered. Pressure of their bodies. Their legs pulling me, trampling me as they fight for their taste of prey.

Heavier. And heavier still.

They pile on top of one another. On top of me.

My breath. Hard to breathe. No oxygen, and lights sparkle in my brain.

This is how I die.

I know this now.

From the darkness bursts a forest of lush green capped by brilliant blue skies. My ancestors step from the woods. Gray wolves. Larger, dark-haired aunts and uncles. Grandparents and farther back. All with kind and welcoming expressions.

From the shadow of the forest, red eyes. I know them well. This is the beast within me. The eyes move closer, growing larger and larger.

As it moves from the trees, the face bearing those eyes reveals itself.

Not a beast. Not a wolf.

It is a man.

How is this possible?

The human with the red eyes smiles warmly, but he is a stranger to me. Large and muscular, with a head of long white hair. A firm jaw and purple scar from brow to chin. Why is this human with my ancestral pack?

As if hearing me, he shakes his head and chuckles softly.

We await you, brother.

But how are you my brother wolf? You are not wolf!

I am. And—he dips his dimpled chin and smiles—*I am not. Like you, I am both.*

Like me?

The man grins wider. As he strokes the head of one of my grandmother wolves, he says, *Yes, like you. You think you were the first? No.*

You?

He shrugs.

But I do not understand.

Your time to join us nears.

I look around as more of my pack emerges from the woods. Dozens. Then hundreds. A lineage going back thousands of years. I feel comfort in my heart and dampness in my eyes.

I say again to the strange human, I do not understand.

Would it help if you did?

I consider his query for a moment. Yes! Yes, it would help. Of course it would help to understand why I am this way!

He shakes his head. *Not now. Not just yet.*

From the horizon, a fog rolls over the distant hills and glens, and I hear a voice call out, "Kane!"

This pack awaits you, but you have another. You must fight for it!

Alas, without the moon to change, I cannot!

The white-haired man steps toward me and presses a finger upon the locket around my neck.

You have everything you need in here.

But it is empty. The locket is empty, my brother.

It is not what is in the locket that matters but what lies beneath it.

I gasp. Yes, I say. My coveralls with the many pockets!

He fixes me with a wry smile. Slowly, the snow-haired man tilts his head. *No, not... not the coveralls. Further deep still.*

Then he turns and follows my wolf ancestors as they return to the woods.

"Kane," I hear the woman call out again. "Kane, get up!"

Emelda.

I must help my friend. My ancestral home fades from view, and the darkness returns. So does the crushing of my body. I take a small gulp of air. Not enough.

"I need you!" Emelda calls to me.

But I cannot. I have been immobilized. Trapped by the weight of the spider swarm.

I feel the first bite. As if they had all been waiting, I feel more of my skin being pierced. The creatures are ravenous. The pain shocks me so that I draw in a short, sharp breath.

I scream, "Emelda!"

But she cannot hear me through their thick bodies. Sharp teeth pierce my legs, my arms, my chest, my entire body made from pain.

More than pain.

Something else. Fire. There is fire in my body now. Poison? What have they—

My chest begins to thump like a drum. Its rhythm quickens. I understand now. Yes. Yes, deep beneath the locket, this is where my power comes from. The beating of my heart.

My wolf heart.

I feel my arms shiver then bulge. My legs buckle and grow. Piercing at my fingertips, but this time from within. No, not piercing.

They are claws.

The claws of the Wolfwere.

Chapter Sixty-Four

I'd been standing in my cage, screaming so loud my throat felt raw. My fists ached from banging on the plexiglass wall, where blood from my arm's cut splattered starburst patterns with each strike.

The writhing mound of spiders, the pitiful *araña*, perversely crawling all over one another trying to get to my friend, exploded.

Black bodies curled and twisted, launched in every direction. One flew toward my cage, and I yanked the door shut. It impacted, leaving green and black goo as it slid to the floor.

A giant, beautiful beast of purple and black crouched low, claws extended, its amber eyes evaluating, calculating. Kane leaped at the monsters, punching, kicking, and slicing the creatures with long, bloodied claws and tearing at them with his teeth.

He sliced off a limb of one creature who'd dared to get too close. Kane grabbed the bloodied leg and smashed two others with it. His powerful jaws clamped down on a spider's thorax, piercing the exoskeleton. The creature thrashed and shrieked, but Kane held firm. It went limp, and he tossed the lifeless husk to the floor.

Another pounced high in the air, and Kane raked his razor-sharp claws across its fleshy underside. The creature's legs clutched as green viscera oozed from its wounds. Still, more spiders advanced.

Kane unleashed a thundering howl that echoed off the walls, a challenge to the arachnid army. This was his territory, his domain. His call was a warning that these eight-legged monsters would learn to fear the wrath of the Wolfwere.

Yeah, I didn't have time for that shit.

"Kane," I shouted. "Let's go!"

As if awakening from a trance, he turned to me, crouched, and leapt in the air to grab a light fixture. Spider bodies writhed beneath him in waves, trying to reach their enemy. They then burst from the center of the room and began climbing the walls to get to their prey.

Hand over hand, Kane advanced toward my cage. He leaped from one light to the next.

Watching his powerful form gracefully traverse the ceiling with enemies all around him, I realized why Covenant had failed. Janus, Hammer, and a billion-dollar corporation had tried to create the ultimate killing machine. The perfect hunter.

Kane embodied that. He was their unattainable goal, and it had destroyed them.

With my help, of course.

I jumped back at the sound of my cage walls rattling. When I looked up, I saw the face of my friend.

"Hello, Emelda."

I smiled at him. "Hi, Kane."

He wrapped his massive beast hand around the cage door and threw it to the wall, taking out a pack of the advancing creatures. They crashed to the floor.

"Time to go," he said.

I climbed out and grabbed his waist. "Don't have to tell me twice."

Chapter Sixty-Five

Kane

I jump from the cage and land on the squishy floor. Ah, this was not floor. My Reebok shoe punched through two spider bodies.

Ha!

The Wyatt coveralls have fallen away but not the Reebok shoe!

"Hold on," I shout to my friend and leap over the spiders, their limbs raking through the air, trying to grab us. As we land, I grip the tracks of my bulldozer with my bare toes, but the rubble makes the footing unstable. We topple forward.

Behind me, I can hear the skittering of thousands of ravenous legs. They are coming.

I stand and assess our options. Countless spiders advance, their mandibles clicking, their many eyes hungry for our blood.

Spinning back to a gap above the crumbled wall, I gesture Emelda toward it. She turns, hesitates, then nods to me. My friend crawls to the top of the rubble and squeezes through. Emelda reaches a hand back and calls to me.

"Come on," she says. "We can still blow this entire facility sky high and end this!"

I shake my head. "I already turned on the robot bomb," I say and hold up my hands. "By mistake. Happened when I tried to use it as footstool."

"What?"

"It did not explode. Only got a bit mouthy."

Emelda's wriggling fingers seek mine. "Doesn't matter. We'll work something out. Let's go."

I reach out and grasp her hand. When she tugs, I hold fast and squeeze it gently. Behind me, I can feel them getting closer. A thrumming sounds as they prepare to attack.

"Thank you, Emelda," I say. "Thank you for being so kind. Thank you for being my friend."

"What—no!" she replies, her eyes full of panic. "What are you talking about?"

I try to release her hand, but she grips me tightly. "Kane," she says, and her eyes turn glassy. "It doesn't have to end like this!"

"You have done the impossible, Emelda. You have taught a forest wolf about love," I say. "And now, I must protect those I love. Like you."

I release her hand, and she tumbles back. Before she can regain her footing, I punch the ceiling. From above, the cement crumbles and collapses the gap.

The spiders scrabble up the front of the bulldozer, knocking plaster and masonry to the floor. One of the chunks rolls over the dead body of the spider I crushed beneath my wheels.

Around this lifeless creature, its black blood mixes with the spilled fuel from its red cannister. Like a river after a dam explosion, streams of the fluid spread out in rivulets.

I touch the locket around my neck. I wish I would have gotten a tiny photo of my friend to put within. However, that may have made me hesitate in doing what I must. And I cannot.

I will protect all those whom I love.

Leaping away from the greedy arms of the monster spiders, I land on the damp floor and drop to one knee. My fingertips moisten in the spilled blood and fuel. Its streams wind and twist all the way to the wall. Right up to red drums stacked to the ceiling. The same fuel barrels the spider had been carrying to the barge.

Ripping the locket from my neck, I gaze upon it one last time then close my fist around it.

The largest of the spiders bursts from the pack, pushing its kin aside. It regards me with its many eyes, its fangs dripping with venom.

As it leaps for me, I slam my palm to the cement floor. There is a spark.

Then, only light.

Chapter Sixty-Six

The blast threw me back, and I landed in the hard dirt. Above me, the dark sky lit up. I rolled into the trees as hunks of concrete rained down, and a massive plume of smoke rose like a nuclear explosion.

I wrapped my arms around my head as the ground rumbled around me. When I looked up again, I saw a wall of fire.

"Kane!"

The only answer was the throaty roar of the flames. I raced around the building, desperately searching for a way inside. I couldn't find one.

Returning to the collapsed wall, I saw black smoke belching out a hole near the top. I climbed over the broken chunks and, ignoring the searing heat, pushed my head through the gap to look inside. Smoke burned my eyes, blinding me.

Choking and coughing, I retreated and spotted another plume of smoke, not from the building but from the bulldozer Kane had smashed through the wall. Its engine was still running.

Covering my mouth with my shirt, I scrabbled up the debris and kicked out the rear window of the machine's cab. I climbed in.

No steering wheel. Two joysticks, so I didn't have a lot of choices. I pulled on the left one, and the machine groaned and shook. The tracks below me kicked rubble into the building as it tried to pull itself out.

Finally, it shook itself free, dragging half the wall with it.

I slammed the joystick forward, and the nose buckled and rocked as I drove over the rubble.

The entire floor was covered with a thick carpet of smoldering bodies. The smell of burned hair and flesh surrounded me. At the far end of the room lay the blackened husk of a woman. Doctor Ilsa Hammer, like all of her creations, was dead.

The smoke made it hard to see, hard to breathe. I rubbed my eyes and scanned the floor, the interior of the building lit by the fires fueled by countless burning bodies.

Then, I saw another form. A large, human-like figure among the dead arachnids.

"Kane."

I leaned into the joystick and pressed deeper into the ruined building, moving the bulldozer closer to my friend. When I stepped out onto the tracks, the heat pushed me back. The floor was still burning. Back inside the cab, I tried the other joystick, and this moved the front scoop.

It took a few minutes and endless coughing fits, but I eventually positioned the scoop under my friend. As it lifted, I shouted through the busted windshield. "Kane! Kane, can you hear me?"

It was impossible to see through the smoke, but I was sure I'd seen his chest moving. At least, I hoped it was.

A minute later, I was pushing the bulldozer at its top speed as it bounced and shook down the wide dirt path, heading toward the shore. His body lay motionless. Smoke whipped off his blackened skin. The drive threw me around so violently, I couldn't tell if he was breathing or if I'd imagined it.

I yelled out, "Hold on!"

Then I heard... laughing? I half stood to get a better look, but my friend had not moved. I was so panicked, I was losing my mind.

When I saw the orange barrier, I put my feet up on the dashboard and braced myself in the bulldozer's seat. We smashed through, and a second later, I drove the machine into the lake.

Vapor hissed from the bulldozer. I hopped out, and the shock of the cold water stole my breath. When I resurfaced, I swam over and grabbed his floating body.

A sob caught my throat. He was so light, like there was nothing left of him inside.

Dragging Kane up onto the rocky beach, I collapsed in exhaustion. The beast's massive body was ruined. Hair singed. His claws melted and curled black.

I pounded on his chest. Then again. And again. Then I put my mouth on his to give him my air.

"No, Kane," I whispered, fighting back stinging tears. "Don't go."

I leaned forward once more, desperately trying to breathe life into his lungs. Nothing. He didn't move, and I put my head to his burned chest. And I wept.

"Am I..." a voice rumbled below me and then rolled into a spasm of coughing.

I shot my head up. "Kane! Oh my God, Kane!"

His eyes cracked open, and black flakes of skin drifted down his gaunt cheeks. "Am I," he said, "a princess?"

Laughing through my tears, I lifted off his chest so he could breathe. "What? What are you talking about?"

"The kissing, yes?" His voice was ragged. Harsh and hollow. "Revive like Disney princess."

"No, no," I said, the joy flowing through me like one-hundred thousand volts of pure electricity. "That's CPR, Kane."

He smiled at me, exposing bloodied teeth. "I think this is how you finally kiss me, but I understand."

"Understand?"

"I am very beautiful," he said, and his eyes fluttered closed. His body slackened.

"Hey, stay with me," I shouted, shaking his shoulders. "I can get you blood! You can heal from this."

"No. Nothing left to do."

I grabbed a sharp rock from the shore and held it up. "You can have mine! Whatever you need!"

He reached out and wrapped his burned hand around my wrist, lowering it. "My time as human is over," he said, his swollen eyes turning damp. "Yours has begun once again."

A wave of anger rolled through me, but then, I read his burned face, and it bled away. Kane had made his choice, and I cared for him too much to deny him that.

I swallowed back a sob. "Just when you taught me how to be an animal."

"You are good human," he said, and his black lips cracked with a sooty smile. "Keep some animal in your heart, yes. But be a good human."

He closed his eyes. I punched him lightly, and a puff of black soot burst from his shoulder.

"No! I don't want this," I pleaded with him. His eyes opened slowly. "Kane, don't go."

"Must."

"But I..." I said, but I could not say the words. I hadn't said those words to anyone in so long.

So I didn't.

Instead, I put my arms around his neck and told him through twitch and shift. Furrow and frown.

I love you. I love you, my best friend.

"Good," he said. "Thank you."

"Thank me for what?" I said, wiping away tears. "You're *dying*."

"Dying while loved?" he said and closed his eyes. "This is a life lived well."

Kane took one last breath and was gone.

Chapter Sixty-Seven

For the next few hours, I sat on the cold, rocky beach. Numb.

It was over. Doc Hammer and her creations were gone. The woman-turned-beast-turned-monster Marata died with them.

And so did my friend.

During the night, the clouds did finally clear. A tiny hope grew in my heart as the moonlight hit his burned body. He shone in that light. Even fried to a cinder, he looked beautiful.

When I'd first met Kane, he'd been unreal. And the more I got to know him, in many ways, the more unreal he became. Not in a bad way. He had grown into one of the best humans I'd ever met.

And I had changed during that time too.

Tears streamed down my face as I stroked his charred body.

And for the first time in years, I had a world of opportunities ahead of me. Kane had told me many times that when this was over, the money in his accounts would be mine to do with what I pleased.

In the days before I'd met him, I would have had endless plans for a small fortune. Traveling. Buying stuff I didn't need. Maybe a house?

Now that I had it... I had no idea.

The sky lightened as dawn approached. Slowly, I got to my feet, and my butt felt numb. How long had I just been sitting there with my friend?

Smoke tendrils still reached into the sky where the building had burned. I walked up the path, unsure where to go. I'd convinced myself I was just checking to be sure the job was done.

Then I realized why I'd felt compelled to return.

I climbed back into the burned building, blinking through the smoke.

"Needle in a haystack," I said, scanning the floor. Thumbing the flashlight on my phone, I cast the light across the carnage. Before me was a sea of smoldering husks; many had coalesced in what looked like cooled lava. Had they reached out to one another in those final moments?

Below, a singular empty spot drew my attention. Its shape curved like a wilting flower, the floor scorched black. I climbed down, crunching carapaces and limbs under my feet, and went to where I'd discovered Kane dying.

That thought brought a lump to my throat, and I brushed away the dew of tears. Something glinted on the floor. I reached down and picked it up.

Kane's necklace.

We'd never gotten him a tiny picture to put inside. Instead, it now held something more precious: the final moments of his life.

Walking back, I tried to come up with some sort of plan for the rest of *my* life, but it all seemed like too much. That voice in the back of my head that would always tell me I wasn't good enough? That I was weak? That the world would crush me?

It was gone.

Now, I had to fill that silence.

Back down the path, I breathed in the first moments of the new day. A new start. When my torn-up moccasins hit water, I realized I'd walked all the way back to the beach. I looked over at my dead friend.

"I'll miss you, wolfman."

I sighed. It was time to leave, but I would have to bury Kane first. I wondered if the water-logged bulldozer had any life left in it.

Then I heard a ticking sound.

What the hell?

A crunch.

I turned to look down the beach. Had one of the spiders survived that inferno? No. They had all burned to a crisp. Every last one.

When I turned back, the sun peeked over the horizon.

Crackle.

I traced the beam of sunlight down to the beach. I stared at the orange light cast upon the body of my dead friend.

Crackle.

My breath caught in my throat. Did it just move?

"Kane?"

I bent down and put my hand to his crispy head. Just my fingertips. He was warm to the touch. Then part of his cheek collapsed and disappeared into the husk below.

Crackle.

Scooting back, I watched as his body broke apart in front of me. My breath hitched in my throat as the blackened skin crumbled and caved in. Then I saw gray. And white. Something was coming out of the husk.

A muzzle.

Whiskers and hair. When I went to reach for it, lips pulled back, and I saw teeth. Not angry teeth but nothing I wanted to lose a finger to.

A head pushed out, soot falling from its fur.

Crab walking in reverse, I watched as the creature lifted itself from the burned body of my friend then shook off the cinders.

A wolf.

A beautiful gray wolf.

"Kane?"

The creature turned its head toward me. It *couldn't* be him. But it was. When those amber eyes fell upon me, I knew I was staring at my friend. But the eyes didn't seem to see me. Or at least, didn't recognize me.

The wolf gracefully leaped out of the husk and padded to the water's edge. It looked back and forth, right through me, then took a drink from the lake. I stood, my heart singing.

For a few minutes, I just watched as the creature sat on its haunches and stared over the water. Its gray-white fur glistened in the dawn's warm sun.

I stood up and slowly walked toward it. I'd said his name a couple more times and got no recognition. But that felt right. It felt good. Kane was a wolf again.

Then I realized where he was staring. North. The wolf was staring north across the water.

"Okay," I said. "Time to get you home."

***

I'd had to dodge around some smaller islands when a couple of border patrol boats caught sight of me. But I was just a woman in a wreck of a boat. They didn't pay me much attention.

I got hailed by a police boat, but before they could stop me, I heard their radio crackle. All available crews were being called to a quarantined island. Some big fire.

Yeah. Sorry about that.

After I'd promised two different boats filled with Canadian authorities that I was just hugging the shoreline to get back to Duluth, I found a bay where I could pull up and set my friend free.

Kane stood on the bow of the boat, staring out into the woods. I knew the moment I got close enough, the animal would bolt, so I cautiously stepped forward.

The wolf didn't even turn to me, his gaze fixed on trees on the shore. I steeled myself, took a deep breath, and slowly dropped to a knee. He turned to me so we were nose to nose.

Furrow and frown.

Calmly, I tried to express I was just saying goodbye. Not a threat. Not that I could be a threat to a forest predator. With slow, liquid movements, I raised my arms and put them around his neck.

The wolf didn't eat my face, so I felt that was a win. Staring into his amber eyes, I tied the metal chain around the back of his neck.

"We never got you an Emelda photo," I said, carefully stroking his fur. That gave me an idea. I plucked out one of my hairs and curled it around my finger. I opened the locket, put the tiny circle of hair inside, and clicked it shut. "There. That's probably as close as you get to a picture in your world."

I backed away to get a last look at him.

"Looks good on you," I said.

I had considered polishing the locket up a bit but decided against it. Its tarnish and dents and scorch marks were as much a part of it as the metal.

Scars aren't just testimony of struggle and hardship. They tell the story of our endurance. Our courage.

Piloting the boat close to a sand spit, I throttled the engine down low. The wolf and I watched as the forest opened its arms before us.

I tried to think of something cool to say but came up short. Then, without warning, he hopped off. The wolf landed on the shore, shaking sand and soot from his body. All that dust catching the morning sun made him glow like some majestic, regal creature.

I smiled. Kane would have absolutely loved that description of him.

The animal looked around then back at me.

"I'll miss you, my friend," I shouted to him. Then I watched the wolf walk into the forest, disappearing into the Canadian wilderness. Searching for his family.

His pack.

Chapter Sixty-Eight

For two days, I cruised along in the old Firebird with no actual destination in mind. I was driving just to drive. Driving for myself and getting my head straight.

I hadn't even stopped at a motel. Just slept in the car and washed up at gas station bathrooms. I could certainly afford proper accommodations. Hell, I could have slept in the best hotels in the state.

Yeah, Minnesota, so that might be a fancy Red Roof Inn, but they were nice too.

When I'd pulled the boat into the marina in Duluth, I'd been ready for whatever was waiting for me. At best, I thought, a few nights in the gray-bar hotel for taking the boat without permission. At worst? Well, I'd long grown accustomed to worst, so I wasn't worried.

Oh, and since I was working on being a better version of me, I accepted that my "taking without permission" was actually called "stealing" by wider society. Better Emelda decided that sort of thing would be behind me.

Within reason, of course. Change takes time.

When I had pulled the boat in, easing the *Glenora* into its berth, Al was waiting for me. A cigarette dangling from her lip, she'd said nothing of my overnight heist. And, in fact, she'd taught me her fancy knot for tying the ropes to the dock piling.

I handed her the boat key, and she gave me my car key.

"Hope you filled 'er up while you were out there," she said.

"I would have," I said. "But I didn't know where the gas cap was."

Before leaving, I'd promised to pay her for the gas. Or whatever they put in boats.

When I stopped a few hundred miles south of Duluth to fill up the Trans Am, I spent some quality time at the ATM. Like Kane had said, there were two accounts I'd never seen before. One labeled "House" and the other "Fund." I'd wondered how he'd even managed any of that money, but he'd had an entire year of BE: Before Emelda.

Maybe the old family doctor, Dr. Fineman, had helped him with it? Or just another kind soul he'd met along the way? He had a way of engendering kindness in others.

I'd blinked at the totals. It was more than I'd ever thought I'd make in my lifetime. Of course, I'd always assumed that wouldn't be very much. Now? Anything was possible.

Funny thing about "anything." Now that I could go anywhere, do anything, I had no idea where I should go.

Turning from the cash machine, I stared out at another tiny Midwestern town. Where I'd once seen them as a succession of dismal cells in my life's prison, they were now stepping stones to the next thing.

Whatever that was.

I realized I was starving and headed to the main drag and found a greasy spoon. Parking out front, I turned off the ignition and waited for the old car to stop running on its own then headed inside.

The waitress who served me had given me a kind smile and a laminated menu. I returned both and asked for a plate of whatever she thought was best.

"Club sandwich isn't bad," she said, tucking the menu under her arm. "And the manager makes his own beer to go with it."

"Any good?"

"The beer or the manager?" Her smile faded a bit on the last word. Yep. I'd been there.

"Sandwich sounds great," I said. "And just a Coke."

I stared out the window at the Firebird waiting for me at the curb. A full tank of gas was a comforting thing. It held promise, and sometimes, that's all you need.

Hushed voices from the bar interrupted my philosophical musings.

"Did you mention my beer? You're supposed to be pushing the lager, Maggie."

I turned my head and watched the exchange. The louder her boss got, the quieter she did. As the manager continued to berate her, she shrank into herself, punched my order into the till, and hit the swinging door to the kitchen.

A moment later, I watched her exit the restaurant and sit on an overturned crate out front. Through the window, I saw her fire up a cigarette and just stare at the smoke.

"You won't find any answers there, Maggie," I muttered to myself. "Trust me, I've looked."

When the sandwich came, I ate it slowly. Enjoyed each bite. Well, I enjoyed it as much as I could. It was good, not great, but I savored the flavors thoroughly. Both of them.

Maggie the waitress asked if I wanted anything more.

I smiled at her. "I have all I'll ever need."

"Ha," she said. "Must be nice."

"Yeah." I nodded. "Yeah, it is."

When she turned back, I heard the creep bar manager asking if I'd ordered dessert. Then he went on about pie or something. With each word, I saw her shoulders fold just a little more. Getting lost in her own mist.

I pulled a pen out of my backpack. Yeah, I'd started carrying a pen. And a notebook. I'd decided I'd start journaling like when I'd been a kid.

Back then, it had been bad poetry and angry lyrics for songs no one would ever sing.

Cracking open the fresh journal, I stared at the blank page. It was time to write a new story. Or maybe just better poetry.

I turned to the sounds of clattering dishes. Maggie had a brown plastic tub on her hip and was clearing dirty plates and glasses from a nearby table. I touched a spot near my own waistline and wondered if I had a permanent dent there from so many years of doing the same.

Watching her perform the monotonous task, one she would repeat a dozen times that day and another dozen tomorrow, I had an inspiration.

I have all I'll ever need.

I'd meant the words when I'd said them. But I only realized in that moment, I hadn't been thinking just about the money. In fact, it had nothing to do with the money at all.

For the first time in my life, I felt like I was enough. *Good* enough. I didn't need to get beaten down by a crappy job at a crappy bar just to squeak by. Never again would I allow myself to be manipulated by someone else to commit crimes so I could pay the rent.

Hold on, no. That's giving me an out.

I committed those crimes. *My* choice. At the time, I felt like I had no other options. Yeah, I had an asshole for a boyfriend, but ultimately, I made the call to sneak into places I wasn't supposed to be to steal shit that didn't belong to me.

No more. That darkness in my life belonged in the past. Lessons learned and all that.

I had a new superpower: I believed in myself. I believed in Emelda Thorne.

And having a fat bank account would only rob me of putting those powers to use. If it was going to be a struggle, so be it. Did I feel I deserved a bit of an easier road? Sure, but now I was at the wheel, and I could pick the roads I wanted to take.

I tore out a sheet from my notebook and wrote a note.

When Maggie came back for the check, she saw more than just the receipt and my bank card. On top, a folded piece of paper. She looked at me strangely, and I put a finger to my lips. She went back to the till to swipe the card. I watched, sipping my soda, as she read the note.

She looked at me.

I nodded.

Maggie looked out the front window then back at me. I smiled. She grabbed the note and went to the front door.

The manager called after her, "What the hell are you doing?"

Without a word, she'd exited the restaurant. I watched her cross the street, getting a horn blast from a semi for not looking. She saddled up at an ATM, and I saw her reading off the note I'd given her. After a few moments, she took a step back. She leaned closer to the screen then read the note again.

I'd given her Kane's bank card. And the PIN to access the three accounts.

I saw her punch a few buttons and then watch, her hands folded to her chest, waiting for what she knew would be bad news. It was a joke. Life playing tricks on her. Her eyes shot down, and she reached out slowly to grab a stack of bills. She flipped through them. Then she did it again as if to make sure they were real.

From across the street, she spun and looked at me through the dirty restaurant window.

Maggie then tucked the card and the cash into her front pocket. I watched her carefully fold the note. Then she unfolded it again and reread it.

Back inside, she walked over and, as I'd requested in the note, handed me a one-hundred-dollar bill. The rest would be hers.

But I did have one condition. She had to do something for me.

She asked me: "Are you sure?"

"Yeah," I said. "Good luck, Maggie."

The waitress hurried back into the kitchen. The door swung open, and I saw the teenage cook's eyes go wide when he'd caught her expression. A moment later, she came out wearing a thin blue windbreaker and a purse slung over her shoulder. She headed for the door then remembered what it had said at the bottom of the note.

At the restaurant door, Maggie stopped, spun around, and faced the bar.

"You ain't done, girl," the manager said. "And you just had a damn break!"

Maggie took a deep breath and gave him the double birds. Elbowing the door open, she smiled and said, "Shove it, Daniel!"

I smiled. Close enough. My suggested language had been a bit more colorful, but Maggie had done it her way.

Good for her.

Chapter Sixty-Nine

My phone buzzed on the dash, and I smiled at it. Sundown in one hour. I hadn't yet turned off the alerts warning me that the moon would soon appear in the sky. I'd never been a sentimental person, but deleting the app felt like erasing my friend entirely.

I was one of those smug people who'd never embraced the selfie lifestyle. An odd source of pride. But, if I was being honest, maybe I just hadn't been flush with moments I wanted to capture in a photo forever. I'd spent all that time with Kane and didn't have one picture.

So, for now, I had my moon warnings. I'd turn them off one day. Not today.

My eyes drifted over to the orange glow of the gauges on the dash. A tiny red stick was hovering over the letter E, ready to smash it.

"I gotta trade you in," I said to the old Trans Am. "Or get you into some AA meetings. You got a serious drinking problem, my friend."

I had about thirty-two bucks left. From a small fortune to enough cash for a half tank of gas. I couldn't remember being happier.

But I did need gas. And maybe a new bandage for my hand. I'd felt pretty badass cutting my palm and spraying Doc Hammer with my blood, but it still hurt like a mother.

I smiled. "Worth it."

A few miles down, I eased off the two-lane highway and pulled into the forecourt of a tiny, small-town gas station. It looked vaguely familiar, but in the Midwest, they all look kind of the same. It was kind of comforting.

Before I could fill up, I'd need to have a conversation. And I was totally at peace with it. Well, mostly at peace with it.

The bell above the door clanked instead of ringing. Just a thunk. It seemed someone had busted it, and the owner had never gotten around to fixing it.

The tiny store was packed to the rafters with everything one would ever need while on the road and a lot of stuff they wouldn't. That thought rolled through my head when I caught my reflection in the glass cases of some frozen bait.

I spun around, looking for the cashier, but no one was manning the store.

"Hello?"

There was a bump, and an older woman came up from under the counter, rubbing the top of her head. She put a heavy box down in front of her and looked out the windows.

"You left your car running, hon," she said.

"Nah, it does that," I said. "You don't happen to have hair dye, do you?"

She blew a strand of her own gray out of her face and nodded to the three overstuffed shelves between us.

"I reckon I got some on that far aisle. What color are you after?"

Smiling, I shrugged. "I'm open. Whatever you got."

She nodded and dug into her box, struggling with a massive jar. For a moment, I thought she might drop it, so I rushed between the shelves and grabbed it to help her out.

"Very kind of you," she said.

"No problem." I cleared my throat, suddenly a bit nervous, but I pushed through it. All a part of the adventure, right? "I'm running low on cash, and I think I'm heading out west, so—"

That got a chuckle out of her. "You think?"

"I'm kind of winging it." I threw a thumb over my shoulder. "I noticed your door chime is busted."

She nodded slowly as she struggled with the lid on the massive jar. Looking around the store, she said, "It's just me here now, and that's one of a thousand things I just can't get to."

I took the opening.

"Well, I'm pretty good with my hands. Any chance I could take care of a couple of those things in exchange for a tank of gas?"

For a long moment, she stared at me, lost in thought. She then returned to working on the lid.

"Tank of gas will only get you to the Dakotas," she said and sighed. "I couldn't in good conscience let you get stranded there."

I held up my hands. "Listen, I'm not asking for charity."

"And I'm not offering," she said. "You really planning on driving all the way to the west coast?"

"That's the plan," I said. "My mom's out there. I haven't seen her in a few years, and I think it's time to mend some fences."

That got a big smile out of her.

"Well, if you can mend that bell and some holes in the drywall," she said, still battling with the jar, "maybe a few licks of paint here and there, we might get you enough to make it all the way."

My vision blurred a little, and I blinked it away. "That would be great."

"Gas ain't cheap," she said. "Might take a few days, I reckon."

"I got time," I said and looked around the store.

The owner told me that before her husband had died, he set up a small office in the back, which she never used. Too many memories. But if I didn't mind the mess, I could crash on the couch.

I reached out and extended my hand. She shook it.

"What do you want me to do first?"

"First, pull that big gas guzzler to the side so people can get to the pumps."

"Easy."

"After that," she said, pushing the big glass container toward me, "you could get this jar of pigs' feet open for me. They always put these darn lids on too darn tight."

"You got it."

She reached under the counter and pulled out a yellow pad. "All right, then. I'll get a list together for you, um..." She scratched her head with a pencil. "I don't even know your name, doll."

I smiled at her.

"I am Emelda."

Chapter Seventy

Kane

Sitting on my haunches, I gnaw at a foot to dislodge a troublesome pebble. I miss my Reebok shoe. Both shoes, actually.

I had watched the sun cross the sky dozens of times over the past weeks. And the moon, too, yes, but she no longer had me under her spell. Now just a big rock circling the Earth. I am the only wolf who knows this about the moon. However, I will keep such conspiracy theories to myself.

I do not want to face banishment like my uncle.

Before I continue my pilgrimage, I once again sing out the call of my pack. I have done this for so long, my throat feels raw. A lozenge would be handy. Cherry flavor, I think.

But cherry throat candies are no longer part of my world. Neither are bubble baths or many-pocketed coveralls.

However, disco fries, these I will have to work out. They are too good to give up.

Can a wolf grow potatoes? Maybe.

Yes, I am sure of it. If any creature could be a hunter *and* potato farmer, it would be an alpha wolf.

No longer second best. I am the alpha.

And I will have disco fries.

With no answer to my call, I start my long walk once again. I look south and recall the last moments with my friend. Should I have said something as well? A final goodbye?

The deception broke my heart, but if Emelda had been aware I was still a man within the wolf, our story together would feel unfinished. At least, this is what I am thinking. I do not understand people psychology very much.

However, it felt right.

"I will miss you, Emelda Thorne," I say quietly and turn back to the forest. I hear a scritching to my right, but I do not fear it. I smelled it long before I heard it. The silly-looking creature chews on a nut as it stares at me.

Did my human sounds surprise it? Maybe. But it is a moronic squirrel, and a shiny rock would surprise it.

My wolf senses pick up a presence, and I halt. Standing there motionless, I breathe in the air. A familiar sent.

Familial scent.

Ah, a delightful play on words and something I wish I could share with my friend! But no, focus. I call out our pack's call and wait. Then it echoes back to me.

She steps out through the trees. Hesitant at first then regards me. Do I still seem like the same Kane who was taken from her? Am I so different she no longer recognizes me?

That would be a bummer.

I recognize her. A beautiful marbling of gray and white and a shock of black just below her left ear. This ear twitches, and I know it is a question. The animal way of speaking.

With gesture and expression, I greet her.

Hello, my wife.

Her beautiful face turns slightly. *Husband?*

I have returned.

She steps closer, revealing her body, a vulnerability that tells me she does recognize the wolf before her. Slowly, she pads forward, her eyes never leaving mine. Then her muzzle caresses my neck, and I feel moisture in my eyes.

I blink this away. This is a human thing, not wolf. But my heart sings! This is human but wolf as well. She presses her warmth against my body for a long moment, but it will never be long enough. I will never let it go again.

She presses her nose to mine, her eyes full of inquiry.

Many suns. Where go?

Looking south for a moment, I gaze back at my wolf wife. I can hardly believe she stands before me, and I am speechless.

Husband? Where?

Ah, yes. I must answer, but I am slightly out of practice. But it returns to me quickly. *I have searched a very long time to return to you. Many dangers along my path.*

Her nose taps the dirty locket around my neck. Again, her expression is a question.

I answer. *A gift from a friend. A friend who helped me.*

She blinks, and her lower lip curls. *A girl?*

"Uh," I say aloud, and my wife's eyes widen. Her ears twitch. Deftly, I recover.

Yes. But—

Her forepaw shifts in the dirt. *A girl friend?*

I lower my body and look up to her. Wolf supplication. Male alpha wolves are proud creatures. Bold. Fierce!

But not stupid.

A human girl who helped.

My wife tucks her chin to her white-and-gray breast, her eyes never leaving mine. *I do not understand. How this?*

Just a friend. A very good friend.

Despite my triumphant return, my wife does not look overly pleased. I try to assuage her concerns.

My only desire was to return to my pack. To come home to you. I battled enemies and traversed vast, difficult terrain. Crossed water and climbed mountains.

My wolf wife steps closer, and her eyes soften.

Rising to my full height, I declare, *Despite these trials, I never stopped. No challenge or foe could stop me from returning to where I belong.*

Of course, she says, and finally, a satisfied look graces her angelic face. *You are wolf.*

I nuzzle the neck of my wife.

"I am home."

THE END

Afterword

Finishing a series feels bittersweet.

Aside from my wife, Emelda and Kane have been my closest friends for the past eighteen months. They are with me when I wake up, when I eat, when I take the dog for walks, and when I lie down at night. I have so enjoyed their enduring company. And even if this series is over, I hope they'll stick around my brain a while.

That is their choice and not mine. Trust me, I know how naff that sounds. By the way, naff is a great word they used here in New Zealand. Basically, it means lame, but I think "naff" really sells the lameness even better.

So, yeah, when I say the characters *make* choices, I know it sounds naff. But they do! And while I have ultimate control to get them back in line, they will not do something that doesn't feel right.

For example, several of my beta readers who read an early draft of *Kane Unmanned* did not like that Emelda gave all that money away. Maybe she could dole it out a bit here and there? Or just keep it because she'd earned it? However, the Emelda in my head wanted to move forward on her own steam. The one thing I did do after getting that feedback was explain her choice a bit more clearly in the book.

I hope I've done that well enough.

Another character that I kind of, um, lost control of? Steve Janus.

I'd had a plan. And it all went pear-shaped (another great expression around these parts).

Let me explain. Late in my other series, *Hell inc.,* a character said something that apparently stuck in my brain. Sally, who is a near-immortal gunslinger, was talking with an Aussie cop named Tara when this moment came up:

> Tara crossed her arms. “Special bullets? Now you’re talking werewolves or something? I don’t want to hear it.”
> “Nah, we ain’t werewolves,” Sally said, chuckling. “But I met one once, a while back. Nice guy. Very tall, great teeth, of course. But he was French, so...”
> The Aussie cop took a few steps to the center of the container.
> “I am really worried that I got hooked up with a crazy person,” Tara said. She wasn’t smiling now. “Immortal gunslingers, ghosts, French werewolves...”
> “Smelled a bit like maple syrup. Mighta been French-Canadian. Hard to tell.”

You may know the impetus for the story behind *Kane* came from the news adage: "Dogs bites man is not a story. Man bites dog? That's a story."

But I wrote that above passage in late 2021. So Kane was already worming his way into my head! When a long-time reader reminded me I'd written that exchange (I'd forgotten!), I thought it would be cool to establish Kane and then bring him into the final book in the Hell inc series, *Hell's End*.

That was the plan. It was going to be fun. Cross-pollinate the series. Bring our hero in when he's most needed.

Nope. Kane was not having it.

It just didn't feel right. I couldn't make that puzzle piece fit. Of course, I only realized this after bringing one of the baddies of Hell inc into the Kane series. Steve Janus. It works fine with Janus here—crazed megalomaniac corporate asshole antagonist. I actually got a huge kick out of writing Janus, which got me primed to start writing *Hell's End*.

So one question you may have after reading the book in your hands now... what happened to the Janus head? Did it burn up with the spiders? Did the power source eventually die out?

No. The Janus head plays a role in *Hell's End*, which I am currently writing. I have a plan for it. Of course, I've had plans before.

As I've wrapped up the Kane series, I've been asked countless times "Is it really over?" Yes, this series is over. But will Kane and Emelda return in another series? Hand on my heart, I do not know. That, as naff as it sounds, is entirely up to them.

Thank you, dear reader, for being a part of this journey. I have both laughed and cried as I've written these five books. And hopefully you have, too, and roughly in the same parts.

Finally, when interviewers ask me to explain what this series is about, I never say it's a werewolf book. Or a supernatural adventure. Yes, it lives in those worlds, but I think at the heart of this series, it's something else. And best described by Kane himself:

> "Most important is to work out your life puzzle... A single piece cannot make a complete puzzle. This requires two. Or three or four or more, yes?"
>
> "You mean I gotta find my pack," I said, nodding.
>
> "If you cannot fit into the surroundings, find surroundings where your piece will fit. You may have to smooth some edges, but this is okay. That takes not just the will to do this but the bravery as well."

I truly believe this. And I agree with Kane that this is one of the most important aspects of life.

Finding those rare people who *really* get you. When you meet good people—good people for *you*—it's not always easy. Great things never come easy. If you've found someone you love, friends or partners, don't let the little stuff dampen that. If they've got a good heart, they're worth fighting for.

Find your pack. And take on the world.

Good luck and God bless,
Dick Wybrow
September 2024
Christchurch, New Zealand

Acknowledgements

Over the past year writing this series, I have been blessed to meet new friends and to get to know old friends better. These books got better because of the smart thoughts from real superheroes. My beta readers.

Usually, it was the little stuff, but often that's the stuff that matters most. A phrase that got stuck in my head and I used far too many times. Names that sounded too similar to other names in the story (note: this is one of the biggest challenges for a writer. Coming up with names. A word of warning: If I come into your store and ask your name, there's a very good chance you will become a character in my book. And, no, you don't get to pick whether you're a goodie or a baddie). Or a simple comment like, "What? She gave *all* the money away?"

My love and thanks to amazing people like Claire Armstrong-Brealey, Peggy Hackett, Joe McCormick, Donna Cronin, Bill Thompson, Ron Daniel, Chris Robinson, Steve Lewis, and everyone else who have been a part of this series.

The amazing editors and proofreaders at Red Adept who help me to not sound like a total idiot. Did you know that lilacs usually bloom in the spring and not the late summer? I didn't, but thankfully Kim did. Bonehead choice averted (and now explains why there are no lilacs in our garden),

Warren Design for these beautiful book covers. I loved all of them and, yes, even have all five hanging on my wall.

And, as always, to my lovely wife who had to put up with me shoving lines at her—spoken, emailed, messaged, or written in the steam of bathroom mirrors—with me asking, "Is this good? Is this funny? What do you think?"

Tiffany, you and I will always be a fierce pack of two.

DEAR LOVELY, GOOD-LOOKING READER...

If you liked *Kane Unmanned*, please take a moment to leave a review on Amazon or wherever you might have picked it up. This allows other readers to discover the novel (and helps the author as well).

Also By Dick Wybrow

THE HELL INC SERIES
Hell inc
Hell to Pay
Hell Raisers
The InBetween
The Night Vanishing
Past Life
Ride the Light
The Hangman
Hell's End
MELODY SUNDAY SERIES
Live Shot

Printed in Great Britain
by Amazon

48482318R00175